Elvi Rhodes was born and educated in Bradford. The eldest of five children, she left school at sixteen and became the main financial supporter of the family. She now lives in Rottingdean and has published four novels: *Opal, Doctor Rose* and the bestselling *Ruth Appleby* and *The Golden Girls*.

Also by Elvi Rhodes

OPAL
DOCTOR ROSE
RUTH APPLEBY
THE GOLDEN GIRLS

and published by Corgi Books

MADELEINE

Elvi Rhodes

CORGI BOOKS

MADELEINE

A CORGI BOOK 0 552 13309 4

Originally published in Great Britain by Bantam Press, a division of Transworld Publishers Ltd.

PRINTING HISTORY
Bantam Press edition published 1989
Corgi edition published 1989

This book is set in 10/11pt Linotron Caslon
by Goodfellow & Egan Ltd., Cambridge

Corgi Books are published by Transworld Publishers Ltd., 61–63 Uxbridge Road, Ealing, London W5 5SA, in Australia by Transworld Publishers (Australia) Pty. Ltd., 15–23 Helles Avenue, Moorebank, NSW 2170, and in New Zealand by Transworld Publishers (N.Z.) Ltd., Cnr. Moselle and Waipareira Avenues, Henderson, Auckland.

Made and printed in Great Britain by
Cox & Wyman Ltd, Reading, Berks.

For Wendy, with love

Acknowledgements

I wish to thank Mr Stanley King and Mr Raymond McHugh for their great help with details of the textile industry in the West Riding of Yorkshire. Both were generous with their time and were mines of information. If I've made errors in this field, they are mine, not theirs.

I am also grateful to the staff of the Bradford Industrial Museum, who started up the machines for me and answered so many questions.

ONE

Walking along the narrow street, her hand resting lightly in the crook of George Carter's arm, Madeleine was filled to the brim with rebellious thoughts. They coursed through her body and tingled in her fingertips until she felt sure that they must be conveyed to the man beside her. The sensation was so physical that she found herself compressing her lips into a tight line as if to prevent her feelings spilling out into words; words which she knew would surprise, even shock, George, coming from some-one on her way home from chapel. But then he was easily shocked, wasn't he? He was so good, so upright. She doubted if *he* had ever had a rebellious thought in his life. And since he continued to walk along without so much as turning to look at her she doubted that he had the slightest inkling of how she was feeling at this moment.

'It was a particularly good class meeting,' George said with satisfaction. 'I felt the Lord was with us. I knew His presence and I was humbled and refreshed. I hope you felt the same, Madeleine?'

The quiet, equable tone of his voice – he always sounded so good-tempered, so unruffled – gave her a quick stab of shame, and at the same time increased her irritation. How could he be so insensitive?

'I thought it was . . .'

She was interrupted by a man, a neighbour, hurrying

towards them. The flagged pavement was so narrow here that she and George had to flatten themselves against the wall to let him pass.

'Evening, Mr Carter! Evening, Madeleine!' the man said. 'Been another nice day!'

Everyone was familiar with her, called her by her first name. She had been born and brought up in Helsdon, in the house at the far end of the street. All eighteen years of her life had been spent in this small, West Riding town. Not so George. He came from beyond Keighley, from the country area where the hills of Yorkshire and Lancashire marched together along the border. A year ago he had come to Helsdon to find work, and her father, seeing a stranger in the chapel, had brought him home. In no time at all George was lodging with them, sharing her brother Irvine's small room, though at present that was the least of Irvine's troubles, since he was far away, fighting the Russians in the Crimea.

They resumed their walking, George offering Madeleine his arm again: not that they were physically close; that would be improper. But though their bodies did not touch, except for her hand on his arm, Madeleine felt the heat coming from him. It had been hot all day, indeed all summer. The July sun shone relentlessly, as it had done since early morning and would for another hour yet. There was no coolness in the evening.

She would like to have been on the top of the moor. There was always a breeze there, even on the warmest day. She could glimpse the moor in the distance, rising high above the smoke pall to where the sky was clear and blue. It made a backcloth to the tall mill chimneys clustered near to the river and the canal in the valley. . . . It was true what they said, that there was no point in Helsdon from which you couldn't see both the moor and the mill chimneys. Even if you stood on the top of the moor and looked down, you looked on to the chimneys, on to the individual clouds of smoke puffed out by each one of them. This was the background to the whole of Madeleine's life so far.

8

'So you, too, found the class edifying?' George said. 'I'm glad!'

It was exactly the kind of conclusion George *would* reach, Madeleine thought furiously. The anger, which had been mounting in her as she had sat mutinously silent through the hymns and prayers and tedious witnessings of the last two hours, resentful that all she could see of the summer evening was a small square of sky through the high window of the chapel, boiled over.

'You are quite mistaken!'

'What did you say?' He had surely misheard her.

'I said, you are quite mistaken. I did not find it edifying. I found it dull! I was not humbled and refreshed. I was . . . BORED! Yes, bored. I was bored stiff!'

'Madeleine my dear, what are you saying?' That startled him all right. He swung around to face her. 'Are you unwell?'

'On the contrary, I never felt fitter. And unless you have cloth ears you know what I was saying!'

She withdrew her arm from his and they faced each other across the pavement. A group of children halted their game of hopscotch in order to watch and listen. It might, just might, develop into a fight. Fights were quite common in Priestley Street. But because the Bates's were chapel folk and chapel folk didn't fight, it was unlikely. Still, you could hope! *She* looked mad enough for anything!

'I think I spoke quite distinctly,' Madeleine said icily. 'I was bored!'

'But Madeleine . . .!'

Though his face was damp from the heat, he had turned quite pale. Madeleine, on the other hand, was flushed with indignation, her dark eyes flashing with temper, her chin held high in defiance. Deep inside she was a little apprehensive about her outburst, but she pushed the fear aside. In for a penny, in for a pound, and it was time someone listened to what she had to say. It was George's

9

bad luck that he happened to be here now, when everything had erupted inside her.

'The prayers were, as usual, too long and very tedious – how you all love the sound of your own voices telling God what you want Him to do! And as for that hymn . . .!'

'But Madeleine, I thought you *liked* that hymn?' She must be ill. A touch of the sun?

'Well I don't! If you want to know, I never have! "Pity and heal my sin-sick soul". Well I haven't got a sin-sick soul. Fat chance I've had of sinning!'

The children had drawn nearer and stood in a rapt circle around the couple. One or two heads popped unashamedly through open windows. All rows in Priestley Street were public property.

'Madeleine, please lower your voice! Everyone can hear you. Take my arm if you please. We must go home. You're not well.'

'I am perfectly well,' Madeleine contradicted. 'And I haven't finished. I was bored, bored, *bored*! And if you felt the Lord was with you, well lucky for you! I certainly didn't. I think He was more likely on the top of the moor, which is where I'd rather be on a fine summer evening, on my only evening off, instead of being stuck in a stuffy old chapel.'

She was shouting now, her voice rising higher and higher. She felt the pricking at her eyes and she just knew she was going to burst into tears any second. She began to run, breaking through the group of children, pushing them aside. She was in a flood of weeping by the time she reached number eight Priestley Street, pushed open the door and flung herself on her astonished mother.

'Why, whatever's the matter, bairn?' Mrs Bates cried.

Tears prevented Madeleine's reply.

'I don't know what it is, Mrs Bates,' George said. 'I think she must have been in the sun!'

There was no way he could repeat to Mrs Bates the dreadful things her daughter had said. It was tantamount to blasphemy. Thank goodness her father hadn't heard her. Thank goodness he was out of the house now, doubtless on some errand of mercy. Joseph Bates was the finest man George knew or had ever known. He would have been horrified at his daughter's outburst.

'Best leave it to me, George,' Mrs Bates said.

'Oh I will, I will! If you'll excuse me I'll go up to my room. I shall pray for you, dear Madeleine, depend upon it!'

'Don't you dare!' Madeleine flung the words after his retreating figure.

'Leave it be, George,' Mrs Bates said pacifically.

In marrying Martha Consett, Joseph Bates had committed the only rash act of his life. He had known at the time that it was unwise, that she would never make a suitable partner for a person such as himself. She was amiable enough, but she was frivolous, not very intelligent, and the things which were the rock-solid basis of his life – his religion, and after that his work – she held only lightly. But she had been the prettiest thing he had ever seen, with her corn-coloured hair and blue eyes, and she had the figure of a goddess. He had quickly tried to put all thoughts of her physical appearance from him, as being unsuitable to his calling in life, but they had proved too strong.

He had journeyed to her village in the first place to preach. Since the age of twenty, in every minute he could spare from his job as a weaver, he had been a local preacher, much in demand. Every Saturday evening, winter and summer, he would set off for some outlying village which lacked the benefit of a regular preacher, let alone a chapel building, and must rely on someone like himself, prepared to walk long distances to bring the Lord's Word. He would preach in houses, in barns, and when the weather was fine, in the open air. He would preach twice, sometimes three times, every Sunday, and always with great eloquence.

On that early spring weekend he had noticed Martha

11

Consett at the Sunday afternoon service, and in the evening she was there again, sitting in the front row. He had marked her attendance as evidence of her devotion to her religion. In fact she had been at the first meeting in obedience to her parents, and at the evening one because she liked the look of this handsome young preacher; and in any case there was nothing else to do.

When the service was over, she waited behind for him.

'I am Martha Consett. My parents would like you to come and eat with us before you set off back to Helsdon,' she said. She had a quiet well-modulated voice, which pleased him.

'I shall be pleased to accept,' he replied.

'Shall you come again?' she asked him later as he was preparing to leave. 'To preach, I mean?'

She blushed prettily as she put the question, and his heart thumped in a way hitherto quite unknown to him.

'If the Lord guides me,' he said. 'And if I'm invited.'

'You're sure to be invited,' she told him. She would see to it herself. She would do everything in her power to help the Lord to guide him in her direction.

'Then I shall accept,' he answered gravely.

She had admitted to herself that it might not be an entirely suitable alliance between them. She was aware of her own shortcomings. And she knew it could come to a match because she had seen the light in his eyes and heard the excitement in his voice, no matter that he had tried to hide them. But she was already twenty-two and there was no one in the village she could marry, and very few visitors came.

'I think that young man will ask for you,' her mother said when they had watched him walk away after that first Sunday.

'If he does,' Martha said, 'I shall take him. I shall be a good wife, even though we might not always see eye to eye. He won't regret it.'

They were married in the September, after the harvest was in, and their first child, Madeleine, was born on the

12

very night that the new young Queen came to the throne. Martha saw that as a hopeful sign and a good omen.

'I dare say I ought to call her Victoria,' she said to her husband. 'But that's what everyone else will call their daughters born today. I shall call her Madeleine. I do so want her to be different.'

'She'll be different all right,' Joseph said. 'And I can't say that I approve the choice. It sounds foreign. Also a much plainer name would have been more suitable, have befitted our life style better. Jane, or perhaps Faith.'

Martha pulled a face. Plain Jane! As for Faith, it was a word she heard too often for her liking in this household.

'Well you have borne the child,' Joseph conceded. 'And I promised that you should choose the name. I won't go back on my word.'

In the eighteen years since then, during which time she had borne six children, though two had died in infancy, she had insisted on deciding what they were to be called, with the result that between them her children had the fanciest set of names in the whole of the West Riding. Madeleine was followed by Irvine, then came Penelope and Emerald. Emerald might become Emmy, or Penelope, Penny, outside the house, but never in their mother's hearing. She wouldn't allow it. She chose the names partly in hate against her own – what could be worse than Martha? – and partly in a barely acknowledged revolt against the soberness of her marriage.

And was a marriage ever more sober? she asked herself bleakly. Apart from fathering their children, which he saw as a duty – 'be fruitful and multiply' – a duty fulfilled without love or understanding, her husband had managed to stamp out, to crush, all those desires of the flesh which had been in him in those first few months. Madeleine was the only one of their children conceived in love and passion.

'What about me?' she had asked him once. 'Don't my feelings, my desires, count?'

13

He hadn't answered. It shocked him that a woman should speak so openly.

The pretty names, the fierce pride with which Martha Bates brought up her children, insisting on good manners and proper speech, were part and parcel of her fight against the dullness and poverty which marriage had brought her. She could have put up with the poverty if theirs had been a loving partnership.

It wasn't her husband's fault that the mills in the Helsdon valley were so often on short time, that there were some weeks when the money he brought home wasn't enough to feed them. That wasn't his fault, and when he was on full time he earned more as an overlooker than did the hands: but what stuck in her throat was that before he handed over his wages he took out what he reckoned was due to the chapel. It was always a substantial proportion, enough to buy a good meal for the six of them, or a pair of new shoes.

'God's work must come first,' he said quietly whenever she complained.

'Not before my children's stomachs,' she protested. 'What sort of god would take the food from the mouths of children?'

He never attempted an answer, nor did he change his ways.

Now, alone with her eldest child – Emerald and Penelope had reluctantly gone with their father to whatever duty called him – she looked with concern at Madeleine, saw the tears like diamonds against her delicately pink cheeks, the long curling lashes framing her dark troubled eyes. It seemed hardly fair that she looked even more beautiful when she cried, whereas Emerald and Penelope would quickly appear swollen-faced, pink-nosed and plain.

She held out her arms to her daughter.

'Now come here, my love. Let me untie your bonnet ribbons, and take my handkerchief to dry your tears. Tell me what is the matter. Whatever can it be, to distress you so much? Surely George hasn't been unkind?'

14

'Oh no, Mam! George is never unkind. It's not his fault, I suppose.'

Mrs Bates nodded. George Carter was the mildest young man, even-tempered, not easily put out. But Madeleine could be provoking, there was no doubt about that. In a way Mrs Bates would have been glad to have seen him show a little more spirit against her daughter. He was almost . . . well, dull! That wouldn't suit Madeleine in the end, if anything was to come of their friendship.

'It isn't his fault,' Madeleine repeated. 'Yet it is partly. He simply doesn't understand the way I feel. He doesn't understand the least bit!'

'Feel about what, my dear?'

'Oh Mam, *everything*! Absolutely everything! What's more, he doesn't want to know. He thinks, he's quite decided, I'm a certain kind of person, and I'm not at all. And he can't see it, or he doesn't want to see it.'

'And what kind of person does he think you are?'

Did he know that her eldest daughter was volatile, self-willed, strong and resolute? All the things she wished she were – and was not? Did he recognize the rebellious spirit which lay beneath the pleasant nature, the affectionate disposition, the habitual obedience she had had to learn in this household? She thought probably not. And if he remained blind it couldn't be a happy future for either of them. She had doubted from the first that he was the right man for Madeleine, but her opinions were never considered seriously, not when they conflicted with her husband's, and he thought George entirely suitable as a future son-in-law.

'He thinks I'm . . . gentle, meek . . . and . . . oh I don't know . . .!' Madeleine protested. 'And he thinks I'm deeply religious, that I live for the chapel, just as he does, and Father. He thinks I'm like my father and I'm not. I'm not a bit like my father.'

She had stopped crying now, but she was every bit as angry. She would say just what she felt, even though it was only to her mother, even though her mother, for all the love there was between them, could do nothing at all about it. Her mother hardly ruled her own life, let alone the household.

'Your father is a good man,' Mrs Bates said loyally. 'He works hard to provide for us all; he cares for us.' She tried, at least, to bring up her children to respect their father.

'I know he's good,' Madeleine said. 'As for caring for us, well I suppose he does in his way – but the chapel is what he really cares about. If it came to a choice between the chapel and any one of us, we both know what would win!'

Mrs Bates glanced nervously at the open doorway, as if expecting her husband to materialize there, as indeed he might do any minute now. She didn't relish Madeleine coming up against her father in her present mood.

'Madeleine, you mustn't speak like that about your father!' she protested. 'I can't allow it!'

'Oh Ma, why must I never speak? Why can I never say what's in my mind? All the week I'm a servant and I have to mind my "p's" and "q's", keep out of sight, not speak unless I'm spoken to, and when I come home for my Sunday afternoon, or for Wednesday evening class meeting I have to keep quiet again, pretend everything's just fine. Well it isn't!'

'Very few of us can speak our minds,' Mrs Bates observed. 'Not people in our position, anyway. And if you want to tell me what's biting you, which you haven't done yet, you'd better get on with it. Your father will be home any minute. You said it wasn't George, so what is it?'

'Well a bit of it's George,' Madeleine admitted. 'But only because he's part of what I don't like . . .'

'Which is . . .?'

'Chapel!'

She spat out the word. She was all defiance now, red lips pushed out, eyes sparking, head tilted back. Tendrils of dark hair had escaped from her usually neat coiffure and curled over her forehead and against her neck.

'Chapel! Oh, my dear!'

She could not have chosen worse, Mrs Bates thought. Though she understood. She certainly did understand.

'It's not that I hate everything about it,' Madeleine explained. 'I don't hate the people, for instance. Most of them are all right – though you'd have to admit that some of them are narrow and some of them are stuffy. But it's summer, and I'm young, and every spare minute I have away from work has to be spent in chapel. Wednesday evenings, Sunday afternoons and evenings. No one gives a thought to what I want to do!'

'You're given a half day every Sunday just so you can go to chapel,' Mrs Bates pointed out. 'The Parkinsons are very good to you about that. Most servants only get a half day once a month.'

'Well I'd rather have it once a month and do what I like with it,' Madeleine persisted. 'I'd like to walk over the moors, or save up and take the coach to Bradford. I'd like to visit friends, if I ever had time to make any. Anything but chapel. And tonight was the last straw. It was hot and stuffy and they droned on and on, all about what miserable sinners they are!'

'What am I to do with you?' Mrs Bates asked helplessly. 'You can't possibly stop going to chapel. You know that, my dear.' It was a step no one in this family could possibly contemplate.

Madeleine crossed the room, turned her back on it and looked out of the small window into the street. It was a long street with identical terraces of small back-to-back houses on each side. They had been thrown up cheaply and quickly, by speculators, when people flocked to the West Riding to find jobs as factory hands in the wool trade. Already they were soot-black, and in need of repair.

The houses at the rear, and the privies and middens which served all the inhabitants, were reached by dim, odorous passages, where rats ran at night (and sometimes in broad daylight) and couples who had nowhere else to go did their courting. Madeleine was thankful to live along the front, and she tried never to have to go through to the privy after dark.

There were no gardens in Priestley Street, no sign of a tree. The house doors opened straight on to the pavement. The roadway was just wide enough for two carts to pass each other with difficulty, but between the cobbles on the road a few tufts of dirty green grass struggled for existence, a reminder that all this had once been green fields. Further down the road Madeleine saw two lines of washing strung across the street between the houses, the sheets hanging limp in the still air. That was Mrs Armitage, who refused to conform to Monday morning washday and did it whenever she felt like it.

Well I'm not going to conform, either, Madeleine thought. I'm not, I'm not! She turned away from the window.

'All the same, that's what I'm going to do, Mother. I'm going to go to chapel just every other Sunday, and I'm not going to class on a Wednesday. I've made up my mind and I'll tell Father myself. I'm not afraid. I shall tell him the minute he comes in.'

But she *was* afraid: not of physical violence, for he had never laid a finger on her. He was not one of those fathers – and there were plenty in Priestley Street – who kept a leather strap handy, hanging on a nail by the fireplace, and used it whenever the mood took them. Her father had no need of physical violence. His will was strong enough to exact all the obedience he needed, and he had used his will, first on his wife, and then on each of his children since the day they were born. As a child Madeleine had thought that the will of God and the will of her father were one and the same thing.

'I'm a child no longer,' she said out loud. 'I'm eighteen, almost grown up. I won't be treated like a child. He can't *make* me do something I don't want to do.'

Mrs Bates shook her head in despair.

'Madeleine, don't talk like that. Remember that until you marry, you are subject to your father, as I was to mine.'

'And then I'll become subject to my husband,' Madeleine said hotly. 'Well I won't, I just won't!' She had seen that in her mother's life and she wanted none of it.

'Why not discuss it with George before you speak to your father?' Mrs Bates suggested. 'Perhaps a compromise . . .' She knew it was no use, even as she said it. 'Compromise' was a word not in her husband's vocabulary.

'I don't need to discuss it with George,' Madeleine said. 'I know my own mind. Anyway, where is George right now? No doubt on his knees wrestling for my soul, instead of here, ready to back me up.'

There was not the slightest hope that he would support her. His ideas, his attitudes, were exactly those of her father. His good points were the same: his honesty, his faithfulness; but his not-so-good points were getting more like her father's every day. No, she couldn't rely on George in this instance.

It was twenty minutes before her father returned, each one of them seeming to Madeleine like an agonizing hour. She alternated between sitting upright at the table, nervously drumming her fingers on the scrubbed deal top, and running to the door to check if he was coming up the street.

'If he doesn't come soon I shall have to leave,' she said. She had to be back at her job by nine o'clock, in time to serve the bedtime beverages.

'Perhaps that would be just as well,' her mother said.

'No,' Madeleine said firmly. 'It would only postpone it. It's no use you thinking I'll change my mind. Good heavens, in any other house except this it would be such a small matter! Here, I shall be made to feel I'm an outright criminal. You know I will.'

Mrs Bates went into the cellar-head, filled the kettle, came back into the living-room and set it over the fire. It was far too hot for a fire, but they needed it for cooking and for heating the water. Her husband would want a cup of cocoa when he came in. She coaxed a little more heat into the cinders and then turned to Madeleine.

'Well,' she said slowly, 'I've decided I shan't try to make

you change your mind, even if I could. I think perhaps you're right.' I should have been as brave as my daughter years ago, she thought.

Madeleine looked at her in astonishment.

'Then you'll back me, Ma?'

Mrs Bates shook her head.

'I can't do that my dear. I can't set myself against your father. It wouldn't be right. Besides which, I have to live with him. And I beg of you not to start on him before Emerald and Penelope have gone upstairs. I don't want them worried.'

'Nor do I,' Madeleine agreed. 'Of course I won't.'

I'm weak, Mrs Bates thought. Why am I always weak? If she hadn't been in the past, if she had taken her son's side when he quarrelled with his father, for reasons very similar to Madeleine's, perhaps Irvine wouldn't have run away and joined the army under age and now be fighting in that hell-hole of Crimea. If anything happened to him she would blame herself.

When Joseph Bates arrived, preceded by his two daughters who ran into the house ahead of him, he stood for a moment in the doorway, filling it. He was tall, broad-shouldered, and though he was thickset there wasn't a spare ounce of fat on him. At forty-three he was still handsome, with only a few grey hairs showing in his beard and in his dark curly hair. It was easy to see where Madeleine got her looks.

Mrs Bates went towards him, took his coat and hat.

'The kettle's on the boil,' she said. 'You shall have your cocoa in a minute. And some bread and dripping. Emerald and Penelope, get you off to bed. I'll bring your cocoa up to you.'

'But it's still light. And I'm not the least bit tired,' Emerald protested. She was fourteen years old and didn't see why she should go to bed at the same time as Penelope, who was only ten.

'You know you have to be up early,' Mrs Bates said.

Much against her will, for she had sworn to herself that

not one of her children should ever go into the mill, Emerald had been put in the spinning. She earned very little, but it helped, and since they worked in different mills, she and her father were not always on short time together.

'You heard your mother,' Joseph Bates said. He didn't raise his voice. There was no need to. It was enough that he had said it. The two girls scuttled upstairs. He went and sat in the only armchair, which was always saved for him.

'Mrs Chambers was pleased to see the children,' he said. 'I'm afraid she is no better, but I read a passage and we prayed with her. By the Lord's mercy I think she was comforted. She is perfectly resigned now to whatever is His will.'

'I had rather you had not taken Emerald and Penelope,' his wife said. 'They are too young to visit a woman as ill as Mrs Chambers. Besides, they might pick up something.'

'No child is too young to visit the afflicted,' Joseph Bates said. 'And the Lord protects those who do His work.'

He turned to Madeleine.

'I had half expected to find you gone. I trust you had a fruitful class meeting; that you were, as always, uplifted and strengthened by it?'

Madeleine took a deep breath. It was now or never. She felt sick, her inside churning. She turned and faced him directly. When she heard her own voice she was surprised that it sounded so strangely high-pitched.

'On the contrary, Father, it was not at all fruitful – not in the way you mean. And I was neither uplifted nor strengthened by it. Quite the opposite, in fact!'

There was a split second in which she saw his face change; his mouth fall open, his dark eyebrows rise almost to his hairline. Then it was gone and he was outwardly back to normal.

'I'm not sure what you mean, Madeleine. Did something go wrong?'

'Nothing more than usual, Father. I hate the class

21

meeting. It's sanctimonious and boring, and the room is as stuffy as the people. Furthermore, I resent giving my free evening to attending it when there are other things I might do. I would like some life of my own for a change.'

The words came out in a rush. It had to be so, or she would lose her nerve. As she spoke she watched her father, and marvelled that he remained so calm.

There was a pause which Madeleine thought would go on for ever. Then he said:

'I sympathize. I know how you feel.'

'You *sympathize?*' She couldn't believe her ears.

'Of course! I have been young, too. I've sat in the class meeting and wished to be out in the open air. But by the mercy of God I recognized these thoughts for what they were – temptations of the devil. And by His mercy and His mercy alone I was strengthened to put them behind me. As *you* will, my dear daughter. The days are gone when we were stoned in our meetings because of our faith, but the devil is no less active against us.'

'You don't understand, Father.' With a great effort she kept her voice as calm as his was. 'You simply don't understand!'

'Of course I do, my child. It is you who are mistaken in believing that there are parts of our life which don't belong to God, parts which we can use for our own pleasure and satisfaction. It is not so. It is not the case at all. Every minute is His, to be used only in His service and to His glory.'

'I can't accept that, Father. I'm not denying God. I just want some part of my life which isn't either spent in work or in chapel. And I have to tell you that from now on I shall not attend the Wednesday class meeting, not ever again.'

He still kept outwardly calm, but now she saw a muscle twitching in his cheek, and a tic beneath his left eye which he couldn't control. She had observed this before and knew it was a sign that he was perturbed. So much the better, she thought. He would have to take her seriously.

'Furthermore, Father, I shall not be going to chapel twice every Sunday from now on. I shall attend only every other Sunday.'

He looked at her with grave eyes.

'The devil has you in thrall, Madeleine. The devil is never more active than in a Christian household, and he chooses for his targets those who are precious to God. But have no fear, Madeleine. I shall pray for you, and you yourself must pray to be delivered. Watch and pray.' He held out his hand as if to take hers, to imbue her with his strength, but she would have none of it.

'I have no feeling for prayer,' she said sharply. 'At present it means nothing to me.'

'God will not punish you for lack of feeling,' he said firmly. 'He punishes no one for offences they can not avoid. We can not, on earth, attain to perfection. That belongs only to the angels. But we must try always to do so. And now my dear I think you should leave or you will be late for your duties.'

'I'm going,' Madeleine said. 'I beg of you to believe what I've said, Father. I mean it.'

He sighed. Perhaps she was not well, or had a touch of the sun. Or perhaps she had that monthly curse of womanhood which made her sex from time to time so inexplicable and tiresome to his own.

'I will believe you for the time being,' he said. 'And on your part you will understand, I am sure, that you must not come to this house on the Sundays when you have not first been to the Lord's house. I have to think of the example you would show to your sisters. I cannot have their innocence corrupted.'

She burned with indignation. It was not so much that she planned to visit her home every Sunday, but to be denied it was another matter. And he was not treating her as a caring father might treat a daughter. He had given her the kind of pious platitudes he would hand out to a stranger. Was there no understanding in him?

She was about to leave when George came into the room.

23

'At last!' Madeleine said scornfully. 'And now perhaps you will ask my father to repeat what I have just told him. I would like you to hear it too.'

'Then I will walk with you to Mount Royd and you can tell me as we go along,' George said.

'No, thank you. I wish to be alone.'

She ran to the door and was almost out of the house when her father called after her.

'God's blessing on you! I shall pray for you. We shall all pray for you!'

'Save your breath to cool your porridge!' she cried. But she was too far down the street for anyone to hear her.

TWO

By the time Madeleine arrived back at Mount Royd, the Parkinson home, she was dog-tired – she had after all been on the go since five-thirty that morning – but curiously lighter of heart. She had not wanted to upset either of her parents, nor George for that matter. Poor George! But having made her decisions about chapel, having stood up to her father on a matter of such importance, though she had trembled all over at the time, she was now left with a deep sense of relief. She didn't really believe, it couldn't possibly be true, that he would ever forbid her the house.

The rage in which she had run out of her home in Priestley Street had subsided during the thirty-minute brisk walk between there and Mount Royd. She felt sad and sorry for her mother, though; as if she was somehow abandoning her. There was no let out for her mother. But perhaps she was happier with her family, restricted though her life was, than she would have been left a spinster in her parents' home in that remote village. Who could tell?

Mount Royd was no more than a good long stone's throw from Parkinson's mill. It was an imposing house by West Riding standards: four-square, solid, well-proportioned; built at the turn of the century when George the Third was on the throne. The front of the house faced away from the mill, looking out over lawns and well-tended flower beds and, at the bottom of the slope, a belt of trees which, except in the bareness of winter, hid the valley and the river. From here the land climbed to the moors on the other side.

That was the front of the house. But from whichever room he cared to stand in at the back, Albert Parkinson could look out of the window at the comforting sight of his own mill. If he cared to employ the small but powerful telescope which he often had handy, he could even see what was afoot; who was coming and going, who was skiving off. He liked to keep an eye on things. It paid to do so. And now, happening to pause by a staircase window to look out, he saw Madeleine returning.

She was a nice lass, Madeleine Bates. A bit too tall, a bit on the thin side for his idea of feminine beauty, though as she walked across the yard he noted the uprightness of her carriage, the slight curve of her breasts against the gingham bodice, the swing of her hips under the wide skirt. She was also a good servant, which was no more than he would have expected from a daughter of Joseph Bates, who had been his weaving overlooker for many years.

He watched her enter the back door of the house, then he turned away and went to join his wife and daughter, and his wife's relatives, in the drawing-room. He must try to stop this nonsense about them going to London, though he found it difficult to refuse his daughter anything once she made up her mind.

'You're nobbut in the nick o' time,' Mrs Thomas said to Madeleine as the latter hurried into the kitchen.

Mrs Thomas had been the Parkinson's cook since before Madeleine was born. Over the years she had seen off more young servants than she could rightly remember, largely because of her sharp tongue; but Madeleine seemed, if not immune to the older woman's gibes, at least able to cope with them, and sometimes to give as good as she got. She had stayed longer than any previous girl – six years now since she had left school at twelve.

26

'It wants five minutes yet to nine o'clock,' Madeleine said evenly. 'Is the milk on?'

'Aye, and likely to boil over if you don't look sharp, young lady! I expect you've been dallying with that young man of yours?'

Without answering, Madeleine set the tray and made the cocoa. Mrs Parkinson and Sophia took cocoa every night, very milky and well-sweetened. Mrs Parkinson's sister, who was visiting with her son, would also take it.

'I'd best lay four cups and do the biggest jug,' Madeleine said, 'in case Mr David wants cocoa. Though I expect he'll be hoping the Master will offer him a drop of his best brandy. Funny how the gentlemen always like a drop of brandy.'

'Don't criticize your betters,' Mrs Thomas said. She said it a dozen times a day and it was like water off a duck's back.

'I'm not,' Madeleine said. 'I'm just saying, that's all. I wonder what it tastes like?' No intoxicant of any kind had ever entered the house in Priestley Street. She doubted whether her father had ever had a teaspoonful of brandy in his life.

'It's not for the likes of you,' Mrs Thomas said. 'Though I have to say it's comforting against the wind, and a specific for the diarrhoea. But don't let me ever hear of you taking a sip or there'll be ructions!'

'Chance would be a fine thing!' Madeleine retorted as she manoeuvred the heavy tray through the kitchen doorway. 'Seeing that it's always kept under lock and key and the Master keeps the key on his watch chain. I'd have to knock him down!'

'And don't be impertinent!' Mrs Thomas called after her. But Madeleine was climbing the steep, narrow stairs which divided the servants' domain from that of their betters.

When she entered the drawing-room, her arms almost breaking under the weight of the tray, David Chester sprang to his feet to give her a hand. She rewarded him with a smile and he thought, not for the first time, what a pretty girl she was. Not beautiful, like his cousin Sophia, of course. Her features were a little too large, too defined. But nice enough for all that. Some fellow was going to be lucky. He wondered if she was walking out with anyone.

The three ladies, deep in conversation, did not even raise their heads. Mr Parkinson was already drinking his brandy, and not looking best pleased about something or other, Madeleine thought.

'I declare I don't know what I shall wear,' Sophia was saying. 'Everyone in London is sure to be exceedingly smart. And there's no time at all to have anything made!'

'Perhaps your papa will take you shopping in London,' her aunt suggested coyly. 'They say the shops there have to be seen to be believed. Far grander than Bradford or Leeds!'

Albert Parkinson glared at his sister-in-law. Why did she have to put her two pennyworth in? His daughter's head was already stuffed full of nonsense.

'I'm going to London for the wool sales,' he said. 'I shall have no time for traipsing around women's shops.'

'That will be all for tonight, Madeleine,' Mrs Parkinson said. 'You may go to bed now.'

'I've got news for you, Mrs Thomas,' Madeleine said, back in the kitchen. 'They're going to London. The Mistress and Miss Sophia with the Master. I heard them talking about it.'

'You've no call to be listening to private conversations,' Mrs Thomas said automatically.

'I wasn't actually listening. I was pouring the cocoa. But you know how they go on, just as if the likes of you and me didn't exist.'

'The Master won't like it,' Mrs Thomas observed. 'He likes his little trips on his own. So when are they going?'

'I don't know. Soon – because Miss Sophia was saying she wouldn't have time to get any new dresses. I must say, the Master didn't look all that happy.'

28

'Well I dare say it'll be all go from now on,' Mrs Thomas said comfortably.

She can afford to sound smug, Madeleine thought. I'm the one who'll have the extra work. Sewing, washing, ironing, packing.

'So what was your class like this evening, then?' Mrs Thomas enquired. 'I hope you've come back a better girl, fitter for work!'

'I'm always fit for work,' Madeleine said coldly. 'I do my work whatever else. I work from morning until night.' Sometimes, when she lay in bed at night, every bone and muscle in her body ached with fatigue.

'Hoity-toity! Well it hasn't done your temper any good it seems. I thought it was supposed to make you all sweetness and light. Not that I've ever been a chapel-goer myself. I've never had the time. You're very lucky that the Master gives you the time off, my girl. I hope you appreciate it.'

'I do. And I hope he appreciates the way I work extra hard to make up for it,' Madeleine said sharply. 'Nothing goes undone that I'm responsible for.'

So would she be allowed the three hours off on Wednesday evenings when she no longer spent them in going to chapel? But would anyone – the thought flashed into her mind – actually *know* that she wasn't in chapel? Couldn't she just leave the house and return at the usual time, no one any the wiser? It was a great temptation, which she must try to put from her. The habit of honesty, inconvenient though it was going to be, was too deeply ingrained in her to be ignored. But she would keep quiet for now. She didn't want an inquisition from Mrs Thomas. It was none of her business anyway.

'Perhaps you've quarrelled with your young man?' Mrs Thomas persisted. There was something not quite as usual about the girl, something in her attitude. She'd sensed it as soon as Madeleine marched into the kitchen – and she prided herself on getting to the bottom of things.

'I haven't,' Madeleine snapped. 'And he's not my young man.'

'Oh pardon me, I'm sure! Excuse me for speaking! I thought you and George Carter were walking out. I thought you had an understanding.' I think I've hit the nail on the head, Mrs Thomas said to herself. A lover's tiff. Now what about, I wonder?

'We were never walking out,' Madeleine said. 'We were simply in chapel together, and since he lodges with my parents, we walked home together. Would you have expected us to have walked home separately?'

'No call to be sharp with me!' Mrs Thomas said. She was quite enjoying herself. It had been a dull day so far.

'I'm sorry. And we don't have an understanding, as you call it. Or at least *I* don't. If there is one, it's in everybody else's heads.'

The truth suddenly dawned on her. Of course that was it! It was her family, the people in chapel, George himself, who had taken this for granted. She had simply gone along without giving it much thought. Nothing definite had ever been said between herself and George, and they had done nothing except walk to and from chapel together. Perhaps George had assumed something more, but if he had, well serve him right for taking her for granted. If necessary she would spell it out for him next time they met, in a kindly way, of course; though in the circumstances who knew when that would be? Anyway, he was better out of it, just as she was, and he'd soon come to see that. The two of them were even worse matched than her mother and father.

'Well you could have fooled me,' Mrs Thomas said. 'In my young day if a man walked a girl home from chapel it was as good as a declaration. How times change!'

'They certainly do!' Madeleine agreed.

She felt sure that times were going to change for her, from now on. She was suddenly free; free of everything which had held her down. But no, she thought, not everything! She was still a servant, tied by the need to earn a living and to help support her family, to carry out other people's wishes, obey their commands. The only way to escape that was in marriage, and at this moment marriage was the last thing she wanted. It was simply another form of slavery.

'I think I'll go to bed,' she said. 'I'm tired out. Good night Mrs Thomas.'

'Good night then. And mind you get out of the right side of the bed in the morning, my lady!'

Madeleine was fortunate in having a bedroom entirely to herself. The rest of the domestic help, mostly wives of factory hands, came in daily from Helsdon, except for William Drake, who looked after the horses, drove the carriage, and lived over the stable. Madeleine's bedroom was at the top of the house, under the roof, and hardly bigger than a cupboard; in fact its twin was the box-room. The walls sloped steeply so that she had to be careful not to crack her head against the ceiling. In winter it was bitterly cold, the window thick with ice crystals, but this evening all the heat of the long, hot summer seemed concentrated within its four walls.

She opened the small window as far as it would go, though not before first snuffing her candle, for she was terrified of the large moths which flew in from the garden. She was never quite sure which frightened her more, the moths which came seeking the light, or the mice which scuttled around in the dark. Either way, she was ready to duck under the bedclothes at a second's notice.

But now, before getting into bed, she leaned over the window-sill, viewing the darkening landscape, trying to get a breath of air. Although her bedroom faced the mill and the town, there were few lights to be seen. Helsdon folk went to bed in good time. There was little to do in the evenings, and anyway they had to be up early. Also it cost good money to light the lamps, and money, except for the few, was always short.

Somewhere out there was Priestley Street. Emerald and Penelope would be asleep; her mother would be lying on one side of the double bed and her father, no doubt, would be on his knees by the side of the bed, saying his lengthy prayers. She supposed he would be praying for her. She wished him no harm, she couldn't help but be fond of him, but if his petitions included her return to the fold, then she hoped God would know better and would not answer. She didn't even think of George.

Somewhere out there also was the whole of Helsdon, and beyond that a bigger world of which as yet she knew nothing. But one day she would, she was sure of it. She turned away from the window, climbed into the narrow bed, and was asleep in minutes, before the first mouse began to stir.

Sophia was in a ferment of preparation. She had tried on every dress in her wardrobe at least twice, and was satisfied with none of them.

'They're going to look so old-fashioned,' she complained to her mother. 'Oh I do so wish there'd been time to have something new made! But in any case, who in Helsdon could possibly make anything fit to wear in London?'

'Miss Compton usually serves us well enough,' Mrs Parkinson said placidly. 'She's a good little seamstress. I don't have cause for complaint.'

Miss Compton came twice a year, in the autumn and the spring, and made their gowns for the coming season.

'Oh Mother, of course you don't!' Sophia said impatiently. 'You don't care about being fashionable, but I do. It's different for me.'

What she meant, and both women knew it, was that her mother was in her late forties and was short and fat, whereas eighteen-year-old Sophia, though no taller than her mother, was slender as a wand and at the same time deliciously curved in the right places. She was also as pretty as a picture with her auburn curls, fine features and milky skin. She had the best of both worlds, for she had inherited her mother's stature and frame – underneath the fat Mrs Parkinson was as delicately boned as Sophia – and her father's good looks and thick auburn hair.

'I would rather be comfortable than fashionable any day of the week,' Mrs Parkinson said.

'I dare say,' Sophia agreed. 'But I wouldn't.' She was prepared to suffer untold agonies for the sake of her appearance.

Now she surveyed herself critically in the looking-glass, her head on one side, her lips pursed.

'So what do you think, Mother? Can I possibly be seen in this thing?' She was wearing a hooped skirt in fine, peach-coloured lawn, with panels at the side, and across the front from waist to hem, rows of deep frills. The bodice was close fitting, with frills at the cuffs and a neckline higher than she would have liked. She was well aware that her bosom was one of her best features, but Helsdon society didn't favour a display of too much flesh.

'I think you look quite delightful,' Mrs Parkinson said truthfully. 'And with your little hip-length jacket if the weather should turn cool, and your bonnet retrimmed, you'll be as pretty as a picture.' Privately, she was convinced that her daughter would outshine anything London had to offer.

'Oh well, I suppose it will have to do,' Sophia said disconsolately. 'And I suppose to go to London without the right clothes will be just about better than not going at all. I can't tell you how much I *long* to go to London!'

'You have,' Mrs Parkinson said. 'About a thousand times. Though how you persuaded your father I shall never know. Of course he'd never have agreed if Cousin David hadn't been able to come with us. Your father won't have the time to escort us, so we must be grateful to David.'

'Cousin David is only too happy to escort us,' Sophia said. 'I dare say he'd accompany us to the ends of the earth if need be!' He was in love with her, and had been since she was in the schoolroom.

'I'm aware of that,' her mother said. 'Sometimes I think you take advantage of him. Why don't you two make a match of it?'

'Well for one thing he hasn't declared himself yet,' Sophia answered. 'And I don't want him to because I can't make up my mind.'

She wanted to be married, of course; to have her own establishment. And David was kind, and very good-looking. The Chesters didn't have much money – Aunt Fanny was widowed – but her father would see to all that.

'Well don't keep him waiting too long. He's an attractive young man and you might not be the only pebble on the beach.'

'And I dare say there might be other fish in *my* pond,' Sophia said. 'Anyway, never mind all that now. What about my bonnet? Straw bonnets are still in, but this summer the straw must hardly show under the lace and flowers, so it will have to be vastly retrimmed. You would think Papa would buy me a new one for the occasion!'

'It's very generous of your father to take us,' her mother pointed out. 'Sometimes you expect too much of him.'

'It gives him pleasure to make me happy,' Sophia said complacently. 'That's why I can't understand him being so mean on this occasion. You'd think he didn't want us to go to London.'

It was quite true that Albert Parkinson didn't want his family to accompany him. It would be deuced awkward. He didn't go to London just for the wool sales. If that had been so he could have sent someone else instead of going so regularly himself. Most men in his position sent someone to buy for them. No, it wasn't the sales. It was Kitty. She was, and had been for three years now, his chief reason for going to London. She drew him like a magnet. Not that he was prepared to upset the apple cart at home, of course. His wife was a nice enough woman, dutiful and faithful; moreover she was the mother of his daughter. But their marriage had early on drifted into a placid relationship. For all her prettiness – which had now largely left her – his wife had very little passion. Kitty was quite different.

Walking home from the mill at the end of the afternoon

he thought about her. He usually walked to and from the mill. It wasn't far, and he could do with the exercise because he had a tendency to stoutness. He often took his spaniel bitch, Bobbin, for similar reasons, and sometimes as they walked, he talked to her about whatever was on his mind. If any dumb animal could understand, then Bobbin could.

'I'll not go to London without seeing her,' he said now. 'I'll not miss out on Kitty!'

At first when he met her he'd almost forgotten her between his visits; she was just someone who belonged to the other world of London. But it wasn't so now. He thought about her a lot, especially as the time for each trip drew near. He longed for her warm disposition, her manifest joy in seeing him, almost as much as for the warmth of her bed.

'I'll not give her up,' he said firmly to Bobbin. 'I'll not give her up, not even for one visit!'

And then, after dwelling on Kitty's charms, soon to be experienced, his mind turned, as it usually did in the end, to business. He was a worried man. He didn't show it outwardly. That wouldn't do. People in the West Riding lost confidence in you if you went about with a long face, and they were sharp to notice. You had to keep up appearances, do things in style, appear successful. He'd always been able to do that, it was something to do with his natural swagger.

Of course he wasn't without a bob or two, and he had the mill – the best worsted mill in Helsdon by a long chalk, and turning out some of the finest cloth in the West Riding, which meant in the world. He wasn't as big as Titus Salt, nobody was; they said his mill covered six acres and he needed 3,500 hands to run it. But Titus wasn't in Helsdon, thank goodness.

The last year or two had been very difficult indeed. The price of wool, especially the price of 'long' wool, which they needed for the worsted, had been all wrong, still was. The war in the Crimea hadn't helped. People in business had been jumpy; had lost confidence because of it. Perhaps I'd have been better in the woollen trade, he thought. It was different from the worsted; they used the sharp staple and turned out coarser, thicker cloth; to his way of thinking, inferior. But they were the ones who'd made money supplying uniforms for the war; it was wool that was in demand here.

Like most of the worsted mills, Parkinson's had been on short time a lot in the last few years. It had been bad for him and worse, he supposed, for his millhands. He didn't know how some of them managed. He'd had to go to the bank to help him out more than once when the bills were due. He didn't like being in debt to the bank.

'Oh well,' he said to Bobbin. 'I dare say it'll all come out in the wash!'

And here they were, home, and he was ready for a good meal, a bit of nice mutton for preference. And the day after tomorrow he'd see Kitty. It would be too late when they arrived in London, but the day after, nothing would keep him from her, choose how.

Albert Parkinson wasn't the only one to be worried by the war in Crimea. That very morning, when Madeleine came down from clearing the breakfast, Mrs Thomas said:

'There's a letter for you, my girl. From foreign parts. Your brother, I shouldn't wonder.'

'Where is it? Give it to me!' Madeleine said quickly. She snatched the letter from Mrs Thomas's hand.

'Oh, Mrs Thomas, it *is* from Irvine! I can recognize his hand. Oh please may I read it straight away?'

'You may, my girl,' Mrs Thomas said graciously.

As Madeleine read the words scrawled on the scrap of paper, her lips trembled and tears came to her eyes. Oh, it was so awful!

'Nothing bad, I hope?' Mrs Thomas asked.

'Oh, Mrs Thomas, you wouldn't believe . . .! It's dreadful! It was written in the winter and it's taken all this time to get here. I just hope things have improved.'

36

But from what they had printed in the *Bradford Observer* she thought it was unlikely.

'He says . . .' She read the letter aloud to Mrs Thomas, who was unable to read.

> 'It gets colder all the time. Two men perished from the cold coming back from Balaclava, and last night a man got frostbite in both his feet and will have to have his toes amputated. We're short of ammunition, there's hardly any food, and it would break your heart to see the condition of the poor horses. Tell Ma I'm well but don't tell her the rest.
>
> Your loving brother . . .'

Tears choked her and she was unable to finish.

'Oh, Mrs Thomas, it's so awful! And Irvine never could stand the cold. Not even in Helsdon!'

'There, there,' Mrs Thomas soothed her. 'Don't take on, love! That was just when he wrote. He'll not be cold now. It's the summer. He'll be as warm as toast.' More like as hot as hell, poor lad, she thought to herself.

'How am I going to tell my mother without showing her the letter?' Madeleine cried. 'If I say I've lost it, or thrown it in the fire by accident, she'll be furious with me!'

'Better than worrying her with the truth,' Mrs Thomas advised. 'But why wouldn't the lad write to his mother?'

'Because he quarrelled with my father. He'd be afraid my father would see the letter first, and open it and keep it from her. But I don't think my father would do that.'

'Well you can slip home to see your mother after they've set off for London tomorrow,' Mrs Thomas said kindly. 'Now, dry your eyes and get back to work. Work's the best cure for sorrow. And try to look on the bright side. They say Sebastopol's bound to fall soon and then the war'll be as good as over.'

Madeleine dried her eyes on her apron.

'Thank you, Mrs Thomas. I have to pack for Mrs

Parkinson and Miss Sophia. I suppose I'd best get on with it.'

For the next hour she smoothed and folded and packed the trunk Mrs Parkinson and Sophia would share between them. Dresses, hose, nightshifts, caps; petticoats laundered stiff as boards with Colman's starch; gloves, slippers. How could anyone need so much for just four days? There were more clothes going into the trunk than Madeleine had possessed in a lifetime. But she was too sad and dispirited to feel any envy. She would have traded everything she had ever owned just to hear that Irvine was safe and well.

'Oh, isn't it all exciting?' Sophia cried – then stopped at the sight of Madeleine's face.

'Why, is something wrong Madeleine? You don't look yourself.'

'It's my brother, Miss Sophia. I've had a letter from the war.'

'He's not . . .?'

'No, miss. Leastways he was alive and well when he wrote it, but that was in February. But it's very nasty out there.' And for all I know, she thought miserably, he might be dead. But she must pull herself together. It didn't do to think like that.

'I'm sorry to hear that,' Sophia said. 'And thankful my brother's not old enough to fight in a war.' Roger Parkinson was fourteen, staying at the moment with new friends he had made at his boarding school.

'Yes, miss. I can't see Master Roger wanting to go for a soldier.' Nor could she Irvine, he'd been such a quiet boy – but he'd gone.

There was a knock at the bedroom door and Mr Parkinson entered. When he looked at the trunk, piled high now beyond the rim, his reaction was the same as Madeleine's.

'Why in the world do you want all that stuff for four days?' he demanded.

'You never know, Papa,' Sophia said. 'It's hot now but it might turn cool; or it might rain. We might go somewhere quite smart, or we might go boating, or to the theatre. I can't possibly wear the same outfits for everything!'

He caught sight of Madeleine and for the first time ever noticed what she was wearing: wide skirt in grey cotton – though the skirt was nowhere near as wide as his daughter's – with a grey cotton bodice, buttoned up to the neck, and on her head a white cap. Did she ever wear anything else? He'd never noticed. He supposed she must have something else to go to chapel in. But then the circumstances were different. His daughter, though inclined to be extravagant, had more needs than the maid. But having looked at Madeleine he noticed the unusual sadness in her face, and since he was a kind man, he spoke to her.

'Is something wrong, Madeleine?'

When she told him about Irvine he said, 'Does your father know? Would you like to go down to the mill and tell him?'

Madeleine shook her head.

'My mother will tell him presently,' she said.

'Very well.'

He turned to Sophia. 'You must see you're totally ready at nine o'clock in the morning. Drake will be waiting to drive us to Leeds for the London train, and if you keep us back we'll risk missing it, and that'll be the end of your trip, young lady!'

'I'll be ready on the dot,' Sophia promised.

'Well see you are,' he said. 'Madeleine, you'd better keep her to it.'

'I will, sir,' Madeleine replied.

At five minutes past nine the next day, with everything packed and secured, they were ready to drive away. Madeleine, who had helped to arrange the ladies' voluminous skirts in the carriage, stepped back to wave them off. She felt in better spirits this morning, lively enough to wish with all her heart that it was she sitting there in the carriage, setting off for London town. Oh, how she longed to do so!

As the horses started to move Mr Parkinson leaned out of the carriage and threw something towards her.

'Here! Buy yourself something!' he called.

It fell to the ground, and when she went to pick it up it was a shilling. She spat on it for luck before putting it into her pocket. She would have a rare treat with that!

THREE

When Madeleine went back into the kitchen Mrs Thomas was all briskness. She had rolled up her sleeves and was wearing a dark 'working' apron instead of her usual spotless white one.

'Well,' she said. 'That's them off. Now perhaps we can get something done!' She sometimes spoke as though her employers perversely existed in order to prevent her finishing things.

She looked the picture of energy, as if ready to overturn the world, but Madeleine was not deceived. Mrs Thomas was the General-in-Command. She would determine the strategy and give the orders. It was Madeleine who would carry them out.

'We'll start with the pantry,' Mrs Thomas said. 'Clear everything from the shelves and then give them a good scrub. Put a drop of ammonia in the water when you come to the scrubbing; it loosens the dirt.'

'Not that there's ever any dirt in *your* pantry, Mrs Thomas,' Madeleine said. 'It looks as clean as a new pin before we start on it.'

It seemed a totally unnecessary job, but Mrs Thomas was good at finding things for other hands to do. In Madeleine's opinion, scrubbing the pantry shelves, and no doubt after that the floor, was not her job at all. She wasn't a charwoman. Mrs Greene came in from Helsdon every morning specifically to do the rough; Mrs Potter every Monday and Tuesday to do the mountains of washing and ironing, though Madeleine usually found herself helping with the latter. Today, for some unaccountable reason, Mrs Thomas had sent Mrs Greene to work at the top of the house and kept Madeleine in the kitchen.

'That's the way I like to keep things. Always have, always will,' Mrs Thomas said comfortably. 'Anybody can inspect my kitchen any time, day or night, it makes no matter. They'll find it clean as a new pin. No dirt hiding in *my* corners!'

'I'll get going,' Madeleine said. 'Sooner started, sooner done.' She emptied the pantry of all its contents, spreading them on the large kitchen table and on every other available surface.

'There's enough stuff here to feed an army,' she said. 'Sugar, rice, flour, pepper, dried fruit, cornflour . . .'

It contrasted sharply in her mind with the two shelves in the cellar-head of her parents' home which served as a larder. These were more than adequate to take all the food they had in the house at any one time. But here, as well as the pantry, there was the larder, with eggs, butter, ox-tongues, even hams hanging from the ceiling; and heaven knew what further good things there were down in the keeping-cellar. But mentioning the army, she thought again about Irvine and wondered if, wherever he was, he had eaten today.

She reminded Mrs Thomas of her promise.

'You won't forget you said I could nip home and tell Ma about Irvine, will you?'

'Of course I won't,' Mrs Thomas said. 'But work comes first. You get through your work and all being well you shall go home this afternoon.'

There was a great deal to get through: not just the pantry to turn out, but the larder, then the kitchen shelves, and finally the big dresser with all its drawers. It was four o'clock in the afternoon before Madeleine brought in the last of the drawers, which, after scrubbing, had been standing out in the sun to dry. She slid it into place, put the cutlery in exact order, and thankfully closed it.

'There! That's that!' She was tired, and far too hot, but worst of all were her hands. They were always rough and red, she thought, scrutinizing them, with the knuckles swollen and misshapen because as a growing child she had had to do too much housework, scrub too many floors; and now they were stinging from the ammonia which had seeped into the small cuts and abrasions from which her hands never seemed quite free.

'Go on, then,' Mrs Thomas said. 'You can have a knob of lard and a teaspoon of sugar to rub in. That'll smooth 'em. Not that it doesn't seem wicked to be rubbing your hands with what some poor soul could put in her stomach!'

Madeleine gratefully held out her cupped hands while Mrs Thomas doled out the lard and sugar. It's all very well for you, she thought. You can keep your hands smooth with all that pastry making and kneading of bread.

'Now get off with you,' Mrs Thomas said. 'Don't be long, mind. Straight there and back! I'm not at all sure that the mistress would like me giving you time off to go home, not if she knew.'

Madeleine was sure she wouldn't have minded. When she remembered, Mrs Parkinson could be quite kind. Anyway, she wasn't here, was she? And what the eyes didn't see the heart wouldn't grieve over. But Mrs Thomas liked to feel she had the power.

'Thank you ever so,' Madeleine said. 'I'll just go and change.'

She ran upstairs to her attic, took off her uniform and put on her gingham skirt and bodice. My but it was hot! She would have liked to have had a long, cool wash, but there was no water in the ewer and she hadn't time to fetch any. When she went down again Mrs Thomas handed her a basket, the contents covered with a white cloth.

'Here, take this for your mother. A bit of oatmeal parkin

43

and a few other things. Might help out a bit. And don't you go forgetting to bring the basket back, *and* the cloth.'

Outside it was warmer, close and sticky as though there might be a storm. Madeleine wondered what it would be like in London, and whether they would have reached there or would still be on the train. She had never been on a train. She fingered the shilling in her pocket. Perhaps that was what she'd do with it; go on a train.

Reaching home, the house door was open, but when she walked in there was no sign of her mother. Then she heard her coming down the stairs. Mrs Bates came into the living-room, grey-faced and looking terribly worried.

'Why, Ma, whatever's the matter?' Madeleine asked. 'Are you poorly?'

'No, but Emerald is. She seems real bad. I've been up half the night with her.' She sat on the nearest chair, burying her face in her hands. She was so weary, so worried.

'What's matter with her, then?'

Emerald was the least strong of all of them. Her mother was used to nursing her through bouts of sickness, but Madeleine didn't remember ever having seen her look as concerned as she did now.

'I don't know. I wish I did. She's not got her usual cough, and though she's been sick a lot, she's stopped vomiting now; but she has a fever and it's not abating at all. She's as hot as a fiery furnace.'

'I'll go up and see her,' Madeleine said.

Mrs Bates put up her hand and caught hold of Madeleine.

'No. No, best not. It might be something catching. There's nothing you can do for her that I haven't already done. What she rightly needs is the doctor.'

Madeleine had no need to ask why her mother hadn't sent for the doctor. A doctor's visit cost money, and in the case of Doctor Hughes, a shilling on the nail. He was seldom sent for in Priestley Street, not because he wasn't needed but because he couldn't be afforded. Even when

44

the women had babies they didn't call on the doctor. The midwife came cheaper or, failing her, they helped each other out. Only if the mother seemed to be slipping away, was beyond their skill, would someone run for the doctor while someone else took up a collection along the street to pay him.

'I've done all I know,' Mrs Bates said. 'I've been sponging her down all day, and Mrs Batley let me have a lemon to make some hot lemon water, but nothing seems to cool her. It's downright wicked that the poor can't call on the doctor when he's needed. There ought to be a law. He could give her a bottle of physic, give her a bit of ease, and perhaps set my mind at rest.' She had lost two children and lived in deep fear of losing another. The older they got, the worse it could be, for with every year that passed they became more precious to her. They were the mainspring of her life.

Madeleine's hand went to the coin in her pocket. She fingered it, turned it over, grasped it. It represented so much. A ride on a train. A visit to Helsdon Fair, which would take place next week. New trimming for her bonnet or some material for a new bodice. While she held it in her hand a whole world of choice was hers.

'Mrs Thomas sent a few things,' she said. 'She's quite kind when she has a mind to be.'

Mrs Bates looked into the basket.

'Perhaps I can tempt Emerald with something later on,' she said. 'A bit of curd tart.' Then she looked up suddenly.

'Why have you come, Madeleine? You don't usually come like this. Surely you haven't . . .?' That was another thing she dreaded, that one day one of them would come home and say, 'I've lost my job.'

'They've gone to London,' Madeleine said. 'Mrs Thomas said I could slip over if I was quick. I've got news of Irvine, Ma!'

All the colour drained from Mrs Bates's already pale face. Her hands, lying on the table, were tightly clenched.

'Tell me at once, Madeleine,' she said quietly. 'I want to know . . .'

Madeleine interrupted her.

'Ma, it's good news! I'm sorry if I startled you. He's fit and well!'

Mrs Bates expelled a long breath. Suddenly she was trembling from head to foot, but now with relief.

'How do you know? Has somebody come across him?'

'I've had a letter.'

Mrs Bates held out her hand.

'Give it to me! Quickly, Madeleine.'

'I can't,' Madeleine faltered.

'Can't?'

'Oh Ma, I'm ever so sorry. It got burnt. Mrs Thomas picked it up by mistake with some rubbish and threw it in the fire!' The words came out in a rush. Please forgive me, Mrs Thomas, for taking your name in vain, she thought.

'Burnt! Of all the stupid . . .!'

'It was an accident, Ma! She was really upset.'

'Oh, how could she?' Mrs Bates cried. 'Then tell me what he said. What did he say?'

'He said he was fit and well. He said conditions weren't all that bad; it had been very cold but now it was warmer.' Madeleine was shocked at the fluency with which she lied. 'And he sent his love,' she added.

If I could have *seen* it, Mrs Bates thought. If I could just have seen his handwriting on the page. But there was no question as to why he hadn't written to her. They both knew the answer to that. Though her husband hadn't, in so many words, forbidden herself and her son to communicate, if they did it would cause a lot of trouble. And because the trouble would fall on her, Irvine had told her when he'd left that he'd write instead to Madeleine.

And all because he had got in with the wrong crowd, she thought bitterly. A set of lads older than he was, who'd offered him a bit of the excitement which was missing from his life. It had come to a head that one night they'd taken him to a public house and got him drunk;

and him only sixteen. Not very drunk – certainly not by Priestley Street standards – but more than enough for his father, to whom a public house was the dwelling-place of the devil. The row which had followed had been terrible. You would have thought the lad had committed murder. She would never forget it, nor the moment when Irvine had stormed out of the house for good. At that moment she would have liked to have picked up sticks and gone with him, but though he was her only son, and the light of her life, she had the girls to think of.

Now her husband acted as though Irvine was already dead. He was never mentioned between them, though she couldn't believe that in his heart of hearts Joseph didn't feel the separation. Somewhere under that rock-hard exterior she knew he had feelings. Or had once had, though each year now they seemed buried deeper. Well, she would tell him nothing of her news. He didn't deserve to know. Her thoughts on the subject were as bitter as gall. And now he was doing all he could to drive Madeleine away. Were all her children to be taken from her, one way or another?

'Has father said anything more about me?' Madeleine asked.

'There's been nothing said, not by George either, though I'd say he's a bit upset and you ought to speak to him. There was a bad atmosphere on Sunday when you didn't turn up for chapel, and the girls missed you. But unless you're going to chapel, it'd be best if you didn't come home, leastways not when your father's in the house.'

'Well, I shall go to chapel once a fortnight and no more,' Madeleine said firmly. 'He's not going to make me. And I'm through with class. They can take my name off the roll.'

There was a sudden loud cry from the bedroom. Mrs Bates leapt to her feet and ran up the stairs, pushing Madeleine away as she made to follow her.

'No! Wait here!'

47

Madeleine could hear her sister's voice crying in distress, and then her mother's trying to calm and soothe. Eventually the cries ceased and all was quiet again. Mrs Bates came downstairs looking totally exhausted and beside herself with worry.

'I think she's delirious,' she said. 'The fever's no better. No better at all.'

'Ma, you've got to send for the doctor,' Madeleine urged. 'Can't father get the money?'

'You know he can't. Not until pay day. And even then his damned chapel will have first claim!'

Hardly ever before had Madeleine heard her mother disloyal to her father, and never before had she heard her swear. She must really be at the end of her tether. And here am I bothering about rides on trains or new bonnet ribbons, Madeleine thought with shame.

'I'll run for the doctor on my way back,' she said. 'I'll ask him to come at once.'

'Don't be silly, Madeleine,' Mrs Bates said in a dull voice. 'You know Dr Hughes'll not come without he sees the colour of your money.'

Madeleine took the shilling from her pocket and held it up in front of her mother.

'There's the colour of my money, then! The Master threw it at me just as they were setting off for London. I couldn't think why, he's not usually that generous. But now I know why. It was Providence, Ma!'

Though the doctor promised to call within the hour, Madeleine returned to Mount Royd troubled. There was so little she could do – though thank goodness she had had the shilling.

'Poor little lass!' Mrs Thomas said. 'We mun say a prayer for her when we go to bed tonight.'

Madeleine did so, though she felt that relations between herself and God were at a low ebb. But if God punished, as her father believed, why would he choose to punish Emerald, who never did a thing wrong? She worried about it until she finally fell asleep, but when she wakened in the morning she felt anxiety still pressing on her like a heavy weight.

'If I could only just go home and see how Emerald is!' she said to Mrs Thomas.

Mrs Thomas pursed her lips.

'I've no wish to be unkind,' she said. 'But there's a lot to get through while the family's in London, and you did have two hours off yesterday afternoon. It wouldn't take you more than five minutes to run down to the mill and ask your father how your sister is. There's no real call to go all the way home when he's close at hand.'

Madeleine could find no answer to that. She had not told Mrs Thomas about the strained relations between herself and her father, nor did she wish to do so. Last Sunday, when the household supposed her to be in chapel, she had spent the time walking over the moor. And now she dreaded having to face her father, but if she wanted to know about Emerald, she would have to do so.

'You can go down to the mill straight after breakfast,' Mrs Thomas offered.

Madeleine set off with a heavy and fearful heart; heavy for her sister and fearful on account of her father. Supposing he refused to tell her anything? Supposing he refused even to speak to her? The field path to the mill ran steeply downhill. Mount Royd was built on the top of the rise, the mill in the valley bottom, on a spit of land between the river and the canal. At her usual pace it would have taken her little more than five minutes to run down – she ran everywhere – but now she dawdled. Anything to put off the moment.

Mr Turner, the man on the gate, knew her.

'Can I go in and see my father? It's urgent,' she begged.

'Well you'll have to come in through t'pennyhoil,' he joked, smiling at her. 'But I'll not fine you this time!'

There was a 'pennyhoil man' at every mill. It was his job to close the mill gates dead on time at the start of each working day. If you weren't inside the gates you had to go through his office, and he took your name and you were fined a penny for the first five minutes late, and worse after that. Some pennyhoil men, Madeleine knew, were kinder than others. If they saw a lass running they would close the gates slowly so she could sneak in. Others would shut the gate in the girl's face. Mr Turner was one of the former.

'Take care, mind!' he called after her as she crossed the cobbled mill yard in the direction of the weaving shed.

She knew her way. As a small child she had been to the mill on several occasions to take her father's dinner. Most of the hands lived close, and ran home for their midday dinner the minute the mill buzzer sounded and the engines were stopped, but her father couldn't manage it there and back in the forty minutes allowed. He took his food in a small hut Mr Parkinson had set aside for the few in the same position. Perhaps she should have waited until his dinner-time before coming?

As soon as you got into the yard you could smell the wool. It was a strange, all-pervading smell, though to Madeleine not unpleasant since, like everyone in Helsdon, she had grown up with it. You could smell it as you walked the streets, or passed the open doors of the mills. Her father said it came from the grease in the raw wool. Some said it was the smell of money, at least for the Masters.

When she stepped into the weaving shed the noise hit her like a thunderous wave, the clack-clack-thump of a hundred looms all working at once. It was a tremendous, terrifying noise, but the people who worked there said you got used to it quite quickly. She spotted her father at once, his buff-coloured overlooker's smock conspicuous among the dark clothes of the weavers. He was standing in the 'gate' between two looms, speaking to one of the hands and examining a piece of cloth. In the interval before he looked up and saw her, Madeleine thought how handsome he was, even in his working clothes, and how much she wanted to love him if only he would let her, if only he would not be so fierce.

50

The moment he saw her he walked across to where she was standing.

'You shouldn't be in here,' he said sharply. 'It's not a safe place with all this machinery about, and you with your hair uncovered!'

He doesn't realize I can't hear him because of the noise, Madeleine thought. Everyone working in the weaving shed quickly learned to lip-read because they couldn't compete with the noise of the looms.

'I can't hear you,' she said. But she could tell by his face that he was cross about something.

He nodded impatiently and led the way out of the shed.

'Don't come in there again,' he said. 'Haven't I told you about shuttles flying off? And all that machinery? It's a dangerous place unless you know what you're doing. What have you come for?'

'I've come to ask about Emerald,' Madeleine said. 'I was worried. What did the doctor say?'

A look of anxiety crossed her father's face.

'He said it was some sort of summer fever. He couldn't put a name to it. He gave her a bottle of medicine. She's a bit better this morning.' His voice softened as he looked at the tense face of his eldest daughter. 'Don't worry, child. She'll be all right.'

'Thank you, Father.' She turned to go and he called after her.

'Come back here a minute, Madeleine!'

She retraced her steps.

'I missed you in chapel on Sunday. Tell me, have you changed your mind? Have you seen the wickedness of your decision, my child?'

'I have not, Father,' she said stonily. 'Nor shall I.'

He shook his head sorrowfully.

'Then I shall continue to pray for you. I shall not cease from doing so until you come out of the darkness and into the light.'

Without a word she turned and ran across the mill yard, out through the pennyhoil without so much as a thank you to Mr Turner, and set off up the hill. Joseph Bates stood where he was, watching her until she was out of sight. Then he went back into the weaving.

Sophia stirred in her sleep at the knock on the door, and then wakened as the chambermaid came into the room with her early morning tea. She raised herself on one elbow, rubbing the sleep out of her eyes, not quite certain for the moment where she was.

'Good morning, miss!' the chambermaid said. 'A lovely day again!' She placed the tray on the bedside table. 'Shall I draw the curtains, miss?'

'Oh yes please!' Sophia sat up in bed, fully awake now. She looked around the bedroom which, with the sun now streaming in through the big window, appeared even better than it had last night. It was the very first time she had slept in a real hotel bedroom. Each year in August they went into lodgings for a month at the seaside, her father staying with them for Helsdon Feast week when the mill was closed; but this was quite different. This was London, and the Hotel Splendid lived up to its name. It had an imposing, pillared entrance, and there were lots of men standing around in dark green livery with brass buttons who sprang to carry out one's slightest wish. It was situated somewhere quite close to the Embankment but Sophia wasn't sure where because she hadn't yet got her bearings.

'I'll be up with your hot water presently,' the chambermaid said.

'Oh! Oh yes, thank you!'

For the next few minutes she lay in bed, thinking about what they'd do today, looking back on yesterday. The train journey had taken several hours but she hadn't been the least bit bored. There was the changing scenery to look at, and she and David found plenty to talk about. She was surprised that her parents should spend so much time nodding off when everything was so exciting.

And then the journey in the cab from the station! She

had never seen such traffic in her life: stage carriages, hackney carriages, slow, lumbering carts, and the horse-drawn omnibuses with people seated precariously on the open top deck. It wasn't that she'd never seen any of these things before. After all, she'd been to Leeds and Bradford several times, but here there were so many vehicles, and hundreds of pedestrians crossing and recrossing the streets, dodging right in front of the carriage wheels in the most dangerous manner. And then there was the noise; not just the noise of traffic, of iron-rimmed wheels travelling fast over the stone setts, but the constant cry of street vendors vying with each other. It had taken their cab ages to reach the hotel, but she hadn't minded a bit.

When the maid brought the cans of hot water, Sophia got out of bed quickly – no time to waste today – stripped, and began to wash. She had hardly started before the door opened and her mother came in.

'Mother, you startled me!' Really, Sophia thought, at eighteen I should *not* be subjected to my mother walking into my room unannounced!

'Breakfast in the dining-room in half an hour,' Mrs Parkinson said. She walked across to the wardrobe and studied the contents. 'What are you going to wear today, my love?'

'I don't know,' Sophia said coldly. Whatever it was, she was going to decide for herself. She really didn't need her mother to choose her clothes for her, just as if she was a small child. 'I'll choose something. But shouldn't you be getting ready also?' Her mother was still in a *peignoir*, and her hair not dressed.

'I thought you might want me to help you,' Mrs Parkinson said mildly. 'You know how difficult those hoops are. And getting the petticoat over just so. Did you sleep well?'

'Perfectly well, thank you. And I'm sure I can manage the hoops.'

'Very well, then. I'll go and put your father's cuff-links

in, and I'll come back to you later to do you up at the back.'

Really, she's like a clucking hen, Sophia thought as her mother left the room. Parents could be such a trial.

At breakfast all the talk was of the day's programme.

'It's so difficult to choose,' Sophia sighed. 'Shopping, a trip on the river – I've never been on a river steamer in my life – or the National Gallery. There might be some quite fashionable people there.'

'Well whatever you decide on,' Mr Parkinson said, 'I shan't be with you. I have to go down to the docks; look at the new wool in the warehouses before tomorrow's sale.'

'Surely that won't take you all day?' Mrs Parkinson queried.

'I've other things to do,' her husband said vaguely. 'People to see . . . that sort of thing. I did warn you before we came, so don't expect to see me until dinner this evening.'

'I shall look after them,' David said. 'You can depend upon it, sir.'

'Of course I think I should like best of all to look at the shops,' Sophia prattled. 'But it won't be such fun with no money to spend. Oh how wonderful it must be to have an income of one's own!'

'Well, that you're *not* having, young lady!' Mr Parkinson took out his purse. 'But here you are. Ten pounds! Mind you spend it wisely.'

'Oh Albert, how generous you are!' Mrs Parkinson cried. 'But what about me? Am I to go penniless while my daughter spends?'

'Ten pounds for you, then.' Having placated his ladies, Mr Parkinson felt much less guilty about the day ahead of him.

As soon as breakfast was over, he left the hotel. First of all he would have his hair and his beard trimmed in the Jermyn Street establishment he always frequented on his visits to London. He wanted, as always, to look his very best. He lay back under the skilled ministrations of the

54

barber, subjected himself with pleasure to hot towels and perfumed oils, and felt soothed and pampered. Then, emerging from the dark seclusion of the barber's shop into the brightness of Jermyn Street, he took a cab down to the docks. It was perfectly true that he had to go to the warehouses. The wool was on show there and he would look at it carefully. There was no buying a pig in a poke for Albert Parkinson. He was, after all, a Yorkshireman!

The wool samples were on the top floor, reached by a rickety wooden staircase. They had to be shown there to get the best light. And you had to know what you were doing, what to look for, and how to judge it when you found it. He was interested in the best and finest merino wool from Australia, with a long, sound staple – quality meant everything to him. He walked around, stopping to look; then he took samples from various bales, holding the stuff in his hands to get the feel; stroking it gently to test its smoothness, then squeezing it hard to gauge its resilience; debating on the yield he'd get. He loved wool, he truly loved it.

So immersed was he in what he was doing that he failed to see the young man standing nearby until, taking a sideways step, Albert bumped into him. The young man was the first to apologize.

'*Excusez-moi*!'

A Frency, eh? Well you got all sorts at the wool sales. They came from all over the Continent.

'I am sorry!' the young man said.

'Nay, I'm sorry. I wasn't looking where I was going.'

'You were concentrating. I think perhaps that you know much about wool.'

'You reckon that, do you?' Albert said. 'Well I suppose you could say I've served my apprenticeship!'

He had taken a handful of fleece from another bale and was pulling it apart between his hands. As well as the length of fibre and all the other qualities, he was looking now for wool which was clean, which had the least possible number of burrs caught up in it, all of which would have to be got rid of at an early stage. He was looking for the crimp in the fleece which determined how well the finished cloth would hold its shape.

'I reckon this might have as much as thirty crimp,' he said out loud.

'That is good,' the young man said. He examined a sample himself and nodded in agreement.

'Aye, well, you can't beat good Australian merino for plenty of crimp,' Albert said. He went once again through all the tests he had already made. It was a good one, this. He made a mental note of the number. Lot 192. This is what he'd buy tomorrow, if the price was right.

He put the sample back in the bale and rubbed his hands together. With the amount of wool he handled his hands were always smooth, because of the lanolin in it.

'When my womenfolk complain about their hands, I tell them to handle a bit of raw wool,' he said to the young man who was still standing beside him. 'But my daughter says she can't stand the smell. Oh, but I forgot, you'll not understand what I'm saying! Well, I'm afraid I can't speak your lingo, not more than the odd word.'

'I understand you,' the young man said. 'Your language it is easier for me to understand than to speak.'

'Nay, you speak it very well,' Albert said.

He was a pleasant-looking young man, handsome even. Quite tall for a Frenchman, and broad-shouldered yet slender. When he raised his tall hat he showed dark, almost black hair, and his eyes were nearly as dark, under strongly marked eyebrows. There was something about the shape of his beard – Albert was knowledgeable about beards – that was distinctly foreign and very smart, as was the cut of his frock-coat with the looser-fitting waist, and the elegant facings of his waistcoat. Oh he was a looker all right – and well-mannered with it!

'Your ladies accompany you?' the young man asked.

'My wife and daughter, and my nephew, are staying in London for a few days. Then back to Yorkshire, where we belong, on Saturday. And what about you?'

'I am alone. I come from Roubaix . . .'

'Ah!' Albert interrupted. 'The Bradford of France they call Roubaix!'

'*Oui, vraiment*! I agree. I live there with my family. Allow me to present my *carte de visite*.'

Albert took the card from him and read it out loud: '"Léon Bonneau". Have I pronounced that right?'

'*Parfaitement*!'

'Well perhaps I'll see you at the sales tomorrow?'

'I hope so,' Léon Bonneau said. 'But I wonder . . . since we two are alone at this moment, would you care to take luncheon with me?'

'Well I'm sorry, young man, but I have a bit of business to attend to.' Being a Frenchman, Albert thought, he'd understand about that.

Leaving the warehouse, Albert took the river steamer to Richmond, where Kitty Shane had a tiny house with a garden which went down to the river. He was as eager to see her as any young man calling on his first love, but that was the effect she had on him. She lived alone, and when he rang the bell she answered the door herself.

'Albert, my dear! How good to see you!' She took his hat and his silver-topped cane and placed them on the hall-stand. 'Luncheon is almost ready. I thought we'd have it in the garden if that suits you? But first I have a bottle of your champagne already chilled . . . How kind you are, Albert!' When he was coming to London he always had a dozen bottles of champagne delivered to her.

'Before the champagne, let me look at you, my dear Kitty.' He took her hands and held her at arms' length, greedily taking in her whole appearance. It seemed so long since the last time. Oh, but she was lovely! He couldn't have described what she was wearing; something soft and flowery, with a low neckline; a sort of apricot colour which enhanced the creaminess of skin and the long line of her throat. Her hair was brown, shot with strands of gold, brushed back from her wide brow and simply dressed.

'You're as beautiful as ever,' he said.

He bent his head and ceremoniously kissed her hands. His wife, if she could have seen him, would not have recognized her blunt Yorkshireman in this gallant mood.

'Come and open the champagne for me,' Kitty said. 'We'll take it into the garden.'

They sat in the garden and drank the champagne over a lunch of poached salmon, watching the boats ply to and fro on the river. The gentle, rhythmic plop of oars in the water and the laughter of holidaymakers on the river steamers floated up to them as they talked.

Everything was simple, yet everything was perfect. It was always the same with Kitty. She made him feel not only attractive and younger, but as if he was the most important man in her life, the one person she had wanted to see. And yet he knew there must be others of whom she never spoke, and he knew better than to ask, for he didn't want to lose what he had.

Later in the afternoon she took his hand and, without a word, led him into the house and upstairs to her bedroom. When they made love she changed from a gentle, pliable woman into a creature of fierce, exulting passion. She gave everything and took everything, not once, but again – and then again, until it was time for him to leave.

'Shall I see you again this visit?' she asked as she dressed.

'It won't be easy, my love,' Albert admitted. 'Not tomorrow because of the wool sales, but perhaps Friday afternoon, if I can think of a reason. But I have to spend a bit of time with my daughter.'

'Of course you must,' Kitty said. 'Her first visit to London – she'll want to be with you.'

'And I want to be with you,' he said. 'I never want to be anywhere else.'

Over dinner in the hotel Sophia was full of what they had done that day.

'We went shopping this morning. Oh Papa, the shops! I

soon spent your ten pounds, I can tell you! And this afternoon we strolled in the park until we were quite worn out. Oh the fashions!'

'And what did you do, Albert?' Mrs Parkinson asked.

'The warehouses,' he answered. 'And saw one or two people. Oh yes, I met a fellow in the warehouses – very nice fellow he seemed. On his own in London. I thought I might ask him to dinner here tomorrow.'

He was about to describe Léon Bonneau when Sophia broke in.

'Oh Papa, not another woolman! Don't say we've come all this way to meet another old woolman; to hear you both talking about staples and yields and warps and wefts!'

Albert Parkinson looked his daughter straight in the eye.

'Well yes,' he said steadily. 'I'm afraid that's what he is, my dear. Another woolman. But I'm sure you'll suffer him for your old father's sake!'

FOUR

The wool sale was under way. Always busy, this afternoon it seemed more crowded than ever. Albert Parkinson was in his usual place. All the regulars had their favourite spots and Albert's was just under the rostrum, where, even in this cacophony of sound and sea of waving catalogues, he could be easily seen and heard by the auctioneer.

Bidding was brisk and the prices were firmer than he'd expected. When Lot 192 was put up there was fierce competition, though he never doubted that he'd get what he wanted. He was always prepared to pay the price for the best, which annoyed some of the other wool buyers, who said they didn't get a look in when Parkinson was bidding.

'Then why bother to bid if you know you're not going to get it?' he frequently said. 'Why send the price up?'

But of course he knew why, and he'd have done the same himself. If he got the wool too cheaply, then he'd be able to manufacture at a lower rate, and that would be unfair competition. It was cut and thrust in the wool business.

At the start of the bidding for Lot 192 he had heard the Frenchman somewhere behind him – you couldn't miss that accent, even though he was only calling out figures – but he'd dropped out well before the final price was reached. When the item was concluded, Albert turned around, picked out Léon Bonneau in the crowd – that again wasn't difficult for he had a distinguished look about him – and waved his catalogue in recognition. When Albert left the saleroom a few minutes later he was followed out into the foyer by the Frenchman.

'*Bonjour*, Monsieur Parkinson! Good afternoon! Congratulations that you got what you desired.'

'I frequently do,' Albert said dryly. The only problem now was that he'd have to pay for it, and within fourteen days at that. It would mean going to the bank again. 'I'm sorry you were unsuccessful,' he said to the Frenchman.

'It is no matter,' Bonneau said. 'Later there is another lot. Perhaps I shall have the good luck then. Who knows?'

'Well I've got what I came for, so I'll be off,' Albert said. Having escaped the sale earlier than he had hoped to, he calculated that he might just have time to call on Kitty. She wouldn't expect him, but no matter.

'By the way, Mr Bonneau,' he said. 'I was wondering if you'd like to have dinner with me and my family this evening? At our hotel – the Splendid. That is if you've nothing better to do.' He wasn't quite sure what these Frenchies got up to in the evenings.

'Why, that is very kind!' Bonneau said. 'I accept *avec plaisir*.'

'Good! At half-past six, then!'

'*Mais oui! A tout à l'heure*! I will see you then.'

Once again, Albert took the river steamer to Richmond. It was grand on the water today, cooler than in the streets. He would like to take Kitty for a trip on the river, hire a boat just for the two of them. But there was no time this afternoon, no time for anything except just to see her and be with her for a few minutes. But every minute was worth it.

'I'm delighted to see you, dear Albert,' she said. 'And glad I was at home. Were it not for the heat I might so easily have been out shopping and you would have had a wasted journey.'

Though she didn't reproach him, it was her gentle way

61

of telling him that he should not call on her without prior notice. Well, he knew that, but the temptation had been too great.

'I can't stay more than twenty minutes or so,' he told her.

'Then I shall make you a cup of tea and we will drink it in the garden.'

The tea, the sun, the scent of the garden and the sounds of the river, but most of all the presence of Kitty, refreshed him more in twenty minutes than anything else could have done in a whole day; but all too soon it was time to leave.

'I *will* come tomorrow,' he said. 'No matter what, I shall come – that is, if you'll have me.'

'Of course I will,' Kitty said warmly.

'Then in the afternoon, my love! And I shall stay longer.'

When Albert arrived back at the hotel his womenfolk were about to go upstairs to dress for dinner.

'I've invited Mr Bonneau,' he told them. 'He'll be here at six-thirty. Wear something pretty, Sophia!'

'Why should I wear something pretty for some old woolman?' she asked her mother as they climbed the stairs. 'Oh it's going to be such a boring evening – and to think, we might have gone to the theatre!'

'It might not be as bad as you expect,' Mrs Parkinson said placidly. 'Anyway, do it to please your father.'

'Oh very well!'

An hour later, when she descended the stairs with her mother and father and Cousin David, in response to a message from reception that a Monsieur Bonneau was waiting for them, she was overwhelmingly glad that she had made herself as attractive as possible, for her father's sake. At first she could see no one who corresponded to her idea of what she expected. There was only one young man standing in reception, and it couldn't possibly be he. No such luck! But when the young man stepped forward and Albert Parkinson held out his hand to greet him, she realized the trick her father had played on her.

She was caught off guard, momentarily confused. The colour rose in her cheeks as the stranger bent to kiss her hand; and what Léon saw before him as he raised his head was an exceedingly pretty young woman in a slight disarray which was infinitely more attractive, had she known it, than her usual cool composure could ever have been. While still lightly holding her fingers, he looked into her thickly lashed, violet-blue eyes. When he let go her hand, he continued to look at her, observing the red gold of her hair, the flush on her cheeks, the powdering of tiny freckles which the sun had brought out on her skin. She was altogether delightful.

'*Enchanté*!' he murmured. '*Charmante*!'

Sophia was speechless. He was the handsomest, most attractive man she had ever set eyes on. And never before in all her life had anyone kissed her hand! And the way he had looked at her, looked into her eyes! She felt her heart pounding with the thrill of it all.

But, oh dear, she thought suddenly, he can't fail to have noticed my freckles! If only her father had given her the proper warning she might have spent at least some of the last hour lying down with slices of cucumber applied to her skin! Also she would have made a much more elaborate coiffure. Thank heaven she had worn her best gown to please her father!

Her father had ordered champagne – what had got into *him*, she wondered, to make him look so pleased with life. He didn't usually care for social occasions.

'Well then,' Mr Parkinson said. 'Shall we go into the dining-room? I'm that hungry me belly thinks me throat's cut!'

'ALBERT!' Mrs Parkinson protested.

Sophia could have died with shame. How could he? Oh, how could he? But Monsieur Bonneau appeared not to have noticed the vulgarity. Perhaps, being French, he didn't understand. She sincerely hoped not.

At precisely the same moment her cousin David and Léon Bonneau both offered an arm to escort her into the dining-room. She smiled apologetically at David while taking the Frenchman's arm. After all, he was a guest. At the table she sat between the two young men, with her mother on the other side of Monsieur Bonneau. Poor David looked unhappy, but it wasn't her fault, was it?

That was the last thought she gave to her cousin that evening. It was her clear duty to concentrate on their guest.

'Do you come from Paris, Monsieur Bonneau?' she asked him.

'No, but I am often in Paris, Miss Parkinson.'

When he smiled, as he did now, he showed the most beautiful teeth: white, strong-looking, even. And his mouth, under his moustache, was all curves, and his beard was so beautifully cut, so crisp and dark, so stylish. Oh, he was entirely elegant! No Englishman she had ever seen could hold a candle to him!

'My home is in Roubaix, close to Lille in the north of France,' he said. 'My family have been there for several generations. We are – how do you say it? – in the wool. Is that correct?'

'Quite correct,' she assured him. 'Does your father own a mill?'

'Alas, my father is dead. My mother lives, and we have two mills which I and my two older brothers manage between us. I also have a sister.'

'You speak English very well,' Sophia said.

'*Merci*. You are very kind. But my accent is not good, eh?'

She wanted to tell him that his accent was divine, that when he spoke it sent cold shivers up and down her spine. Instead she said:

'Your accent is very good, monsieur! As for me, I don't speak a word of French!' What good would French have been to her in Helsdon?

'Then I must teach you!' he said with a smile.

He turned and spoke to Mrs Parkinson.

'Is Helsdon, where you inhabit, a beautiful place then, madame?'

'Not what you'd call beautiful,' Mrs Parkinson said. 'But it suits us. We've always lived there, you see.'

'I think Helsdon is a very nice place,' David put in suddenly. 'I see nothing wrong with it at all!'

'I comprehend, monsieur,' Léon Bonneau said agreeably. 'It is the same for Roubaix with me.'

'Yes, well, there you are!' David said, mollified.

Albert Parkinson, concentrating on his meal, had said little so far. Now he looked up from his plate and spoke.

'You should pay us a visit, young man! Come and see the place for yourself, come and look around the mill. You never know, you might learn something from us slow Yorkshire folk!'

'I am certain of it,' Léon agreed.

Oh if only he would, Sophia thought. If only he would! But it would all come to nothing, just as his remark about teaching her French would come to nothing. There was no time. Only this evening and then she would probably never see him again. She was desolated by the thought.

'And have you been to the theatre?' he was asking her now.

'Oh no, monsieur.' To think that if she had had her way she would have been at the theatre this very moment, and she would never have met him!

'Oh, but it is imperative, mademoiselle! All who come to London should visit the theatre!' And it would lighten his last evening, tomorrow, he thought, if he could do so with this enchanting little creature. He spoke across the table to his host.

'Perhaps, Monsieur Parkinson, if you would allow it . . . a visit to the theatre . . .?' He saw the wary look in Albert Parkinson's eyes. 'That is, I mean your family also. All who are here. *Naturellement*!' He supposed he would have to include the so-dreary Monsieur David who was in love with the little Sophia who did not care a fig for him?

'Oh Papa! Oh Papa, do say yes!' She supposed it was unladylike; you were meant to hang back, but the words were out before Sophia could stop them.

'It would be very pleasant,' Mrs Parkinson said. 'We could go to a matinée.'

'No, not a matinée,' her husband said quickly. 'That is, not if you want me to go with you. I have business to attend to in the afternoon.' He turned to Léon Bonneau. 'But a visit to the theatre tomorrow evening would be very nice. Especially as it's our last evening here.'

'The pleasure would be to me!' Léon said.

'Papa I *must* have a new dress!' Sophia said, immediately they had seated themselves at breakfast next morning. 'I cannot possibly appear at the theatre in anything I have. Dear Father, if you love me and pity me, please say I may buy a new dress!'

'My word, it *is* a serious matter, and all before I've had a mouthful to eat!' Mr Parkinson said.

'Papa, please don't tease me!' Sophia begged. 'Please say I may have it!'

Albert Parkinson looked into his daughter's pleading eyes, saw the trembling of her lips, and sighed. How could he refuse her? And yet he knew she only wanted the dress to impress the Frenchman, and he had not yet made up his mind about Monsieur Bonneau. Oh he supposed he was all right, he seemed nice enough, but they didn't know a lot about him, didn't know what commitments he had back in France, did they? It was quite clear his little girl was smitten by the fellow and he didn't want her to get hurt. Still, he'd agreed to the theatre visit, so he supposed he'd have to go the whole hog.

'Very well, then,' he agreed. 'Only don't spend too much.'

Sophia leapt from her chair and rushed around the table to fling her arms around his neck.

'Oh, you are the most wonderful father in the world!' she cried.

'I'm sure I don't know where we shall find anything at such short notice,' Mrs Parkinson demurred.

'Nonsense, Mother!' her husband said. 'I'm sure the

shops will be full of suitable gowns. But don't let her choose anything improper mind; nothing too fashionable!'

'If you're going to be buying clothes,' David said, 'I think I shall pay another visit to the Academy. I wouldn't in the least mind seeing Mr Millais' new painting again. I consider it a fine piece of work, no matter what some say.'

Sophia pulled a face. She had disliked the painting very much – firemen rescuing little girls – and had dragged David away from it long before he was ready to go.

'You do that,' Sophia said. 'Mother and I will be perfectly all right on our own. You would only be bored.'

When Albert Parkinson looked at his daughter that evening he told himself that his money had been well spent, and it was also clear that Bonneau was very taken with her. She'd chosen a summery confection in deep blue taffeta. It suited her, though he thought the neckline was a bit low, and of course the skirt was too wide. You couldn't get near women these days for the width of their damned skirts. He was glad Kitty, with whom he had spent a wonderful and satisfying afternoon, didn't go in for these extremes, though she always looked elegant, and to his mind, fashionable.

'It is the blue of your eyes *exactement*!' Léon Bonneau said softly to Sophia. 'Except that – oh, how to say it? – the shine on the silk of your *robe* does not approach the shine in your eyes. I hope I don't offend you? It is not easy to find the words.'

And the fine lace at the neck was the same creamy colour as her bosom, though he would not say that to her. He was not sure how far he might venture with an English Miss, though this one must surely know how attractive she was to his sex.

'Thank you kindly,' Sophia said. Of course no one but a Frenchman could have paid such a compliment. She would have liked to have told him that in her eyes he looked wonderful; better even than he had last night, for now with his well-cut tailcoat he wore a waistcoat of white satin, braided and decorated around the edges, and a white carnation in his buttonhole. Everything he wore emphasized the slimness and shapeliness, as well as the masculinity of his figure. But she could only tell him so with her eyes, and hope that he understood.

This one does not need to be taught how to flirt, he thought. She is a pretty little *coquette*.

'I have taken a box at the Olympic where there is a revival of your so clever *School for Scandal*,' he said. 'I had thought of *The Templar* at Sadler's Wells, but it is all about Scottish history, kidnapping, bloodshed, violence. I thought it would not be suitable for a young lady like yourself.'

'I am happier to see what you have chosen,' Sophia said. It was not entirely true. A frightening play, in the company of such a man, had its possibilities. Oh how sickening that she was going back to Helsdon tomorrow, and he to France. She must, above all, persuade her father to issue a definite invitation to Helsdon and pray that Léon Bonneau would accept. Otherwise, she thought she would just pine away!

The play was wonderful – too wordy perhaps, and she couldn't follow everything – but the settings and the clothes, and the position of their box, made her feel almost as if she was on the stage. In the interval, champagne was brought to them; one glass alone enhanced the sparkle in her eye and gave wings to her tongue. In the heat of the theatre her hair came just a little loose, and strands fell over her cheeks and neck in what Léon Bonneau thought was the most entrancing way.

'I have thought much about your so kind suggestion that I might visit with you in your home. If you were serious, then it is my pleasure to accept.'

'Well, yes, certainly!' Albert said. He wasn't quite sure that he had been serious; he doubted that he actually *had* invited him. But if he said so . . ., and a man didn't go back on his word.

'Then a thousand times, thank you,' Léon said. 'I shall learn a lot, that is certain!'

He turned and smiled at Sophia as the curtain went up for the next act.

It was late when they reached Leeds on Saturday. A derailment of trucks had held up their train. Drake was waiting patiently for them and they were soon in the carriage and away, but even so midnight had struck before they reached Helsdon. Madeleine was drowsing, her head sunk on her folded arms on the kitchen table. At the sound of the carriage wheels on the flagstones, she wakened and jumped to her feet. Mrs Thomas had been in bed this past hour, but Madeleine had been deputed to wait up. Now she went out to the carriage to give a hand with the luggage.

'Welcome home, ma'am!' she said. 'Welcome, sir – and Miss Sophia!'

'Thank you, Madeleine,' Mrs Parkinson said. 'It's nice to be back.'

It's no such thing, Sophia thought, but she was too sleepy to argue. She had hated leaving London, and the fact that Léon – she allowed herself to think of him as Léon – had come to the railway station to see them off had in a way made her feel worse than ever. The only bright spot on the horizon was that a date had been fixed for him to visit Helsdon. Only another ten days and she would see him again. She believed he was looking forward to it as much as she was.

'Shall I make a jug of cocoa?' Madeleine asked.

'That would be very nice,' Mrs Parkinson said. 'And perhaps a sandwich. It's a long time since we ate, though we had a hamper on the train.'

'I'll have mine in bed,' Sophia said. 'I'm quite desperately tired. I shall have a long lie in in the morning.'

By the time Madeleine took the tray to Sophia's bedroom, the latter was already asleep. For a moment Madeleine looked at her as she lay there, observed the auburn hair tangled against the white pillow – she had clearly omitted its nightly one hundred brush strokes – the thick lashes lying against the delicate, almost bluish skin beneath her eyes; her hands – smooth, white, delicate – against the coverlet. She was really very pretty, and in sleep her expression was sweet and innocent, not at all the spoilt, petulant look that Madeleine was used to seeing.

I'd better leave the tray, she thought, in case she should waken and feel hungry; but she looked settled enough to sleep the clock round. It was the thing Madeleine envied her young mistress most: the opportunity to stay in bed as long as she wanted. She would envy her even more when five-thirty tomorrow morning came. No, this morning, come to think of it, and if she didn't get a move on it would be here before she'd got off to bed!

It was dinner-time before Sophia came down next day, the Sunday roast already on the table and Madeleine standing by to serve the vegetables.

'There you are, my dear,' Mrs Parkinson said. 'Well I must say you look rested! And I think the visit to London has done you good. Don't you think so, Albert?'

'I dare say,' Albert Parkinson said. 'I dare say.'

He doubted it was London which had put the sparkle in his daughter's eye; it was who she had met there. And if his womenfolk took the trip as a precedent, then they were in for a disappointment. He'd soon put a stop to that. It had been hard for him to leave London, it got harder every time. The only thing which cheered him was the thought that he could go back there, and on his own – that, and the fact that he'd be back in the mill come tomorrow morning. If he couldn't be with Kitty, then he was happiest in the mill. He'd have to go to the bank, though.

'We must start at once getting things ready for Monsieur Bonneau's visit,' Sophia said.

Madeleine pricked up her ears. So who was Monsieur Bonneau when he was at home? She'd never heard of him before.

'What do you mean, get things ready?' Mrs Parkinson queried.

'Oh all kinds of things, Mama! For instance, we badly need a new dinner service. I suppose this is all right for Helsdon but I'm sure it's not what Monsieur Bonneau is used to. I expect he eats from the finest French porcelain!'

'He'll eat from this and like it!' her father said. 'And there's no French porcelain can come up to English Wedgwood, young lady.'

'And the covers in the drawing-room definitely need replacing,' Sophia said, ignoring her father. She would get around him later. 'And Mrs Thomas really *must* learn to do some French cooking. We must have some proper menus. We really can't be offering Monsieur Bonneau roast beef and Yorkshire pudding.'

'I've got news for you, Mrs Thomas!' Madeleine said when she returned to the kitchen. 'You're to learn to do French cooking, no less! That'll be a bit of a lark!'

'What *are* you talking about?' Mrs Thomas said.

'It seems there's a visitor coming, a Frenchman. I suppose a business friend of the Master's.' She paused. 'Though why would Miss Sophia want the house turned upside-down for a friend of her father's? She's not usually that considerate.'

'Well if they think they're going to get me on cooking frogs' legs and snails, they've got another thought coming!' Mrs Thomas said vehemently. 'They can have my notice first!'

The day after the Parkinsons' homecoming was the Sunday Madeleine had set aside to go to chapel in the evening. It was four o'clock before she had finished her chores – there was no one in from Helsdon to help out on a Sunday – and in view of the fact that she meant to attend chapel, she thought she might be welcome to visit her family first, to have tea with them. She badly wanted to check on Emerald, of whom she had had no news; to see how she was faring. In fact, though it was only ten days since she had last been in Priestley Street, she had missed

71

everyone more than she had ever expected. Perhaps it was because she had been barred that she wanted all the more to be there.

Her father was in the house when she arrived. She had hoped that he might be out on some mission; he often went sick-visiting on Sunday afternoon. When she stood at the open door he rose from his seat, and from the stern look which came over his face at the sight of her she thought he was about to forbid her to enter.

'I'm going to attend chapel, Father,' she said quietly. 'I told you I would do so every other Sunday, and I mean to keep my word. I hoped I might be welcome to see my family beforehand.'

'Very well.'

There was scant courtesy and no warmth in her father's words, but like herself he was keeping his side of the bargain.

'Of course you're welcome, love,' Mrs Bates said warmly. 'Nobody more so! How have you been? Are they all back?'

'They came back last night,' Madeleine said. 'But never mind them. How is Emerald?'

'Much better. She's sleeping just now. The doctor says she must get plenty of rest, and she can't go back to the mill for at least another fortnight.'

Which, Madeleine knew, meant two more weeks without her sister's wages. They were little enough, but they made a difference in this household.

'And what about you, Penelope? Are you all right?' Penelope was sitting at the table, frowning at a picture of Moses giving the ten commandments.

'I suppose so,' Penelope grumbled. 'I want to go and play out with the others but I'm not allowed. And I've looked at this stupid book until I'm sick of it!' She glowered at her father as she spoke.

I wouldn't have dared to speak to him like that when I was ten years old, Madeleine thought. But Penelope, perhaps because she was the youngest, got away with it –

though never to the extent of being allowed to do as she wanted, only to grumble about the restrictions.

'You know very well that you are not allowed to play in the street because it is Sunday,' Joseph Bates said patiently. He was willing to instruct his children in the ways of righteousness as long as was needful, and without ever growing weary of the task.

'Well I don't see what harm it does,' Penelope said rebelliously. 'Any more than all the other things I'm not allowed to do, like sewing or knitting or reading a book which isn't religious.'

'It is not a question of doing harm,' her father said. 'It is that everything we do on the Lord's own day must lead us directly in the path of true holiness.'

'Well I don't want to go in the path of holiness,' Penelope cried. 'And I'm sick of silly old Moses, so there!'

Then with one movement she swept the book to the floor and stood, red as a beetroot, furious and defiant, in front of her father.

'Go at once to your room!' His voice was icy. 'Tell God you are sorry; and when you have well and truly repented of your sin and propose to do better, and not before, you may join your family again.'

Penelope turned and marched out of the room and thumped up the stairs, banging her small feet on every tread. There wasn't an ounce of repentance in her stubborn little body, Madeleine thought. If it wasn't so serious, such an oft-repeated occurrence, it would be comic.

Joseph Bates turned to Madeleine.

'I cannot but think that your own attitude has in some measure helped to shape your youngest sister's. Had she had a good example in you, it would have been easier for her.'

'And had you not . . .,' Madeleine began furiously, but her mother put out a hand and restrained her.

'Please Madeleine! Let it be. We all know that Penelope has been insubordinate since the day she was born.

73

And I don't want Emerald to hear any of this and to be upset by it.' She turned to her husband. 'I beg of you, Joseph, let us have peace on the Sabbath.'

'"I came not to bring peace, but a sword,"' Joseph quoted.

'You make that abundantly clear,' his wife said coldly. 'Now Madeleine, tell me how the Parkinsons fared in London.'

Years of practice had made Mrs Bates adept at guiding the conversation into safer channels. Madeleine found it more difficult to put aside her anger, but for her mother's sake she did so.

'Well as far as I can tell, the highlight of the trip seems to have been the meeting with a Frenchman, a Monsieur Bonneau. He's been invited to visit Mount Royd in about ten days' time and it's quite clear the whole house will have to be turned upside-down and inside-out on his account. I think he's a friend of the Master's, but I'm not clear about that.'

'Why not?'

'Well Miss Sophia seems mighty perky about his visit and she doesn't usually think much of her father's friends. Anyway, never mind them. Shall I help you to make the tea?'

'Thank you, love. Lay for George as well. He should be in any minute now. He's gone to visit one of his class members who's not well.'

Madeleine had spread the cloth and was laying the table when George returned.

'I hoped you were coming this afternoon, Madeleine,' he said quietly. 'I trust you are well?'

'Very well, thank you, George.'

She was struck by how pale and serious he looked. He didn't get out and about enough, she thought; never had any fun. His work as a sales assistant in a furniture shop in Helsdon meant that he was incarcerated there six whole days a week; and the seventh day, as well as most of his evenings, was devoted to the chapel. In a way she felt sorry for him, though she supposed it was what he wanted out of life. Well it wasn't what *she* wanted.

'Tea won't be a minute,' she said.

This being Sunday tea they sat down to bread and jam, currant teacake, and a curd tart kindly given by Mrs Thomas. A tray was laid and set aside for when Emerald wakened and Madeleine kept back a piece of curd tart on her plate to sneak up to Penelope later. It was the rule in this house that if you were sent to bed in disgrace, you also forfeited whatever meal was going. And poor little Penelope, Madeleine knew, though she was so small and thin for her age, had the hungriest appetite of any of them.

When the tea was over it was almost time for chapel.

'Bring Penelope down, Mother,' Joseph Bates said suddenly. 'She must go to chapel; nothing could be better for her.'

'But she's had no tea,' Mrs Bates protested. 'You know she's not had a bite! How can you expect her to go to chapel on an empty stomach, a little girl like Penelope? If she's to go to chapel, then she must be allowed some food first.'

She began to pile bread and jam on to a plate, but her husband held up his hand to stop her.

'No, Mother! I forbid it! She sinned grievously and she must take her punishment. She knows that. When she has repented, then she may eat.'

Madeleine snatched the plate from her mother's hand.

'I'm taking it to her,' she cried. 'Father, how can you make a child go hungry when there's food on the table?'

'You will not help your sister by defying me,' Joseph Bates said coldly. 'The sooner she repents, the sooner all this will be over.'

Mrs Bates put a restraining hand on Madeleine's arm. 'Don't, Madeleine,' she said quietly. Though she knew that Madeleine was right, she also knew that, in the end, such an action wouldn't help Penelope. It would simply prolong her punishment. It was better, in the long run, to give in.

Reluctantly, Madeleine put the plate back on the table,

75

then faced her father directly. She would at least have her say. She would not be cowed.

'Don't you realize that what you get from Penelope won't be true repentance? You'll get no more than lip service from a little girl whose stomach can hold out no longer. There will be no repentance in her heart. You know that, and I dare say God knows it too!'

Her voice shook, her whole body was trembling with anger. What had come over her that she could speak to her father like this? But she might as well *not* have spoken; he gave no sign that he had even heard her.

'We must start for chapel in five minutes,' he said.

When she had left Mount Royd earlier, Madeleine had fully meant to attend chapel in the right frame of mind. Now everything was changed. In the pew she sat, stood, bowed her head at the right times, but her movements were automatic. Inside herself she felt only anger and resentment. She could not sing a word of the hymns, nor listen to the scriptures.

But the worst came when her father began to lead the prayers, his strong, resonant voice penetrating every corner of the little chapel. She had expected him to commend all sinners to God, to bring them to repentance, but not this, not this!

'Look upon Thy sinful child, Penelope,' he intoned. 'Cleanse her of her wickedness, forgive the depths of her iniquity, drive the devil from her! Cast her not into the darkness, but bring her to true repentance. Of Your grace, Oh God, be merciful to this sinner. Bring her to the light . . .'

His voice rose, pleading. Sin must be rooted out – and the sins of his own family weighed heaviest on him, above all others.

As the words echoed around them, Madeleine was conscious of heads surreptitiously turning to look at her little sister. She was filled to the brim with bitterness against her father, and moved to put an arm around Penelope. It was too late. In a paroxysm of sobs, Penelope leapt to her feet.

'I'm sorry! I'm sorry!' she cried. 'I *will* be a good girl! Oh I will be, always! And oh, I'm ever so hungry!'

Still sobbing, she threw herself into her mother's arms.

'The Lord be praised!' Joseph Bates's voice rang out as he brought his prayers to a triumphant 'Amen'.

More than anything in the world, Madeleine wanted to rush out of the chapel, get away into the open air. She felt physically sick. She half rose to her feet, then sat down again. She couldn't desert her sister.

When the service was over, when they were outside again, Joseph Bates took Penelope's hand.

'I praise God that He has guided you to the light,' he said, 'as He always will if you call on Him. So now come along home, my child!'

God has done no such thing, Madeleine wanted to scream. She has given in to hunger.

'I'll go straight back to Mount Royd,' Madeleine said. She was sure that if she went home with her father and Penelope in her present mood she would only make matters worse.

'Then please allow me to accompany you, Madeleine,' George said.

'Thank you, but I shall be quite all right on my own.' She didn't want anyone with her.

'Please Madeleine!' he said quietly, out of earshot of her father. 'There's something I want to say to you.'

He was going to propose to her. She just knew it! It was the last thing in the world she wanted to hear. Hadn't she already decided that she must tell him there could be nothing between them? But perhaps this was as good an opportunity as any. She would get it over and done with. Naturally she would be as kind as she could. She didn't want to hurt his feelings, poor George!

They walked in silence for a while. George was the first to speak.

'I have missed you in class, Madeleine. We all have. When are you coming back?'

She stared at him.

77

'Never! You know that!'

'I know you said so, in the heat of the moment; but I hoped you had been led to change your mind.'

'Certainly not!' How could he know so little of her? 'What's more, after today it will be a great effort to me to come to chapel at all. You can see my father's attitude. How can I bear with that?'

'Oh, Madeleine . . .' He spoke hesitantly at first, but then with earnest conviction. 'Your father is right. It is *you* who are mistaken. Why must you be so stubborn, Madeleine? Why do you make things so difficult? Oh Madeleine, I had hoped . . . I had hoped with all my heart that one day you and I . . . We seemed to have so much in common.'

'George . . .' Madeleine began.

'But it's no use is it, my dear?' he continued. 'And that is what I have to be firm enough to tell you. I know that, like me, you have always believed that we had an understanding, that one day in God's good time something must come of it. I am therefore all the more sorry that what I have to say must disappoint you, as it does me . . .'

What *was* he going on about? Did he think he was addressing a class meeting? She stopped him in mid-flight.

'George, please say whatever it is you have to say!'

'Very well, then. I am afraid the truth is, Madeleine, that I could never marry you; not while you turn your face so resolutely from God!'

They had been walking slowly along in the fine summer evening, crossing the fields towards Mount Royd. Now Madeleine stood stock still and stared at him for a moment in astonished silence. Then she found her voice.

'George Carter, I wouldn't marry you if you were the last man on earth! I wouldn't marry you if you were hung about with gold! I wouldn't— How *dare* you say you could never marry me! How dare you!'

She turned away, picked up her skirts so as to run the faster, and left him standing.

An hour later, when she served the Parkinson's cocoa, she was still fuming inside, though she had taken pains to hide her feelings from Mrs Thomas. Sophia was going on, as she had done ever since she'd landed home, about the amazing Monsieur Bonneau. She was getting to be quite boring about it.

'He's so handsome! Don't you think he's handsome, Mama? And so charming! We shall so enjoy having him to stay.'

Well I won't for one, Madeleine thought. Some silly French fop – who wanted him? She disliked him already. She hated all men!

FIVE

The next few days were every bit as bad as Madeleine had expected. Urged and prodded by her daughter, Mrs Parkinson agreed, in honour of Mr Bonneau's visit, that the whole house should be thoroughly cleaned, and wherever she could get the money from her husband, also refurbished. Thus, though there were to be no new covers for the drawing-room furniture, fresh cushion covers made their appearance everywhere: and though nothing Sophia could say moved her father to buy a new dinner service, he gave in at last over the purchase of a silver coffee pot, in search of which Mrs Parkinson and Sophia made a most successful trip to Bradford.

'The French drink coffee all the time,' Sophia explained. 'I doubt they ever touch tea!' She was learning everything she could about the French, though information wasn't easy to come by. So far as she could tell, no Frenchman had ever set foot in Helsdon before.

'We must have a party – and perhaps one or two dinners,' she said to her mother. 'We must on no account let Monsieur Bonneau be bored.' Also, she couldn't wait to show him off to her friends.

'It's the mill he's coming to see, lass. Not Helsdon's high society,' her father reminded her.

'Oh the mill!' She dismissed the idea at once. He could

see the mill in a couple of hours. There was all the rest of a whole, glorious week to think about.

'Whatever shall we do if it rains?' she asked, suddenly worried. 'It can rain even in July. Especially in Helsdon.'

'We shall put up our umbrellas,' Mr Parkinson replied. 'And if it should happen to snow, we'll go sledging! For heaven's sake stop fussing, Sophia!'

The domestic staff were required to clean everything within an inch of its life, from the rooftops to the cellars.

'I really can't see why!' Madeleine grumbled. 'Who in their right minds thinks Monsieur Whatever-he's-called will go down in the cellars – or up in the attics for that matter?'

'Ours not to reason why!' Mrs Thomas reproved her.

'Why not?' Madeleine demanded. 'Why shouldn't we question things?'

'Because it's not our place, that's why. Our place is to serve our betters; and be thankful we have the opportunity.'

'Well, I'm not thankful!' But Madeleine muttered the words under her breath. She could go so far and no further with Mrs Thomas.

Every day seemed so long now, and so hardworking. She was bone weary. And then when she got to bed, instead of falling into the sleep her body craved, she lay awake worrying about her family. It was her thoughts about her family which were at the bottom of everything. Though her father had always been strict, and often as a child she had resented it, she had never before been openly at such cross-purposes with him. Indeed, though he didn't show it overtly, she had always known that she was his favourite child; there had been a special bond between them. Now she felt his love for her had vanished, and that as far as the rest of her family was concerned, all she did these days was stir up trouble for them. They were better without her, yet she loved them all so very much.

Lying in the hot little attic, she ached with longing and

love for her home in Priestley Street. She knew very well that many servant girls didn't see their families from one year's end to the next, but she couldn't have borne that. She would just never have worked a long way from home. Helsdon people seldom did. They remained close to their families, kept an eye on each other, supported one another through thick and thin.

Then on the day before she was to leave school her father had come home with the offer of a place for her in the Parkinson household.

'But I don't want to go into service,' she'd protested. 'I'd rather go to the mill with you, come back home at the end of the day.'

'Nay lass, I've never wanted you to go in the mill,' he'd replied. 'And you'll do well at Mount Royd. Mr Parkinson is a good Master. Any road, you can get home oft enough.'

But little by little since then, because she was shut out from their daily lives, she had felt the gap widen between herself and her family; and now, because of the quarrel with her father and the business of the chapel, she felt a million miles from them.

Partly out of habit and partly from a deep need, she had continued the practice of saying her prayers before she climbed into bed at night; but more often than not, the only words she could manage were those of her earliest childhood prayer:

'Look upon me from above
Bless the home I dearly love.'

She doubted that God heard her. She was calling into a void. There were many nights now when, overcome by loneliness, she cried herself to sleep.

On Wednesday morning, Mrs Thomas said to Madeleine:

'I'm afraid you won't be able to go to your class this evening. The Mistress has given me a list as long as my arm of things to be done. The fact is, I came here as cook, *not* as housekeeper. Now I'm expected to take on both, and not a penny extra paid!'

'Same here,' Madeleine agreed. 'I seem to spend half my time doing jobs which have nothing to do with being a parlour maid. But it's not like you to grumble, Mrs Thomas.'

'Well sometimes I feel like grumbling,' Mrs Thomas said. 'It's the most we can do. We can't say nowt outside this kitchen. Servants are ten a penny!'

'As a matter of fact,' Madeleine confessed, 'I've stopped going to class. Oh, I was going to tell you when I got a minute.' Now was not the time to say she hadn't been for the last two Wednesdays.

Mrs Thomas stopped short in the act of rolling pastry, the rolling pin suspended six inches above the table.

'Not going to class? I don't believe it! Whatever for? Whatever's brought that about?'

'One thing and another.' Madeleine didn't want to discuss it with Mrs Thomas. 'Anyway, I'm not going again.'

Mrs Thomas narrowed her small black eyes, pursed her lips.

'Your dad'll not be best pleased. And what does George Carter think?'

'George Carter has nothing to do with it,' Madeleine said quickly. 'We both know where we stand, George and me. I've told you before, Mrs Thomas, there's nothing between us! I wish people wouldn't make out there was!'

'Keep your hair on!' Mrs Thomas said. 'No call to be shirty!' A lover's quarrel was certainly at the bottom of this, let the girl protest how she may. 'So what does your dad say, then?'

'He's disappointed,' Madeleine admitted.

'I should just think he is! You're not giving up chapel, I hope?'

Mrs Thomas liked the fact that Madeleine went regularly to chapel. She never went herself – well where would she get the time? – but she felt that a little of Madeleine's devotion might somehow reflect on her, count in her favour.

'No. But from now on I shall go only every other Sunday evening. You don't suppose the Mistress will stop me having the evening off the Sundays I don't go to chapel, do you?'

Mrs Thomas shook her head doubtfully.

'I couldn't say, I'm sure. It was my belief you were given the time for that special reason. Do you want me to have a word with her?'

'No. I'll speak to her myself. But not while she's got her mind on this silly Frenchman's visit. She'd be sure to say no.' It was Madeleine's plan also to ask Mrs Parkinson if, providing all the work was done, she might also go out for an hour on Wednesday evenings. But it would have to wait.

Monsieur Bonneau was due late in the afternoon of the following Tuesday. The carriage would have to go to Leeds to meet him from the train.

'Why cannot *I* go in the carriage to welcome him?' Sophia begged. 'Please let me, Mama!'

'Certainly not,' Mrs Parkinson said with unusual firmness. 'It would look very forward indeed. Men do not like girls who are forward. How often have I told you that, Sophia? Even I shan't go in the carriage. It's quite enough that your father goes.'

At seven o'clock in the evening the party had still not arrived from Leeds. Mrs Thomas had had to keep back the meal from its usual time of six-thirty, which didn't please her, and left everyone in the house faint with hunger. Mrs Parkinson and Sophia, taut with anxiety, were constantly in and out of the kitchen, issuing fresh instructions, peering into pans, lifting the covers of dishes.

'The soup smells delicious,' Mrs Parkinson said. 'Well, thank goodness that won't spoil with waiting! Now remember, Madeleine, when you take round the soup, you start from the *right* of the Master, and when he carves

84

the lamb you must stand on his *left*. And as we are a small party, do not remove any plates until all have finished the course, then remove mine and the Master's last of all. And take the parsley sauce around at the same time as the fish. Oh dear, perhaps we should have engaged someone to help you! Are you sure you will be able to manage the serving?'

'Yes thank you, ma'am,' Madeleine said. And she'd do it all the better if she didn't have so many instructions. 'I'll be all right, ma'am, don't worry!'

'We should have hired a butler,' Sophia put in. 'I said so from the first.'

'For only a small dinner, your Aunt Fanny and Cousin David the only other guests, that would have been ostentatious,' Mrs Parkinson said. 'And I think you had better leave the kitchen, my dear. You are becoming quite pink from the heat. Go and cool down in the drawing-room while I check that everything is perfect in the dining-room.'

'Thank heaven for that!' Mrs Thomas said when the two ladies had left. 'I don't like people interfering in my kitchen, prying and poking into everything. It's not as if they knew the first thing about it!'

'Well it isn't often Miss Sophia favours us with her presence,' Madeleine said. 'She looked very pretty, didn't she?'

Mrs Thomas snorted.

'Handsome is as handsome does. Hire a butler indeed! They'll be wanting a French chef next!'

Madeleine surveyed herself in the small square of looking-glass which hung on the wall by the door. It was there so that she could check that her cap was straight and her hair tidy before she appeared in the dining-room. Yes, she thought, like Miss Sophia, I'm a bit pink from the heat. But there the resemblance ended. She was as dark as Miss Sophia was fair. Miss Sophia was so much more delicate-looking, like an expensive china doll. Madeleine couldn't see that her own face had twice the character of the other girl's, that her features, though not as delicate, were strong and chiselled and harmonious, and would always be so, since they were not, like Sophia's, dependent on the temporary beauty of youth.

'That's enough looking in the glass!' Mrs Thomas called out. 'One of these days the devil will come out and get you!'

As Madeleine moved away they both heard the sound of the carriage on the drive.

'Here they come!' Madeleine said. 'Let's hope they start their meal right away and get through it quickly. I'm that hungry my front's touching my back-bone. Why do we always have to wait to eat until they've finished?'

When, not long after, she handed around the plates in the dining-room she would have liked to have snatched at the food and eaten it there and then. And when she took the not-quite-empty dishes back to the kitchen she did just that, stuffing her mouth with the leftover succulent new potatoes which had accompanied the saddle of lamb.

'Well what's he like then?' Mrs Thomas asked impatiently. 'You've hardly told me a thing!' She was putting the final touches to a large dish of apricot cream, one of her special puddings.

'I haven't had a minute, have I? Rush, rush, rush! Wait until I've served this and we can have a breather.'

'Not until I've done the savoury, we can't. Herring roe on toast. Who wants that after all the rest?'

'I shall if there's any left. I'm starving!' Madeleine said.

But Monsieur Bonneau, she'd noticed, had eaten only a spoonful or two of his apricot cream and took only a mouthful of the savoury.

'Please excuse me that I do not do justice to this so excellent repast,' he apologized to his hostess. 'It is that the journey was so long . . . It is many hours since I left Calais . . . And then there was the storm in *La Manche*! *Horrifique*!' No wonder, he thought, the French didn't come much to England with that revolting stretch of water between them. And why had he let himself in for travelling so far north? Could it possibly be worth it? Would it even be civilized? But the meal, had he felt fit to eat it, had certainly been better than he'd expected.

'Poor Monsieur Bonneau!' Mrs Parkinson sympathized. 'Then you must allow yourself an early night!'

'Thank you, madame,' he replied. 'With your permission I shall. And please call me Léon. It is what I should prefer.'

Does that include me? Sophia thought quickly. Well I certainly shall. His name would come easily to her tongue since it was how she had thought of him since the night at the theatre.

'And in the morning I look forward to inspecting your mill,' Léon said to Mr Parkinson.

'I shall accompany you, Léon,' Sophia said.

He looked at her in surprise.

'How very pleasant! So it is possible you know all about the making of cloth? The ladies in my family do not make themselves familiar with it, I must say!'

She doesn't know a thing, Mr Parkinson thought, amused. She's never taken the slightest interest in the mill. She doesn't know a spinning frame from a loom. Serve the little minx right if he left her to show the Frenchman around.

'Well, I . . . that is . . .' Sophia began.

'I'd like the pleasure of showing you things myself,' Mr Parkinson interrupted. 'But you may come along if you wish,' he said to Sophia, his lips twitching in a smile.

'Well that's it!' Madeleine said. Having at last served the coffee in the new silver coffee-pot, she was free to sit at the table with Mrs Thomas and eat her fill. There was something of everything left and for once they reckoned that the Mistress wouldn't want an account of what had become of it. It wasn't until Madeleine was halfway through her meal that she stopped eating long enough to answer Mrs Thomas's impatient questions about Monsieur Bonneau.

'Well, he's taller than I expected. His hair is dark and

he has a moustache and a beard. He's a bit pale, but from what I can tell he had a bad journey. He has a nice way of speaking.' Yes, she had liked his voice: deep, strong yet not harsh, almost musical. And, surprisingly, it hadn't been difficult to understand the few French words he'd used.

'And did he like my dinner, then?' Mrs Thomas wanted to know.

'He did indeed. He ate it with enjoyment,' Madeleine said, stretching the truth. Well he would have, wouldn't he, if he'd been feeling up to scratch?

'There now!' Mrs Thomas was pleased. 'Perhaps the French aren't all bad,' she conceded. 'But I don't forget that they're the enemy, always have been. And don't you forget it neither! I remember Waterloo, you know. I was only a little mite of five, but I remember the rejoicing in the streets when the old Duke trounced them. *And* I remember the wounded when they came back from France. That was a sorry sight, I can tell you!'

'We can't blame Monsieur Bonneau for that,' Madeleine said sensibly. 'He wasn't born. I'd put him at no more than twenty-three. My word though, Miss Sophia's struck on him! You should just see her, making up to him!'

'I won't see anything will I, stuck down here in the kitchen,' Mrs Thomas complained. 'Did he speak to you?'

'Speak to me? Good heavens no! He didn't even see me!'

At quarter to eight next morning, holding the heavy copper jug filled with hot water, Madeleine knocked on the door of Monsieur Bonneau's room. Since there was no reply she assumed he must still be asleep, and entered. In fact he had risen, and was standing at the far side of the room, looking out of the window. He wore a long dressing-gown of dark blue brocade, and even at this hour of the day he managed to look elegant.

'Good morning, sir! Here's your hot water.'

He made no reply, gave not the slightest sign that he

had heard her, just continued to stare out of the window. Well his dressing-gown might be elegant, Madeleine thought, but his manners weren't up to much. Noisily, on purpose, she banged the jug down on the marble top of the washstand before marching to the door. Her hand was on the doorknob as he called out to her.

'I would like some tea. Will you bring me some tea, please?' He had turned his head and was looking at her over his shoulder, the way people did look at servants, as if they weren't really seeing them.

'Yes, sir. I could bring coffee if you'd prefer it.'

'No. Tea.'

'Very well, sir!'

When she had gone he looked out of the window again. The view surprised him. He had expected a landscape cluttered with mills and chimneys, and houses of blackened stone, but from this window he looked over undulating countryside with fields of golden stubble where the hay had been harvested, belts of trees in heavy summer foliage, and in the distance high, purple-tinged hills. There were just a few scattered houses in sight, and not a single mill. He was not to know that this was because he had been given the best guest-room at the front of the house, and that if he had looked out of any of the back windows he would have seen exactly the landscape he'd expected, and one not vastly different from the one he had left behind him in Roubaix. The principle was the same too. Here, it seemed, they turned their backs on the town and faced the view. In his own country they built the blind side of the house towards the street and concentrated all the beauty at the back.

He left the window and crossed to the washstand, poured the hot water into the basin, stripped off his dressing-gown and nightshirt and started to wash. When Madeleine entered the room, having given a swift knock which she assumed he wouldn't bother to answer, he was mother-naked. After one startled glance she lowered her gaze, concentrating on the tray of tea as she crossed to

89

place it on the table. She felt her cheeks burning, but if she kept her head down she hoped he wouldn't notice. Meanwhile, he nonchalantly took a towel from the rail and wrapped it around his waist, seeming in no way disturbed.

'Your tea, sir,' she said. 'Shall I pour it?' She was glad that her voice came out cool and calm. No way would she let him think that the sight of him naked had surprised her in the least. Anyway, he probably thought, in common with the rest of his class, that being a servant she neither saw, heard, nor understood.

'If you please. No milk.'

'I'll leave it on the table, sir!'

'*Merci*! How do you call yourself?'

She looked up, slightly confused.

'What is your name?'

'Madeleine, sir.'

'Madeleine? But that is surely unusual?'

He means it's too fine for me, she thought.

'My mother reckoned that she was free to choose whatever names she wished. She never gave a thought to what was suitable.'

He heard the edge in her voice. So! He had somehow insulted her! He smiled a little as he looked at her. She had a mutinous face.

'I meant that it was a French name. I didn't expect to find it in Yorkshire. Your mother has French blood, perhaps?'

That would explain the fact that to him she didn't look English. Sophia was his idea of how an English girl should look; blue-eyed, delicate. This one looked . . . Italian. Yes, that was it – like something in one of those paintings in the Louvre. Did she have an Italian figure, curved, voluptuous? It was impossible to tell under that stiff, enveloping uniform.

'Not that I know of, sir. Will that be all, sir?'

The skin on his body was smooth and white, except that he had dark silky hair on his chest and arms. His shoulders were wide and his waist narrow. Well if he

90

would stand in front of her with no more than a towel around his hips, how could he expect her not to notice?

'Yes thank you. What time is breakfast?'

'Half-past eight, sir.'

'So is he going to want a tray of tea every morning?' Mrs Thomas enquired when Madeleine was back in the kitchen.

'I suppose so.'

She said nothing more. She was reluctant to discuss the Frenchman with Mrs Thomas, which was surprising because it was such little titbits of gossip which lightened their days. But Mrs Thomas would make too much of the fact that she had seen the man naked, if only for a second. She would be shocked. Madeleine had been embarrassed but somehow not shocked, though she had never seen a member of the opposite sex without clothes before; not even her brother, certainly not her father. It was something not to be thought of in her home. But on subsequent mornings, she thought, she would wait until he answered her knock before entering his room. She wouldn't risk it again.

Léon Bonneau quickly fitted into the household. He suspected, rightly, that the Parkinson family went out of their way to entertain and impress him. Mrs Parkinson was not always sure of herself and the little Sophia – though delightful in her own way – tried too hard. She had not yet learned the sophistication she so clearly and ardently craved, and from what he had seen of it so far, from the houses they visited and the neighbours who called at Mount Royd, she wouldn't learn it in this little West Riding town of Helsdon. But she was teachable, he was sure of that. It only needed the right person; in Sophia's case the right man.

'We plan to take the carriage to Ilkley and on to Bolton Abbey today,' Mrs Parkinson said, coming into the kitchen after breakfast on the Thursday. 'Will you pack us a picnic hamper, Mrs Thomas? What can you offer us?'

'Well, there's a nice raised pie in the larder. And there's the ham. Of course if I'd had notice I could have done a cold fowl, but there's no time now.'

'The pie and the ham will do nicely. And perhaps a gooseberry tart and some strawberries. And fresh bread of course. We shall leave immediately after lunch.'

'Get on hulling those strawberries,' Mrs Thomas instructed Madeleine when Mrs Parkinson had left the kitchen. 'It's going to be all go again. I'm glad we don't have visitors every week, that's all.'

'But it does give you a chance to cook absolutely delicious meals,' Madeleine said. 'I think you enjoy it, secretly!'

'I'd enjoy it more if I ever set eyes on the gentleman,' Mrs Thomas said. 'It's all right for you, you see all the visitors a great deal of the time. There's scarcely one ever sets foot in my kitchen, and I don't suppose this French Monsieur will be any different!'

But he *was* different, Madeleine thought, though not in the way Mrs Thomas meant. There was something about him. An air, a style, that she'd not seen in any of the men she'd met before. It was no wonder Miss Sophia was head over heels for him – and showed it far too clearly to Madeleine's way of thinking. That wasn't the way to get a man. But what do *you* know about getting a man, Madeleine Bates, she asked herself? Nothing at all, she concluded; but instinctively she recognized that it wasn't the right way with Monsieur Bonneau.

Not that she knew a lot about him, even now. She took his hot water and his tea every morning. His manners had improved since that first occasion. He passed the time of day with her, called her by her name, sometimes made a remark about the weather, or asked her a question. Aside from that he naturally didn't notice her at all.

But in fact, had she known it, he did. Each morning when she came into the room he looked at her to see what sort of a mood she was in – for she was a creature of moods, he had discovered that. Sometimes her face was as sunny as the July weather, sometimes as clouded and brooding as a day in November. And because he knew next to nothing of her, he could never account for either face. Nor could he get her to talk, nothing more than conventional monosyllables in reply to his questions. He knew she had been embarrassed on that first morning, but it hadn't been his fault. The English were such prudes!

But why is it, he asked himself, that women of the peasant class are so much more attractive, more exciting, than born ladies? It was the same in France. Such a pity!

'And now you tell me they're going to the concert in Bradford tomorrow night and that they're in Leeds on Saturday!' Mrs Thomas said. 'What a rackety life they do lead, to be sure!'

'I wish I did,' Madeleine said enviously. 'I wish I could just go to one exciting place, just one! But Monsieur Bonneau does spend a lot of time in the mill with the Master,' she added. 'It's my opinion that's what he likes best. You can see his face light up when the two of them are talking about wool.'

She was quite right, it was what he liked best. And he could have had no better guide to Parkinson's mill than its owner, who painstakingly and with great enthusiasm took him through all the processes. They discussed everything at length, comparing notes with total frankness on the similarities and differences in methods between the Parkinson factory in Helsdon and the Bonneau factory in Roubaix. But when Léon expressed a tentative wish to go into other mills in Helsdon, it was another matter.

'Nay, we keep out of each other's way,' Albert Parkinson said. 'We play our cards close to our chest in the wool trade; we don't like the other fellow to know what we're doing all the time. It's not that we're unfriendly, you understand – but when it comes to manufacturing, or selling, or getting orders, we like to keep ourselves to ourselves. We'd not mind knowing the other man's business, mind you, but we don't want him to know ours!'

'And yet you are so open with me?' Léon said. 'How is that so?'

'Because you're too far away to threaten us,' Albert said. 'You can't sell better quality or cheaper in this country – for a start we make the best in the world – and we can't sell our good stuff in France because of your country's lousy tariff.'

Léon smiled.

'Well, I agree that you can't be beaten on quality, my friend. Yours is the best. But I think perhaps we have better patterns!'

'That's as may be,' Albert said. 'We won't quarrel about it.'

'Not about that or anything else,' Léon agreed. 'Now, can we go back into the weaving shed? I would like to talk to your – overlooker is it not? – again.'

'Joseph Bates? Yes, I dare say he could teach you a thing or two. His daughter's our parlourmaid – Madeleine. Did you know that? She's very like her father; straight as a die, honest as the day – and as stubborn as a mule.'

Léon nodded. It was an opinion which coincided exactly with his own.

At the dinner table on Sunday evening Albert Parkinson engaged Léon in talking about wool yet again, though Léon was conscious of the boredom of the others with the subject – Aunt Fanny Chester and Cousin David as well as Sophia and her mother.

'It surprises me that you do not attend the Paris Exhibition, Mr Parkinson,' he said. 'There is much there that would interest you; and many trade exhibits from this part of the world.'

'Oh I know!' Albert said. 'There's several stands from the West Riding. Titus Salt is very prominent – and there's others.'

'Then why do you not come?' Léon asked.

'Nay, I've never really bothered me head about it,' Albert said. 'And from what I've read in the newspaper, it's been a bit of a shambles.'

'It was at first,' Léon agreed. 'But now all is ironed out and it goes swimmingly. People from many places are visiting. September would be a perfect time. Paris is beautiful in September. And it would be a pleasure for me to come to Paris myself to be with you, to show you around.'

'Oh Papa! Paris! Oh Papa, we must go, we must!' Sophia cried.

'You mean for the sake of the mill, lass?' Albert asked innocently. 'You think it'll be good for trade, do you?'

'Papa you're teasing me again! Of course I think it will be good for trade, but I long to visit Paris. It is the dream of my life!'

Or has just become so, Albert thought. But she looked so bonny when she was excited; eyes sparkling, cheeks flushed.

'Mama, isn't it just the dream of your life?' Sophia demanded. 'Don't you just long to go?'

'Well . . . now that you mention it . . .' Mrs Parkinson was at first hesitant, but then the idea quickly took root. She had been reluctant to go to London, and just look how much she had enjoyed that. 'Yes! Yes, indeed, I think I would like to go! And September would be suitable, Léon. Our son will be back at school.'

David Chester raised an anxious face from Mrs Thomas's caramel blancmange he was so enjoying.

'Sophia, my dear, you are too hasty. And you also, Aunt, if I may say so. It would be not at all suitable for two ladies to be disporting themselves around Paris; and you know I cannot go with you for I start in my new post at the beginning of September.'

'Oh what a fusspot you are, cousin David!' Sophia cried. 'Of course we shall be all right and quite safe. I dare say most of the time we shall be with Father. And you have heard Monsieur Bonneau promise that he also will be there.' She turned to her father. 'Oh Papa, please say that we may go!'

Madeleine cleared the empty plates and went back to the kitchen.

'Well it looks as if they're all off to Paris next, Mrs Thomas. I'm sure Miss Sophia will get her way – as per usual!' She envied them all from the bottom of her heart.

'It'll make life easier for us for a few days,' Mrs Thomas pointed out.

'But I don't want life to be easier,' Madeleine protested. 'I want it to be . . . well, more exciting.'

On the last morning of Léon Bonneau's visit Madeleine took his hot water and his tray of tea, as usual. He was gazing out of the window and she thought at first that he hadn't heard her come in. Then, as she poured his tea he turned around and came towards her.

'I shall be sorry to leave,' he said. 'There is something about Helsdon that I quite like.' He was afraid he sounded condescending – he wasn't sure of the language. She was so touchy. 'I suppose you like Helsdon very much.'

'I do – or I did,' Madeleine agreed. 'But I suppose it's easier to like a place when you know you can get away from it if you want to.'

'And do you want to get away, Madeleine?'

'I don't know,' she admitted. 'I used to think I wanted to spend my whole life here in Helsdon. Now I'm not sure what I want . . .'

She broke off. She was saying too much, and he didn't really want to know.

Léon Bonneau felt in his pocket, held out his hand, and gave her a coin. Without looking at it, she knew at once by the feel that it was a half-sovereign. In the whole of her life she had never had so much money.

'Thank you kindly, sir!'

'Thank you for looking after me, Madeleine.'

When she had left he took his cup of tea over to the window. I shall be sorry not to see that funny little girl again, he thought.

On her way back to the kitchen, Madeleine took the coin out of her pocket, rubbed it with the corner of her apron to bring up the shine. She would never see the giver again, but when she came to spend the money, on something absolutely marvellous, she thought she would remember him.

SIX

It took Sophia, after Léon Bonneau's departure, no more than the inside of a week, during which time she brought up the subject on every possible occasion, to persuade her father that a visit to Paris was absolutely essential.

'You surely don't want to be left behind by the other millowners, Papa!' she said. 'It's always been so important to you to keep ahead.'

'So it's for the sake of the mill you want me to go?'

'Well . . . yes. Yes of course, Papa!'

'Perhaps you're right,' Mr Parkinson said thoughtfully. 'It's true that a lot of the chaps I know have shot off to Paris this summer.'

'There you are, you see!' Sophia said. She tried not to sound too triumphant. She'd discovered she couldn't push her father, only guide him, persuade him.

'Mind you, I can't recall that they've taken their wives and families with them,' Mr Parkinson continued. The expression on his face was bland, his voice smooth as cream.

Sophia caught her breath. He couldn't, he just couldn't go without them. It would be too cruel. How could she bear to see him go without her, to know that he was to experience the delights of Paris in the company of Léon Bonneau. But there were times when she couldn't quite decide whether her father was serious or teasing, and this was one of those times.

'However,' Mr Parkinson continued, 'if I decide to go – and think on I've not made my mind up yet – then I dare say you and your mother might as well come along!'

Sophia flung herself at him, held her arms tightly around his neck and gave him a big kiss.

'Oh, you are the loveliest father in the world!' she cried.

'Steady on, lass,' he cautioned, though he couldn't help feeling pleased. 'I told you I haven't decided yet. There's no rush.'

'Oh but Papa, there is!' Sophia contradicted. 'There'll be so many preparations to make. Dresses, bonnets, shoes – and I definitely need a new parasol . . .'

'I'll not have you running me into a lot more expense,' her father warned. 'You've got the new dress I bought you in London. And remember, this is a trip – if we make it at all, that is – to visit the exhibition. It's not for you to flaunt yourself around Paris dressed to the nines.'

'Oh I know, Papa! I do understand.' She was all acquiescence. There was no point in going on at this stage about all the things they would quite certainly need for the trip. That could come later when she had finally persuaded him to make up his mind.

She was not to know, it was something he would never bother the women's heads with, that he was worried about the cost of it all. Money was getting tighter all the time. The bank had met him over the wool he'd bought in London at the last sales, but, unless he'd imagined it, and he didn't think he had, the bank manager hadn't been quite his affable self. The trouble was that the cloth they were making – and it was good cloth, there wasn't any doubt about that – wasn't selling fast enough. There was too much of it piled up in his warehouse. He cursed the war, dragging on in the Crimea, making everyone nervous; he cursed the French who put the tariff on the cloth he'd like to have sold to them. Sometimes it was difficult to see his way clear.

Nevertheless, two days later, as they were getting ready for bed, he spoke about the proposed visit to his wife.

'I've decided,' he said. 'You can get yourself and the lass fixed up for Paris in September. Nothing extravagant, mind. I trust you to keep Sophia in check. I'm not made of money!'

'Of course I will, Albert!' Mrs Parkinson smiled happily. She knew he wouldn't deny them a thing they needed. He was quite generous, in spite of always saying he was short of money. She was almost minded to go and give Sophia the good news right away, but no doubt she was already asleep. It would have to keep until morning. She adjusted her nightcap, climbed into bed, turned on her side and was fast asleep in two ticks. Not even the thought of Paris could keep Mrs Parkinson awake once her head had touched the pillow.

While his wife snored gently beside him, Albert Parkinson lay awake, his thoughts turning, as they so often did, to Kitty Shane. Now if he was taking Kitty to Paris . . .! He'd never been there, but they said it was a place for lovers. But perhaps young lovers, he thought; not a middle-aged, putting-on-weight, going-a-bit-grey fellow like himself. Though what they didn't know, the young ones, was that you could love as passionately when you were knocking on for fifty as you could at twenty; and perhaps more deeply. It came too late, that was the devil of it. But he would see Kitty again before Paris. Somehow or other he'd make a trip to London. He was as set on that as his daughter was on Paris.

'It's not fair,' Roger Parkinson said bitterly. 'Why couldn't they go before I had to go back to school? Then I could have gone as well. Stupid school! It interferes with everything a chap wants to do.'

He was in the kitchen, grumbling to Mrs Thomas and Madeleine because he'd said it all to his parents and his sister to no avail whatsoever. Apart from the fact that his father said September suited him best, it seemed they'd be invited to go at that time by this Frenchman his mother and sister were full of. That was that, and there was no changing anyone's mind.

'Never mind, Master Roger,' Mrs Thomas consoled him. 'You've got all the time in the world to go to Paris, and a dozen other places too, I shouldn't wonder. Have another bit of my chocolate cake!'

'Well I still say it's jolly unfair,' he said, biting into the cake.

'Who said life was fair, Master Roger?' Madeleine demanded.

Both she and Mrs Thomas quite liked Roger, perhaps because when he was home he came into the kitchen and talked to them, as if they were real people. Sophia had never done that. Even as a little girl she'd been too much on her dignity. Or perhaps he just came for the food? He was tall for his fourteen years, thin, lanky, and always hungry.

'That was jolly good, Mrs T.,' he said, polishing off the last crumbs. 'Is there anything else?'

Mrs Thomas shook her head.

'I reckon you've got hollow legs, Master Roger! But there's a piece of apple pie Madeleine can fetch you from the larder – and that's the lot! I don't know what your mother would say to me, feeding you up like this!'

'Well she won't know, will she? Not unless you tell her, and I'm sure you won't.'

He took the piece of pie from Madeleine, ate it in one minute flat, and left the kitchen.

'He's a caution, that one,' Mrs Thomas said. 'But sometimes I feel sorry for him. He doesn't get his fair share of attention, sent away to school like that.'

'I'd be hopping mad if the rest of my family was going to Paris and I couldn't,' Madeleine agreed. 'Not that there's a snowflake in Egypt's chance of that either way!'

She continued to worry about her family, especially about Emerald. Knowing of the younger girl's slow recovery, Mrs Parkinson had given Madeleine time off to go

101

home to see her, and Madeleine had persuaded Mrs Thomas to let her do this during the afternoon, when her father would be out at work. She knew she would not be welcome in Priestley Street if he was there and she was half afraid that he wouldn't let her into the house.

When Mrs Bates saw Madeleine in the middle of the afternoon her face lit with an expression which was half hopeful, half apprehensive. Her eyes widened in a mixture of joyful expectation, and fear.

'You've heard from Irvine?'

'No, Ma, I haven't. But we must tell ourselves that no news is good news.'

Madeleine tried to sound more cheerful than she felt, but at Mount Royd the previous day's papers were sent down to the kitchen where Madeleine read them avidly, especially the war news; and there was never anything good.

'They say that when Sebastopol falls, that'll be the beginning of the end,' she told her mother.

'But when will that be?' Mrs Bates wondered. She sometimes felt she would wait for ever, that she would die waiting for news of her son which never came.

'I came to see Emerald – and you of course,' Madeleine said. 'Where is she?'

'She went out for a little walk, to get some air,' Mrs Bates said. 'I'm surprised you didn't pass her on the way.'

'So how is she?'

Mrs Bates shook her head. 'She's mending too slowly for my liking. I'm worried about her going back into the mill, though I suppose she'll have to before long. But it's not suitable. On her feet all day, never a chance to sit down, and a stuffy atmosphere which does her chest no good.'

'I'm sorry, Ma,' Madeleine said. 'Try not to worry. I'm sure she'll pick up soon. She always has.'

'It's never taken so long. And our Penelope's not helping. I don't know what's got into her these days, she's that awkward.'

102

'I wish I could do something,' Madeleine said. 'As it is I can't even stop long. I'll have to rush back. I promised Mrs Thomas I wouldn't be long. She's sent an egg custard for our Emerald.'

'Well it's brightened my day, seeing you,' her mother said. 'And thank Mrs Thomas for the custard. She's not a bad sort is she? I'd be happier if Emerald could find a place like yours.'

Madeleine, running most of the way, arrived back at Mount Royd hot and breathless, flopped into a chair and began to fan herself with a newspaper.

'On your feet, girl!' Mrs Thomas said. 'You're in the nick of time! Miss Compton's arrived. You're to take a tray of tea to the Mistress's room.'

The usual neatness of Mrs Parkinson's bedroom was transformed by a clutter and confusion of dress materials, rolls of braid, silk fringing, half-finished garments, laces – and in the middle of it all stood Sophia in her white-embroidered shift and drawers, and over them the metal frame which would bear the weight of her voluminous skirts and make them even wider-looking. Miss Compton, brandishing a pair of scissors, hopped around like a frightened bird, and the sounds which came from her when she did venture to speak were not unlike the cheep-cheep of a sparrow.

'Now try this on, Miss Parkinson,' she twittered. 'I'm sure it's going to be quite beautiful!' She lowered the dress carefully, arranging the skirt over the frame. 'There! I do declare you'll turn all heads!'

But when Sophia surveyed herself in the mirror her face dropped in dismay.

'The skirt is not *nearly* full enough!' she protested angrily. 'It's Paris I'm going to, Miss Compton! Paris! Not Helsdon Town Hall!' She could have screamed at the stupidity of the woman. Why oh why did they have to employ Miss Compton?

Miss Compton flinched.

'I should have thought myself that it was quite wide

enough, Miss Parkinson, quite wide enough; but if you think not, then I can insert some extra material at the hipline. It won't take long now that I have my beautiful new sewing-machine.' The thought of her new sewing-machine quite cheered her up. She was so proud of it. It was one of the very first in Helsdon.

'Don't stand there, Madeleine,' Mrs Parkinson said tetchily. 'Put the tray on the table. I'll pour presently.' She made no attempt to hide the loud sigh which escaped her.

She hoped Sophia wasn't going to be as difficult as this from now until September. Sometimes, just occasionally, she wished they weren't going to Paris, that Monsieur Bonneau had never issued the invitation. She was tempted to wish that her daughter would just settle down, marry her cousin David, and start a family, and the sooner the better so that she could have a bit of peace herself.

'Miss Sophia ought to be smacked!' Madeleine said, back in the kitchen. 'She's got that poor Miss Compton all of a dither. Doesn't she realize how lucky she is – a week in Paris *and* new dresses into the bargain! And what a beautiful dress that one was!'

'Not to mention the French Monsieur when she gets there,' Mrs Thomas said. 'You're forgetting him. I suspect that's what most of the fuss is about.'

But Madeleine had not forgotten him. In the end, she thought, he had been quite nice. And she still had the half-sovereign he had given her, tucked away at the back of her handkerchief drawer. She had no plans yet about what to use it for. It was a lot of money; the spending of a sum like that required careful planning.

The days flew by in a riot of preparation, with Sophia ever more demanding, Mrs Parkinson short-tempered and Miss Compton hardly ever out of the house. Mr Parkinson took himself off to London for a short visit, and returned looking much better for it. On 3 September Roger, still protesting, was packed off to school, and on the same day

Cousin David went off to take up his new teaching appointment at a school in Ripon. He didn't look forward to it, but with a widowed mother, not well off, and the hope in his heart that one day he would be able to marry, it was essential for him to earn a living.

'I shall miss you so much, Sophia,' he said on his last evening at Mount Royd. 'Promise me you'll write to me?' He would have liked to have declared himself there and then, but it was impossible.

'Of course I will! But not until after we return from Paris. It's going to be such a busy time!'

It was only a week away now. She could hardly contain herself for the excitement of it. In the end silly old Miss Compton had come up with some quite nice new dresses, and tomorrow, because Bradford had yielded nothing fine enough, she and her mother were going to Leeds to buy a smart new parasol.

They found the perfect thing in a shop in Briggate. The frame was covered with cream silk moiré, adorned with appliquéd motifs of flowers, braided around the rim, and as a final, wonderful touch, from the centre of each appliquéd flower hung a small tassel of brown silk.

'Oh Mama, it's quite beautiful!' Sophia cried. 'Oh please say I may have it!'

'It's very lovely,' her mother agreed. 'But my dear, the price! I don't know what your father would say!'

'He'd want me to have it!' Sophia said quickly. 'You know he would!'

She was right. Mrs Parkinson hesitated for only seconds longer.

'Very well then,' she said to the shop assistant. 'You may wrap it for us.'

'No! Don't wrap it. I'll carry it. You may wrap my old one.' Sophia took the parasol from him, ran her fingers over the smooth ivory handle, and could hardly get out of the shop fast enough to put it up. Oh it was so handsome!

But it was really the parasol which caused the accident. Sophia walked down Briggate conscious of nothing except the canopy of beauty she held aloft. She walked head in the air, gazing upwards at the silhouette of the flowers through the silk moiré, watching the movement of the dainty tassels. Then, at a particularly crowded part of the narrow pavement she bumped into her mother, which would not have been so bad had her mother not been walking too near the pavement edge. Mrs Parkinson stumbled, fell off the pavement into the gutter, and gave an anguished cry.

'Mama! What is it? Oh Mama, what has happened?' She put out a hand to help her mother to her feet, but Mrs Parkinson shook her head.

'It's no use! I can't stand. Oh dear me! Whatever shall I do?'

A small crowd had gathered and a man pushed his way through to Mrs Parkinson.

'Allow me to help you, madam,' he said. 'What seems to be the matter?'

'I think I've broken my ankle,' Mrs Parkinson said faintly.

'Oh no!' Sophia cried. 'It's not true, Mama! You can't have!'

'I'm afraid I have,' Mrs Parkinson said.

'Don't worry,' the man said to Sophia. 'A broken ankle is painful and inconvenient, but it is not serious.' How concerned the poor girl looked.

Not serious, Sophia thought! Not serious? If only he knew what it meant!

'But we must get you to a doctor at once,' the man said to Mrs Parkinson. He appealed to the bystanders. 'If another gentleman will help me, we will make a chair with our hands and carry this lady to the nearest doctor!'

'No!' Mrs Parkinson said. 'Our carriage is only just a few yards away. If you can help me to the carriage, then I would rather be taken home. Perhaps it is no more than a sprain.'

Sophia's face brightened.

'I dare say that's it, Mama! A nasty sprain – and a day or two's rest will put it right.'

'Don't you think you should see a doctor?' the man said doubtfully.

'You are extremely kind, but I would rather go home,' Mrs Parkinson said. 'I will call my own doctor at once.'

Doctor Hughes came to Mount Royd the moment he was sent for, by which time Mrs Parkinson was in considerable pain. The journey home, the movement of the carriage over the rough road, had been agony.

'You've broken it all right,' he said. 'I don't doubt it for a moment. I shall put it in plaster and I'm afraid you'll be off your feet for several weeks!'

He looked up in time to see Sophia, who was standing nearby, turn quite white and sway on her feet. He took her by the arms and sat her down in the nearest chair.

'Your mother will be quite all right,' he said. 'And once she's in plaster it won't hurt nearly so much. It will just be a matter of rest.'

But before he had completed the sentence Sophia had jumped to her feet and rushed out of the room. He stared after her. He had known her all her life and it had never occurred to him that she could be so filled with compassion as to almost cause her to faint. Well, he must revise his opinion!

Soon after Doctor Hughes had left, Mr Parkinson, summoned from the mill, came home. When she heard his tread in the hall, Sophia, who had run to her own room in a state of rage and bitter disappointment, came downstairs again. She knew what she must do. There was only one thing for it. She must persuade her father to take her to Paris without her mother. She could not, would not, miss it!

'Well, this is a right to-do!' Mr Parkinson said as Sophia came into the drawing-room. 'I go off in the morning, everything fine, and come home to find your mother with her ankle in plaster!'

'Are you feeling more comfortable, Mama?' Sophia

107

asked. She wanted to cry, 'What about Paris? What about Paris?' But she must wait.

'I am, thank you,' Mrs Parkinson said. She looked at her daughter with apprehension. She knew perfectly well why Sophia had turned pale and rushed from the room, and it had nothing to do with concern for her mother. She was genuinely sorry for her daughter's disappointment and she dreaded the days which must follow, not for her own pain, but for all the misery the girl's frustration would bring to the household.

'Well this puts a different complexion on things,' Mr Parkinson said. 'I must inform Léon Bonneau at once. Thank goodness we can now telegraph to France!'

'Papa, you don't mean . . .?' Sophia began.

'Yes, love?'

'Papa you don't mean, you can't mean, we're not going to Paris?'

He stared at her in astonishment.

'Of course that's what I mean! Isn't it obvious? How can you possibly go to Paris without your mother?'

'But Papa, you and I could go! You know very well you ought to go. You agreed it would be a good thing to do. It seems so wrong to give it up so easily. And . . . and Monsieur Bonneau will be so disappointed if you don't go!'

Yes, that was what was at the bottom of it, Albert Parkinson thought. The Frenchman. Well, all the more reason why he wouldn't let his daughter go without her mother to chaperone her. There was no way he could be with her every minute of the time, and heaven knew what she might get up to in a place like Paris.

'Well, he'll have to bear with his disappointment,' he said. 'For one thing, I'll not let you be in Paris without your mother. You're much too young. And for another, you'll be needed here to look after her. You do admit she'll need looking after?'

'Of course,' Sophia agreed. 'But Aunt Fanny will do that far better than I could – especially now she hasn't

Cousin David at home to look after.' She turned to her mother. 'You'd be happy enough with Aunt Fanny wouldn't you, Mama?'

'Of course I would, but that's not the only point your father's making, is it?'

A thought occurred to Sophia.

'Well then, supposing we got a nurse to look after Mama, and Aunt Fanny chaperoned me to Paris?'

But Aunt Fanny, who arrived at exactly that moment, gave the answer to that.

'Apart from the fact that my place is with my dear sister, and I wouldn't dream of deserting her – quite apart from that, I say – *nothing* would induce me to go abroad. Nothing in the world. I wouldn't cross the sea if you paid me a king's ransom!'

Sophia looked from her aunt's implacable face to her mother. Persuade her, she wanted to say. But her mother was white-faced and clearly in pain, not wanting to argue with anyone. Sophia looked to her father. He was her only hope. He seldom refused her anything. Before she could speak he shook his head.

'It's no use, lass. I'm not taking you on your own, and you've heard what your aunt says. I'm sorry you're disappointed. Perhaps we'll go some other time.'

For the second time that day Sophia turned and ran out of the room; ran to her bedroom and threw herself face down on the bed in a paroxysm of angry tears, beating her clenched fists against the pillow.

'I *will* go, I *will* go!' she cried out loud.

Through her noisy sobs she didn't hear Madeleine come into the room.

'Why, Miss Sophia, whatever is it? I came to turn the bed down. Whatever's to do?'

'I can't go to Paris!' Sophia cried. 'They won't let me go to Paris! It's cruel! It's unfair! And all my new dresses! And my parasol! The most beautiful parasol in the world, and now I can't go.'

'I'm sorry, miss,' Madeleine said. 'I truly am. I understand how you must feel, Miss Sophia.'

Sophia rounded on her.

'How can you possibly understand how I feel? You've never been faced with the chance of going. How can *you* understand?'

'The fact that I've never had the chance doesn't mean I wouldn't want to,' Madeleine said as sharply as she dared. 'And I can imagine, Miss Sophia. I can dream!'

Sophia stopped crying as suddenly as if a tap had been turned off. As the thought hit her she sat bolt upright on the bed and stared at Madeleine as if she was seeing her for the first time. Yes, that was it! That was the answer!

'How would you like to go to Paris, Madeleine? How would you like to chaperone me? As my maid, of course.'

Madeleine stared back at Sophia, open-mouthed. Just for a moment, for a split second, she had thought . . .

'Well?' Sophia said impatiently. Her cheeks were flushed, her eyes bright with a new-found enthusiasm.

'I . . . I don't understand, Miss Sophia,' Madeleine said. 'How could I . . .?'

'It's simple enough,' Sophia said impatiently. 'My father won't let me go to Paris without another woman to chaperone me; my mother can't go, my aunt won't. But a young woman can travel if she's accompanied by her maid. Everyone knows that. So what do you say?'

Madeleine tried to still the excitement which was now running through her so that she could hardly breathe. She mustn't let herself believe it because, of course, it couldn't happen. The Master would never agree to it. The Mistress would forbid it. Mrs Thomas would say she couldn't manage without her. There'd be a dozen reasons why it could never happen, and so she mustn't let herself think for a moment that it could. She took a tight hold on herself and tried to control the trembling of her voice as she replied.

'I would be more than willing to go, Miss Sophia, but of course it's not possible!'

'Why not?'

'Well for one thing, the Master would never allow it.' There was no need to go into the rest. That one reason, above all others, was enough.

'Leave him to me,' Sophia said. 'I think he *will* agree.' He would simply have to. She was determined on it.

In the end, to her great surprise, it was easier to persuade her father than she had expected. At first he had demurred, but in the end it seemed his good opinion of Madeleine was the deciding factor.

'She's a sound, sensible girl, and I trust her,' he said. 'But we'll have to see what *she* thinks, won't we?'

'Oh she'll be quite agreeable,' Sophia assured him. After all, the girl was a servant, she'd do as she was told even if – and such was not the case – she didn't want to. 'And of course she needn't stay with me all the time, not when I'm with you and Léon.'

'Oh no! I'm not having that, young woman!' He was adamant. 'I have a duty to her as well as to you. I'm not leaving her in Paris on her own, any more than I would you. No, if she goes, it's as your maid-companion. She accompanies you everywhere and she's one of the party. Understand that from the start, or I'll have none of it.'

'Very well, Papa. I only thought—'

'In this case I'll do the thinking,' Mr Parkinson said firmly. 'Now send Madeleine to me and I'll see how she feels about it.'

When Madeleine stood before him and listened to what he had to say she could hardly believe her ears. She, Madeleine Bates of Priestley Street, Helsdon, going to Paris!

'Well, what have you to say?' Mr Parkinson demanded.

'Oh, sir, it would be wonderful. And I'll take the greatest possible care of Miss Sophia, I promise you that!'

'I know you will, otherwise I'd never have agreed to it. So all I have to do now is to ask your father's permission. I couldn't take you abroad without that. So I'll see him at the mill tomorrow.'

An ice-cold wave of disappointment swept over Madeleine. In all the obstacles which had occurred to her she had not once thought of her father. He would never let her go. He wouldn't let her go as far as Leeds – a city of sin, he called it – let alone Paris. For a moment she hated her father.

'What is it, Madeleine?' Mr Parkinson asked. 'Is something wrong?'

'I'm not sure that my father will agree,' she said quietly.

'Indeed! Well let's see, shall we?' he replied.

From the minute Albert Parkinson began to put the proposition to Joseph Bates he realized that Madeleine had been right. Here was an awkward customer and no mistake! Bates stood before the desk in his office, rigidly straight, his arms by his side as if he was on parade. His mouth was closed in an obstinate line, his brows drawn together. His face was as dark and ominous as a thundercloud.

'Well, Bates?' Albert Parkinson demanded. 'What do you say, then?'

'I don't like it, sir. I want none of my family going off to Paris.'

'And why not?'

'It's a sinful place, sir!'

'So you are saying that I'm leading my own daughter into sin, are you?' Albert Parkinson queried sharply.

'I didn't say that, sir.'

'As good as, Bates; as good as! Or are you suggesting that you don't trust your own daughter? That after the upbringing you've given her, you still can't trust her?'

'I didn't mean that, neither!' The man was somehow twisting his words, giving them the wrong meaning. And because he was his boss he didn't feel free to argue.

'I should hope not,' Albert Parkinson said. 'I must say, I've always found your daughter an honest, trustworthy sort of girl.'

'She is that, sir. There's no denying that.'

'Then are you suggesting perhaps that I won't look after her properly? If so, you're wrong – because I shall look after her exactly the same as my own daughter. Come along now, Bates. Unless you allow Madeleine to go, my Sophia can't go. You'd be doing us all a favour!'

What does he care that Paris is a godless city, a Babylon, Joseph Bates thought. But he has me in a cleft stick. I'm beholden to him for too much.

'Very well, sir,' he said truculently.

It was less than a week now, and for Madeleine there were so many things to settle, from the matter of who would cover her work in the house to what she could possibly wear that was fit for Paris. Apart from her uniform she had only one dress, and that, to put it mildly, had seen better days. But she would solve these problems, or get around them. She was grimly determined on that. The way she felt, she would go to Paris in her shift, if need be!

Her mother suggested the solution to the help in the house.

'Our Emerald could come,' she said. 'She was going back to the mill next week, but I'd be glad for her to help out at Mount Royd if Mrs Parkinson was agreeable.'

'Oh I'm sure she would be,' Madeleine said. 'But will they keep Emerald's job at the mill if she's away another week?'

'I dare say. She's a good little worker. But we'll meet that when we come to it. I have to say, your father's not best pleased about you going to Paris. He'll be home any minute now.'

'Then I'll wait and see him,' Madeleine said bravely. She had this feeling of wanting things to be right with her father before she went abroad, even though it was only for a week.

He came into the house a few minutes later, carrying a parcel under his arm.

'I'm glad to see you, Father,' Madeleine said. 'I wanted to thank you for saying I might go to Paris.'

'I didn't want to,' he said stonily. 'I don't hold with it. As it is, I shall just have to trust you.'

'Oh, you can, Father,' Madeleine assured him. 'You know you can!'

His reply to that was a grunt – and then he handed the parcel to her.

'Here, open this!' he said. 'It's for you.'

Madeleine looked from her father to her mother in wonderment. In all her life he had never given her a present.

'Well, open it,' he repeated.

Her fingers trembled as she unknotted the string and unwrapped the parcel. What she revealed was a length of fine worsted material in a rich, dark green, woven in a herringbone pattern. Oh, it was beautiful! She gasped in amazement.

'This is for *me*?'

'I'll not have a daughter of mine going off shabby,' he said gruffly. It was a matter of family pride. Deep inside himself he had experienced a moment's pleasure in the act of giving his favourite child a present; but he had quickly squashed the feeling.

'The Master let me have it at cost,' he added. 'You'll have to get it made up in time.'

'Oh Father!'

She wanted to fling her arms around him, but she couldn't. He had never encouraged, never even allowed, his children to be demonstrative with him. He had never kissed her, not even when she was small – and now she felt she was denied the chance of showing him how much at heart she really loved him and of expressing her gratitude for the gift.

'Oh Father, it's so good of you!' Words didn't seem enough, but they were all she was allowed to offer.

'I'll make it up for you,' her mother offered. 'If I sit up every night between now and the weekend, I'll see you have it ready. Now we must discuss styles, Madeleine!'

'Before you discuss any such thing, I'd like my tea,' Joseph Bates said.

SEVEN

Madeleine stood in the stern of the ship, leaning against the rail, the spray wet on her face though they were scarcely out of the harbour. Mr Parkinson and Sophia stood nearby, but she was barely conscious of them as she strained her eyes towards the little port of Newhaven, set into the impressive curve of white cliffs. They had stayed there last night, after the long journey from Helsdon, in a small inn close to the dock, so as to be in good time for the morning steamer. Now, as the town and the coastline receded into the distance with every second, with every wave which broke against the little ship, she felt she was leaving behind the whole of her life; her family, her friends, even her country.

It seemed so much more than Mr Parkinson had described it – a few miles, a few hours across the English Channel, was what he'd said. But the way she felt they could have been sailing away for ever, to the far ends of the earth. It was a new and strange sensation and she was loving every minute of it.

'I'm getting wet,' Sophia complained. 'Must we stand here, Papa? Can't we go down into the saloon?'

Her father had booked first-class all the way from Helsdon to Paris, which meant they had entry to the saloon in the stern, and also a cabin for herself and Madeleine.

'We can,' Albert Parkinson said. 'Though why we should sit in a stuffy saloon when we could be up here on deck, filling our lungs with the sea air, looking at the scenery, I fail to see.'

'What scenery, Papa? Only a line of white cliffs after all – and grey sea, and all these quite frightening seagulls swooping around.'

Sophia had no time for the scenery. She wasn't interested in the travelling, only in getting there. Paris was her goal and anything which stood between her and it was simply tedious. She already knew she was going to hate the steamer with its oily smell, its uneven deck, its narrow, precarious stairs and gangways which were far too narrow for her wide skirt; and everything, even the line of the horizon, was beginning to go up and down in the most alarming way.

'Perhaps I'll go to my cabin and lie down,' she said.

Mr Parkinson glanced at his daughter. She *was* looking a bit pale.

'Well if you think so, love, but it seems a pity to miss all this. Anyway, Madeleine can go with you and I'll stay up here for a bit.'

To travel in the stuffy little cabin was the last thing Madeleine wanted. This morning was the first time in her life she had seen the sea – it had been dark when they'd arrived at the inn last night – but already she felt an affinity with it. She was excited by the fact that it was beginning to get a bit rough, the waves white-topped with foam. She felt a thrill go through her body each time an extra large wave thudded against the side of the ship, testing its strength. But, she reminded herself, she wasn't here for her own pleasure. She was here to look after Miss Sophia and she must do it with a good grace.

'Certainly, sir!' she said.

Sophia had not in the least wanted to share a cabin with Madeleine, and really it was against the ship's rules, which decreed that servants must travel in the less comfortable bow of the ship; but her father had been adamant.

116

'Madeleine is going with us to look after you,' he'd said. 'She'll do everything needful. But for this trip she's to have the status of a companion. We've gone into all this, so don't argue.'

'But she's not a companion, she's a servant,' Sophia protested. 'How can you expect me to share everything with her?'

'Well you will,' he said. 'And that's that!'

In a dozen ways, sometimes subtle sometimes, if her father was out of earshot, quite blatant, both before they had left Helsdon and since, Sophia had made her feelings plain to Madeleine. Madeleine bit her lips and took it all, but rebellious thoughts churned inside her. If you think I actually want to be your companion, my fine Miss, she wanted to say, then you're quite mistaken. I don't want to share with you any more than you do with me. But it would be worth it. To see Paris would be compensation enough for both of them. And there would be the added pleasure, though for Miss Sophia rather than for herself of course, of meeting Monsieur Bonneau again.

In the cabin Madeleine helped her mistress off with her bonnet, her mantle and her top skirt. Really, she didn't look at all good, though they'd been no more than half an hour at sea.

'You might feel better if you loosened your stays,' Madeleine suggested. 'Then lie down on your bunk. Can I get you anything to drink – some milk, or a cup of weak tea?'

'I couldn't take a thing!' Sophia moaned. 'You can have no idea how awful I feel! That is the worst of a refined nature; one is so much more sensitive!'

'Yes,' Madeleine said lightly. 'There are advantages in being of peasant stock!' Fortunately her mistress wasn't sensitive enough to recognize sarcasm when she heard it. 'Then I'll just sit and read my book while you try to go to sleep, Miss Sophia.'

She didn't look forward to that either. It was a book of

pious sermons her father had given to her before she left, and she had promised him that she would read a little each day. She would keep her promise – he had been good to her in giving her the dress length, and allowing her to come – but nobody was going to make her enjoy it.

'There's no need for you to remain,' Sophia said. 'I'd sooner be on my own.'

'If you're sure,' Madeleine said eagerly. 'And I'll come back from time to time to make sure you're all right. In the meantime, if you need me just ring for the steward and he'll fetch me.'

The next minute Sophia was asleep. Madeleine thankfully closed her book and went up on deck. Mr Parkinson was nowhere in sight. She presumed he had gone for a walk around the ship, which she also would do presently. For the moment it was enough to stand against the rail, watching the ever-changing movements and colours of the sea, the September sun sparkling like diamonds carelessly scattered on the water. Oh it was glorious! She had never felt quite so alive! A gust of wind came and almost took her bonnet with it, so she untied the ribbons, took it off and held it in her hand; and when some of the pins fell out of her hair so that strands of it came down around her shoulders, she didn't care. She turned her face to the wind and let it blow about her as it would. She stood so a long time, and it was there that Mr Parkinson, in his perambulation around the deck, found her.

He saw her before she was aware of him, and for a moment he caught his breath at the sight. She stood tall, upright, her body leaning into the wind, her face glowing with life, her dark hair streaming out behind her. She was no longer a north-country servant on a shabby cross-channel steamer. She appeared to him as a proud figure-head at the prow of a ship, sailing to who knew where? He was still looking at her when she turned around and caught sight of him.

'Oh, Mr Parkinson, sir! Miss Sophia said I wasn't to stay in the cabin. But in any case she fell asleep. I'll go down and see her again.'

He held up his hand, shook his head.

'No need. If she's asleep, best let her be. But it seems you're a good sailor. Are you enjoying this?'

'Oh I am, sir, I really am! It's the best thing that's ever happened to me!'

'So far,' he said. 'So far. There's a lot more to come and I hope you're going to enjoy it all.'

'Oh I shall, sir!' Madeleine said. 'I know I shall.'

'Well let's hope so. There's just one thing . . .' He hesitated.

'Yes, sir?'

'Be patient with Miss Sophia, Madeleine! I know my daughter isn't the easiest person in the world and she hasn't your common sense – I say this in confidence, of course – but bear with her. If at any time she's – well – a little bit awkward, then put up with it for my sake.' His voice was gruff, as if he found it difficult to say the words.

'Oh sir, you can count on me! It will be no trouble at all! It's the very least I could do.'

She was fond of Mr Parkinson; he was such a kind man. Also she felt at this moment that she could take on the whole world, however awkward it turned out to be.

'Good! Then we'll all have a good time I dare say.'

He turned away and resumed his promenading. His thoughts on the journey from Helsdon had not been easy ones. His mind had been often on Kitty Shane and his longing to be with her rather than to visit Paris. What was to happen about Kitty? It had all started out so lightly, in such an uncomplicated manner, and now there were days when the thought of her obsessed him so that it was all he could do not to run down to Helsdon railway station and jump on the next train for London.

Then cutting deep into his thoughts of Kitty had been the worries about his business. Only he and the bank knew the difficulties he was in. Nothing in the daily conduct of his life gave the slightest hint to anyone, nor must it. Until the tide turned for him, as he told himself desperately it must, it was imperative to appear as prosperous as ever – which was why he had not put a stop to the extravagances of his wife and daughter, notably the expensive trip on which he was now engaged. But now, walking briskly around the decks, buffeted by the breeze, open to the elements, he had begun to feel better. It was as if the wind had taken his doubts and fears and blown them away into the high, clear atmosphere. They knew what they were talking about when they said a sea voyage was good for you. By the time they reached Dieppe his natural optimism had reasserted itself. Everything would work out, he was sure of it.

A few minutes before the steamer docked, Madeleine shook Sophia gently awake.

'We're here, Miss Sophia! Time to get dressed!'

Sophia rubbed her eyes, turned as if to go to sleep again, then suddenly sat up.

'We're here? We're in Paris?'

'Why no, miss! We're still on the ship. We're in Dieppe – and you've slept all the way across the channel!'

'Oh, Dieppe! Then we still have to take the train to Paris. Oh, what a bore!' Sophia said, yawning.

'It won't take all that long,' Madeleine said. 'Here, let me help you on with your skirt. And in Paris Monsieur Bonneau will be there to meet us.'

It was as if someone had lit a lamp in Sophia. She was suddenly wide awake.

'Oh do help me to do my hair, Madeleine!' she implored. 'I'm sure I must look a fright, and I absolutely must look my best!'

'You don't look a fright at all, Miss Sophia,' Madeleine assured her. 'In fact you look a good deal better than when we came on board. The sleep has done you good.'

120

In fact, neither of them had slept much since leaving Helsdon, but in Madeleine's case she felt it didn't matter in the least. Life was far too exciting to waste time in sleep. 'We'd better hurry, though. The Master will be waiting for us on deck.'

But not until Madeleine had helped her mistress to arrange her thick auburn hair in a becoming manner, topping it with her pretty straw bonnet, over which she fussed inordinately about the exact tying of the bow beneath her chin, would Sophia leave the cabin. When the two of them joined Mr Parkinson on deck, everyone waiting impatiently for the boat to be tied up, it was Sophia who saw Léon Bonneau first. He was standing on the quayside, waving to them.

'It's Léon! It's Monsieur Bonneau!' she cried. 'Look, there he is, Papa! He's waving to us! Oh my goodness! Thank heaven I took the trouble to do my hair!'

She and her father waved back energetically. Madeleine restricted herself to a raising of her hand in greeting. It would not be seemly for her to wave enthusiastically to a friend of her employer, though she was nevertheless pleased to see him.

When they came down the gangway he was there at the foot to meet them. He greeted them warmly, bending low over Sophia's hand as he raised it to his lips, shaking Mr Parkinson's hand with enthusiasm.

'You remember Madeleine?' Mr Parkinson said.

'But of course!' Léon Bonneau replied.

Naturally, he did not kiss her hand, but there was no lack of warmth in the smile of recognition he gave her. Madeleine bobbed a curtsey to him.

'Madeleine has come as a companion and chaperone to my daughter,' Mr Parkinson said.

'And as my maid,' Sophia said firmly. 'Mama thought it would not be fitting for me to travel abroad without a maid.'

'But we didn't expect to see you in Dieppe,' Mr Parkinson said. 'We thought you were to meet us in Paris.'

'It seemed to me that it would be easier for you if I were

here,' Léon Bonneau said. 'I have already engaged a porter to see to the baggage and our train leaves for Paris in fifteen minutes, so we have plenty of time.'

'Well it's very kind of you,' Mr Parkinson said. 'I really do appreciate that – and I'm sure the ladies do.'

'It's quite, quite wonderful!' Sophia said, taking Léon's arm as they walked along the jetty in the direction of the railway station. Madeleine walked behind, carrying various small items of luggage which Sophia had thrust upon her.

'I have reserved rooms for you in an hotel in Faubourg St Germain,' Léon said as the train rattled towards Paris. 'It was impossible to find rooms any nearer to the exhibition. Paris is quite full; they say every *chambre*. I do hope you will find it to your liking.'

'Oh, of course we shall!' Sophia enthused. 'I'm quite sure you wouldn't choose anything unsuitable!'

She chattered incessantly with Léon Bonneau while Madeleine gazed out of the window. The landscape was a bit disappointing: flat and uninteresting, nothing like the steep green hills of her native Yorkshire. But don't be so silly, she admonished herself. All places are different – and anyway, I've come to see Paris, and very soon now we'll be there.

Sophia tried hard to hide her disappointment when the carriage they had taken from the station drew up at the hotel. The entrance was insignificant, the building shabby, high, squeezed in between other buildings in a narrow street. It was not the least bit like the Hotel Splendid where they had stayed in London. And the lobby, when they entered, was equally unprepossessing with its black-and-white tiled floor and high wooden counter behind which the receptionist, an elderly lady in black, sat with her back to a board hung with a selection of the largest keys Sophia had ever seen.

She managed to hide her feelings, smiling sweetly at Léon as he went to speak to the woman at the desk. Perhaps this was what French hotels were like; perhaps it was just that Paris was so full for the exhibition. Perhaps the rooms themselves would be quite splendid.

'I inspected the rooms when I reserved them,' Léon Bonneau said, turning to Mr Parkinson. 'I hope you will find them clean and comfortable, though perhaps not luxurious.'

A porter appeared, took the two large keys which the receptionist offered him, and gathered up more items of baggage than Madeleine would have thought it possible for any one person to carry at a time.

'He will show you the way,' Léon said. 'And if you will permit it, I will call at seven o'clock this evening when I will take you out to dine. Except for breakfast, the hotel does not provide meals. But it is much more interesting to eat in a restaurant – do you not agree?'

'Oh yes, indeed!' Sophia said. 'I much prefer it!'

'*Bon*! Then I will see you later. In the meantime, *au revoir*, and I hope you will all have a rest.'

When the porter unlocked the door of the room assigned to herself and Madeleine, one of several along a narrow, dark passage on the third floor, with Mr Parkinson right next door, Sophia was once again disappointed. The man opened the shutters to reveal a chamber sparsely furnished with two narrow beds, a washstand with a ewer and basin, a wardrobe and a small chest of drawers. Though everything was pristine clean, the only trace of luxury was the pretty quilted counterpanes. She struggled between expressing her disappointment and not wishing in any way to criticize Léon Bonneau's choice for them.

'Well!' she exclaimed – but her face said it all.

'I'm sure this will do us very nicely,' Madeleine said.

She had never seen the inside of an hotel before and she had no comparisons to make. Except that she must share it, it was certainly better than her room at Mount Royd. The ceiling was high, the window was large, there would be lots of light and air, and the flowered counterpanes were the prettiest she had ever seen.

'I shall take the bed nearest the window,' Sophia said. 'You may unpack for me at once. Please be careful how you hang my clothes in the wardrobe. I should not like anything to be creased. Perhaps madame behind the desk will show you where you can do some ironing for me if necessary. And while you are unpacking I shall rest.'

'Yes, miss,' Madeleine said obediently.

It was what she herself longed to do. She was now desperately tired and the sight of the bed was almost too much for her. Oh, what bliss it would be to take off her boots, loosen her stays, lie down flat and sink into oblivion. But as on a thousand previous occasions when she had felt too fatigued to do another stroke, she took a deep breath, squared her shoulders, and set to work. Sophia, from her bed, watched Madeleine through half-closed eyes.

By the time Madeleine had hung Sophia's dresses in the wardrobe and disposed of her underwear neatly in the drawers, Sophia was asleep again. The temptation to lie on the bed was now too much for Madeleine. She had not unpacked her own clothes, but there were very few of them and they could wait. Apart from her underwear, some of which was her mother's lent to her for the occasion, there was only one dress, and that a cast-off of Sophia's. Mrs Parkinson had insisted that her daughter should give it to Madeleine so that she should have a change from the green woollen dress when they went out in the evening. She knew she ought to take it out and hang it to get rid of the creases, but she was so very tired. She took off her boots, lay on the bed, and was asleep at once.

She was awakened, it seemed in no time at all, by Sophia roughly shaking her shoulder.

'For goodness' sake wake up, Madeleine! It's already six o'clock and Monsieur Bonneau is calling for us at seven. How dare you go to sleep like this? Please get up at once and help me with my toilet.'

'I'm sorry, Miss Sophia,' Madeleine said, jumping to her feet. 'I lay on the bed and I must have dropped off.'

'Well, please hurry and get my things ready. I'll have the blue dress – or would the grey silk be more suitable for dinner in a restaurant? I wonder? Yes, I'll have the grey! And my grey kid shoes. I have washed. I did that while you were asleep – I don't know how you can sleep so!'

'I'm sorry,' Madeleine said, 'I was very tired.'

'Well, you will be able to get plenty of rest while we are out this evening,' Sophia said.

In the act of removing Sophia's dress from the wardrobe, Madeleine stood quite still, her face buried in the soft material.

'Do you mean, Miss Sophia, that I'm not to go with you to the restaurant?'

'Well we shan't need you, shall we? I shall be well accompanied by my father and Monsieur Bonneau.'

'But I thought—'

'I'm sure my father only meant you to accompany me when he and Monsieur Bonneau were engaged in business,' Sophia said smoothly. 'Besides, I'm not sure you would enjoy yourself. It will most likely be a very smart restaurant.'

You mean I won't know which knife and fork to use, Madeleine thought furiously. Well you're wrong, miss! Haven't I been laying the table for you for years and years. I know as well as you do what's what on a table! She wanted to say it out loud, to shout at her young, horrible, impossibly selfish young mistress. But she wouldn't. She remembered her promise to Mr Parkinson, and kept quiet. All the same, she was sure it wasn't part of his plan that she should be left behind. Also, what about her supper? She was by now terribly hungry.

'Very well, miss,' she said. 'What shall I do about my meal?'

'Oh! I hadn't thought about that! Well I suppose there must be some little café hereabouts. I'm sure you'll be quite safe. And I'll give you some francs to buy yourself something. Now do hurry, Madeleine, and help me with my toilet.'

In silence, for she couldn't trust herself to speak, Madeleine helped Sophia on with her dress, brushed her hair into ringlets, fastened the single strand of pearls Mrs Parkinson had lent her daughter around Sophia's neck. She did look beautiful, there was no denying it. But handsome was as handsome did, and she had the manners of a pig.

Madeleine was putting the finishing touches to Sophia's hair when there was a tap at the door.

'May I come in?' Mr Parkinson called.

'You look very nice, my dear,' he said to his daughter. 'And are you almost ready, Madeleine? Monsieur Bonneau will be here in ten minutes. We don't want to keep him waiting.'

'I didn't think it was necessary for Madeleine to come with us, Papa,' Sophia said quickly. 'I don't need a chaperone this evening – and I'm sure she's very tired.'

Mr Parkinson gave his daughter a long, cool look before turning to Madeleine.

'Are you too tired to come and eat a meal, Madeleine?'

'No sir!'

'Then naturally you must eat with us. It's thoughtful of my daughter to consider your fatigue,' he said dryly. 'But to leave you alone here is not what I had in mind – nor, I am sure, did Sophia. Can you be ready in ten minutes?'

'Certainly, sir!'

There would be no time to change into her other dress, but never mind that. She would wash her hands and face and brush her hair and that would have to do.

'Then I'll take my daughter along to my room and leave you to it,' Mr Parkinson said. 'Be as quick as you can and join us the moment you're ready. Come along, Sophia!'

With a face like thunder, Sophia followed her father.

126

Madeleine quickly emptied the water Sophia had used from the basin into the slop bucket and picked up the ewer to pour herself some fresh. The ewer was empty; Sophia had used it all. Gritting her teeth, Madeleine washed herself in the water Sophia had used. Poor people, she knew only too well, saved water in this manner, but however short they had been her mother had always seen to it that each of her children had fresh water to wash in. Madeleine hated what she now had to do. It was the first and last time she would suffer it, no matter if it led to words with Miss Sophia about the matter.

Less than ten minutes later she glanced at herself in the mirror over the washstand. Her mother had made a good job of the green dress and Mrs Thomas had lent her a cream lace collar which added a nice finishing touch. The colour suited her clear skin and dark hair.

'You'll do,' she said out loud. But of course she could never hold a candle to Miss Sophia.

The restaurant, like the hotel, was less smart than Sophia had expected. Madeleine, on the other hand, was thankful that it was not at all pretentious. She felt quite at ease there. Her green dress was right for the occasion, while Sophia looked slightly overdressed. Not that the Frenchwomen there weren't smart. They were – but in a different way, with gowns beautifully cut and not at all flamboyant. What did surprise her was their make-up. Almost every woman was powdered and painted, something Madeleine had never seen in Helsdon; yet not one of them had a skin half as good as Miss Sophia's.

'You will find the food good,' Léon Bonneau said.

Madeleine devoured everything that was put before her, enjoying the different textures and flavours, though half the time she didn't know what she was eating. When she looked up and saw Monsieur Bonneau smiling at her she blushed with shame. She was eating like the peasant Miss Sophia thought she was.

'I like to see a young lady enjoying her food,' he said.

'My mother would be pleased with you. She begs my sister to eat more.'

Sophia pouted. She had eaten daintily, leaving a little of everything on her plate, as fashion dictated.

'I'm afraid I have a teeny, teeny appetite,' she said. 'But then I'm a teeny person, ar. I not?' She tilted her small head, held out her small, beautifully shaped white hands and gazed at them ruefully. Madeleine dropped her own hands out of sight, on to her lap.

They were on the last course, fine, ripe peaches piled high in a basket lined with leaves, when they heard the noise outside in the street: a tide of sound, drawing nearer, getting louder. Sophia looked at Léon Bonneau in consternation.

'What is it?'

'I don't know. Perhaps I should go and see?'

'Oh I beg of you, please don't! Who knows, it might be quite dangerous!'

As Sophia was speaking a group of people charged into the restaurant, calling and shouting, cheering, waving papers; not looking the least bit dangerous, but smiling and laughing, and in the case of one woman, crying, but happily. They were all talking away, everyone speaking at the same time.

'Oh, how frustrating not to understand a word they're saying!' Madeleine cried.

But Léon was already on his feet.

'Sebastopol has fallen!' he cried. 'Oh my dear friends, Sebastopol has fallen at last! Oh, but this is wonderful news, both for your country and for mine!'

Madeleine heard no more than the first three words: 'Sebastopol has fallen.' Irvine! The war would be over! Irvine would come home!

She gripped the edge of the table, her face as white as the cloth which covered it.

'Why, Madeleine, what is it?' Léon Bonneau asked. 'Are you feeling ill?'

His voice was so kind, his concern so real. It was all

too much for Madeleine. Tears of relief, which she couldn't keep back, raced down her face and Mr Parkinson leaned across the table to lend her his handkerchief.

'Her brother is fighting in the Crimea,' he explained. 'This news means more to her than to any of us.'

'I'm sorry,' Madeleine gasped. 'Please excuse me! It's stupid of me to cry at such wonderful news.'

'Your tears are natural,' Léon Bonneau said. 'They will not be the only tears of joy shed tonight. Oh dear, I wish you could all understand exactly what is being said, but I will translate. Sebastopol, they say, has been left a heap of ruins. The Russian fleet is destroyed. Nothing now remains in the harbour. This will be the beginning of the end of the war, that is surely so!'

All the customers were standing now, many of them on chairs, and one man, who had over-indulged, in the middle of a table, waving his napkin.

'Come, my friends, we will drink to this victory, and to a speedy end to the war!' another man called out.

Léon Bonneau looked at Madeleine. 'And to the safe return of our loved ones!' he added.

Dear me, what a fuss, Sophia thought. And what an exhibition Madeleine has made of herself. Nevertheless, like everyone else in the restaurant, she raised her glass. She turned to Léon, but he was smiling at Madeleine and didn't see her.

Later, accompanied by Léon, they walked back to the hotel through streets which were thronged with shouting, singing, cheering crowds. The theatres had long since emptied but no one, it seemed, had gone home. Every window in every building was lit, and the streets seemed as bright as day.

'A wonderful end to your first day in Paris!' Léon Bonneau said as he made his farewells. '*Dormez bien*. Sleep well, and I will call for you all at ten o'clock in the morning.'

Long after she had snuffed the candle, and Sophia was asleep, Madeleine lay in her bed listening to the rejoicing crowds. There was only one small corner of her mind which did not rejoice with them, one small voice which she couldn't still. Supposing, just supposing that for Irvine it was already too late? Dear God, she prayed, let him come home safe. Only let him come home safe and I'll be good for ever.

'There are open-topped omnibuses going directly to the exhibition in the Champs Elysées,' Léon Bonneau said when he called for them next morning. 'I think you might prefer that to a *fiacre*. And we would see more of Paris.'

'Oh yes, indeed!' Sophia agreed. And on the top of the omnibus she would sit under her beautiful parasol, which Léon had not yet had a chance to see. 'I think that's a splendid idea!'

The streets were heavy with traffic, but whenever there was the slightest space the horses broke at once into a fast trot, so that the passengers on the omnibus had to cling tightly to their seats: but much of the time they were slowed down, hemmed in by the density of the traffic.

'I'm afraid this will be a slow journey,' Léon Bonneau apologized.

'Well I for one don't mind in the least,' Madeleine said. 'It gives us all the more time to see the people on the pavements!'

Such fashionable clothes they wore – the men and women were equally splendid: parasols, elaborately trimmed bonnets, top hats, white-gloved hands waving.

'It's wonderful,' she said.

Sophia's look told her she was talking too much, but she didn't care.

She had never seen a sight so colourful or heard such a cacophony of sound. It seemed as if everyone in Paris was on holiday, everyone celebrating. And when the omnibus reached the Champs Elysées and they dismounted, a smiling Sophia assisted every inch of the way by a gallant Monsieur Bonneau, and when Madeleine saw the magnificent white stone building which was the Palais de l'Industrie rising up in front of them, and when they actually stepped inside, Madeleine simply could not help clapping her hands. She felt that they had indeed entered into another world.

'Oh!' she cried. 'I don't believe it!'

They stood there, the three of them from their small corner of Yorkshire, staring. The size of everything: the width, the breadth, the space; the balconies, the arches, the feast of colour in the exhibits and the elegant clothes of the people; but more than anything and high above all, the great domed glass roof; it was overwhelming.

'It's magic!' Madeleine said.

It was enchantment; she was dreaming and any minute she would wake up! It was more than she could have imagined in a thousand years.

'Well, this is a bit of all right and no mistake!' Mr Parkinson said.

Léon Bonneau was beaming with pride, as if he had built the whole scene with his own hands, especially for them.

'Oh it's wonderful! It's splendid!' Sophia cried.

'And what do you think, Madeleine?' Léon Bonneau asked.

'I think it's . . . like fairyland,' she said. 'It's just the best thing I ever saw in my life!'

'Oh, what shall we look at first?' Sophia cried. 'Oh, I want to see absolutely *everything*!'

In fact, she discovered, she did not. There was too much, far too much. Oh, it was all right at first. She hooked her small hand firmly through Léon's arm and dragged him hither and thither, never stopping for long in one place. He didn't seem to mind, and laughed at her cries of enthusiasm when some pretty thing caught her eye. And the soldiers! So marvellous in their splendid uniforms!

'Each day the commanding officer of the garrison sends a number of men to view the exhibition,' Léon explained. 'They looked splendid, I agree!'

She was entranced by the elegant clothes of the women

there, the width of their skirts, the depths of the frills on them. How right she had been to object to silly Miss Compton's idea of fashion!

But after the first hour or so, during which the small party followed in her wake wherever she chose to go, her father called a halt.

'I'm sure it's all very nice, but I want to see the textiles, the machinery, that sort of thing,' he said. 'After all, it's what I came for.'

'You are quite right,' Léon Bonneau said. 'And so we shall. Look, we come to them now!'

It was from then on that Sophia began to feel bored. She had little interest in textiles, and none at all in machinery. How could she be expected to enthuse? The trouble was, the men were far *too* interested. Even Madeleine seemed genuinely taken by it, which in her mistress's opinion was most unfeminine. Sophia felt herself quite neglected.

'Oh, do look at this!' Madeleine cried. 'There's a machine here weaving two wide ribbons at the same time. They're the prettiest ribbons and they have portraits of two people woven into them!'

'The Emperor and Empress of France,' Léon said.

'Aye, but it's an English machine!' Mr Parkinson pointed out. 'Don't forget that. Made in Coventry. And have you noticed? It hardly needs any looking after? That lad in charge only gives it an occasional glance!'

'You English are very clever with machines,' Léon said. 'I admit that. But as you and I have discussed before, I think we French are better at patterns. I think we have newer ideas. We are more – how to say it – audacious about blending colours. Come and regard the exhibits from Roubaix and I will show you what I mean.'

My father would enjoy all this, Madeleine thought! She followed close behind the men, studied the textiles as they did, listened carefully as Mr Parkinson and Léon Bonneau discussed and argued about the respective merits of the cloths. Yes, her father would love this, and

132

so did she. Anything to do with weaving had always interested her, and here in the exhibits from Roubaix she saw designs which were quite different from anything woven in Parkinson's mill. Not necessarily better, but different. Exciting, almost.

'Well, I see what you mean,' Mr Parkinson was saying to Léon Bonneau. 'And it's a challenge. I don't deny it. But I still say we could teach you something also. Perhaps you should come over and spend some time with us at Parkinson's. I don't mean a week. A few months. It would be for the benefit of both of us. And when you went back home, happen you could take one of our men to see what you do in Roubaix.'

For the moment, engrossed in what was the main-spring of his life, the production of fine cloths, he forgot his financial worries, forgot that the next few months might not be the best time to take this Frenchman into his mill.

'Oh, what a perfectly splendid idea!' Sophia cried, suddenly alive to what they were saying. 'Oh, do say you will, Léon!'

Léon laughed. She was such an attractive little thing, and quite transparent. Obviously there was money there too. Mr Parkinson was clearly a rich man with a pros-perous business. It was a fact not to be overlooked. He wouldn't be averse to spending more time with the pretty Sophia, he could grow quite fond of her; but living in Helsdon for several months was another matter. Could he possibly bear it?

'I shall have to think about it,' he said. 'Speak with my family. But I promise I shall do that.'

He turned back to Mr Parkinson and they continued their tour of the machinery, Madeleine and Sophia in tow. It was getting terribly hot, the noonday sun beating down through the glass roof. Madeleine felt the perspir-ation running down her back, and her hair was damp underneath her bonnet. Of course her dress was far too warm for the occasion, but the main trouble was that

133

there was no air. It looked as if no ventilation had been built into all that vast area of glass.

'That's a nice bit of carpet there,' Mr Parkinson pointed out. 'Made by Crossleys of Halifax. I shouldn't wonder if they got a medal for that!'

Madeleine looked at the rich purples, blues and greens of the carpet; at the skilful weaving of shade into shade. Then as she looked, the colours began to merge into one and whirled and spun like a Catherine wheel in front of her eyes. And while they were still spinning, all the colours, and everything around her, turned black.

EIGHT

When Madeleine came to, the first person she saw was Léon Bonneau. His arm was around her shoulders, supporting her, his eyes were full of concern. For a moment she was sure she was dreaming, otherwise why would she be in the arms of this handsome stranger? Nothing like this happened in real life. Then he spoke, and she recognized his voice, and knew it was not a dream. She was covered in confusion. What had happened? Had she done something stupid? But he sounded kind enough, anxious even.

'Madeleine, are you all right?'

'Yes. Yes thank you, sir. I'm quite all right, though I don't understand what happened.' She began to struggle to her feet and he helped her up, seated her on a chair someone had brought.

'You fainted. It was the heat, I'm sure. It is very oppressive in here.'

'I'm very sorry, sir,' Madeleine said. 'I've never done such a thing before in all my life. I'm sorry to be such a trouble.' She felt a fool.

'You are no trouble,' Léon Bonneau assured her. 'I blame myself that I have kept you ladies far too long in this heat.'

Of course you're a trouble, Sophia thought angrily! All this fuss and bother, all this concern! She herself might

135

well have fainted, the heat was every bit as bad for her, but she had more self-control, more consideration for others. Well, she couldn't say what she thought now but she certainly would later.

'Perhaps you should go back to the hotel, Madeleine.' She struggled to keep her voice level.

'I will, if you don't mind,' Madeleine agreed. She felt strange, weak, not quite sure of herself. The last thing she wanted was to cause any more fuss. She was deeply ashamed of what she had done.

'Then we'll put you in a cab,' Sophia said.

'Oh no!' Léon contradicted. 'I think she must not go back alone. One of us will accompany her. I am ready to do so.'

'Well, if you think it *really* necessary . . .' Sophia began doubtfully. She would go with them, of course.

'Of course it's necessary!' Mr Parkinson interrupted.

'Then I'm sure Papa will take her!' Sophia said brightly. Actually, this could turn out better than she had hoped.

Albert Parkinson gave his daughter a sharp look. He was sorry for Madeleine – she looked very pale still – and he'd have been quite willing to accompany her, but if Sophia thought she was going to be left alone with the Frenchman, she had another thought coming!

'No, I think we'll leave it to Monsieur Bonneau,' he said. 'He knows the ropes. He'll be there and back in no time. You and I will take a stroll in the fresh air and we'll arrange a place to meet up later.'

'I shall be perfectly all right on my own,' Madeleine protested. She felt like a parcel no one wanted to deliver. Also she could guess what Sophia was thinking. It was certain she'd be made to pay for all this later.

'It is not to be thought of!' Léon Bonneau said emphatically. 'Now if you are well enough we will leave at once, get you out of this heat.' He quickly made arrangements to meet up again with the Parkinsons, then took Madeleine's elbow and guided her through the crowd.

'Such a palaver!' Sophia said irritably, watching them go. 'Trust a person of that class to cause a fuss about nothing!'

'Sophia! I'd remind you that your great-grandfather was a farmhand,' Mr Parkinson said sharply. 'He cleaned out pigsties for a living. And my father was a self-made man and proud of it. So come off your high horse, my lady!'

Oh she was so cross! She could cry with the frustration of it all, but her father wouldn't be impressed by that and she'd end up with a blotchy face. Why was everyone so unkind to her? It wasn't turning out a bit as she'd expected. She'd been as good as gold – and here she was, stuck with her father, while Madeleine, a servant, who had been a nuisance to everyone, only they were all too well-mannered to show it, had gone off in a cab with Léon. It was so unfair!

In the cab Léon turned his head a little to look at Madeleine. She lay back against the seat, her eyes closed, thick lashes splayed against cheeks into which the colour was already returning. He could look at her now without hindrance, and did so. He had been right in Helsdon in thinking that her beauty was not English. Her dark looks fitted much better into this Continental scene. She could have been taken for a native, except that her dress would never pass muster in Paris. It was quite hopelessly provincial, only redeemed by the dignity with which she wore it, as if to her it was something special.

Apart from this air of dignity, which he thought was natural to her at all times, she was different from the girl he had observed in Helsdon. There, in spite of being a servant, she had been her own person. Here in Paris, though she was treated as an equal – except by that pretty little minx Sophia – she was too quiet, too subservient. This surprised him, even irritated him a little. He had marked her out from the beginning as a young woman who would know how to use every opportunity.

She was able to cope in general of course; she had conducted herself very well in the restaurant. But it was only this morning when they were looking at the textiles that she had actually come alive, emerged as a real person. He had enjoyed that brief glimpse.

In one quick movement, no fluttering of her eyelashes, she opened her eyes and was staring into his before he had time either to turn away, or to disguise the intensity of his scrutiny. Had he been a man ever to have been embarrassed, he would have been so now.

'I thought you were asleep,' he said.

'I'm sorry!'

'Why are you sorry? It would be a very natural thing to do on this warm day. I wouldn't have been the least put out.'

'It would seem very rude,' Madeleine said. 'And I'm already taking up your time with my foolishness.'

'Do not apologize,' he said. 'It is not necessary. A little fainting fit could happen to anyone.'

But it happened to me, Madeleine thought. It just would.

'I had not thought you would apologize too much,' Léon said. 'You were not like that in Helsdon.'

And what could he mean by that?

'Sir, are you suggesting that I'm ill-mannered?' she asked coldly.

'No, no! It is not that. What I try to say is that there is no need for you to be so – humble. I prefer you as you were in Helsdon.'

'I'm sorry . . !' Madeleine began. Then they both laughed.

'Promise not to use those words again!' Léon said.

'Well, perhaps I was wrong in Helsdon,' Madeleine suggested. 'A servant has to be submissive. And I *am* a servant. Perhaps for the moment you had forgotten that, sir?'

'Perhaps. I don't know. Does it matter?'

'Oh, yes sir!'

When he talked to her so freely she was in danger of forgetting it herself, and that wouldn't do. Though never in her life had she felt submissive inside, she couldn't afford to show that. And she didn't trust those above her, employers and the like, especially when they offered equality. They held it out to you, and when you were on the point of taking it they snatched it back and were affronted that you could ever have thought it was yours. So she knew she must tread carefully, which was a pity, because she quite liked Monsieur Bonneau; though she was sure that deep down he was exactly like the rest.

She is right, Léon thought irritably. It does matter. To trifle with a servant, even to make love with a servant, was not forbidden – but with a servant of one's friends it was both ill-mannered and foolish. Not done, as the English said. And aside from that, there was something about her which would stop him. She was damned attractive, but she was . . . well for one thing too serious. There was no feminine coyness, no flirtatiousness in her. While he was pretty certain that he could have the lovely Sophia with the minimum of effort, it would not be so with her maid. Pity! There was passion in her, he was sure of that. He recognized it in her eyes and in her voice, and it was all the more exciting because she herself was almost certainly unaware of it. He envied the man who would one day arouse that passion.

'Ah! Here is your hotel,' he said. 'I will see you in.'

'There's not the slightest need, Monsieur,' Madeleine said. 'I can do that very well myself, and you can keep the cab and go back to the others.'

'Are you sure you are recovered?' he asked. 'Will you promise me you will lie down for an hour or so?'

'I'll do that – though I'm perfectly all right now. I thank you very much for your kindness, Monsieur.'

'Then I will say *au revoir*. I hope you will be quite fit for the theatre this evening.'

'Oh I'm sure I shall be,' Madeleine replied.

He watched her enter the hotel, then at a word the driver flicked his whip and they drove away.

For the next hour Madeleine lay on the bed, her head

resting uncomfortably against the hard pillow roll, and allowed herself the luxury of thinking about Monsieur Bonneau. Yes, he was definitely attractive, not only in his looks and his figure, but in other ways. He impressed her as purposeful, strong, a man who would get what he wanted. In her mind she compared him with George Carter, who outside her family was the only other man she had known. Beside Monsieur Bonneau, George Carter was a pale ghost; nothing. How could she ever, for one second, have contemplated marrying George?

With such thoughts chasing around in her head, Madeleine fell asleep; and what she dreamt, when she remembered it on waking, caused her to blush – yet to wish she could fall asleep and dream it all over again. Instead, she rose, sluiced her face in cold water, and decided to go out.

'I'm going for a walk,' she said to the woman at the desk as she handed in her key.

She had no idea which way to go, but if she noticed every turn surely she couldn't get lost? She had this strong desire to be on her own, away from everybody. She wished, for a little while, neither to serve anyone or to be beholden to them.

She had walked along no more than half a dozen narrow streets when she came across a small park, a pretty place, where nurserymaids pushed babies in carriages, parents held children by the hand, older couples strolled slowly along the wide paths, though no one, she noticed, ventured on to the green, velvety lawns. She walked a little, then presently she sat on a seat, leaned back, tilting her face towards the sun. In spite of the number of people, it was peaceful here in the little park. She wished she could bring her mother here.

Sitting there, she forgot the passage of time until the air on her face felt suddenly cooler, and when she looked around there were fewer people. The nurses with babies and the parents with young children had gone. The sun was low in the sky.

She jumped to her feet at once and began to walk

140

quickly, hoping to goodness she could remember the way back. If the Parkinsons were back before her she'd be in trouble. No one would know where she was. She doubted if the *concierge* had understood a word she'd said. But the time spent in the park had been worth it. For a brief period she had felt freedom.

Sure enough, Mr Parkinson, not looking at all pleased, was pacing the lobby.

'I'm sorry, sir,' Madeleine said. 'I felt the need of fresh air. I didn't mean to be away so long.'

'I was worried,' he said gruffly. 'Anything could have happened to you. I wouldn't have known where to look!'

'I'm truly sorry, sir,' she repeated. 'It won't happen again.'

'I hope not. Well now that you are here, get upstairs quickly,' he said.

And I'll get it in the neck from Miss Sophia, Madeleine thought, climbing the stairs to the bedroom.

'Oh there you are at last,' Sophia said.

'I'm sorry, miss. I went for a walk.'

To Madeleine's relief and surprise there was no further reference to her absence. Sophia seemed to be in a particularly happy mood.

'Did you have a pleasant afternoon?' Madeleine ventured.

'Oh, quite wonderful! We went to the Palais des Beaux-Arts. That's the Palace of Fine Arts,' she explained kindly. 'Painting, porcelain, that kind of thing. So much more interesting than silly old machinery and textiles, at least to me. But I expect you're interested in cloth because your father's a weaver.'

'And I suppose the Master and Monsieur Bonneau are interested because they manufacture it,' Madeleine said smoothly.

Sophia gave her a sharp look.

'Monsieur Bonneau was most interested in the paintings,' she said. 'He is a man of great culture and refined taste. And afterwards he took us to the most delightful

141

café and we had hot chocolate and plate after plate of scrumptious little pastries. Yes, it was a very satisfactory afternoon. Much better than the morning.'

'I'm glad you enjoyed it, miss,' Madeleine said. She was laying out her mistress's clothes for the evening. 'Shall I help you to get ready now?'

'Yes. I must look my absolute best this evening. I want you to take a great deal of trouble with my hair; as many ringlets as you can possibly coax it into.' She had every hope this evening of persuading Léon to take up her father's invitation and come to Helsdon. He had been most attentive to her all afternoon.

When she was ready, wearing her very finest dress, her hair like burnished copper, her eyes sparkling and her cheeks pink from excitement, she looked truly lovely. Surveying herself in the mirror, Madeleine standing behind her, she was really quite pleased.

'Of course there is absolutely no need at all for you to go to the theatre if you don't want to,' she said to Madeleine. 'I'm not at all sure that you will enjoy it – and of course it will be entirely in French.'

Of which you, madam, don't know one word more than I do, Madeleine thought.

'You might feel much happier here, reading your book,' Sophia suggested. 'My father would have a meal sent in for you.'

'Thank you for your concern, miss,' Madeleine said smoothly, 'but I'd quite like to go to the theatre. I'm looking forward to it.'

Sophia shrugged.

'Oh very well! Then get ready quickly. Don't take long about it.'

Sophia sat in the armchair, buffing her nails on a pad of chamois-leather, while Madeleine changed her clothes. For the visit to the theatre she was to wear the evening dress which Sophia had reluctantly passed on to her before they left Helsdon. It was nowhere near as fine as Sophia's present dress, but it was nevertheless beautiful. It had the

142

lowest neck Madeleine had ever worn, with fine cream lace at the breast and down the front of the bodice. When she stepped into it the soft material caressed her body. She felt like a princess of the blood royal.

Of course it was too short. It revealed her shabby boots, which even spit and polish couldn't redeem. She must just hope that everyone would be so taken with her top end that they wouldn't look as far down as her feet.

She was fastening the last hook when there was a knock at the door.

'See who it is,' Sophia ordered.

Madeleine went to answer it, and returned bearing two almost identical, elaborately wrapped boxes.

'What is it?' Sophia asked.

'Boxes from the florist, Miss Sophia. The surprising thing is . . . one for you, and one actually addressed to me!' She could hardly believe her eyes. Nothing like this had ever happened to her before.

Really, Papa is going quite mad, Sophia thought, sending flowers to a servant. There's a limit to equality. In fact, he seldom sent flowers to anyone.

'It's not like my father to give flowers,' she said. 'Paris must have gone to his head!'

Madeleine had already opened her box and was reading the card. She gasped, and looked up in bewilderment.

'They're not from the Master,' she said hesitantly.

'Then who . . .?' Sophia snatched up her box and tore it open. Tucked into the most beautiful spray of orchids she had ever seen was a white card. 'Miss Sophia Parkinson, from Léon Bonneau.' For a moment she almost swooned with pleasure, and then the truth hit her.

'I don't believe it,' she said. 'There must be some mistake. The flower shop has made an error. They must both have been meant for me.'

'I don't think so, miss,' Madeleine said firmly. 'My name's quite plainly written here.'

Sophia darted towards Madeleine and snatched the card from her hand. 'To Miss Madeleine Bates, from Léon

Bonneau.' How could he? How could he do such a thing? It was almost an insult, and would have been so entirely had not her own corsage been bigger, and clearly more expensive, than the one lying in Madeleine's box. Oh there was more to this than met the eye! Furiously, she tore Madeleine's card into tiny pieces and threw them to the floor.

'You cannot possibly wear it, of course!' she cried. 'Who ever heard of a maid wearing an orchid?'

That had been precisely Madeleine's own thought. It was wonderfully kind of Monsieur Bonneau to think of her, but not very sensible. She had decided almost at once, though reluctantly, that she wouldn't wear the orchid. It would not be seemly. She would put it into water and keep it until it faded, but not wear it.

All it took to change her mind was Sophia's words. How dare she say such a thing! I shall wear the flower now, no matter what, Madeleine decided. Deliberately, she took a pin from the tray on the dressing-table and fastened the corsage to her dress.

'What are you doing?' Sophia shouted. 'Take it off at once I say! You can't wear it! You look quite ridiculous!'

'Oh, but really I think I must,' Madeleine said quietly.

'Do you dare to defy me!' Sophia was beside herself with rage.

'I don't like to, miss. It's not my way, as you know. But the gentleman sent it to me. It would seem very rude and ungrateful if I were not to wear it. He might think I didn't know how to behave.' She spoke calmly, but inside she was shaking. For a moment she had wondered if the words would actually come out.

'So! What did you do to earn this?' Sophia demanded. It was clear to her now that Léon had been inveigled into all this. 'Oh don't think I didn't see you this morning, making up to him; pretending to faint. What happened in the cab? What favour did a servant give him that he sent an orchid? Take it off! I order you to take it off!'

She stood facing Madeleine, her pretty face flushed with anger. Madeleine neither moved nor spoke.

144

'Then I'll take it off for you!' Sophia yelled.

She lunged towards Madeleine, grabbed at the flower, and in her rage tore the fine material of the dress from the neck to the waist, so that Madeleine was left with her breasts bare. Then she threw the orchid to the floor and stamped on it.

Madeleine could bear no more.

'How dare you!' she yelled. 'How dare you! I shall never forgive you for that!'

Then she seized her mistress roughly by the shoulders and shook her until the pins fell from her hair and it cascaded around her shoulders.

'You are nothing but a spoilt brat! Someone should have taken a slipper to your backside years ago!'

Sophia tried hard to fight her off, raining blows with her clenched fists on Madeleine's bare breast, while Madeleine pulled at Sophia's bright hair. It was only the appearance of Mr Parkinson who, hearing the row, entered the room without knocking, which stopped them both.

Madeleine quickly crossed her hands over her breast, trying to hide her nakedness.

'What in the name of thunder is going on?' he bellowed.

'Ask her!' Sophia shrieked. 'She attacked me!'

He turned to Madeleine and saw the state she was in.

'Who tore your dress?' he demanded.

Madeleine remained mute. He turned back to his daughter.

'I did,' Sophia said. 'She asked for it.'

He was as red as a turkey-cock with anger. Madeleine thought he would have a stroke. But he took a deep breath, clenched and unclenched his hands and tried to speak calmly.

'You are both aware that we're due to leave for the theatre very shortly. So pull yourselves together and get ready at once. At once, do you hear? But don't think this is the last you'll hear of this little lot. I've never seen a more disgraceful affair, not even among rough men. We'll speak of it later, make no mistake about that!'

'Sir!' Madeleine said.

'What is it?' he barked. 'There's no time for explanations now.'

'I can't go to the theatre,' she said. 'Even if I had the materials to mend my dress, there isn't time. And I can't go in my day dress, sir.'

'*That* is for certain,' Sophia drawled.

If it had not been for the note of triumph in his daughter's voice, Albert Parkinson might have left it at that, let Madeleine stay behind. As it was he didn't.

'In that case, Sophia, you will lend Madeleine one of your new dresses. She may choose whatever she likes from your wardrobe, except the one you are wearing. Either you will lend her a dress, or you will not go to the theatre yourself. The choice is yours!'

She hated him! She absolutely hated him! How could he do this, how could he humiliate her so in front of this wretched servant girl? But she couldn't bear to miss seeing Léon, or have him miss the sight of her in her new dress.

'Be quick about it!' her father said. 'I need to let Monsieur Bonneau know if we're not going. What's your choice?'

'I'll lend the dress,' Sophia said sulkily.

'Sir, I would rather not . . .,' Madeleine began.

Mr Parkinson silenced her. 'I'm afraid you have no choice, Madeleine. You'll do as I say. Just get ready quickly.'

When he had left the room Madeleine knelt down and picked up the damaged orchid. She would never wear it, but she would press it in her book. She gathered up the pieces of card which lay on the carpet like confetti and put them away in the small drawer which was hers. When this visit to Paris was over she would not see Monsieur Bonneau again. But she didn't care. She never wanted to see any of them again. When they came back from the theatre she would give in her notice to Mr Parkinson before he could sack her. Oh, he had been fair to her in the last few minutes, but she wouldn't be let off scot-free.

146

She was sick of being a servant. She would never be a servant again, never as long as she lived. She was sick of Paris too. All she wanted now was to be home with her family. But when she thought of home she remembered that her father would not welcome her.

She had little spirit now for dressing up in Sophia's clothes, she would far rather have stayed in the hotel, though yet again she must do as she was told. But she would never again kow tow to that little cat Sophia.

She opened the wardrobe door and surveyed Sophia's dresses.

'I'll wear this one,' she said cheekily.

She had deliberately chosen a gown Sophia had not yet worn. That way she could feel for a little while that it was her own.

'It won't suit you,' Sophia said savagely. 'You'll look a fright – and serve you right!'

Madeleine stepped into the dress. The delicate pale green of the silk and the ivory lace at the neck suited her dark colouring to perfection.

'I think it quite becomes me!' she said pertly.

'I shall never wear it now!' Sophia declared. 'How could I? After my servant has worn it.'

'I am not your servant, I am your father's,' Madeleine retorted. 'For the moment, and until we get back to Helsdon, I am your companion – a position I dislike every bit as much as you do. I just hope we can both behave so as not to ruin everyone else's evening!'

She was shaking in every limb. Only the rage boiling inside her enabled her to spit out the words – words she couldn't have believed she was capable of.

Sophia looked at her open-mouthed.

'Are you daring to tell me I don't know how to behave?'

'I most certainly am!' Madeleine said. 'But since I *do* know how to behave, I will rearrange your hair for you.'

'And since you ruined it – so you should!'

After that there was silence between them while

Madeleine, with what she considered to be true nobility dressed Sophia's hair even more beautifully than before.

The delicate white skin of Sophia's shoulders still showed red from Madeleine's fierce grasp, and on the upper part of Madeleine's chest, so that she had to disguise it by a rearrangement of the lace collar, a bruise showed as a result of Sophia's pummelling. How disgusting we both were, Madeleine thought. But when she looked at the ruined beauty of the orchid she didn't feel the least bit repentant for what she'd done.

When Mr Parkinson came to collect them he couldn't keep the spark of admiration out of his eyes at the sight of them both.

'Just think on you behave as fine as you look, the pair of you,' he said grimly. 'I want no hanky-panky!'

He needn't have worried. Sophia was so immediately engrossed with Léon Bonneau, and his admiration for her was so plain to see, that every other thought went out of her head. Madeleine had vowed, as far as manners would permit, to remain aloof and remote from everyone. This was made easier by the fact that she was not wearing her own clothes, she was dressed in unaccustomed finery, and therefore felt quite a different person, not herself at all. Was this what beautiful clothes did to you, then?

Léon Bonneau eyed both girls appreciatively as they stood in the foyer before the start of the performance.

'You must be the two most charming ladies in Paris this evening,' he said.

For a moment Madeleine felt sure he was about to kiss her hand, as he had Sophia's, and she at once clasped her hands firmly, one in the other, holding them tight against her body, so that he couldn't.

She was not, Léon Bonneau noticed, wearing his flower – and wondered why. Perhaps it had been a mistake to send it? In the florist's shop, against his better judgement, he had yielded to a sudden impulse. Ah well, he'd meant to be kind but perhaps he'd simply been foolish!

Madeleine saw him glance at the lace at her neck, and

148

wondered if the bruise was showing. She put up her hand to cover the place, then realized that he was looking for the orchid. Since Sophia's attention was for a brief moment elsewhere, Madeleine spoke.

'Thank you for the orchid. It was beautiful – and a most kind thought.'

'But you are not wearing it?'

'It – it met with an accident,' she said quietly. 'It was damaged. I'm very sorry.'

'What a shame! But this evening you have no need of flowers to enhance you!'

And at that moment Sophia turned to him again, linking her arm through his in a proprietorial manner.

'Should we not go to our box?' she suggested. 'I would so like to be able to look at people before the lights go down.'

And to be looked at, Madeleine thought unkindly – though it was true that in her fine dress she was drawing as many admiring glances as Sophia. But she would be glad to go into the box, for there she could hide her feet in their awful boots.

Mr Parkinson offered her his arm and escorted her to the box, for all the world as if she were a lady.

From the moment the lights went down she was totally immersed in the play. It was *The Lady of the Camellias*, and it didn't matter in the least that it was in French. Somehow she understood it. She *was* Violetta. In the happy parts she rejoiced with her, and when Violetta suffered, as she seemed to much of the time, every pang was Madeleine's own. She was glad of the darkness of the theatre which hid the tears she couldn't keep back; and when the tears caused her to give a small sniff she was grateful for the beautiful white silk handkerchief which Monsieur Bonneau surreptitiously passed to her.

'Are you enjoying it?' he asked during the interval.

'Oh it's wonderful, monsieur!' Madeleine assured him. 'It's the first play I've ever seen, and if I live to be a hundred I shall never forget it!'

The second half was equally absorbing, and sadder than ever. She was glad Monsieur Bonneau had not reclaimed his handkerchief.

'It was splendid, quite splendid!' a dry-eyed, applauding Sophia said when the lights went up. 'Did you not think so, Léon?'

'I found it very moving,' he said.

'And we'd better move, too, if we're to get some supper,' Mr Parkinson remarked. He'd enjoyed it up to a point, but of course he hadn't understood a single word, and really a good music-hall was more in his line.

Madeleine did not enjoy the supper which followed the theatre. For a start, she was still affected by the sadness of the play they had seen but, in addition, she was now deeply troubled by the thought of what Mr Parkinson would have to say when they were back in the hotel. The enormity of what she had done had suddenly swept over her. Mr Parkinson wouldn't gloss over what had happened, that was for sure; and it was natural she'd have to take most of the blame.

She wouldn't change her mind about giving in her notice. She was quite sure about that. But when she left Mount Royd where would she go? How would she live? Would the Master even give her a reference? Without one she'd find it almost impossible to get another job.

Apprehension overwhelmed her like a tidal wave. There was no way she could eat. She laid down her knife and fork and pushed her plate away.

Sophia, on the other hand, was as bright as a butterfly on a summer's day – and as pretty, Madeleine thought. She laughed and chattered, ate and flirted, without a care in the world. Well no doubt she could twist her father around her little finger – and Monsieur Bonneau too by the way he was looking at her.

It was Sophia who mentioned again the invitation to Helsdon.

'I do so hope you're going to say "Yes", Léon,' she said.

'Of course Helsdon isn't Paris, but we shall do everything we can to entertain you.'

'If he comes, it'll be to work,' Mr Parkinson put in. 'Not to be entertained. Of course we'll be very pleased to have you. Don't think we won't.' He spoke hastily to Léon, aware that he had been rather bad-tempered all evening.

'Well then,' Léon said, 'I have already decided that if my family is agreeable, and I think they will be because what I learn will be of value to them also, then I shall come. But I will write to you finally when I have been back to Roubaix for a day or two.'

Sophia squealed with delight.

'Oh, how marvellous! And no matter what Papa says, it certainly won't be all work and no play. I shall see to that myself!'

She tries too hard, goes too far, Madeleine thought. Well thank heaven she wouldn't be involved in any of it herself. But what would she be involved in? That was now the question uppermost in her mind.

'Tomorrow,' Léon Bonneau said, 'there is to be a special service of thanksgiving in Notre Dame cathedral, for the victory at Sebastopol. The *Te Deum* will be sung, and it will all be very splendid. As it will be your last full day here, though I know you are not Catholics, I thought you might like to attend.' He turned to Madeleine. 'It would be most appropriate for you, with your brother in mind.'

'We should be delighted to be there!' Sophia said eagerly.

'Are you a Catholic, then?' Mr Parkinson asked Léon Bonneau.

'But of course.'

A slight frown crossed Albert Parkinson's face. 'I hadn't realized,' he said.

Back at the hotel, standing in the foyer, Mr Parkinson said, 'It's too late now for anything but bed. Go up to your room, the pair of you, and I'll talk to you in the morning after breakfast. But don't think I've forgotten that disgraceful scene, because I haven't!'

'If you please, sir,' Madeleine said. 'I'd like a word with you now!'

'I've just told you, girl, it's too late,' Mr Parkinson said. 'Surely it can wait until morning?'

'I'd rather not, sir, if you don't mind. I'd like to speak to you alone.' It took all her courage to persist.

He looked at her keenly. He could guess what it was, of course. She thought she was going to be sacked and unless she could put her side of it she was going to worry all night. Well, he'd no intention of sacking her. She'd done wrong, he didn't doubt that, and she couldn't be allowed to get away with it, but he was equally sure that Sophia had provoked her. Still, he could put her out of her misery about the sacking.

'Very well,' he agreed. 'Sophia, take the key and go on up. Madeleine won't be more than five minutes.'

'Well?' he said, when Sophia had gone.

'I want to give in my notice,' Madeleine said. She couldn't help it that her voice trembled. She was determined enough inside. 'A month's notice, sir – though I know you would only have to give me a week.'

So he was right. She was sure she was going to be sacked, but if the initiative came from her she might get three weeks extra work. It was a sorry system, but he wasn't responsible for it.

'There's no need for that, Madeleine,' he said. 'I'm not going to give you the sack. We'll talk about it all in the morning, that much I promise. So you can go to bed and go to sleep!'

At the kindness in his voice she almost broke down. But it wasn't the Master she was leaving, it was his hateful daughter, coupled with the whole life of being a servant. She was sick of it.

'That's very generous of you, sir! But I still want to give in my notice, if you please. I don't want to go on being a servant for the rest of my life.'

'But you won't,' Albert Parkinson said. 'Before you know where you are some young man will come along and marry you. Then you'll have your own home.'

'I don't think so, sir,' Madeleine said stubbornly.

He sighed. It really was very late. He was tired. He hadn't enjoyed the evening. And now this!

'Well I note what you say, Madeleine. We'll talk about it in the morning and perhaps you'll have changed your mind by then. We don't want to lose you. But run off to bed now.'

'Thank you, sir.'

She slept better than she had expected to, but when she wakened to the new day, though she had not changed her mind about leaving Mount Royd, she was filled with foreboding about her future. Certainly she felt in no mood for a service of thanksgiving, though she reminded herself, as they drove towards Notre Dame cathedral, that it was for Irvine, and for the war about to be ended, not for herself.

Mr Parkinson had seen the two girls separately after breakfast and had told them in no uncertain terms what he thought about them. Madeleine had repeated her notice.

'Well, I suppose I'll have to accept it,' her employer said, 'though I don't want to, and I think you're making a big mistake.' His wife wouldn't be pleased that they were to lose a good servant, one she'd trained over the years. She would blame him entirely.

Whatever the Master had said to his daughter, Madeleine thought, it had run like water off a duck's back! Sophia was her usual self: chattering, demanding, looking fresh and lovely in yet another new outfit.

Madeleine's first impression when they entered the cathedral was of the tremendous height – the walls seemed to stretch upwards forever – and then, in spite of all the windows, of the darkness. The only light was in the shafts which came through the stained glass, beaming their way on to the pillars, the pews, the floor, catching the milling, dancing particles of dust, illuminating and colouring them.

'Come with me,' Léon said quietly. 'I will find seats.'

That he did so, and ones from which they could see the high altar, seemed nothing short of miraculous to Madeleine. She had never seen a place so crowded. All Paris must be here, yet still people were streaming in.

'You will not understand the service since it will be in Latin,' Léon said. 'But never mind!'

Madeleine quickly found that she had no need to understand the words. They were superfluous. The sights – the magnificence of the priests in their embroidered robes, the acolytes with their lighted candles – the sounds, the singing of the choir, pure voices which rose until they were finally lost in the great height of the roof, and the chanting of the priests, all combined to amaze and delight her. But most of all the smell, the wonderful, heady scent of the incense, spicy and aromatic, rising in a fog from the swinging censers, swirling around the congregation and finally ascending to the roof to join the voices, to a point where it seemed as if earth and heaven might meet, were more than enough, infinitely satisfying.

Léon Bonneau, glancing sideways, caught his breath at the sight of her enraptured face and wished he could enter into the experience which at this moment was hers. But he looked away, feeling himself an intruder.

Madeleine was unaware of his gaze. She was caught up entirely in something beyond herself. Time seemed suspended. Nothing mattered except what was happening here and now. There was no need to think beyond the moment because everything would be for the best, now and for ever. Irvine would be safe. She herself would be all right.

She was brought back sharply to reality by Sophia's fit of coughing.

'It's the incense!' Sophia gasped. 'I just can't stand it!'

When they emerged from the darkness of the cathedral into the bright sunlight, she found herself standing beside Monsieur Bonneau.

'Well, Madeleine?' he said quietly.

She could hardly speak.

154

'I can never thank you enough,' she said quietly. 'I can't explain!'

He put his hand on her shoulder.

'Do not try. I understand.'

She turned and looked directly at him. She was totally unaware of anyone else, of the fact that Sophia was impatiently twirling her parasol and Mr Parkinson was looking at his watch. All she knew was how it had been in the cathedral, and now the look in Monsieur Bonneau's dark eyes as they met hers.

'Do you?' she said. 'Yes I believe you do. Perhaps better than I do myself.'

Long after they had left the cathedral, after they had left France and were once more within sight of the cliffs of England, the memory of the service, and of those few moments afterwards when she had spoken with Léon Bonneau, stayed with Madeleine. She felt a different person. Though her personal circumstances were every bit as bad, she felt hope, new confidence.

It was this confidence which enabled her, when they were on the steamer, to make a request of Mr Parkinson. In the intervening hours she had spent most of the time thinking about her situation, and had come to a decision.

'What I would like to do is to learn to weave,' she told him. 'Is it at all possible, sir, that you might give me a job in your mill?'

'In the mill?' He couldn't hide his astonishment. 'Nay, lass, you'd surely not want to go into the mill? Whatever would your Ma and Pa say to that?'

'They'd say I was better off in service,' she admitted.

'Aye, and they'd be right!'

'I don't want to be in service,' she said stubbornly. 'If you'd give me a job in the mill I'd work hard, serve you well.'

'Though you'll no longer do so in my house?'

'Not just your house, sir. Any house! I want to be independent.'

155

'And what makes you think you'd be independent in the mill?'

She had no answer to that, none she could give him. She couldn't tell him she wanted to be free of being at the beck and call of his wife and daughter, even of Mrs Thomas, all day long.

'I'll have to think about it,' he said.

NINE

Immediately after breakfast, on the morning after they had arrived back in Helsdon, Madeleine was summoned by Mrs Parkinson. She had realized as she served breakfast that her mistress was not in the best of moods, and now she sat in her high-backed armchair in the morning-room, her ankle propped on a footstool, her face as black as Egypt's night. Madeleine stood before her, mute, arms held straight by her sides, eyes lowered, fixed on the toecaps of her boots.

'Is what Mr Parkinson tells me true? Can it be true – that you have given in your notice?'

'Yes, ma'am. If you please,' Madeleine replied.

'Well I don't please. I'm severely displeased. What can you be thinking of? It's a most inconvenient time for me. All the entertaining of the autumn and winter to come, and now the possibility of Monsieur Bonneau paying us a long visit. Mr Parkinson should never have taken you to Paris. It was a foolish gesture and it has obviously unsettled you!'

Yes, Madeleine thought, it was Paris which unsettled me. There had been something in the air, a feeling of freedom, a hint that the world was a wider place than Helsdon dreamed of. But Paris had been only the final spur. She'd not been settled for a long time now. Apart from those few occasions when she'd stolen a little time to walk over the moors, to be totally free of everyone, she wondered when she'd last been truly happy. Yet she was sure she could be, it was there inside her, if only everyone would stop trying to rule her life.

'You have chosen a very strange way to repay our generosity,' Mrs Parkinson rattled on, her voice getting higher and shriller with every word. 'I hadn't thought you would do such a thing.'

'I'm sorry for the inconvenience, ma'am!' Madeleine said. 'I do know if you want her to, my sister Emerald will take my place.'

'That's no solution!' Mrs Parkinson snapped. 'I had already thought of taking your sister on in addition to you. She's willing enough, but of course she's quite untrained. Think of the years I have spent, training you!'

For what? Madeleine wanted to ask. So that I could be a better slave to your family, to your insufferable daughter? You didn't train me for *my* benefit! She couldn't say it out loud, but she raised her head, gave Mrs Parkinson a defiant look – then looked away again. She must go carefully. She desperately needed Mr Parkinson to give her a job in the mill, and what if Mrs Parkinson set him against her? Also she mustn't jeopardize Emerald's position. Her sister, she had already found out, was anxious to stay here.

She stood there, outwardly submissive, while Mrs Parkinson carried on.

'Well, you had better take a couple of hours off. Go and tell your mother of this foolish, headstrong decision of yours. I'm quite sure she won't approve, and perhaps she'll make you see reason. I'll give you until this evening to come to your senses. Tell Mrs Thomas she can let you go home for a short time when it suits her best.'

Mrs Thomas was not amused. 'You must be mad, giving up a place like this to go and work in the mill – always supposing you get a job,' she said. 'I always knew it was a mistake to go to Paris. It's given you ideas above your station!'

'Most people will reckon working in the mill is *below* my station,' Madeleine retorted. 'Anyway, I shall like it. I was very interested in the exhibition, and more in the textiles than anything else there.'

'Exhibitions!' Mrs Thomas snorted. 'What have exhibitions got to do with real life? You won't find working in the mill 'owt like a Paris exhibition. It'll be hot and noisy. Smelly, I shouldn't wonder. You'll work from morning 'til night, and for no more than you get here. You'll mix with a lower class of person instead of with your betters. And you'll never be as well fed as you are now. You'll miss *that*, my girl! I know how you like your belly!'

That bit at least was true, Madeleine thought. One good thing about Mount Royd was the food. Even a week of it had made a difference to Emerald's appearance.

'Well I suppose if the Mistress says so, you'd best get off home,' Mrs Thomas said. 'Think on you come back and tell me you've changed your mind. You do that, then nothing more need be said. I'm not one to bear grudges, as even my worst enemy would admit.'

It was a pleasant autumn day as Madeleine set off for home, the sun shining brightly, but a nip in the air and the trees already beginning to change from green to red and gold. She walked with her usual long, easy stride, glad to be out in the open air, pleased at the thought of seeing her mother, though nothing dulled her anxiety. The plain fact was that she had thrown up her job without having another to go to, and in Helsdon, with things as they were, that was about the most serious thing anyone could do. Her mother might understand the reason, though she couldn't be expected to condone the action.

But it was the thought of her father which worried her most, which had gnawed at her since the moment she had given in her notice to Mr Parkinson. He had made it plain that she was no longer a welcome visitor at home, so could she expect him to let her live there again? And if he wouldn't have her, where could she go?

'But I won't change my mind!'

She said the words out loud as she turned into Priestley Street, and a woman who was hanging out washing across the street stopped and stared at her.

'Nay, Madeleine love, they take folks away when they start talking to theirselves!'

Madeleine smiled at the woman.

'Nice drying day, Mrs Gregg! Bit of wind!'

She desperately hoped that soon she would be coming home every day to Priestley Street. In spite of its grim poverty, she liked it there, liked the friendliness of the people. There was no one toffee-nosed in Priestley Street, they'd nothing to be toffee-nosed about.

Martha Bates's face lit up as Madeleine walked into the house.

'I'd been hoping Mrs Thomas might give you an hour off to come and see me,' she said. 'Well, how have you been, love. What was it like? But first off, did they know about the fall of Sebastopol in Paris?'

'Know about it, Ma! I should just think they did! Why, everybody was celebrating, in the streets and everywhere – I even went to a thanksgiving service in the Catholic cathedral!'

Mrs Bates's eyes widened in horror.

'The *Catholic* cathedral? Oh Madeleine, you must never tell your father that!'

'He's the last person I'd tell. But isn't the news wonderful, Ma? And I'm sure Irvine's going to be all right. We'll hear from him any day soon, I feel certain.'

'Oh I do hope so!' Mrs Bates's voice was husky with longing. 'It would be the answer to my prayers.'

For a moment she was unable to continue. Then she said:

'But tell me your news, love. Were you seasick on the steamer? Did you feel smart in your green dress? What was the exhibition like? Do they have the same weather as us, in Paris, or is it hotter?'

'Whoa, Ma!' Madeleine held up her hands in protest. 'One question at a time, *if* you please!'

'Well you can't expect me not to be eager,' Mrs Bates said. 'I don't know anyone who's been to Paris – and when I think that it's happened to *my* daughter . . . Well!'

For several minutes Madeleine answered her mother's questions, but all the time it was the real reason for her visit home that was uppermost in her mind. In the end she could wait no longer.

'Ma, there's something I've got to tell you. Nothing to do with Paris. Oh, you're not going to like it, but please try to understand.'

Mrs Bates listened in shocked silence to Madeleine's news, shaking her head in disbelief.

'But love, that's terrible! What were you thinking of? Whatever made you do such a thing, throw up a good job in service to work in the mill?'

'I was so angry,' Madeleine confessed. 'I was beside myself with anger.'

'Oh, that's all fine and dandy! But people like us can't afford to get angry – or at least we can't afford to show it. You know that, Madeleine.'

'Yes I do,' Madeleine said. 'And that makes me angrier still. But I *did* get angry, and I *did* give in my notice – though that not before I'd cooled down a bit. If it hadn't happened then, it would have happened sooner or later. Oh Ma, I've been so unhappy! I'm just not cut out to be a servant!'

'Well, we can't spend time mooning about what we're cut out to be!' her mother said sharply. 'We have to take what we can get and be thankful. You're no different from the rest of us, my girl! Surely working for the Parkinsons is a mile better than working in the mill? Emerald seems very happy. Why can't you just go straight back and tell them you've come to your senses?'

'I came to my senses when I gave in my notice,' Madeleine snapped. 'And I'm not Emerald, I'm me. And I don't want to stay at Mount Royd a minute longer than I have to. Don't worry, Ma. I'll get a job in the mill. If not Parkinson's, then some other.'

'If you're lucky! People like us don't often strike lucky. As for tempting Providence the way you have . . .'

'You won't turn me away, will you Ma?' Madeleine pleaded. 'You will let me live here?' Suddenly she wasn't sure even of her mother.

Mrs Bates was worried sick, no use pretending otherwise; but Madeleine *was* her daughter.

'I won't turn you away,' she said, more gently. 'It's your home and you've a right to be here – and I shall like having you. But I can't speak for your father. I can't speak for him at all. Not unless . . .'

'Don't suggest I go back to chapel!' Madeleine said quickly. 'I won't do that. Only once a fortnight. And definitely not to class.'

Mrs Bates sighed deeply. 'It would make things so much easier. But if you're determined . . .'

'I am, Ma! I won't do it! Oh Ma, you stuck by me when I decided that. Please say you'll still do so!'

'Well I will, love. But you'd best leave your Dad to me. It'll not make it easier, you telling him. And happen you ought to be off now.'

All evening Martha Bates tried to broach the subject with her husband, and couldn't. She didn't know how to begin. In the end she waited until they were both in bed, and the candle snuffed, hoping it would come easier in the dark, when she couldn't see the look on his face. He might even, if God were good, be too tired to argue, and therefore give in more quickly.

The first few words were hardly out of her mouth before he shouted at her.

'*What* did you say, woman? Did I hear you right?'

She steeled herself to keep calm.

'I expect you did. I said, Our Madeleine has given her notice to leave Mount Royd. She's asked Mr Parkinson for a job in the mill!'

He sat bolt upright in bed and relit the candle.

'Then I hope you told her to stop all that nonsense, to

get straight off to Mount Royd and take back her notice?' he barked.

'I did. She refused.'

'Refused? What do you mean?'

'She said she wouldn't do it. What else could I mean?' Your daughter gets her stubborn streak from you, she wanted to say. There was no denying it.

'And supposing the Master doesn't give her a job,' he challenged. 'Jobs don't grow on trees in Helsdon, and she's blotted her copy-book with him.'

'Madeleine seems to think he will.' She hoped she sounded more convinced than she felt.

'The Master's said nothing to me.'

'Happen he's waiting to see if she'll change her mind,' Mrs Bates suggested.

'She'd better!' he threatened.

'Promise me one thing, Joseph,' she pleaded. 'Promise me whichever way it goes, you'll let her live here; in her own home with her own family.'

She couldn't bear to think of the alternative. She herself would take in her daughter, job or no job; would share the last crust, or go hungry herself, to feed her, and this she would do, in spite of what she saw as her daughter's terrible folly, just because she *was* her daughter. But if her father wouldn't have her, the alternative was simple. If she had no position and no money, then it was the workhouse. Surely even Joseph Bates wouldn't condemn their daughter to that? But she couldn't be certain.

'Please Joseph!' she begged. 'Please Joseph, promise me!'

There had been a time when she'd known how to plead with him, how to cajole, how to reach what little softness was at the centre of him; but that time was long past. Now, though from necessity they shared a bed, they lived as brother and sister. He no longer touched her, or kissed her; and endearments, which had never been plentiful, were a thing of the past. If at this moment she could have tempted him with her body into being lenient with their daughter, she would have done so. But it was no longer possible.

'I can't promise,' he said roughly.

'I'll manage,' she said quickly. 'I'll make do. Even if she doesn't get a job, I'll see *you* don't go short, Joseph!'

'There are other things to be considered,' he said.

'What else is there?' She was genuinely puzzled.

'Must I remind you that Madeleine has turned aside from God?' he said. 'Is it right that we should shelter the ungodly, even in the person of our own daughter? The Lord thy God is a jealous God – and is not our daughter's soul more important than her body? How can we save her soul by condoning her wrongdoing? I don't speak of her giving up her job, important though that is. I speak of her rejection of God Almighty!'

She stared at him in horror. Was he mad? She wanted to hit him, to beat him with her fists into some show of humanity. But there was no humanity in him. There was no love. Duty, discipline, obedience – obedience to whatever god *he* chose – were what counted with him. Love must be rooted out, lest it be seen as a weakness.

'Joseph Bates I would like to kill you!' she cried. 'You have robbed me of my son, and now, to placate some vengeful god I don't even recognize as the one I know, you'll rob me of my daughter! For believe you me, if Madeleine is sent away, she'll never return!'

The words welled up from the very depths of her bitterness. He was staring at her, his face suffused with anger.

'Be quiet, woman! Hold your tongue and get to sleep!'

'I shall not be quiet – and I'll not go to sleep. Why are you always right? Do you think God speaks only to you, that you're the chosen one?'

For a second, she saw indecision come into his face, and then go again in the same instant.

'God speaks to those who listen,' he said arrogantly. 'He who hath ears to hear, let him hear!'

164

'Well God speaks very differently to me, I can tell you that! I would like to leave you, Joseph Bates. I would like to leave your bed this very minute and never return. I would have liked to have done it when Irvine left. But you have me trapped, don't you? I'm powerless – because in the next room there's Penelope – and I have nowhere to go and no money. But you can't stop me hating you. That I can do every day 'til the end of your life!'

'You're beside yourself!' he said roughly. 'You must have a fever on you.'

'Oh no!' Martha Bates said. 'I never saw things clearer. So let me tell you this, Joseph: if you turn Madeleine out of her rightful home, I shall stand up in chapel and I shall denounce you! That much power I do have. And I'm no longer afraid of you. I despise you. Unless you give Madeleine a home, whether she has work or not, I shall inform your chapel friends, in public, what a despicable man you are. And what will they think of a man who turns his own daughter away because she won't go to chapel?'

'You're talking wildly,' he said. 'What's come over you?'

'Courage!' she said. 'That's what's come over me! And I'll soon show you whether I'm talking wildly or not!'

She leapt out of bed.

'I'm going downstairs for the rest of the night. I don't want to be in the same room as you!'

Only one night of her life had been as bad as this, she thought as she stirred the dying embers of the fire, trying to coax a little warmth from it. That was the night her son had left home, driven out by his father. Well he wouldn't drive Madeleine away, not without a fight.

In the morning she made her husband's breakfast, packed his jock tin and handed it to him, as usual, as he was leaving.

'Remember what I said,' she warned him.

Joseph Bates paused on the doorstep.

'Pray to the Lord, who has power to change all hearts,' he said, 'and through whom our daughter might even now see the light.'

And how about you seeing the light, Martha Bates thought, watching her husband walk away down the street. As for praying – well if worrying herself witless all day was prayer, she'd certainly be doing that.

As Joseph Bates walked to work he thought of nothing except the matter between them. For a man so sure of the Lord's way, so certain of what was right for himself, for his family, indeed for all mankind, since it was quite plain in the Scriptures, it was torment to realize that he did not know what to do. Madeleine was his daughter, and when she had been smaller and more biddable, she had been especially dear to him. He acknowledged his responsibility towards her. But she had turned aside from God, and it was God to whom he must answer.

'Show me the way, Lord! Show me the way!' In his agony, he cried the words aloud as he walked.

As he neared the mill he tried to calm himself, and as always, on the threshold of the weaving shed, he paused and made his regular silent prayer:

'Lord, save my workmates. Preserve them from swearing, from lying, and from every evil practice. Amen.'

Halfway through the morning, Albert Parkinson sent for him.

'This is a sorry business, Bates,' he said. 'You know your Madeleine wants to leave our service. My wife is very put out, but it seems nothing will make Madeleine change her mind. Have you spoken with her?'

'No sir, but my wife has,' Joseph Bates said. 'She's of the same opinion, that Madeleine is determined. I'm very sorry, sir.'

'So am I, Bates. I have a certain regard for Madeleine. She's served us faithfully. But I have a daughter of my own and I know how headstrong they can be. So it looks like that's that!'

'Yes sir!'

'You know she's asked to be set on in the weaving?' Albert Parkinson continued. 'If she won't stay at the house, then I've nothing against her going into the weaving, if you think that's suitable.'

'It's very good of you, sir, in the circumstances. I don't know whether she'll be suitable or not. She'd have to learn everything from the beginning – and no favours given.'

'Well I'm sure I can rely on you for that,' Albert Parkinson said dryly. He was a cold fish, Joseph Bates, no mistake about that. 'She'll have to work out her notice, of course. And Emerald can stay with us. My wife tells me she's coming on well.'

'Very well, sir! Thank you, sir.'

Joseph Bates turned to go. He was confused as to whether he had done the right thing, but he seemed to have had no choice in that. His greater problem remained: should Madeleine be allowed to live in the house in Priestley Street, influencing his youngest child, leading her astray? Penelope was easy to lead astray, and his wife seemed to be possessed by the devil. He could think of no other reason for her behaviour. If she stood up in chapel and denounced him, that much would be clear to everyone.

Not without sorrow, he foresaw that soon his whole family might be against him. How could it happen so? Hadn't he always been a good man, a good husband and father? Hadn't he always lived by the Good Book, loved God? But the Lord chasteneth whom He loveth, he reminded himself. Now he must pray more diligently than ever for guidance.

His wife was looking out of the window when he came back from work. She'd been worried sick, gnawed with anxiety all day.

'Madeleine has not changed her mind,' her husband informed her. 'The Master has said she may have a job in the weaving. I've agreed to that. It seemed that there I had no choice.'

167

Martha Bates breathed a sigh of relief. One fence climbed!

'And she may come home?'

'It's Penelope I worry about,' he said. 'She'll come too much under Madeleine's influence. I don't want that. I don't want this family disrupted, led into bad ways, any further. First your son, and now your eldest daughter.'

He speaks as though they weren't his, Martha thought. They are only his children when they go his way.

'Then what will she do if you won't have her here?' she asked levelly. 'What can she possibly do?'

'I don't know. Perhaps she could find lodgings.'

'In Helsdon? While she has a home here? What would everyone think to that? Who ever heard of anyone in Helsdon going into lodgings when they had a family? And she's little more than a child, though she thinks she's grown up. Oh Joseph, I beg of you to let her stay! Give her a chance, and I'll see to it myself that she doesn't influence Penelope in any wrong way. I'll make her promise. Please, Joseph!'

'Serve my tea,' he said.

'But if you don't,' she added, 'remember what I said. I meant every word of it.'

'I cannot allow threats to influence me,' he said. 'Threats are of the devil. I shall be guided by God.'

When he had finished his tea he pushed back his chair and said: 'I'm going upstairs.'

He was going to pray; she knew that. Oh God, she thought, I don't know how to pray as well as he does, but listen to me also.

It was the better part of an hour before he came down the stairs again. His wife looked at him, searching his face for a sign.

'You can tell her she may live here,' he said.

Madeleine thought the remaining time of her month's notice would never pass. The days dragged by; it was clear that Emerald had now taken her place and Madeleine was of little account. Though the sisters got on well together, Madeleine knew that Emerald longed for the moment when she would have the little bedroom, which for the last four weeks they had been obliged to share, to herself.

'Well that's it!' Madeleine said. 'I don't think I've left anything behind, and if I have you can bring it over on your first day off. So the best of luck, love. Don't let them work you too hard — especially Miss Sophia, who's a slave-driver if ever I saw one.'

'I don't think you're fair to Miss Sophia,' Emerald protested. 'I get on very well with her. She gave me a scarf yesterday.'

'Then watch out for what she wants in return!' Madeleine advised. 'Anyway, ta-ta love! I'm glad you like it here.'

'Much better than the mill,' Emerald said. 'I think you're crazy.'

On the Monday morning Madeleine wondered if her sister hadn't been right. At five o'clock her mother shook her by the shoulder and stood over her while she got out of bed.

'Ooh, I'm so tired!' Madeleine yawned.

She put on her new mill skirt, one of two which her mother had made her from strong brown cotton.

'You need two in case one get's torn from catching in the machinery,' her mother had explained. 'Be careful it's no more than your skirt gets caught!'

Over her skirt she fastened a holland apron, and round her head she tied a scarf.

'You'll have to hurry,' her mother urged. 'Your father leaves at twenty to six sharp. He'll not want to wait for you longer. And you're not going out without a cup of hot tea inside you.'

She was to walk to work with her father this morning, but only the once, because it was the first day. Her mother had explained that her father liked to walk alone to his work because that was his time for meditation. He was welcome to it, Madeleine thought. She'd just as soon be on her own, or perhaps she'd make friends with some of the other mill-girls from Priestley Street. All the same, she was determined to be as pleasant and cooperative as possible where her father was concerned. She knew nothing of the scene which had passed between her parents.

'Here, don't forget your breakfast and dinner sandwiches; and there's a mashing of tea. I've mixed the sugar in with it – you'll be provided with boiling water – but you'll have to learn to drink it without milk.' She touched Madeleine lightly on the shoulder. 'Well, good luck, love!'

It was a pitch black October morning when they left the house. When she had to make the journey on her own, Madeleine thought, she would carry a lamp, but her father seemed to have no need of one. It was so quiet, too; the only sound the rhythmic clang of her father's steel-tipped boots on the stone setts. But as they drew nearer to the mill other people appeared, dark shadows emerging from doorways and side streets. By the time they were almost there the street was thronged, and noisy now, with the chatter of voices added to the clatter of boots.

Then suddenly there came an ear-splitting sound, a long, shrill wail like an animal in torment. Though Madeleine knew what it was – she had heard the mill hooter every day at Mount Royd, telling the people that they must soon be at their machines – its close proximity took her by surprise. She jumped almost out of her skin, and clutched at her father. He made no response and she let go his arm immediately.

In the weaving shed he called across to a woman standing by a loom, and she came over.

'This is my daughter. She's starting work today. See to her, will you?'

'Right you are, Mr Bates. Come on then, love.'

As they moved away he called after them.

'And no favours because she's my daughter, think on!'

* * *

'Before we go any further, tie that scarf tighter round your head, tuck all your hair inside,' Mrs Barnet said firmly. 'Never mind about looking pretty. You'll look a sight worse if you get scalped – and it has been known.'

There was so much to learn. She quickly discovered that although her father had been a weaver all his life, and although the idea appealed to her and she'd been so interested in the weaving at the Paris Exhibition, really she knew next to nothing.

'Now come and stand by me and I'll show you what's what. No, not there love. A bit closer to me.' She indicated the narrow space between two looms. 'If a shuttle flies off we don't want you to be dead in line. We mustn't have an accident on your first morning, must we? Now first off, do you know the difference between warp and weft?'

'Oh, yes,' Madeleine said confidently. 'The warp thread runs the length and the weft goes across the cloth.'

Mrs Barnet nodded approvingly.

'That's right! We usually call the weft the "pick". And it's the shuttle throws the pick thread side to side through the warp. Well at least you know something!'

It took Madeleine no more than five minutes to realize that that was about all she did know of weaving. Expressions like "setting the frame", "beam", "warping fault", "picking straps", "loom-tuning", and a dozen others gushed from Mrs Barnet's lips in a fast-flowing stream. Aside from the fact that it's a whole new language, how shall I ever learn it in all this noise? Madeleine asked herself. With the exception of the one Mrs Barnet was demonstrating, every loom in the weaving shed was thumping and clacking away like nobody's business.

'How many looms are there in the shed?' she shouted.

Mrs Barnet smiled.

'I can tell you're yelling by the look on your face. But there's no need, love. You can speak as quiet as you like because I lip-read. All the weavers lip-read, and you'll soon learn. There's seventy looms here. It's a bit noisy until you get used to it. I won't set this one until after breakfast, but I shall have to then because there's work to get through.'

From six o'clock starting time to eight o'clock breakfast time, when the machines were turned off for half an hour, seemed an eternity to Madeleine. Just before eight o'clock a boy came down the shed, pushing a trolley.

'Have you brought your tea mashing and your pot?' Mrs Barnet asked Madeleine. 'Give it to him and he'll put the water on. We have a half-hour for breakfast and you can sit over there on one of those buffets if you want. Mr Parkinson's very considerate, providing the buffets.'

Madeleine was unbelievably glad of the break, but she nevertheless took only ten minutes to drink her tea and eat her sandwiches before going back to the loom. She absolutely must learn something while there was a bit of peace.

'Eh, you!' a girl called out. 'What do you think you're doing? We don't work in us breakfast time!'

'Leave her be, Alice!' Mrs Barnet called out. 'She's new. She has a lot to learn, and she can't hear everything when t'looms is going.'

She walked across and joined Madeleine.

'The sooner you learn, the better for your own sake,' she said. 'As long as I'm teaching you, you'll have to pay me out of your wages for the time I spend wi' you. I'm on piece work, you see – we all are – and I'd lose money, else. And you won't be earning much, will you, until you turn out some work?'

'I didn't realize,' Madeleine said.

Mrs Barnet gave her a sharp look.

'Didn't your father tell you, then?'

'No!' He hadn't told her a thing, not a thing. It was as if he wanted nothing to do with her. She wasn't welcome in his home and he didn't want her in his weaving shed. She was only on sufferance in either place.

'I see!' Only Mrs Barnet didn't see. Oh, she knew he wanted no favours for his daughter, which was right and proper, but you'd have thought he'd have said a few words to the lass in the privacy of the home, put her in the way. But he was a law unto himself, Joseph Bates was; no two ways about it. A good overlooker, a good loom-tuner – none better – but a strange man; serious, no jollity. She liked a man who could crack a joke as well as crack the whip.

'Well, I'll learn as quickly as I can,' Madeleine promised. 'Can I just ask you one or two things before the machines start up again?'

''Course you can, love. Ask away! And if you like I'll sit wi' you at dinnertime an' tell you a bit more. Owt I can do to help. The sooner you learn, the better for me as well as for you.'

She was a good weaver, Harriet Barnet, one of the best, with two looms to mind – which was why Joseph Bates had put his lass to her; but being a good weaver was one thing and teaching it was another, and she didn't fancy herself as a teacher.

'How long will it take me to learn?' Madeleine asked.

'To weave – just to do it – not long, love. But to be a good weaver, and only then if you apply yourself, it'll be a year. And after that you'll still go on learning.'

So all that day and for several days afterwards Madeleine stood by Harriet Barnet's loom, trying to catch the words she said, learning very quickly to lip-read the essential words, asking questions, hearing from her teacher the long catalogue of things which could go wrong. It seemed that weaving was beset with those.

'Mostly it's the pick thread that breaks,' Mrs Barnet said, 'and that's a nuisance, but not too serious. But if a warp thread goes wrong, or gets missed or summat, and it has to be stitched in, it could mean seventy yards, a whole piece, two or three days' work. So mind you allus keep both eyes on your work, love.'

'Oh I will, Mrs Barnet,' Madeleine assured her. 'I'd be scared stiff to look away!'

Towards the end of the third day Mrs Barnet let Madeleine have a go by herself on one of the looms.

'I'm nearing the end o' the piece,' Mrs Barnet said. 'It's not likely owt'll go wrong. But watch out!'

Madeleine felt herself charged with an awesome responsibility. What if she ruined the whole piece, all seventy yards of it? What if a thread broke? What if the picking stick or the shuttle flew off and hit her, or worse still, hit Mrs Barnet. But in the end, nothing went wrong.

'It's a bit o' reight!' Mrs Barnet said, smiling. 'That's what we say when we reach the end of a piece and it's gone well.'

'A bit o' reight!' Madeleine repeated. She felt elated; full of achievement. 'Thank you very much, Mrs Barnet. You've taught me such a lot.'

'Well, you've been a good pupil,' Mrs Barnet answered.

At the end of each day, though she was enjoying her job, Madeleine was unbelievably tired. She was glad, like all the other girls, to escape when the final hooter went and the machines stopped. They flew out of the building then as if the place was on fire. If you'd been coming the other way you'd have been mown down and trampled underfoot!

She never once walked home with her father, and after the first day she didn't accompany him in the mornings. At the end of the day it was his duty to stay behind until everyone was out of the weaving, and then inspect to see that everything was safe. Throughout the mill there was always the risk of fire from the grease in the wool. You had to be viligant, and he was.

Madeleine was relieved not to have to walk with him, for these days they had nothing to say to each other. Or, rather, he had no word for her. She longed to be closer to him, for them to be true father and daughter as they had been until a few months ago. She would have liked to have talked to him about the weaving, but he gave her no encouragement. She hated the distance between them but there seemed nothing she could do about it.

At the end of the first week Emerald came home to go to Sunday service. It seemed strange to Madeleine to hear the news of Mount Royd from someone else's lips, though she felt no envy of her sister. Mount Royd already seemed another life and she had no wish to return to it.

'What do you think?' Emerald asked, all excitement. 'That Frenchman is coming to stay! Monsieur Bonneau. In November. Miss Sophia is all of a doodah, I can tell you! The way she talks, *I* think they've got an understanding. Do you think they have an understanding, Madeleine?'

'I'm sure I couldn't say,' Madeleine replied. 'He was taken with her, that's for certain. But Miss Sophia exaggerates, as I'd have thought you'd have found out by now.'

'I can't wait to see him,' Emerald gushed. 'Is he as handsome as Miss Sophia says he is?'

Madeleine considered her answer, conjuring up the sight of him in her mind; remembering his black hair, his dark, twinkling eyes, the curve of his mouth under his moustache, his indefinable, exotic foreign air. She remembered, too, the way he had escorted her back to the hotel when she'd fainted; the fact that he'd sent her an orchid, now pressed in her bible. He had treated her like a lady. But most of all she remembered the few words they had exchanged outside Notre Dame. She had felt for that brief period that he had understood her as no one else ever had.

'Is he handsome?' Emerald repeated.

'Yes,' Madeleine replied. 'He's very handsome. Kind, too.'

She doubted she'd ever speak to him again. He'd come into the mill, of course. She'd see him, but there was no reason why he would speak with her.

It was the week she had chosen to attend chapel and she walked along Priestley Street between Emerald and George Carter. It was strange how she'd lived in the same house as George for the last week and really hardly noticed him. She left the house before he was up in the morning, and since the shops in Helsdon kept open until eight o'clock, she didn't see much of him in the evening. When he was in he was very quiet and, she thought, rather dull.

George Carter had noticed Madeleine. He had been strongly and acutely aware of her, every moment of the short times they had spent together. The beauty of her face and hair, the grace of her figure, the whole strong aura of her femininity disturbed him more than he could ever have thought possible. He didn't understand it. But then he had never lived in the same house before, never spent a night under the same roof. Now when he lay in bed at night he was aware that she lay just a yard or two from him, separated only by a thin wall. Her presence seemed to fill every corner of his mind, every place he was in. He thought of her all the time: turbulent, tumultuous thoughts which he didn't know how to quell or what to do with.

TEN

Madeleine, sitting in chapel between Emerald and George Carter, gave up listening to the sermon, which seemed to have been going on for ever, and as far as she could without turning her head, looked around her. The chapel was small, and plainly furnished, built and maintained by the hard work and financial contributions of its members. The money which came in each week was for the most part sacrificial, offered by those who found it difficult to make ends meet, to eat well enough or to clothe themselves adequately. The Lord loveth a cheerful giver, they were frequently reminded, and they braced themselves and gave with a smile.

So it was wrong of her, Madeleine thought, to compare this austere place with its whitewashed walls devoid of pictures or any decoration, its windows of plain glass, its bare oak table instead of an elaborately draped altar, its officials dressed in plainest black, its congregation soberly suited, with the cathedral of Notre Dame and its fashionable congregation. It was quite unfair. What could you expect a little chapel in Helsdon to have in common with a famous cathedral?

Yet in her heart she couldn't help making the comparison. And though she knew she ought to prefer this simplicity to the opulence of Notre Dame, the plain fact was that she didn't. But it hadn't just been the opulence, the richness, the well-dressed congregation: there had been something else. She couldn't define it. It was in the atmosphere. She had breathed it in with the heady smell of incense. It had spoken to her, moved her to her depths. There was no one to whom she could speak of it, but it remained in her, hidden yet strong.

She suddenly realized by the upward tone of the preacher's voice that he was coming to the end of his sermon. She rose to her feet with the rest to sing the final hymn. Well, that was something they could do all right, this small, Yorkshire congregation; they could certainly sing.

'We must hurry home,' Mrs Bates said when it was over. 'There's the dinner to see to. Come along, girls!'

They gave quick greetings to the people they knew, and were on their way. The men, including George, lingered.

There was always business for the men to discuss. George didn't want to stay behind, he wanted to walk home with Madeleine. For the last hour-and-a-half he had sat beside her, her shoulder or arm sometimes touching his in the confined space, sending a sensation through him quite out of keeping with the solemnity of the place and the occasion. From time to time he had turned his head and glimpsed her profile from under her bonnet. She was so beautiful. Why had he never noticed before quite how beautiful she was?

Halfway along the road Emerald turned off to go to Mount Royd.

'If I'm late there'll be ructions,' she said. 'Mrs Thomas says I'm dead lucky to be let off once a fortnight for morning chapel instead of always for evening service, like you were, Madeleine. But if I don't get back to help with the dinner, then they'll stop it. So, ta-ta everybody!'

'She's chirpy enough,' Madeleine remarked.

'She's a changed girl,' Mrs Bates agreed.

Perhaps because she got away from Priestley Street, Madeleine thought. Well I prefer to be back here.

Once in the house Mrs Bates quickly set to. She removed the pot roast from the slow oven, then raked the embers under, built up the fire and pulled out the dampers. The oven had to be at its very hottest for the Yorkshire pudding. Thank goodness the wind was in the right direction!

By the time Joseph Bates and George Carter returned, the pudding was already in the oven, and twenty minutes later it was on the table, cut into crisp, high, golden squares, surrounded by rich, aromatic onion gravy. Madeleine was ravenously hungry. She prayed that her father wouldn't embark on one of his more lengthy graces, and her prayer was answered.

'For these and all his mercies. God's Holy Name be praised,' he intoned briefly.

Martha Bates always made plenty of Yorkshire. The more pudding you ate, the less meat you needed, and the joint of brisket was a very small one. Enough for a good helping for the men, of course, but not much for herself and the girls. And it had to do at least tomorrow, and perhaps Tuesday. We shouldn't be short like this, she thought, yet again; not with a man in work, and a lodger. But if the man gave too much to the chapel and the lodger paid so little, what could you do?

Madeleine watched her father carefully carving the joint.

'I don't want any meat, Father,' she said.

She was deeply conscious of the fact that she'd made no contribution to the household this week. What little she'd earned had gone straight to Harriet Barnet – and she still owed her. The least she could do was to eat less.

'Very well,' her father said.

'There's no need . . .' Mrs Bates began.

'I don't want any!' Madeleine said firmly.

She took the empty plate from her father and helped herself to potatoes and cabbage. She hated cabbage, but it filled the corners.

'I wondered,' George said, looking to Mr and Mrs

179

Bates, 'I wondered if I might take Madeleine for a walk this afternoon? That is if you agree!'

What about me? Madeleine thought furiously. What if I *don't* agree? She was about to speak up and say she didn't want to go, but then she thought again. She was still bone tired, she would like to go to bed – but to do so in the middle of the afternoon would certainly not be countenanced. If she went with George at least she'd be out of the house, away from the oppressive Sunday atmosphere.

'Would you like that, Madeleine?' Mrs Bates asked.

'Thank you, yes,' Madeleine said. 'Perhaps we could walk up to the moor?'

'Certainly!' George said. 'That would be splendid!'

'And we could take Penelope,' Madeleine added.

'I think you'd better not,' Mrs Bates said. 'It's a chilly day, and she looks a bit flushed to me.'

'I thought so myself,' George said quickly. 'We wouldn't want her to catch cold. But another time, certainly.'

As soon as the dishes were cleared, George and Madeleine set off. Fifteen minutes brisk uphill walk from Priestley Street, climbing all the way, brought them to the edge of the moor. The built-up area of Helsdon ended abruptly where the last street of back-to-back houses had been put up for the mill workers, and there also the road ended, giving way to a track which passed no more than a cottage or two and a farm before they felt the rough, tufty moorland under their feet.

'It's a sharp afternoon,' Madeleine said. 'A nip in the air!'

'Winter's on its way,' George replied.

Winter came early in these northern hills. The glory of the heather was over but its seed, fallen to the ground, provided food for a grouse which shuffled about, hiding from its enemy, the crow. Overhead curlews cried mournfully.

'They always sound as though they're searching for something,' Madeleine said. 'Seeking in vain, never

180

finding. Did you know that when the winter comes they'll move to the coast?'

'I didn't know,' George admitted. 'I don't know much about nature.'

'I wonder if they'll find what they're after there,' she queried. 'Or if they'll go on searching for ever?'

Much of the time the two of them walked in silence. Madeleine had little to say, and George, who had so much he wanted to say, couldn't find the words. Is it possible, is it just possible, he wondered, that we might come to an understanding? He knew she wasn't suitable as a wife, he had thought all this out months ago and she hadn't changed. She was wilful; she was not obedient, not pliant as a wife should be. There was the vexed and important question of her attitude towards the chapel. But above all this was the fact that she had become utterly irresistible to him. He wanted to touch her, to hold her in his arms; he wanted to do things which had not yet taken shape in his mind. Could it be that under his own good influence she might become a suitable wife? Moreover, could it also be that in her present circumstances she would be grateful for the chance? He wanted desperately to make her his own.

When they reached the summit of the moor, before the track led down into the next valley, Madeleine stopped.

'The sun's beginning to dip,' she said. 'I think we should turn back, don't you? We don't want to be on the moor in the dark.'

It was now or never, George thought. When would he have her to himself again?

'Madeleine!'

'Yes George?'

'There's something I want to ask you, Madeleine.'

'Well ask it, then.' She wasn't really listening. She was gazing ahead, looking down into the next valley. The air was so clear that, even at this time of day, you could see for miles.

'Madeleine, do you think we could . . . well . . . what I'm trying to say is . . . do you think we might have an understanding? I know I said it wasn't possible, I know you said you'd not have me – but things have changed. Why can't we walk out together, Madeleine?'

Astonished, she swivelled around and gave him her full attention.

'Walk out? Have an understanding, you and me? I thought you'd decided that I was quite unsuitable? You could never marry me, you said. Have you forgotten?'

'I was wrong, Madeleine! I admit I was wrong.'

'You meant it then all right!'

'I've changed, Madeleine. And I know you'll change. Once we're married I know you will. Marriage will improve us both. Oh it can't be for a long time yet, but . . .'

She couldn't believe her ears! The cheek of him!

'George,' she interrupted. 'I shall *not* change. Moreover, I don't want to change to fit in with some idea you, or anyone else, might have of what a wife should be like. If ever I marry, which seems unlikely, it will be to someone who loves me as I am, doesn't want to improve me. And I remember I told you I wouldn't marry you if you were hung about with gold – well, that still goes.'

'Then *I'll* change!' he said eagerly. 'Madeleine, I'll do anything!'

Suddenly he went down on one knee, clutched at her hand and covered it with kisses – but in the act of snatching her hand away, she upskittled him. He lost his balance and fell back on to the tufty ground. It was too much for her. At the sight of him on his back, his legs in the air, it was just too much! She burst into a gale of laughter and held out her hand to help him up.

He brushed her hand aside and struggled to his feet, his face dusky red with anger and shame.

'Oh, I'm sorry!' Madeleine said. 'I'm really sorry, George! I shouldn't have laughed, but you did look so funny!'

He couldn't speak. Rage such as he had never known burned in him, poisoned him. Rage and humiliation. How dare she! Without looking at her, without a backward glance, he set off down the hill towards Helsdon. Madeleine at once ran after him.

'George, don't be so silly!' she called out. 'Surely we can be friends?'

He ignored her. Finally she fell in a pace behind him, and in that fashion they reached Priestley Street and home.

Over the next week or two, things went on as before. Her mother and Penelope clearly enjoyed her company. They had many a good laugh between them, but only when her father wasn't present. When he was there he never spoke to her and the atmosphere for all of them was strained.

'I feel guilty that I'm spoiling things,' she said to her mother.

'Don't you dare say such a thing!' Mrs Bates said fiercely. 'If there's any guilt in this house it's not down to you! Ignore him!'

Madeleine stared at her mother in amazement. She had never, in all her life, heard her speak so of her father.

Since the Sunday of their walk George had ignored her, not speaking unless circumstances forced him to. It seemed as if he had dismissed her from his life. Well that's fine and dandy by me, Madeleine thought. She could never really take George seriously.

'I wish we could hear from Irvine,' Mrs Bates said. She spoke of her son only when her husband was out of the house. 'November already – I'd have thought we'd have had a letter.'

'I expect they're moving around a lot,' Madeleine said. 'Why, he might even be on his way home right now!'

Her words were more optimistic than her thoughts. The silence had been too long. She had begun to be afraid of what might have happened to him, but she would never let her mother see her fear.

'Perhaps you're right,' Mrs Bates said. 'Well, when Irvine does return, George Carter will have to go, no matter what your father says. This is my son's home and he shall have his room back.'

Madeleine thought it unlikely that her brother would ever want to live with his family again, or at least not with his father, but that was another thing best left unsaid.

'I'd be quite glad for George to go,' Mrs Bates said unexpectedly. 'He's not the person he was. Sometimes I find myself almost disliking him!'

At the mill, Madeleine was becoming adept at learning to weave, and was even beginning to bring home a little money for the family purse. She was quick, especially at spotting flaws, and worked hard and conscientiously.

'I'm reight pleased wi' t'way you've come on, love,' Harriet Barnet said. 'I'm sure your dad must be pleased wi' you?'

Well if he was he hadn't bothered to say so, Madeleine thought.

'Are you liking it here?' Mrs Barnet asked.

'Oh yes, thank you, Mrs Barnet. Sometimes I wish we could weave something a bit more colourful, something with a bit of pattern, instead of all this grey. But apart from that . . .'

'Aye well, we've got this big order for the grey,' Harriet pointed out. 'We make what sells, you see. And it's beautiful quality cloth, you can't deny that!'

'Oh no, I don't,' Madeleine assured her.

She wondered whether, when Monsieur Bonneau came, which must be very soon now, he might persuade Mr Parkinson to experiment with more designs? If so, they might come to Mrs Barnet, who was one of the best weavers; in which case she herself might be involved, for she would be under Mrs Barnet's wing for some time yet.

The work was going well enough in the mill, but she had made no real friends among the other girls. They were civil, but nothing more. She was never included in their conversation at breakfast- and dinner-times, they never shared with her their numerous jokes over which they shrieked with laughter, and though they frequently called out to each other as they worked at the looms, no one called to her.

'Why don't they like me?' she asked Mrs Barnet.

'Nay, it's not that they don't like you, love,' Mrs Barnet answered. 'It's down to the fact that your t'overlooker's daughter. However good he is – and they respect your Dad – t'overlooker is their natural enemy.'

'But he never comes near me, let alone shows me any favours,' Madeleine protested.

'Well, no he doesn't, not in t'weaving shed,' Mrs Barnet conceded. 'But I dare say they think you might talk to him at home.'

If only they knew, Madeleine thought! She felt that he was every bit as much her enemy as theirs; he had made himself so.

'Another thing is, lass,' Mrs Barnet continued, 'you don't join in the singing! As you've noticed, there's nowt these lasses like better nor a good sing-song as they work, and perhaps as you don't join in they think you're being a bit above yourself, a bit stuck up like.'

'But that's not true!' Madeleine objected. She loved to hear the girls sing. They sang comic ditties, sentimental ballads, patriotic songs, and several to which they fitted their own words – and since every day she improved her lip-reading, these she could now understand. 'It's not true! I just don't know the songs. We've only ever sung hymns at home. We're not allowed to sing songs!'

'Well, I never!' Mrs Barnet looked at Madeleine in shocked disbelief. Fancy not knowing any songs! 'Well, love, you could soon learn. And if your Pa's not going to object I'm sure the girls'll be pleased to see you join in!'

'He'll never even notice,' Madeleine said pertly.

So, from that moment, Madeleine joined in the singing and felt happier for it, though goodness knew what her father would think of some of the words the girls made up instead of the proper ones! Downright cheeky they were! And sometimes she'd catch the eye of another girl as they were singing at the looms, and they'd give a smile and a

185

wink. But still she longed for just one or two of the girls to talk to her.

There was a girl she felt particularly drawn to. Sally Pitt was younger than she was, and quite different to look at, being small, fair, and rather plain. One day at breakfast time Sally came over and sat by her.

'How are you getting on then? Do you like it here?' she asked.

'Yes I do. I think I'm getting on all right. There's a lot to learn, though.'

'You'll soon get used to it,' Sally said.

Madeleine nodded.

'I expect so.'

'You live in Priestley Street, don't you?' Sally asked. 'I live in Waterloo Street. It's in the same direction. We could walk home together if you like. I'd be glad of company now that it gets dark early.'

'Oh, so would I!' Madeleine said eagerly. Perhaps at last she had found a friend.

It was a week or two after this conversation, during which period she and Sally had walked home together until the younger girl turned off at Waterloo Street. They didn't always talk much – sometimes Sally was particularly silent – but they enjoyed each other's company.

And now Madeleine was at home, preparing to have a bath. Her mother and father and Penelope were leaving to attend a meeting at chapel. There was to be a lantern lecture, and a special missionary speaker, which was why Penelope was to be allowed to go. To his great disappointment, George was working very late on the shop's annual stocktaking, and would have to miss the occasion. Madeleine had refused to accompany her family and the air was heavy with her father's disapproval.

'There'll be refreshments afterwards,' Mrs Bates said. 'But we shan't be very late.'

'Don't hurry back,' Madeleine said.

She didn't mind how long they were away. It would be a chance to have a long leisurely bath, seldom possible with two men in and out of the house. When the door closed behind them she took the bath down from its hook in the scullery and, placing it on the hearthrug, proceeded to fill it with jugfuls of steaming hot water taken from the fireside boiler. She had mended the fire in good time, so that now the coals glowed red, giving off a fierce heat, and the heavy curtains were drawn against the November night. It was all quite cosy.

Madeleine lowered herself into the bath, and with a sigh of pure pleasure began to wash away the fatigues and the aches of the day. As she soaped her body, she sang the hymns which habitually accompanied her bath.

> 'Oh happy harbour of the Saints!
> Oh sweet and pleasant soil!
> In thee no sorrow may be found,
> No grief, no care, no toil.'

The words exactly described her feelings for this lovely bath she was having! Then she remembered a song the girls had been singing in the weaving shed that day, and she began to sing it. She remembered a second, and a third, and all the cheeky words which went with them. Oh, she had never enjoyed a bath so much in all her life! Her father would have had a fit if he could hear her – but he couldn't, could he?

As she stepped out of the bath and began to dry herself, she sang the songs over again. She sang them with abandon, at the top of her voice. She was still singing when she finished drying herself, draped the towel over the fireguard to dry, and looked around for her nightshift.

It was perhaps because of the noise she was making, perhaps because she didn't expect it, that she failed to hear the door latch. He was already in the room, staring at her, and she was facing him, mother-naked, not a stitch on her. For a moment she was so transfixed that she did not even have the power to turn around and grab the towel, but continued to stand there, naked, held fast in his gaze.

187

George had never seen a naked woman before, never believed that such beauty existed. In what seemed an eternity but was in reality, seconds, he observed and experienced every part of her, his eyes riveted first to her breasts, so round, so proud, the darkness of the nipples and the softer pink circles which surrounded them in such contrast to the whiteness of her skin. His eyes skimmed the slenderness of her waist and the curving mound of her belly before dropping to the triangle of dark hair below.

Everything he had felt, for days, weeks, months, surged inside him. The demands of his body and the invitation of hers were the only reality in the world.

'Madeleine!'

He shouted her name, then he was at once in front of her, grasping her roughly. She wanted to seize something to cover her awful nakedness – somewhere, on the fireguard, there was a towel. But she was paralysed by fright, rooted, unable to move. Her body refused to obey the commands she gave it. And then his hands were on her body, all over her body; hard, exploring, painful. It was when his hand dug and squeezed her breast and he lowered his head to bite her nipple that she came to life again, screaming with the pain of it.

'No! No! Let me go! Please let me go!'

She fought and writhed now, beat him with her fists – but her strength was nothing against that which possessed him. She clawed at his face, scratched until the blood showed in a thin red line down his cheek, and at that he flinched momentarily and she almost escaped. But he had her again at once, and now she was powerless against this terrible thing which was happening to her; impotent with fright as he pushed his face into hers and his mouth opened like a red cavern and fastened on her mouth.

There was nothing he couldn't do, George thought. He was all-powerful, the world was his; and the world was all contained in the softness and roundness and warmth of this body, which he would subdue and conquer with the pulsating hardness of his own. And what she didn't know

188

was that the more she struggled, the more pleasure and excitement it gave him to conquer her. And there was no doubt that he could. He could conquer the world!

She was crying now; moaning and sobbing. He covered her mouth with his hand to silence her, and then he pulled her to the floor. He could wait no longer.

He prised open her thighs, and entered her, while at the same time his finger dug deeply into her breasts again and his mouth bruised hers; his lips bit her lips until he tasted her blood.

Her cry, her shriek of pain and terror as he penetrated her, went unnoticed. The beating of her clenched fists against his body felt no stronger to him than the faint touch of a moth's wings, and as easily ignored. When the act was over, when he knew at last that it was this to which his thoughts had been leading him all these weeks, he scrambled to his feet. He couldn't look at her, lying there on the floor. He closed his ears to her sobbing. He half-ran, half-stumbled up the stairs to his room, and flung himself on the bed.

For several moments Madeleine lay on the floor. She tasted the blood on her lips, felt the wetness on her thighs, breathed in the smell of him; but it was the pain, the pain. She had never known such pain. But worse than the pain, and over and above the pain, was the terrible shame, the violation. She lay with her face buried in the rug – and wanted to die. She wanted never to have to open her eyes and face life again. She was filthy, desecrated, spoiled. Her whole body was one large blemish, one great foul sore which would never heal.

But she was not going to die. Nothing was so easy. She was going to go on living, and the only way she could live was if no one, but no one, ever, ever knew. It was that thought, for that reason alone, that she slowly dragged herself to her feet. She washed in the water still in the bath, scrubbing until her white flesh turned red, scrubbing as if she could never get herself clean. Drying herself, she saw there was blood on the hearthrug, and that she cleaned, and the rug being dark, it didn't show.

With the mechanical movements of someone sleep-walking, she emptied the bath, put everything in the room to rights, and went to bed. The most important thing for now was that she should be in bed, her face turned to the wall as if she was asleep, before her family returned. She never asked herself what George was doing, never gave him a thought. It was as if some quite impersonal force, not a man she knew, had done this thing to her. She couldn't possibly think of George, she could think only of the filth that was herself.

After that evening in November, Madeleine went only once more to chapel. It was not difficult to avoid George Carter in the house, presumably because he was as averse to setting eyes on her as she was to seeing him. Just once, two days after it had happened, she had found herself for a moment alone with him. She saw the scratch on his face and wondered what story he had invented to explain that. She didn't care. It surprised her that she didn't feel afraid of him. Her only feeling was ice-cold loathing.

'Madeleine, I have to talk to you! I don't know what came over me. I can't begin to tell you how I feel!'

'Please don't,' she said tonelessly. 'Don't ever speak to me again as long as I live. Oh, you needn't be afraid I shall tell my parents! I couldn't bear for anyone in the world to know my shame. All I want is for you to leave this house, get out of my life.'

She had expected that he *would* leave, but he showed no sign of doing so. On that first Sunday she had wanted to go to chapel. She had felt that perhaps there, in the prayers, in some word of the preacher's in a place dedicated to the presence of God, she might find some peace, some forgiveness for what she thought of, inexplicably, as her guilt. Or rather, did not think of, but felt. She was all emotions, no rational thought.

She might have found some solace in the service had

190

she not sat, as she had hitherto always done, next to George. She had tried to avoid this when they arrived, but she had been innocently out-manoeuvred by her mother. Therefore, beside him, she stood for the hymns, sat for the sermon, bowed her head for the prayers, her body trembling so that she could scarcely keep it in check, her inside churning with sickness. But when, towards the end of the sermon, his shoulder inadvertently touched hers, she felt his body against her, she could bear it no longer. Before the preacher had quite finished she jumped to her feet and ran out of the building.

'I can't stand it, I can't stand it!' she cried as she ran.

As Mrs Bates half rose in her seat to follow Madeleine, Joseph Bates gripped her arm to prevent her. He felt deeply angry and humiliated, but nothing would allow him to leave before the service was over. When it was ended and they came out of chapel a few minutes later, there was no sign of Madeleine. Tight-lipped, Joseph Bates marched his family home, not stopping to speak with anyone. Madeleine was there, looking composed, but pale.

'And what is the meaning of this, madam?' he demanded.

'I'm sorry, Father. I just couldn't stand it another minute.'

'So we heard. So everyone in chapel heard. I repeat, what is the meaning of your behaviour?'

'I can't explain, Father. I repeat, I'm sorry!'

On her face he saw the familiar stubborn expression, but Martha Bates saw something more. Under the unyielding look she saw the unhappiness in her daughter's face. It wasn't the first time she had seen it recently.

'Do you feel ill, Madeleine?' she asked.

'No Mother, I'm quite well.'

How could she explain that the sight of George Carter, going through the motions of piety in God's house, had sickened her to the core, that she had looked around her and wondered about every person there, and that when his body had inadvertently touched hers she had felt herself to be the most defiled of them all; that simply by being there she was desecrating the place.

No, she couldn't explain to her parents. She would never be able to do so. Nor would she ever be able to walk into the chapel again.

'You have disgraced your whole family,' her father said. 'Most of all you have disgraced yourself. If you will not pray, humbly, for forgiveness, then we must do so for you. Here and now, while your sin is so strongly on you.'

While he motioned to the three of them to bow their heads, Madeleine's great relief was that George had not returned from chapel with them. That she could not have borne.

'Dear Lord in Heaven, [Joseph Bates intoned]
We ask Thee to forgive this Thy erring child.
Be merciful to her, a sinner. Cleanse her heart
from wickedness and her ways from evil. Wash
her till she be whiter than snow, and bring her
finally to Thy throne of heavenly grace. For
Christ's sake, Amen.'

Yes, pray for me, Madeleine thought. I have need of that. But I can never be cleansed. All the washing in the world will not clean me.

After dinner Joseph Bates went out sick-visiting, taking Penelope with him. Mrs Bates was glad to be alone with Madeleine.

'There's something wrong, Madeleine love,' she said. 'I'm sure of it. I've watched you. Can't you tell me?'

'There's nothing,' Madeleine said.

'Is it something at work?' Mrs Bates persisted.

'I've told you, Mother, there's nothing!'

Madeleine spoke shortly. With part of her she wanted nothing more than to confess to her mother, but it was impossible. Her mother would feel in duty bound to tell her father, and what Madeleine dreaded most of all, more than anything in the world, was that because of what happened they would make her marry George Carter. She would rather die, she would kill herself, before she would marry him.

It was because she was so turned in on her own thoughts that she didn't notice the change in Sally's mood. They walked in near-silence now. Madeleine blamed herself for the silence and was not able to break it.

When, therefore, she looked across from her loom one morning and saw Sally, white-faced, with eyes red-rimmed and swollen from crying, she was startled. She wanted to go across to her at once, to try to comfort her, but she couldn't leave her loom.

'What do you think's wrong with Sally?' she asked Mrs Barnet. 'She looks very upset about something this morning.'

Mrs Barnet looked at Madeleine in surprise.

'You mean you don't know, love? And you a friend of hers?'

'I don't know what you're talking about,' Madeleine said.

Mrs Barnet shook her head sadly.

'She's in t'family way, poor lass! Did you really not know?'

Madeleine stared at the older woman in disbelief.

'You mean she's having a baby? But she's not married.'

'Well that's the trouble, isn't it?' Mrs Barnet said. 'And she's beginning to show. The minute Mr Bates twigs, she'll be out on her ear.'

'You mean my father will sack her? But that's terrible!'

'Any overlooker would do the same,' Mrs Barnet said, 'though some would turn a blind eye for a bit longer than others. It shows the trust she has in you, that she didn't expect you to go running to your father.'

'Nor would I ever,' Madeleine said. 'But I wish she'd told me.'

'Happen she thought you knew. We keep quiet as a rule, whether the lass is single or married, so as to give her

193

a bit longer to work afore it's noticed. I've known one or two women work right up to the day afore they gave birth – because they knew how to disguise it, see. But that won't be the case with Sally. Her being so small, she'll look like a balloon afore long. I think she's realized she can't stay here much longer and that's what's upset her.'

'Poor Sally!' Madeleine said. She wanted to cross the floor and put her arms around her friend. 'Won't she get married?'

'Who? Who's to say who the man was? He could have scarpered or he could be a married man, lying low.'

Privately, she had her own ideas about who the baby's father was, and you wouldn't have to go outside the family to find him. But there was nothing to be said. It was a common enough situation, and not her business.

'That family is as poor as church mice,' she observed. 'A tribe of kids and a no-good father. What they'll do without Sally's bit of money, let alone keeping another bairn, I shudder to think!'

It had not occurred to Madeleine until that moment that she herself might be pregnant. The truth was that she had thought clearly about nothing. All she had were feelings; terrible feelings which had to be kept hidden. Now – looking across at Sally Pitts, seeing her wan face, noticing for the first time the curve of her stomach under her pinafore – with horror in her heart she faced the fact that she might be in the same condition; that her stomach would swell until she eventually gave birth. And when she did give birth, it would be to a monster. It could not be otherwise. Only a monster could be born of that experience.

And what would happen to her? Her father would sack her from her job the minute he knew. There would be no mercy for her. She had little doubt that he would also turn her out of the house. Her only refuge then would be Helsdon Workhouse, and that was the end of hope for anybody.

She couldn't let it happen! She must plead with him.

She must seek out every shred of compassion which might possibly be hidden somewhere under that hard, austere exterior. But to begin with she must do it for Sally Pitts. She saw herself as the only one who could plead for Sally Pitts, and in doing so she would be pleading for herself.

'I'll ask my father to let her stay on as long as possible,' she said to Harriet Barnet.

Mrs Barnet looked at her in consternation.

'Nay lass, you mustn't do that! The second he knows, she'll have to go. As long as he doesn't know, she'll get a few weeks extra work. You mustn't tell on her, love.'

'Very well, Mrs Barnet. I won't.'

She would never mention Sally's name, she'd never give him the slightest clue, but there was a question she had to ask her father. She *had* to. She had to know. She didn't know how or when she would do this, but to carry out her intention became an obsession with her.

The opportunity came sooner than Madeleine expected. There was an evening during the following week when she found herself alone in the house with her father, Penelope in bed and her mother not yet returned from a sewing meeting for the missions. Her father was sitting at the table reading a book of sermons. Not knowing how to begin, for she had never had an intimate conversation with him and now there was a gulf between them, she plunged straight in.

'Father, there is something I have to ask you.'

'Well?' He continued with his reading. She was glad he wasn't looking directly at her.

'If a girl in the weaving was in trouble, would you sack her for it?'

Then he did look up. He knew the phrase 'in trouble,' knew what it meant when the women used it, but on his daughter's lips it couldn't mean the same thing. His daughters had been brought up in goodness and in innocence. Even Madeleine, the most troublesome of them, knew nothing of that dark side of life.

'It would depend what the trouble was,' he said evenly.

'If she had brought it upon herself. If she had been dishonest, stolen something for instance . . .'

'What if it was something done to her?' Madeleine interrupted.

He looked at her, frowning.

'I could answer you better if I knew what this trouble was.'

Madeleine summoned up all her courage.

'If she was having a baby, Father? And she wasn't married.'

His face darkened.

'You should not speak of such matters. That they happen is deplorable, but they should not, and will not, ever touch you; should not ever be in your thoughts or on your tongue.'

'But what would you do, Father?' Madeleine persisted.

'I would sack her on the spot! Her sin would be a great one, for which she should not go unpunished. Are you telling me that you know of an employee in the weaving shed who is in this sinful condition? If so, speak up and tell me her name!'

'There is no one, Father. No one at all. I just wanted to know what you would say.'

He didn't believe her. Clearly there was someone, but he knew at once that she would never tell. But he would find out who it was. In any case, time would show – and he would keep his eyes open. In the Lord's name he would eradicate all sin from those in his charge; cast it out, root and branch.

At the weekend Emerald came home in the highest of spirits and bursting with news.

'Monsieur Bonneau is to arrive on Tuesday! Oh, everyone is so excited, and there's no holding Miss Sophia! I must confess, I can hardly wait to see him! Oh, Madeleine, you know him, and I do so want to do things right. How should I treat him? What should I do?'

For the first time in the last few days, Madeleine

smiled. Emerald came like a breath of fresh air into the little house. She was so enthusiastic, so innocent.

'Just treat him as you would any guest,' Madeleine advised. 'He might be French, but he's still a human being – a man like any other. Oh yes, when you take him his morning tea, knock on the door and wait for his answer before you go in!'

She had been neither shocked nor afraid when she had seen Monsieur Bonneau without his clothes. If such a thing were to happen now, or ever again, she would be terrified, revolted. She would run from the room screaming.

ELEVEN

Léon Bonneau drew back the heavy curtains and looked out of the window. It was the window of the same room he had been given on his previous visit to Mount Royd, but the view today was quite different. In fact, there *was* no view. Instead of the hilly countryside – the oddly shaped, walled-in fields, the belts of trees, and in the distance the moors – all of which he remembered – all he could see now was a sodden lawn, and beyond it vague shapes of shrubs and trees, drained of colour and almost obliterated by the thick blanket of fog which hung over the whole of the West Riding.

He shuddered, and turned away. How could he possibly have come to such a place, and with the prospect of the whole winter, perhaps every day like this one, before him? He must be mad! Yet he knew he wasn't. He had his own compelling reasons for coming to Helsdon in late November.

Hearing a tap on the door he called, 'Come in!' He half-expected to see Madeleine Bates, but instead the girl who entered was the one who had served at dinner last night.

'Good morning, sir!' Emerald said.

'Good morning! But not a very nice one. I have been looking out of the window.'

'Oh, the weather, sir! Well it's November isn't it?' She

never took much notice of the weather herself. Now that she didn't have to turn out to go to the mill it didn't bother her.

'And is it always foggy in Yorkshire in November?' he asked.

'Oh I think so, sir. It can be a good deal thicker than this, though. Sometimes you can't see your hand in front of your face.'

'How very unpleasant!' he said.

'I'm sorry, sir!'

He smiled.

'I am not blaming you for the weather! Please tell me, do you know Madeleine Bates? She was working here when I paid my last visit, and she visited in Paris with Mr Parkinson and Miss Sophia, but now I see no sign of her.'

'I know her very well,' Emerald said, 'seeing as she's my sister. I'm Emerald Bates, if you please. Madeleine left Mount Royd after she came back from Paris. She's gone to work in the mill, learning to be a weaver.'

'*Work in the mill?*'

Why in the world would she have done that? He had sensed, though nothing was ever said, that matters had not been amiable between herself and Sophia in Paris, but to give up a job here, in the house, for the drudgery of the mill, was surely extreme? He had observed the girls in his own family's mill. It was a hard life.

'Shall I pour your tea, sir? Without milk, I believe.'

'How do you know that, Emerald?'

'Madeleine told me, sir.'

'Your sister remembers well!'

He was remembering too. He remembered the impassive look on her face – the face which he had thought so Italian-looking – on that first morning when she had walked into the room to find him naked. He smiled at the memory, and wondered if she had warned her sister. The sisters didn't look the least bit alike. Emerald was small and waif-like, with straw-coloured hair.

He remembered Madeleine in Paris, too; recalled her

interest in the textile exhibits, the beauty of her face and form on the evening of the theatre, in what must surely have been one of her mistress's gowns; the rapt expression on her face in Notre Dame when she had been unaware of being observed. Yes, considering the fact that she was a servant, he remembered quite a number of things about her.

'Tell your sister I hope she is well.' He gave Emerald a nod of dismissal and began to think about other things. He must dress, and go downstairs for that barbaric English breakfast. How could anyone eat so much at this hour of the day? Perhaps because they served such atrocious meals the rest of the time. Would his stomach endure all these months of English cooking?

Sophia was already down, looking as enchanting at breakfast as she did at all other times of the day.

'Good morning Léon!' she said. 'I do hope you slept well? I'm afraid it's not a very nice day, today.'

'But who will care about the fog outside in the sunshine of your presence!' he replied.

She blushed a pretty, rosy pink, adding to her attraction. Who but a Frenchman could pay such compliments – and with such evident sincerity?

'What would you like to do today – in spite of the fog?' she asked.

'He's going to the mill with me,' her father put in. 'Isn't that what he's here for?'

'Oh Papa, how can you be so mean? I'm sure Léon is quite tired after yesterday's journey. I'm sure he'd prefer to rest, or perhaps to go somewhere interesting.' She was quite prepared to devote her whole day to him, though where they could go in Helsdon which was not the least bit interesting, let alone in the fog, she didn't know. She greatly favoured a day spent indoors.

'I am in your hands!' Léon said.

But whose hands his non-committal smile did not indicate. It was important to be on good terms with every member of the Parkinson family. He went to the sideboard to help himself from the various breakfast dishes, averting his head from the sight and smell of most of them. Kidneys! *Mon Dieu*! Who could eat kidneys at nine o'clock in the morning? He eschewed porridge and helped himself to a portion of lightly scrambled eggs as being the least uncivilized dish he could find.

'Let me pour you some coffee!' Sophia offered.

'No, no!' he protested. 'I will take tea! When in Rome . . .' The truth was, the English had no idea how to make coffee. It was always weak.

'Well then, what's it to be?' Mr Parkinson demanded. 'How are you going to spend the day, Léon?'

'I think it would be a good idea,' Mrs Parkinson said, 'if you two men went to the mill this morning. . . . No, Sophia, not you. We have plenty to do at home. . . . And in the afternoon perhaps the fog will have lifted and we can go for a nice walk. Or if it doesn't lift, then we can have a little music. Sophia will play for us. What do you think?'

'I think that is an excellent suggestion,' Léon said. 'The best of both worlds!'

He would have been happy to spend all day in the mill, the work truly interested him, but it would not be sensible to neglect Sophia, or her mother. It was Sophia, not the mill, which was his main reason for being here. With luck, and with application on his part, he might accomplish what he had come for in less than the six months he had allowed himself. He devoutly hoped so.

He looked around the room in which they sat. Though only the breakfast-room, and therefore the least opulently furnished room in the house, everything in it was of the best, from the thick soft carpet, the beautiful walnut table and chairs, the lavish display of silver on the heavy sideboard, to the exquisite china which graced the table. Yes, there was money here; perhaps not always the best of taste, but certainly money.

He did not begrudge the Parkinsons one penny of their money. Albert Parkinson had without a doubt worked for it. He liked and admired his host. No, all he wanted, all he aspired to, was the marriage settlement which would undoubtedly accompany Sophia. Her dowry, her *dot*. As the only daughter of a very fond father it couldn't fail to be a good one – and without a doubt there would be an allowance to follow. And later on, in the fullness of time when Mr Parkinson had joined that mansion in the sky, Sophia would inherit.

He did not see himself as a *coureur de dots*, a fortune-hunter – not at all. He would make Sophia happy. To live in France would appeal to her, he thought – though Roubaix wasn't Paris, it certainly wasn't Helsdon! Nor did he wish Mr Parkinson to quit this life one minute sooner than nature decreed. What he wanted, in fact badly needed, was a lump sum of money enough to put into the family business in Roubaix.

The business was not as profitable as it could be. New machinery was needed – he had seen the very thing at the Paris Exhibition – but his family lacked capital. There were so many demands on the business; his two brothers and their wives, his mother and sister, all took their share, leaving little for him. Perhaps, after all, when he had the money, it would make sense to start up a business of his own? He would make more money that way.

All this went through his mind as he toyed with his scrambled eggs, ate a slice or two of toast with a surprisingly pleasant orange preserve, and drank yet more tea.

'Then we'll leave in half an hour,' Albert Parkinson said.

'I shall be ready,' Léon promised.

'We have time for a little sojourn in the conservatory,' Sophia suggested. 'We have some interesting new plants since you were last here.'

And it will be warm, Léon thought. The English heated their plants more consistently than they did themselves.

'I should like that!' he agreed.

It would be no great penance to marry Sophia, he

202

thought, following her into the conservatory. None of the women in France with whom he might have contemplated marriage had their 'portion' sufficed, been as attractive as this little English miss, from her ugly northern town. It would be a pleasure to make love with her, expecially as she was clearly in love with him and would wish to please. Whether, apart from her physical charms, she would be an interesting wife, was another matter and could be left to the future.

'It is so pleasant to be with you in here,' he said after a while. 'I would willingly spend several hours so. But alas, duty must come before pleasure and your father will be waiting for me!'

'Then come back soon,' Sophia said boldly. 'Don't let Papa keep you for hours and hours!'

Oh, he was so handsome, so attractive! When he stood close to her like this, she could have swooned into his arms. She swayed a little towards him and the scent of her clean shining hair came into his nostrils. He raised his hands and would have laid them on her shoulders, but stopped himself in time. As yet, the mother and father were more important. Sophia was a ripe fruit which would fall into his hands at a touch, but he was not sure that that was, as yet, true of her parents. So instead he took her hand and raised it to his lips.

'*Au revoir*, Sophia!'

'*Au revoir*, Léon!' She was quite determined to learn French.

'First off, we'll take a look around,' Albert Parkinson said when they reached the mill. 'Just to refresh your memory.'

They went first into the wool-sorting.

'If I had to work in the mill I think wool-sorting would be my choice,' Albert said. 'Every job in the mill has its own skill, but there's something about this one that appeals to me.'

'And that is probably why you are such a good buyer when you go to the sales,' Léon said.

'Ah yes, the sales!' He'd not be going again until into the New Year. He couldn't afford to buy, for one thing. But he was missing Kitty badly and wondered if he might find an excuse at least to go up to London.

'I think I would like the scouring least of all,' Léon observed as they continued. 'I can never get used to the stench. When I come into the scouring I would like to put a peg on my nose!'

He left the scouring with relief. They visited the dusty wool-combing shed, where only men were employed, and later went on to the humid atmosphere of the spinning, kept so because if the yarn became too dry it would fly into the air.

'Now the twisting,' Albert Parkinson said.

Léon put his hands over his ears and raised his eyes to heaven in mock despair as they entered the twisting.

'Terrible, the noise!' he said. 'How does anyone stand it for hours on end?' The twisting machines made a high-pitched, whirring sound, especially hard on the ears. 'It is always the noisiest place in the mill!' But he didn't need to shout to make himself heard; both men, like their workpeople, could lip read.

'I don't know how they stand it, but they do,' Albert Parkinson said. 'We never have trouble setting people on.'

Léon stopped for a moment at a machine where the operator was twisting two colours of yarn together.

'Brown and green,' he remarked. 'The result is nice, but not unusual.'

'Heather mixture,' Albert Parkinson said.

'Yes. I see that. What I would like to do while I am here – if you agree of course – is to experiment with twisting very differently coloured yarns together. Could we, do you think, get the dyers to dye the tops in some more bold or unusual colours? You send the white tops for dyeing, do you not?'

'Aye, that's right. I daresay you could do that, though you might have to stand over them to get the shade you wanted.'

'I would do that. It is only if we get the yarns in the right colours that we shall get the effect I want in the woven cloth.'

'What's it going to cost?' Albert Parkinson asked.

'Not a great deal to begin with. We could work with small quantities.'

But it was when they moved on to the weaving that Léon showed the greatest interest, felt most at home. This, for him, was where everything came together. As soon as they entered, Joseph Bates came forward to meet them.

'I dare say you'll remember Mr Bates, our weaving overlooker,' Albert Parkinson said.

'Of course I do! Good day to you, Mr Bates.' Léon held out his hand and Joseph Bates took it reluctantly.

'Good day, Monsieur Bonneau.'

He had been told that Monsieur Bonneau would be spending quite a lot of time in the weaving over the next few months. He didn't look forward to it. Giving credit where it was due, he acknowledged that the man knew his job; he'd seen that at once on his last visit. But he didn't want any interference. He ran a tight ship here in the weaving. He didn't want any foreigner – and a Frenchman at that – putting his oar in.

'Who do you reckon's your best weaver?' Albert Parkinson asked his overlooker.

Joseph Bates didn't need to think about it.

'Mrs Barnet, bar none!'

'Right! Then when Monsieur Bonneau is ready, which won't be just yet, I want you to let him have Mrs Barnet for whatever he wants doing. Has she got someone helping her?'

'My daughter,' Joseph Bates said reluctantly.

'Madeleine!' Léon cried. 'Of course! Her sister told me she was here. If you will permit, I shall say "hello" to her.'

'Well, Bates, take Monsieur Bonneau over to Mrs Barnet,' Albert Parkinson said. 'He can talk to her about what he's likely to want in the future. I'll leave you for a while. If you want me, Léon, I'll be in my office.'

Léon Bonneau followed Joseph Bates to where Mrs Barnet was at two looms and Madeleine was minding a third one under the older woman's supervision.

'I am told you are Mr Bates's best weaver!' Léon said when he and Mrs Barnet were introduced. 'I look forward to seeing what we can achieve together.'

'Thank you, sir. You just set up the patterns and I'll do my level best!' Not many compliments came her way. Mr Bates didn't believe in praise, but it was nice to have a bit for a change.

'And here is Madeleine,' Léon said. She hadn't looked up from her work at his approach, and he wondered why. *Bonjour*, Madeleine! I was surprised when your sister told me you had left Mount Royd.'

Joseph Bates frowned. The man's tone was too friendly. He didn't like any of his hands, and his daughter in particular, being singled out. People should stick to their work, and to their own station in life. The Frenchman's place was one thing, his daughter's quite another. She'd never been the same since she'd returned from Paris. He was convinced that something there had changed her. She never *would* be the same, never the daughter he'd once had, until she put it all behind her and returned to God.

'How are you, Madeleine?' Léon Bonneau asked.

'Very well, thank you sir.'

She seemed reluctant to lift her head to reply, but when she did so he was shocked by her appearance. No matter what she said, she was far from well. He observed the pallor of her skin, the dark circles around her eyes – they seemed larger and darker than ever in her white face, eyes which were frightened. What could cause such fear? Why was she changed, and in so short a time?

Can he tell when he looks at me, Madeleine thought?

Can he see I'm filthy and dirty and spoilt? She felt that everyone who looked at her must know, that it must stand out on her like the mark of Cain. And somehow it mattered to her that he should see her like this.

As each day passed, and now it was almost Christmas, Madeleine's fear grew. She had little doubt now that she was pregnant. Her period had been due only a few days after that terrible evening, but that was several weeks ago now and there had been no sign of it. She could see no way out of her predicament, no way out at all. Sometimes she wished she had not put Sally Pitts's case to her father, for he had confirmed her worst fears. She knew there was no hope where he was concerned. He would be harsher towards his own daughter even than to one of his mill-hands.

One evening, walking home arm-in-arm with her in the dark, Madeleine had plucked up courage to speak to Sally about her predicament, though she could never mention her own.

'I'm ever so sorry to hear of your trouble, Sally. Mrs Barnet told me. I hope you don't mind.'

'No. I suppose everyone else knows – except Mr Bates, that is.'

She spoke as if he had no relation to Madeleine, until she suddenly remembered. Madeleine felt the arm through hers tighten.

'Don't worry, Sally,' she assured her. 'I wouldn't tell my father in a thousand years!'

Joseph Bates had discovered nothing though he still suspected that Madeleine had been talking about one of his weavers, and he'd since kept a close watch on every girl in the shed.

Two days later Sally didn't turn up for work. Her mother came to see Joseph Bates at breakfast time.

'Our Sally's got bronchitis,' she informed him. 'She'll be back inside a week. If there's any wages due to her I'd like to take them. We're a bit short.'

Mrs Barnet recognized Sally's mother and when she left the weaving shed, and as it was breakfast time and the looms were stopped, she ran after her and walked with her to the gate. When Mrs Barnet returned a dozen heads lifted, a dozen pairs of eyes asked the same question.

'Sally's baby was born prematurely – five-and-a-half months,' she said quietly. 'He was dead, poor scrap. And now we'd best get back to work. Buzzer'll be going any second. And try to look cheerful. It's bronchitis she's got, remember!'

Sally was back at her loom less than a week later; paler than ever, thinner, saddened – but no longer in danger of losing her job. The general feeling in the weaving was that she'd been lucky.

'If you can call it lucky, losing a bairn!' Mrs Barnet said to Madeleine. 'Myself, I'll call it luck if she doesn't get in the family way again. Some men ought to be castrated!'

Mistaking the cause of the stricken look on Madeleine's face, she had apologized.

'I've no right to be saying such things in front of you. Take no notice of me, love. Even though you are eighteen, it's my belief you don't know the first thing. And best keep it that way, if you ask me!'

Will I be as lucky as Sally? Madeleine asked herself. Perhaps I'll miscarry, then no one will know. Was that something she could live through on her own? There were ways, there were women who could do things – she was not as ignorant as Mrs Barnet supposed – but who? And how? Sometimes, she'd heard, they killed you.

She was at home, sitting at the table mending her work skirt. Her parents and Penelope were out on one of those missions to do with the chapel which seemed so frequent at this time of the year. They were distributing gifts to the poor, a task which Madeleine knew her mother did with bad grace.

'Who is poor?' Mrs Bates had demanded. 'Who will bring gifts to *my* children? How will *we* feast at Christmas?'

Nevertheless she had gone. George was working very

late every night of this Christmas week, the shop being open. At least Madeleine had no fear that he would arrive back before her parents. She had grown to hate George Carter. In the first few days after the rape she had had no room in her mind to think of him as a person, only as a thing, but now she hated him with an all-consuming, frightening intensity. Sometimes she found herself on the verge of praying for some terrible punishment to fall on him, but at the very edge she drew back, fearful that it would rebound on herself. God clearly punished the innocent equally with the guilty, or why would she be going through this?

In the New Year, she thought, she would begin to show. That would be when her father would turn her out. Already she had started to save coppers as and when she could so that she should not be entirely destitute. Then at the thought, which came so often now, of leaving her home, her mother and her sister, it was suddenly all too much for her; she was overwhelmed. She bent her head over the table and wept, tears coursing down her cheeks, her body rent with great sobs.

'Please God save me!' she cried. 'Dear Lord, in Your mercy, save me!'

It was her cry of despair which Irvine heard as he opened the door and came into the house. He was at once by her side and she was in his arms, her slender body shaken by her rasping sobs, the front of his uniform wet with her tears. He held her close, stroking her hair, not speaking, until at last her strength gave out and her weeping ceased.

'A right homecoming!' he said gently. 'Tell me what it's all about, Madeleine love.'

'I can't tell you!' she said. 'But oh, Irvine, I am so glad to see you!'

'What do you mean, you can't tell me? You must. It's not like you to cry. I've never seen you in a state like this. Come on, love!'

She wanted to tell him. She longed desperately to tell

him the whole horrible thing, from start to finish. It wasn't that he could help her – but just to tell another soul . . .

'Come on,' he insisted. 'I'm waiting.'

'Then will you promise never to tell anyone? Not mother or father or anyone? Will you promise?'

'If that's what you want, I will,' he assured her.

She saw the horror growing in his face as she told him. He leapt to his feet, his face suffused with anger, ready to strike out at anything, anybody.

'Where is he?' he cried. 'Where is he?'

'He's at work,' Madeleine said. 'He works at Nevill's in the town. They keep open late this week. But Irvine, you can't do anything. If you did, mother and father would know about it. They'd make me marry him, if only for the baby. I can't do that, Irvine. I can't do it!'

He sat down again.

'Yes. I see. So what *can* I do, Madeleine?'

'Nothing. But for the moment, just for the moment, I feel better for having told you. Oh Irvine, I can't tell you what it's been like, bottling it up inside! Oh I'm so glad you're home.'

'You're not to tell anyone I'm back,' he said suddenly. 'You're not to tell a soul, do you hear?'

'But Irvine, what about Ma? She's waited so long.'

'Not yet, Madeleine. You're to tell nobody you've seen me. I'll come back in a day or two, but until then, nothing. I promised to keep your secret, now you must keep mine. Do you understand?'

'Not really,' Madeleine confessed. 'But I'll do as you ask. Just tell me one thing, Irvine – are you in trouble?'

'No,' he said. 'I'm not in any trouble. I've been given Christmas leave – and I promise you I'll be back to spend Christmas here. But I'm off now, before they come back. Take care of yourself, Madeleine, and try not to worry. We'll think of something.'

But what? he asked himself as he left the house. What

could he do which would actually help Madeleine? As yet he saw no answer to that.

It was ten o'clock at night, pitch dark, and more than a little foggy when George Carter, together with Eddie Broom, a fellow-assistant, emerged from Nevill's shop.

'Another day over!' Broom said. 'I'll be glad when it's Christmas and we get a day off. What about you?'

George's reply was little more than a grunt.

He's a rum fellow, Broom thought. Never has a civilized word for anyone these days. The two of them walked in silence for a couple of hundred yards, until it was time for Broom to turn left.

'Well, see you tomorrow, George,' he said. 'Glad I don't have to go as far as Priestley Street in this stuff!'

It was a twenty-minute walk to Priestley Street, first through the old part of Helsdon, then across a piece of waste ground. In the summer, thick belts of gorse brightened the waste ground with yellow flowers, but now the shrubs were no more than blurred shapes. The fog was thicker here, and the path was visible for no more than a few yards ahead. Not that that mattered to George Carter. He had walked this path so often in the last year that he could have found his way blindfold.

Irvine Bates had watched George Carter leave the shop. He knew who he was; he had been in the shop yesterday and had identified him. He'd been disappointed that this evening he was not alone, but when the other man turned off Irvine breathed a sigh of relief and scurried through the back streets of Helsdon, which he had known since childhood, arriving on the waste ground a few minutes ahead of George Carter. He was glad of the fog. Though Carter didn't know him – he had already been in the army before George Carter arrived in Helsdon – he'd as soon the man didn't get a good look at him, not when he was wearing the Queen's uniform, not when he was going to give him the hiding of his life!

The attack was almost too easy. Walking with his head

down, George Carter didn't see his assailant come from behind the belt of gorse, wasn't aware of him until he almost walked into the large shape which blocked his path.

'What in the world . . .?'

He had no time to finish the sentence before Irvine's fist caught him full in the face and the blood spurted from his nose. He reeled back, losing his hat, but was prevented from falling to the ground when his attacker grabbed him by the lapels and set him on his feet again.

'Oh no, you don't lie down yet!' Irvine said. 'I haven't finished with you, not by a long chalk.'

He seemed to have the size and strength of a giant. Even while he was speaking he was raining more blows, mostly to George's head. It was, however, a fist in his midriff, with Irvine's full weight behind it, which felled him.

'Thank your lucky stars I didn't kill you, you scum!'

They were the last words George heard, followed by the sound of his attacker's footsteps fading into the distance, before he lost consciousness.

He was not sure, when he came round, how long he had been lying there. He thought it could not have been long for, in spite of the fog, his clothes were not particularly damp. His body was one enormous mass of pain. He opened his mouth to breathe in the air – his nose was clogged with drying blood – and realized that his lips were so swollen, his jaw so painful, that he could hardly do so. He tasted the blood in his mouth and longed, above everything, for a drink of water. He must get up, he must find water somewhere. It was no use waiting for help. No one would pass this way until morning.

With difficulty he got to his feet, then slowly set out for Priestley Street, which was not far, though every yard seemed like twenty. Later, he thought as he trudged the last half-mile, he would think about why he had been attacked by a stranger, who had made no attempt to rob him. He *was* a stranger, he was certain of that, yet there had been something familiar about his voice, and he had a local accent.

In the dark George had seen nothing of how the man looked, though he thought he might have worn a uniform. There had been a moment when he had grabbed at the man's coat and felt a metal button, embossed. He had wrenched it hard as he was falling backwards. But he couldn't think about it now. His head was throbbing. He felt as if he would die with the pain.

When he came into the house Joseph Bates jumped to his feet and Mrs Bates screamed.

'What in the world . . .!'

Madeleine felt the colour drain from her face and clutched at the table, fighting off the wave of nausea which swept over her. But it was not the sight itself, dreadful though George Carter looked, standing there in the room, his face still bleeding, his eyes blackened with bruises, which caused her almost to faint; it was the knowledge in her heart, as certain as if she had witnessed the event, of how and why this had happened.

'I was . . . attacked!' George croaked. 'On the waste ground. . . . A drink of water!'

'At once!' Mrs Bates said. 'Oh, you poor boy!'

Joseph Bates helped George into his own armchair while Mrs Bates fetched him first a drink, and then a bowl of water to wash his cuts. Madeleine stood by.

'Who?' she whispered. 'Do you know who?'

'No. It was all so quick. It was too dark to see.'

'You've no idea?'

'Don't bother him with questions, Madeleine,' Mrs Bates said impatiently. 'Can't you see he's not in a fit state?'

'I've no idea,' George said.

Thank God at least for that! Madeleine tried not to show her relief.

'We must inform the police,' Jospeh Bates said. 'We must do that at once. Whoever has done this must not be allowed to go free!'

'No!' George protested. 'I don't want that. I don't feel able . . .'

'Of course he doesn't,' Mrs Bates agreed. 'The minute I've attended to him he must go to bed. The police can wait until morning.'

'But the attacker should be found, and punished,' her husband said.

'I beg of you, no!' George said.

His head was fuzzy and his whole body racked with pain, but he knew quite clearly that he didn't want the police. There was something about this attack which frightened him even more than the blows, though he couldn't put a name to it yet.

'Whoever it was, he'll be miles away,' Mrs Bates said. 'Goodness knows where he'll be!'

Where *will* he be? Madeleine wondered. Where will he be on this winter's night?

Two days later, when Madeleine came out of the mill at the end of the day, Irvine was waiting for her at the gates.

'Irvine! Where have you been?' She scanned his face for signs of bruises. There was nothing. Surely if he'd been in such a fight he would have some mark? But she was clutching at straws. In her mind she had little doubt about the matter.

'Never mind where I've been. I told you I'd be back, and here I am. As far as anyone else knows, I've just turned up today. Don't you forget that, Madeleine.'

'I won't. But don't think I'm fooled.'

She was neither glad nor sorry about what her brother had done to George Carter, except that she didn't want him to be caught. It had changed nothing. George was still there, in the house all day at present, because with his face so bruised he couldn't work in the shop. Her state was no different, neither better nor worse. Irvine was the only satisfaction. Yet, she thought, she *was* a little different. The blind hatred she had felt for George, the intensity of her bitterness, had, as she had seen him standing there, the picture of abject fear, with blood streaming down his face, not abated – that was too strong a word – but it no longer consumed her like a fire.

'Come on, love. We're going home!' Irvine said.

When Irvine walked into the room in Priestley Street Mrs Bates was fiddling with the oven dampers, her back to the door.

'Hello, Madeleine love,' she called out.

Irvine quickly laid a finger across Madeleine's lips.

'Hello, Ma!' he answered.

She swung around with the speed of a bullet. He stood quite still, a smile on his face, though he felt the tears stinging his eyes. Then he opened his arms wide and she rushed into them. He lifted her off her feet and swung her around in the small space.

'Oh Irvine! Is it true? I'm not dreaming?'

'It's true, Ma,' he said gently. 'You're wide awake and I'm home for Christmas.'

'Oh Irvine, I've prayed for this day! Are you all right, love? Tell me you're all right?'

'Not a scratch on me. The only thing is, I'm hungry, Ma! And I can smell one of your hotpots in the oven.'

'You certainly can,' Martha Bates said, wiping her eyes with the corner of her apron. 'And you shall have some at once! Your father won't be here for a quarter of an hour yet, but we'll start without him.'

It was a bold decision. She noted Madeleine's raised eyebrows. No one ever ate in this house until Joseph Bates was at the table and had been served. But be blowed to him! Be blowed to him! And if her son was hungry and wanted a large serving, then the rest of them would go a bit short. Including you, Joseph Bates, she thought. There was fresh-baked bread in the crock; they could fill up on that.

'Madeleine, take your brother's coat, and fetch Penelope – she's next door. Irvine, you sit to the table at once. Oh Irvine, there've been times when I've wondered if you'd ever sit at my table again – and here you are!'

They were well into the meal when Joseph Bates walked in. It was difficult to say which surprised him more – the fact that they were eating before him or the presence of his son.

His greeting was cool; a brief handshake before he joined them at the table.

'I presume you said grace?' he asked.

Mrs Bates put a hand to her mouth.

'Oh dear, we forgot. It was the excitement. And if ever there was an occasion for saying grace, this is it! Let me say it, Joseph.'

She laid her hand on Irvine's as he sat next to her.

'For these and all His mercies, God's holy name be praised,' she said.

'Who is going to tell Emerald?' Penelope asked after supper.

'Well not you, not tonight,' her mother said. 'It's too dark for you to walk to Mount Royd.'

'I will go with Penelope,' Joseph Bates said. He would feel more comfortable away from the house for a spell.

'Our Emerald will be transported!' Mrs Bates cried. 'But be careful, Joseph. Remember what happened to George!'

'I have no fear for the pestilence that walketh in the darkness,' Joseph Bates said. 'God is a lamp unto my feet, and a light unto my path.'

'Well, He didn't do much for George!' Mrs Bates said boldly. But there was no acid in her words; she was too happy.

'Now we must sort out where you'll sleep for the time being,' she said to Irvine when her husband and Penelope had left. 'George Carter has your room, but I shall give him his notice this very evening, when he comes in from chapel. You're my son and it's your room, but I can't turn him out at once, of course.'

'Of course, you can't, Ma,' Irvine agreed. 'Anyway, I've found lodgings in Helsdon which will do me for the time I'm here.'

'But surely you're back in Helsdon for good?' his mother cried. 'Surely you can come out of the army now?'

'I doubt I'll be sent back to the Crimea,' Irvine said. 'But I'm staying in the army for a while. It suits me. Anyway, I could never live at home again, Ma. With you – yes – but not with my father.'

The door opened and George came in. The two men stood staring at each other without speaking.

'This is my son, Irvine,' Mrs Bates said proudly. 'He's been fighting in the Crimea, as of course you know. Now he's going to be with us for Christmas! Poor George was attacked on his way home from work,' she added, turning to Irvine.

Mrs Bates didn't notice, but Madeleine did, that the two men made no attempt to shake hands.

'Well, that's quite a mess he made of you!' Irvine said to George. 'Now I wonder why anyone would do a thing like that? Don't you know any reason why it happened?'

'No. No I don't,' George said nervously.

'And you don't know who the fellow was? You wouldn't recognize him again?'

It was Irvine Bates who had attacked him. George knew that now for certain. He had recognized the voice the minute Irvine had spoken – and it had sounded familiar because it was like Joseph Bates's voice.

'You don't know who it was?' Irvine repeated.

'No I don't,' George lied.

'Well,' Irvine drawled, 'I don't suppose it would do you any good if you did know.'

He turned to Madeleine.

'What did you do with my coat, love? I've got a present in the pocket for Ma.'

'Here you are, Irvine.' She handed him his greatcoat. 'You've got a button missing.'

'Now where could I have lost that?' Irvine asked, looking at George.

The next evening when George left work Irvine Bates was waiting for him outside. George felt his insides turn to water. He thanked God that Eddie Broom was with him. Surely he was safe in Eddie's company?

'I was on my way to Priestley Street,' Irvine said smoothly. 'I thought I'd walk along with you.'

'I . . . I was thinking of calling in at Eddie's place – this is Eddie Broom – for a cup of cocoa,' George stammered.

'You never said!' Eddie cried. 'I'm sorry, old sport. I'm going to my mother-in-law's. You wouldn't want to come there, I can tell you!'

'So it's you and me together,' Irvine said. 'Best foot forward then!'

While they walked through the streets George was not so afraid. It being near to Christmas, there were plenty of people about. But when they reached the waste ground he was terrified. He walked beside Irvine, his legs trembling, his whole body in a sweat. Suddenly – they had gone no more than a hundred yards on the waste ground – Irvine stopped. He grabbed George by the coat collar and swung around to face him, thrusting his face within an inch of the other man's.

'Don't! Please don't! I'll do anything you say!' George pleaded.

'You certainly will, you snivelling little rat! And the first thing you'll do, the minute your shop closes down for Christmas, is you'll leave Helsdon. You'll leave and you'll never come back!'

'Anything!' George promised.

'I'm capable of killing you,' Irvine threatened. 'I've been learning how to kill, and I'd kill you with no more compunction than I'd swat a fly. If I don't do it it's for my mother's and my sister's sake – and it's for their sake I'm not beating the living daylights out of you this minute. So get off with you, you bastard! And if there's sight or sound of you in Helsdon after Christmas Eve, then you know what to expect!'

He picked up George by his shoulders and gave him a final shake before dropping him to the ground, then he turned smartly and began to walk back to Helsdon.

218

The next day George Carter announced that he was going home for Christmas.

'It's a long time since I saw my parents,' he explained. 'I've decided I ought to go.'

'In that case,' Mrs Bates said to Madeleine, 'Irvine can have his room while he's away.'

She was surprised when she went to prepare it to find that George had taken all his personal possessions with him. Then, shortly after Christmas, when he should have been back at work and was not, a letter came.

'I shall not be returning to Helsdon', he wrote. 'I find that my parents have need of me here.'

For Madeleine, it was as if a ton weight had rolled off her. The worst was still to come – she knew that – but somehow she would face it. She would face it a thousand times more easily without the constant reminder which George's presence in the house had been to her. That night, with true sincerity, she thanked God on her knees for this lightening of her load and prayed for strength to meet the future.

On New Year's Eve her period returned. Feeling the wetness on her thighs, she ran upstairs. When she found that it was true she lay on the bed and cried as if her heart would break; tears of relief and thanksgiving. Mrs Bates, rushing upstairs to see what ever was the matter, was at a loss to understand.

'I think you've been overdoing things, Madeleine! That's what it is – you've been working too hard!'

TWELVE

'Good morning, Miss Sophia! Happy birthday!' Emerald said.

Sophia stirred in her sleep, then came to slowly as Emerald drew back the curtains.

'What?'

'I said, "happy birthday," Miss Sophia. Here's your morning tea, and just take a look at what's on the tray!'

Sophia sat up quickly. Beside the delicate china cup and saucer lay a single, beautiful red rose. She cried out with pleasure at the sight of it.

'Oh! How ever did that get there? Is there no message with it?'

'Well I'm sure I didn't put it there,' Emerald said, smiling. 'Who ever did it must have sneaked into the kitchen. And there's no message, miss!'

It was from Léon, of course. Sophia had no need to ask. Who else would be capable of such a wonderful gesture?

Emerald was equally certain Monsieur Bonneau had put the rose on the tray, though she hadn't seen him come into the kitchen. Frenchmen were so romantic. She wondered if, when Miss Sophia and Monsieur Bonneau married, they would live in France, and whether they'd take her with them and she'd meet a handsome Frenchman herself? Oh what heaven that would be! Of course they weren't engaged yet – but it couldn't be long now.

Everybody knew it would happen. Perhaps this very day, it being Miss Sophia's nineteenth birthday.

'Have you seen Monsieur Bonneau this morning?' Sophia asked.

'He left for the mill as usual, miss. He should be back any time now for breakfast.'

'Is it so late? You should have wakened me earlier,' Sophia grumbled. 'You know how I dislike dressing in a hurry!'

'I thought you could do with the extra sleep, Miss Sophia. It's going to be a busy day for you, what with the party and all.' It was going to be a busy day for all of them. She had been up since half-past five, and Mrs Thomas not much later, there was that much to do.

'Well you thought wrong!' Sophia snapped.

She hated getting up in the morning. Most days she missed family breakfast and instead had it brought up to her room at a civilized hour; but today was different. Today was her nineteenth birthday and she must, she absolutely must, see Léon at breakfast.

'Put the rose in water,' she ordered. 'Monsieur Bonneau must have gone to a deal of trouble to get a rose in May.'

'It wouldn't be no trouble to him!'

Emerald sighed. She reckoned he'd have got that rose if he'd had to climb to the top of a mountain for it – though that wouldn't be the right place, come to think of it.

'I'll fetch your hot water, Miss Sophia.'

Sophia had no doubt about what to wear on this special morning. It was to be one of the two new gowns Miss Compton had made for her birthday; a dress of fine printed wool in shades of cream and brown, with wide cuffs falling from the elbow, undersleeves of cream silk, and a deep frill of cream lace at the neck. The colours, she thought, surveying herself in the mirror, were a perfect foil for her auburn hair. She would wear the other, even more elegant dress of green watered silk, for the party this evening.

And on second thoughts, she would wear the rose at breakfast. She was sure Léon would want her to do so. She took it from the glass, dried the stem carefully, then pinned it to her bosom – placing it exactly over her heart. She hoped that Léon would realize the significance of its position.

She was already at the table when he came in. He crossed the room and kissed her hand.

'A happy birthday, my dear Sophia!'

'Thank you Léon.'

Her violet eyes, soft and limpid, met his, while her fingers strayed to the rose at her bosom.

'And who am I to thank for this beautiful flower?' she asked archly. 'Could it have been you, Papa?'

Albert Parkinson grunted.

'I thought not. Then it must have been . . .'

'I plead guilty,' Léon said.

Mon Dieu! She had read too much into it!

That was the trouble with Englishwomen. Their own men were so stolid – and nowhere more so than here in Helsdon – that if they were paid what to a Frenchman would be the slightest attention, a matter of no more than politeness, they saw it almost as a declaration of love.

Yet was there a certain logic in Sophia's view? he asked himself guiltily. Since part of his plan on coming to Helsdon had been to woo Sophia, and since over the months of his stay he had paid her every attention, how could she, with her English outlook, be blamed for thinking of him as a serious suitor? That, in the beginning, was certainly what he had set out to be.

Oh dear, I am the one to blame, he chided himself. He should have left Helsdon several weeks ago, when it came to him that he didn't want to marry Sophia. He didn't want it at all. But what he did want was her money, which on marriage would come to him. He wanted that, and two months ago he had still believed that he could struggle against his growing aversion to the marriage in return for the *dot*.

But this morning he had realized, finally, that he couldn't go through with it. This, Sophia's birthday, was the day he would be expected to propose. He couldn't do it. It was impossible! Much as he wanted and needed the money, he could not bring himself to marry Sophia.

Oh, she was pretty enough! Her figure was perfection; she was in many ways quite adorable. He would willingly have taken her as a mistress, had the English understood such things – but as a wife, as someone with whom he must spend the rest of his life – well, it was impossible.

He could have coped with her appalling selfishness, and he'd soon have dealt with her temper tantrums; he took it for granted that she would embrace his religion; but the plain fact was that she bored him. She bored him to death, and boredom he could not bear.

But damn it man, he asked himself, why have you let the affair drag on? Why hadn't he put a stop to it two months ago? Well, he would have to do so now. He would have to make it plain that there was nothing doing, and the sooner the better. A pity it hadn't worked out. Now he must seek for money elsewhere, preferably this time in his own country.

'That is a most charming gown, Sophia,' he said. 'I have not seen it before.' Even now he couldn't stop himself paying the compliments which came so naturally to his lips.

'Miss Compton made me two new gowns for my birthday. You will see the other this evening. But alas, Miss Compton is the best that Helsdon has to offer! I'm sure it's not what you are used to!' She pouted a little, inviting his denial.

'Nonsense! You look as *chic* as any Parisian lady!'

'Oh I do so wish you didn't have to go back to the mill after breakfast,' she cried. 'Papa, *must* Léon go back to the mill? After all, it *is* my birthday.' She turned to Léon. 'We could go for a walk. It's a beautiful day.'

They could be alone together. It was so seldom she had him all to herself for more than two minutes at a time.

223

How could he say what she *knew* was in his heart when they never got a chance to be together? And surely this was the day he would say something – her nineteenth birthday?

'I'm not the young man's keeper,' her father said. 'But he's got plenty on in the mill. Not everything can stop because it's your birthday. And it being Saturday, we'll both be home by half-past two.'

'Your father is right,' Léon said. 'I'm sure I must go to the mill. Perhaps we shall find time for a walk before tea?'

That they must do, he decided. He must see Sophia on her own, get it over with quickly. Some sixth sense warned him that if he didn't do it before the excitement of the party, before all her friends and relatives were present and the air full of expectation, he could be . . . trapped. So no more shilly-shallying. But he would let her down as lightly as possible, dear little Sophia. He would be kind, but firm. And afterwards it would be teatime, and the present-giving, then the guests would begin to arrive. She would have plenty to occupy her, no time to brood. Yes, he must do it this afternoon.

'Oh, very well then,' Sophia said.

She wondered what Léon's present would be. They had decided to have the presents at tea, make a ceremony of it, because there was so little time at breakfast. Would it be . . . would he today give her what she hoped for? As discreetly as she could she placed her left hand on the table and studied it. A well-shaped hand, she congratulated herself; white as a lily, smooth as silk. Any ring would look well on her hand, though she couldn't help preferring a diamond.

The morning passed. She found plenty to do. She bathed her face and neck in rich cream, which Emerald brought from the kitchen, then lay on the bed to let it dry. It did wonders, they said, for the complexion. In the meantime her mind wandered in its usual direction, a jumble of wedding dresses, rings, bridesmaids and so on. Of course there was the small question of religion. She would have to take up Léon's, but that didn't matter – except that she supposed she'd have to be married in a Catholic church and the only one in Helsdon was very poor, not the best of settings for a wedding.

When the cream had dried to a thick, smelly mask, she got up and washed it off, then rang again for Emerald.

'I'd like some slices of cucumber, Emerald. I've already got freckles from yesterday's sun.' If she rubbed them vigorously with the cucumber they might just show less. Freckles were so common!

'I'll bring it as soon as I can, miss,' Emerald said. She was wanted for a hundred jobs in the kitchen, in the dining-room, in the drawing-room.

'Bring it *at once*!' Sophia demanded.

Then there was the question of her hair. She had decided to dress it in a new and fashionable style, and that took ages, for every ringlet must be perfection. When she was married, she wondered, might she have a lady's maid who would do all this sort of thing for her? She sincerely hoped so.

Albert Parkinson and Léon were home by half-past two. Luncheon on a Saturday always waited for the return of Mr Parkinson, and was therefore late.

'Take the vegetables in,' Mrs Thomas said to Emerald.

'All right, Mrs Thomas. My but I'm tired!'

It felt like a hundred years since she had crawled out of bed that morning. She was also light-headed with hunger, for they couldn't have their own meal until the family had been served. In the dining-room, with a face as red as pickled beetroot from her exertions in the kitchen, she handed round the vegetables. Moving from Mrs Parkinson to Sophia with a dish of floury, boiled potatoes, she caught her foot against a chair leg and went sprawling. Potatoes flew in all directions. It was not her fault that a couple landed right in Miss Sophia's lap.

Sophia leapt to her feet, screaming.

'Oh, you stupid idiot! You've ruined my new dress! You've scalded me!'

225

Emerald lay on the floor. The colour had drained from her face. She was chalk-white, her features contorted with pain.

'I'm sorry, Miss Sophia,' she whispered. 'I caught my foot . . .'

'What good is being sorry?' Sophia shouted. 'Look what you've done to my dress! Now get to your feet and clean this mess!'

'Sophia! Control yourself!' Mr Parkinson thumped the table, glaring at his daughter.

'But she's ruined my dress! For heavens' sake, get up girl!'

The tears were rolling down Emerald's face.

'I'm sorry, miss,' she whimpered. 'I'm sorry, sir. I don't seem to be able to get up! I think I've twisted my knee.'

Léon sprang to his feet and pushed past Sophia.

'Then let me help you.' He knelt down beside her. 'Can you clasp your arms around my neck? I'll lift you as gently as possible. Hold on now.'

'Take her into the drawing-room. Lay her on the sofa,' Mrs Parkinson said. She turned to her daughter. 'As for you, miss, you should be ashamed of yourself, speaking to anyone, even a servant, in such a manner!'

Léon was carrying Emerald into the drawing-room. He hasn't so much as looked at me, Sophia thought angrily. I might be quite severely scalded, hot potatoes in my lap! Her parents were following Léon into the drawing-room. Did no one care in the least about her? Not mind that her new dress was spoilt? She remained alone at the table, her feet surrounded by boiled potatoes. She was still sitting there, angrily drumming her fingers on the table, when Léon reappeared.

'Your father has sent Drake to fetch the doctor,' he reported. 'It looks as though poor little Emerald will be well and truly laid up. She cannot move her right leg at all!'

'She *can't* be laid up!' Sophia cried. 'She absolutely *can't*! She'll just ruin my party!'

Léon stared at her.

'What *do* you mean, Sophia? How can a little servant girl, twisting her knee, ruin your party?'

'Because she's needed for a thousand jobs, not least to help to serve. Who else will do it? We never have enough servants in this house! A cook, a maid, a coachman, two gardeners and a couple of women from the village. What sort of an establishment is that?' She was beside herself with rage, oblivious to the effect she was having on Léon.

'If the worst comes to the worst,' he said coldly, 'I myself will help with the serving. It is not beyond my capabilities.' And so could you, his look said.

'You can't possibly!' she protested. 'How would it look?'

'Does that matter?' he asked.

Mrs Parkinson came back into the dining-room.

'Poor Emerald! I can imagine how she feels. I know how I felt when I fell and broke my ankle.'

'But how are we going to manage? What about my party?' Sophia insisted.

'We shall manage, that's all,' Mrs Parkinson said. 'And I'm sorry to see that your attitude is exactly as it was when I had my accident. You thought only of how it would affect you.'

'But it's my birthday!' Sophia wailed. 'It really isn't fair.'

'Léon, would you be kind enough to carry Emerald up to her bed?' Mrs Parkinson asked. 'Since Drake has gone off for the doctor.'

'Of course!'

Emerald lay back in Monsieur Bonneau's arms as he carried her up the two flights of stairs to her attic room, followed close behind by Mrs Parkinson. If it were not for the pain, which was really quite nasty, this would be a taste of heaven.

'If you please, ma'am,' she said to Mrs Parkinson when Monsieur Bonneau had laid her, oh so gently, on the bed, 'if you please, ma'am, you could ask Madeleine if she'd come in my place, just for the evening.'

'Why, so I could! Madeleine would know exactly what to

do. Now who shall I send? The moment Drake gets back he has to take my husband to an important appointment. And Mrs Thomas is up to her eyes.'

'Look no further,' Léon said. 'I will go with pleasure.'

When Mrs Parkinson and Léon joined the others downstairs Mrs Parkinson said, 'Emerald has suggested that we should ask Madeleine to come and help us out.'

'Well, I'm not going to fetch her,' Sophia broke in quickly. 'I wouldn't set foot in Priestley Street at any price. Nasty horrid place – who knows what I might catch?'

'Who knows, indeed,' Léon said smoothly. 'But don't worry, Sophia. I have already arranged to go.'

'Oh!' She looked confused, dropped on. 'I didn't mean . . . that is, if you would like me to —'

'To go instead of me?' Léon interrupted.

'Well, no . . . that is . . .'

'I wouldn't dream of it,' he said. 'I am quite happy to go alone – and I am not in the least afraid of catching anything!'

Anger surged in Sophia: against Emerald for falling, against her father for not employing enough servants, against her mother for wasting sympathy on Emerald – even against Léon, who had wrong-footed her – but anger also against the whole world which was treating her so badly. She stood in the window and watched Léon set off, walking briskly down the drive. She could have been with him. She could have had all of twenty minutes alone with him had she not played her cards so badly.

Léon was glad to be out of the house, especially relieved to be away from Sophia, who on this occasion had excelled herself. If he had needed anything to strengthen his resolve to speak to her on marriage, or rather on the impossibility of their marriage, she had given it to him with both hands.

It was the first time Léon had seen Priestley Street; mean, drab, reeking of poverty. No doubt there were streets like it in Roubaix, perhaps not built in such long straight lines as these in Helsdon, perhaps not so monotonous, with the stone so smoke-darkened; but equally poor, and equally crowded with small children playing in the puddles left from yesterday's rain, and the older children playing hopscotch, or whatever the French equivalent was.

He stepped carefully around a hopscotch game, chalked on the pavement. The children, even the one who was standing on one foot, stopped what they were doing to stare at him. He was a bit of a swank for Priestley Street.

'I'm looking for the Bates's house,' he said. 'I don't know the number.'

A couple of the children giggled at the sound of his accent, but an older girl pointed down the street.

'Number eight, mister! Down yon end.'

There were clean curtains at the windows of number eight and the brass door knocker was polished. While he waited for the door to be answered he hoped that Mr Bates wouldn't be at home. Joseph Bates he had found to be good at his job, but he was a surly tyrant, with seldom a kind word for anyone.

The woman who came to the door was so like Emerald that he knew at once he was at the right house.

'Mrs Bates?'

'Yes.'

'I have come from Mount Royd. . .'

She gave a little cry.

'Something's happened to our Emerald.'

'Oh no, Mrs Bates – or at least nothing serious. She has fallen and twisted her knee, but otherwise she is quite well.'

Madeleine heard him and came to the door. She was in her mill clothes, not long home.

'This is Monsieur Bonneau, Ma.'

'Oh! I beg your pardon, sir! Won't you please come in?'

He was aware of two things as he entered the house. The first was the obvious poverty, linked with an austerity that he was sure came from Mr Bates – only one armchair, the rest hard and upright; no cushions, no ornaments, no pictures, only texts, on the walls; one rag rug on the stone

229

floor. Surely they were not so poor, with Joseph Bates a weaving overlooker? The second thing which struck him was the utter cleanliness of everything – the floor flags swept, the deal table scrubbed white, not a speck of dust anywhere.

'Please sit down, sir.' Mrs Bates motioned him to the armchair. Madeleine stood at the other side of the table, waiting in silence for him to speak.

'Well,' he said. 'I'm sorry to say that Emerald has twisted her knee. The doctor was fetched and there is nothing seriously wrong, but she will be off her feet for a few days.'

'Oh dear! Shall we need to get her home then?' Mrs Bates asked.

'Not at all. She is as comfortable as possible where she is, and will be well looked after. No, I came at Emerald's own suggestion to ask if Madeleine would do the favour of taking her sister's place, just for this evening. As I daresay you know, it's Miss Sophia's birthday and there is to be a party. Mrs Parkinson had counted heavily on poor Emerald to help with the refreshments and other things.'

Mrs Bates looked at her daughter.

'What do you say, love? Will you go?' She knew her daughter was tired after a week standing at the loom. But it was difficult to refuse a request from Mount Royd. They were more or less beholden to them.

To her own surprise, for when she'd left she'd wanted never to set foot in Mount Royd again, Madeleine quite liked the idea. Being a party, it would be more interesting than staying at home, and certainly a sight more cheerful. She could do with cheering up. Also she'd get something nice to eat and a shilling or two in her pocket.

'I would come,' she said. 'But I don't have a suitable dress. The one I used to wear is in the wash and Emerald's won't fit me at all. I only have my dark green one.'

'If that is the dress you wore in Paris,' Léon said, 'I'm sure it will do admirably.' Does that mean I looked like a servant in Paris? Madeleine asked herself. No matter. She would wear it and she would go.

'Mrs Parkinson said I should tell you that there would be a bed for the night. You would have no need to return home until tomorrow's daylight.'

'Very well,' Madeleine said. 'Please tell Mrs Parkinson that I'll be there shortly after you. I only have to change.'

'Then in that case I will wait for you and we can walk back together,' Léon said.

She didn't want to walk back with him, she thought as they set off together. She would rather have been on her own. She saw him quite often in the mill because Mrs Barnet was working on his designs, and recently she herself had begun to do so, now that she was more skilled. She got on well enough with him, but there was never much conversation between them; just the time of day and an occasional instruction. Mostly he conversed with her father or with Mrs Barnet. But she'd found it easy to talk to him in Paris, hadn't she? Anyway, Paris was one thing, Helsdon was quite another. Things had changed.

'Is Miss Sophia enjoying her birthday?' She was fishing around for things to say.

'I'm not so sure,' Léon said, smiling. 'She was rather upset by your sister's accident.'

But not for Emerald's sake, Madeleine reckoned. That was for certain. She didn't look forward to meeting up with Miss Sophia again, but in so short a time she needn't have much to do with her.

She wondered if the rumour was true – Emerald had brought it home with her – that Sophia and Monsieur Bonneau would announce their engagement today. It wouldn't surprise her. Miss Sophia had had wedding bells in her ears since the moment she'd set eyes on Monsieur Bonneau – and she usually got what she wanted. Well, she was welcome. I shall never marry now, Madeleine thought. Never.

'We can take a short cut between those houses,' she said presently. 'It chops five minutes off the time.'

Léon glanced sideways at her. She looked better than when he'd first returned to Helsdon last November, less anxious; but she was still too quiet, too subdued. He had watched her in the mill as she stood at her loom. She was pleasant enough, she clearly got on well with Mrs Barnet and the other girls but, caught unawares, she had a withdrawn look.

'When is your birthday, Madeleine?' he asked.

'It was in April, sir.'

'And am I permitted to ask how old you are?'

'Nineteen. Just a month older than Miss Sophia.'

And there all similarity ends, he thought.

They had left the houses behind now and were walking over the field path. When they came to the stile he went over first, then turned and held her wrist to help her down. At his touch, she jerked her hand away from him as if she had been stung, and when their eyes met the stark fear in hers shocked him, so that for a second he stared at her in disbelief. After that they walked the rest of the way to Mount Royd without speaking, and when they reached the house and he went in at the front door, Madeleine left him and continued around to the back. It was just starting to rain.

Half an hour later, Madeleine entered the drawing-room with a message for Mrs Parkinson. Sophia, a sulky look on her face, was staring out of the window at the rain, now coming down in torrents. Léon was sitting on the sofa, reading the Bradford *Observer*, as if nothing mattered.

'Mrs Thomas says could you spare her a minute in the kitchen, ma'am? It's a question of when to serve the trifle, I think. And one or two other things.'

Sophia turned around and looked at Madeleine.

'What in the world are you doing, wearing a green dress?' she asked sharply. 'Green is not the colour for a maid to wear when she's serving in the house.'

Madeleine met Sophia's rude stare boldly. She was independent of this spoilt girl now. She had nothing more

232

to fear than a tongue-lashing, and that she could cope with – indeed if it came to a contest she could give as good as she got, but for the sake of Mr and Mrs Parkinson.

'I'm sorry, Miss Sophia, I don't have anything more suitable. You see, I'm not a maid now!' That she couldn't resist.

'Of course not! I forgot. You're a mill-girl!' There was the utmost contempt in Sophia's voice.

Madeleine tilted her chin, clenched her fists. She was tempted, oh yes she was tempted! She was tempted to say, 'I helped to make the money that clothed you in that fine dress.' Instead she spoke politely, though the look she gave Sophia was scathing.

'That's right, miss. I'm a mill-girl now!'

'Tell Mrs Thomas I'll be with her at once,' Mrs Parkinson said nervously. Really, she didn't know what had got into Sophia. She was being very naughty.

Thank heaven for a few minutes alone with Léon, Sophia thought when her mother had left the room. But there was no sense in staying in the drawing-room. Her mother would be back in no time at all. Not only that, but Aunt Fanny Chester and cousin David were due any minute now. David had taken a weekend away from his school especially to be present on her birthday, and they were both to arrive before the party proper. What a bore it was, and how sickening that the rain continued to pour out of a most unseasonably leaden sky.

'Why don't we move into the conservatory?' she said pleasantly to Léon. 'Any minute now we shall be surrounded by relatives. I know you'll hate that as much as I shall!'

She was flattered by the alacrity with which Léon rose to his feet.

'Certainly, my dear.'

It was now or never! She was right about the relatives. He absolutely had to get things straight before they arrived. When she led the way to the conservatory he followed.

'How delicious it smells in here,' Sophia enthused. 'I do so love flowers, above all else. And Léon, let me thank you again for my beautiful rose.' She touched it again where it lay, now drooping a little, against her bosom. 'Time may wither it, but I shall keep it always; I shall press it in my bible.'

'You are very kind,' Léon said swiftly. 'I hope it will remind you of me when I am gone!'

'GONE!' She shrieked the word at him in fear and trembling. He wasn't . . . he couldn't be . . . 'Are you ill?' she cried.

'Ill? Of course not! Oh my dear little Sophia I didn't mean "gone" in that sense. What a little goose you are! I meant when I have gone back to France, which must be soon, now.'

'Gone back to France? But I thought . . .'

Clearly he was talking about a visit he must make. Of course, that was it. He would have to tell his family about her. 'But you won't be away long? Léon, please say you won't be absent long, that you'll return quickly!'

He took her by the arms and turned her gently towards him. She raised her beautiful eyes to meet his, opened her mouth slightly, put out a pink tongue to lick her dry lips, then swayed a little towards him.

'I shall not return, *chère* Sophia,' he said softly. 'I cannot do so.'

She jerked away, stood back and stared at him.

'You mean . . .?' What *could* he mean? 'I don't understand.'

'I'm afraid,' he said sadly, 'there is someone in France who waits for me.'

The idea had come to him in a flash of inspiration, but God forgive me for the lie, he thought. Still, it was the kindest way. No need to tell Sophia that he wouldn't marry her if she was draped in diamonds.

'But I thought . . . you and I . . .? You never mentioned another.'

'And in that I was gravely at fault,' he said. 'But I am

bound to her by the strongest ties. It has been arranged so since we were children.'

'But surely . . .?' She cast around for the smallest hope.

'No, Sophia, for you and me it will all too soon be farewell! But I shall always remember that you have my rose!'

Anger, blinding anger, came to her aid, taking over swiftly from bitter disappointment. She tore the rose from her bosom and flung it at his feet.

'That much for your rose!' she cried. 'And that much for you, you two-faced, horrible monster!'

Then she burst into loud tears, turned and ran out of the conservatory and up the stairs to her bedroom, passing her astonished mother on the way.

'What ever has got into the child?' Mrs Parkinson said out loud.

Twenty minutes later Madeleine came to Sophia's room.

'Excuse me, Miss Sophia. The Mistress says would I tell you that your aunt and cousin have arrived. She'd be obliged if you'd come down.'

She's been crying, Madeleine thought. Her eyes are all swollen and red. But she couldn't feel sorry for her. It was no doubt another of her temper tantrums, something she wanted and couldn't have.

'I'll be down in a few minutes,' Sophia said sullenly.

She bathed her eyes and tidied her hair. Looking at herself in the mirror, she pinched at her cheeks and bit her lips to make them less pale. Then she drew herself up to her full five feet and squared her shoulders. She'd show them! She'd show them all – especially *him*. Oh, the monster! She loathed him! But if he thought he could get her down, he was mistaken. If he thought he was the only pebble on the beach, he'd soon know different.

With head held high and a bright smile on her face which cost her a great deal of effort, and with the hope in her heart that the swelling around her eyes was not too noticeable, she went downstairs and entered the drawing-room. No one, but no one, must suspect that anything was the least bit amiss.

For a moment all eyes were on her. There was a short silence and then everyone began to speak at once.

'Happy birthday, Sophia love,' Mrs Chester said. 'Come and give your old aunt a kiss, then!'

Sophia pecked her aunt on the cheek, then turned to her cousin David, who was standing with his hand out-stretched.

'Happy birthday, Sophia!' He took her hand in his but, to his great surprise, she leaned forward and kissed him. Well, she *was* his cousin, but she wasn't in the habit of kissing him. He flushed with pleasure.

'Thank you, David. And thank you for taking the weekend off to come for my birthday. I can't tell you what it means to me!' Nor could she, for until a few minutes ago she hadn't given it a thought. But in fact, she supposed, he was quite nice; rather good-looking in his fair, English way; always very attentive.

The two sisters looked at each other with raised eye-brows. Mrs Parkinson shrugged her shoulders. She wished she could understand this daughter of hers for ten minutes together.

'I've brought you a present,' David Chester said. 'I hope you like it!'

It was a shawl of the finest cream cashmere, deeply fringed.

'Why, it's beautiful, David!' she enthused. She crossed to the mirror, draped the shawl around her shoulders, pirouetted this way and that. Of course it didn't really go with her dress and she would never have chosen it, but that couldn't be helped.

'I shall wear it from this minute on,' she promised. 'Thank you a thousand times, David!'

David was wreathed in pleasure; he had never had such success with a present before. Sophia was not the easiest person in the world to please, but he'd clearly done it this time.

'And this is my present,' Léon Bonneau said, handing her a small packet, beautifully wrapped. It was not now, since they were not to be affianced, appropriate. It was too expensive. But there had been no time to exchange it for something else.

'Oh do open it!' her aunt cried.

Sophia tore off the wrapping and threw it to the floor. Inside a white velvet box was a necklace of exquisitely enamelled links of green, blue and gold. It was beautiful – but she controlled her pleasure at the sight of it, remaining stony-faced. For a fleeting moment she thought of the diamond ring she had expected – and then put the thought from her mind, and the necklace from her hands, on to the sofa table.

'Thank you,' she said. 'It's very pretty.'

If he thought she was going to wear it he was mistaken. She would never do so. She would like to have thrown it in his face.

When she had opened her aunt's present – a book she would never read – and her parents' – a gold bracelet – she turned to her cousin.

'The rain has stopped, David. Shall we take a turn in the garden? It's still daylight. And it's so long since you were here.' She took his arm, clinging to him as they left the room.

So that's it, Léon thought, watching them go. She is trying jealousy. But it won't work.

Hanging on his arm, Sophia walked around with David Chester until they reached the far corner of the garden where there was a seat, hidden from the house. Putting out of her mind that she had so often sat here with Léon, and the compliments he had paid her then, she drew David towards it and they sat down.

'I have missed you so much, cousin David,' she said. 'I had no idea, until you went away, how much I . . .' she hesitated.

237

'Yes, dear cousin?'

'How much I depended on you. You've always been there, David. You've always been such a support. And when you left . . .'

'Absence makes the heart grow fonder!' he said.

'Indeed it does!'

He could scarcely believe his ears, scarcely credit his good fortune. In all the time he had been teaching those wretched boys in Thirsk there had never been a day when he hadn't thought of his beautiful cousin – but always in the belief that he wouldn't be in *her* mind for a minute. Now she was telling him that she had actually missed him, was glad to see him back! It was a miracle!

'Can I believe . . .?' he began.

'What, cousin David?' Her hand was on his arm, she was gazing at him so that he felt he was swimming in her soft eyes.

'Oh Sophia! Sophia, you know how I've always cared for you. You must know . . .'

'I dared to hope,' she murmured.

For a second he stared at her in astonishment, then he took his courage in both hands. There would never be a better moment.

'If I never asked you to marry me it was because I couldn't bear the thought of your refusal . . .,' he began.

Then with one swift movement he was on his knees on the wet grass.

'Sophia, will you marry me? Oh say you will! Say we can be engaged. Make me the happiest man in the universe!'

There was a smile of triumph on her face as she took both his hands in hers and started to pull him to his feet. In her wildest dreams she could not have believed that it would be so easy. In that moment she put all thoughts and dreams of Léon Bonneau away from her.

She didn't doubt that she and David would get on quite well. He doted on her; he'd always let her have her own way. And she'd be delighted to get away from Helsdon, the sooner the better, away from all those people who had

238

expected her to marry Léon Bonneau. She and David would settle in Thirsk. They'd have a nice little house and she'd be her own mistress. Anything was preferable to reaching the age of nineteen without even being engaged, let alone married.

'I *will* marry you,' she said. 'But if you don't get up from the wet grass you'll have pneumonia on your wedding day! And we can be married quite soon, can't we David? There's no reason to wait.'

'You know that's what I want, dearest,' he said. 'But there is the question of . . . well . . . money. As yet I don't earn much, though later I'll do better.'

'Oh, you don't have to worry about that for one minute,' she assured him. 'Papa will see to all that. Why, I daresay he'll buy you your own school, if that is what you'd like! So let's go in and tell the others. We both know how pleased our families will be.'

For a few seconds there was an astonished silence when, hand-in-hand with Sophia, a stammering yet proud David made the announcement. Then everyone seemingly recovered and the confused hearers voiced their congratulations.

You poor devil! Léon thought, eyeing David Chester. You poor, innocent devil!

Sophia was pink with excitement. Her eyes, meeting Léon's briefly before she looked away again, glittered with triumph. No wonder you are blushing, he thought. No wonder!

'We want to marry quite soon,' Sophia said, darting a coy glance at her new fiancé.

'So eager, dear children!' Mrs Chester gushed.

It was more than she'd ever hoped for, certainly much more than she'd expected. Sophia wouldn't be an easy daughter-in-law, she was only too aware of that; but Sophia was what her son had always wanted, and if she could have, Mrs Chester would have given him the sun and moon on a plate.

Mrs Parkinson hardly knew what was happening. It was

239

the last announcement she had ever expected to hear. She glanced across at her husband, who looked as confused as she felt.

When, a little later, Sophia went up to her room, Mrs Parkinson followed.

'I don't understand, Sophia,' she said. 'It's all so sudden. I thought . . . I was almost sure . . . that you and Léon . . .'

Sophia rounded on her mother.

'Me and Léon Bonneau?' she cried. 'Why, what ever can you be thinking of? I've never, ever felt that way about Léon!'

'I don't think I shall ever understand you,' her mother murmured. 'I just hope you're doing the right thing, that's all.'

'Of course I am, Mama! David and I will be very happy together. All you have to do is persuade Papa to let us marry soon. We thought the middle of June, as soon as David's term ends.'

'But that's only a month away!' Mrs Parkinson protested.

'I know,' Sophia agreed. 'But who wants a long engagement?'

When Mrs Parkinson told her husband he shook his head in disbelief.

'I can't fathom the girl,' he said. 'David's a nice enough lad; upright, honest, kind. But I don't see him being a match for Sophia.' She'll run rings around him, he thought.

'Well she seems quite sure of herself,' Mrs Parkinson said. 'And certainly it's what David has always wanted. That being the case, and if you give your consent, I suppose there's no reason why they shouldn't be married in June.'

To tell the truth, she would be quite relieved to have Sophia married and in her own home. After that perhaps she and her husband could settle down to a peaceful existence.

'Very well,' Albert Parkinson said.

The intervening weeks for Sophia and her mother were rush, rush, rush. Every time Emerald came home to Priestley Street it was with news of some arrangement or other: bridesmaids, ushers, the reception, the bridal gown.

'It must be costing Mr Parkinson a fortune,' she said.

'Well he's a very generous man. He never stints,' Madeleine said. 'And I daresay he can afford it.'

'Me and Mrs Thomas are to be allowed to go to the wedding,' Emerald said. 'We're to sit at the back of the church and slip out before the ceremony's over, so as to be in time to help at the reception.'

'I hope all goes well on the day,' Mrs Bates said.

All did go well. The sun shone. The bride looked beautiful. If there were those in the congregation, which included Léon Bonneau, who wondered what that minx Sophia Parkinson was doing marrying her mild-mannered cousin David, and at such short notice, then no one was impolite enough to say anything.

In a few days' time, Albert Parkinson thought as he circulated amongst his guests, I shall be in London. He had written to Kitty to tell her he was coming. He could hardly wait to see her. He knew there was no fool like an old fool, but some days now he just couldn't get her out of his mind.

THIRTEEN

'Meet the train on Thursday afternoon. Mind you're not late.'

Albert Parkinson was speaking to Drake, who had driven him over from Helsdon to Leeds.

'I'll not be late, sir!' Drake promised.

The Master had no call to say that. He was never late, not unless something went wrong with one of the horses, which wasn't his fault. But he'd been a bit tetchy lately, the Master. Not his usual self. Maybe he'd come back from London in a better frame of mind. Drake handed the luggage to one of the porters hovering near the carriage.

'The London train,' he instructed.

'Corner seat, back to he engine,' Albert added.

Minutes later he settled into the seat, glanced briefly at his fellow passengers, of whom there were only two. One, a man sitting opposite, held a watch in his hand, which he consulted, nodding approvingly as they drew out of Leeds station.

'We're leaving on time,' he said with satisfaction.

'Good!' Albert replied.

There was someone like this on every train journey. The man would sit with his watch in his hand all the way to London, scrupulously timing every section; and no doubt when they got out in London he'd go and examine the engine. Well let's hope he doesn't talk about it all the way, Albert thought, settling himself behind the *Yorkshire Post*.

His reading was perfunctory; he couldn't concentrate on the close-printed columns, couldn't settle to it at all. Perhaps later.

The truth was, he was too excited at the thought of seeing Kitty again after all these months. When he tried to read, the memory of her lovely face came between him and the print. He had longed for her, and now in a few hours he would see her. But what a silly old fool he was; pining like a lad, mooning worse than a love-sick calf! He folded the newspaper and laid it on the seat beside him, then he closed his eyes and let the rhythm of the train take over, beating through his body.

Quite apart from Kitty, though, he was glad to be leaving Helsdon for a while. It hadn't been an easy year so far, and with Sophia's wedding on top of everything else, it had been an expensive one. Ostensibly, he was going to London for the wool sales, and of course he'd call in, meet a few people, but this time he couldn't afford to buy. He couldn't go to the bank yet again. They wouldn't stand for it.

Anyway, he'd not think about that now. He was going to have a wonderful time, during which he wouldn't give so much as a thought to what was going on in Helsdon. He settled further back into his seat and, after a little while, fell asleep. When he opened his eyes the man opposite was still holding up his watch.

'Doncaster!' he exclaimed. 'We're making good time!'

'Fine!' Albert replied. The sooner they got to London the better.

From the station he took a cab straight to his hotel. He had written to Kitty to tell her he was coming and had suggested taking her out to dinner that same night. There was no way she could let him know, but he hoped it would be all right. He hoped also to be able to spend much of the day with her tomorrow, and an hour or so before he left for home on the following day. He would have liked them to have spent the nights together but it was something, so far, she wouldn't hear of.

At a quarter to seven he rang for a whisky. He was unaccountably nervous. Supposing he wasn't welcome? Supposing she had grown tired of him – and why shouldn't she? He was nothing special: a middle-aged Yorkshireman; all right; smart enough, not bad-looking a nervous glance in the mirror told him – but nothing special.

When the whisky came he poured himself a stiff one and said to the waiter, 'Ask someone to call me a cab. I want to go to Richmond.'

An hour later, sitting in Kitty's drawing-room, he wondered why he had worried. Nothing could have been warmer than the welcome she'd given him, greeting him with a wide smile, eyes sparkling. Within seconds they had been in each other's arms.

'Eeh, Kitty lass, I've missed you!' Albert said. Emotion, as always, intensified his Yorkshire accent.

'And I you, Albert! It's been a long time, too long.'

'I shall see to it that it's never so long again. You can count on that!'

'Come and sit down, my dear,' she said. 'Are you tired after your long journey?'

'I was,' he admitted. 'But not any longer. Not once I've seen you.'

He seated himself in the armchair and she sat on the rug at his feet, leaning back against him. He stroked her hair, feeling the silkiness of it, noting the way the lamplight brought up the gold lights in the rich brown. Contentment wrapped him around like a blanket.

Presently Kitty said, 'Need we dine out, Albert? Wouldn't it be nice to stay here? I could make an omelette if that would suit you.'

'It would suit me down to the ground,' Albert said. 'I just thought you might like to go out.'

'Perhaps tomorrow evening. But for this evening it would be nice to be alone, I think. You shall open the champagne you so thoughtfully sent!'

244

And now they were drinking it, from elegant crystal glasses.

'Everything in your little house,' he said, holding the glass up to the light, 'is elegant and graceful. A perfect setting for its owner!'

She smiled with pleasure at his compliment.

'I hope the wine is chilled enough for you. It only arrived a short time before you did.'

'It's perfect!'

The truth was, he hardly cared. It was so wonderful to be here that a glass of cold water would have tasted like nectar.

But before they had finished the second glass he drew her into his arms again, and this time she took his hand and led him upstairs to her bedroom.

'How can it be?' he said in wonderment, after they had made love. 'How is it possible that a woman like you – so rare, so special – can love someone like me? You do love me, don't you Kitty?'

'You know I do, Albert.'

'I can't for the life of me think why,' he said.

'If anyone else said that they'd be fishing for compliments,' she told him. 'But not you, my dear. Never you! Why do you not believe that you are lovable?'

She traced the outlines of his face with her finger, smiled into his eyes.

'The truth is,' she said, 'I don't know why I love you. You're kind, thoughtful, generous. When we make love you're powerful and exciting – yes, I mean that! But it isn't for any of these things that I love you. It's because you are you. I love the essence of you.

> '"And love me still but know not why
> So hast thou the same reason still
> To dote upon me ever!"'

'Who wrote that?' he asked.

'No one knows. But that's how I love you, Albert.'

'I'm the luckiest man in the world,' he said quietly.

Later, she made an omelette, which they ate in front of the fire – and then it was time for him to leave.

'You know I don't want to go,' he said. 'Kitty, just this once, couldn't I stay?'

She shook her head.

'Don't think I don't want you to, my love. That's far from being the case. It's just that – don't laugh at me, will you – there are some things which belong only to marriage, and to wake up in the morning with your man beside you is one of them. Perhaps it's a strange notion on my part, and I know it makes what I do allow illogical, but it's the way I feel.'

'Very well,' he said. 'I might not understand that, but I'll respect it because I respect you.'

'Come tomorrow the minute you are through with the wool sales,' Kitty said. 'We shall have the rest of the day and all the evening together.'

Albert spent only a little time at the wool sales next morning, greeted a few friends and acquaintances, made no bids.

'How is it you're not bidding, Parkinson?' one of them asked him. 'Do you know summat we don't?'

'That would be telling!' he said.

The last thing he wanted anyone to know was how hard-pressed he was. There were samples at the sales he'd dearly have liked to bid for, but what credit he could raise, with difficulty, would have to be saved for the tops; dyeing the tops for Léon Bonneau's new patterns. They were coming on fine. The hope in Albert's heart was that the new pieces, unlike anything anyone else was turning out in the West Riding, would take on. They had to find the markets. They were beginning to open up, but there was a long way to go.

'Tell me about this young Frenchman,' Kitty said that afternoon.

They had eaten lunch and were sitting in the garden in the warm June sunshine.

'He's a very clever young man,' Albert acknowledged.

'Very clever. I wasn't so sure I wanted him to come to Helsdon; I invited him on the spur of the moment. But I'm glad he did. He's going to make a difference. I've got two weavers – one of them a girl who used to be our parlourmaid – turning out some lovely stuff from his designs. The only thing is . . .' He hesitated.

'Yes?'

'Well . . . I'm not sure his visit's done my daughter any good.'

'In what way?'

'She fell for him. Oh, nothing was said, and she denies it now, but it stuck out a mile. And when Sophia wants something she thinks she can have it, just like that! She goes at it bull-headed, which is enough to frighten any man off!'

'But she's married now?'

'Yes. But too quickly. All decided and done in a rush. And is her Cousin David the right man? He's wanted her ever since she was a little lass, but I suspect she married him on the rebound. Still, as in everything else, there was no holding her once she'd made up her mind. And in a way I'm glad to have her married. I confess, Kitty, I don't really know how to deal with my daughter. I think somehow we've brought her up wrong.'

'Perhaps it will turn out for the best,' Kitty said. 'I hope so.'

'Happen it will. But never mind that, I didn't come all this way to talk about Sophia. Now love, what would you like to do this afternoon?'

'Anything you like, Albert dear. There's an exhibition in Richmond by a new young painter. Would you care to see that?'

'Why not, eh?'

He liked paintings. Sometimes he thought he'd have liked to have been a painter; mixed the colours, applied them to the canvas one against the other to build up the picture. There was a little bit of the same thing in blending wool to make cloth, especially when you saw what young Bonneau could do. His patterns glowed with colour. Sometimes the designs stood out almost as if they'd been painted.

They were halfway around the exhibition when they saw the painting and even from several feet away the colours sang out to them. But it was not only the colours, the deep, brilliant yet soft purples, pinks and greens, which spoke to Albert.

'Why, it's the Yorkshire moors!' he exclaimed. 'It's for all the world like the moor just above Helsdon! I could swear to it!'

'It's beautiful! It's quite beautiful! Just look at the heather! Is it really so picturesque?'

'Every bit,' Albert said. 'Oh Kitty, I wish I could show it to you! When the heather's in bloom it's like a great big sheet of colour thrown over the ground, as far as the eye can see!'

'Let's ask the gallery owner what he knows about the painting,' Kitty suggested.

'It *is* Yorkshire moorland,' the gallery owner said. 'Though just where I've no idea.'

'Well I dare say it could be any bit of it,' Albert conceded. 'But it looks mighty like Helsdon moor to me. How much are you asking for it?'

'Ten guineas.'

Albert turned to Kitty. 'Would you like it then? Would you like to have it?'

'Oh Albert, of course I would!' She flushed with pleasure. 'But it's frightfully expensive.'

'Never mind that. I shouldn't have asked the price in front of you. But there's a Yorkshireman for you. No tact!'

He turned to the gallery owner.

'Have someone wrap it up, then, and we'll take it with us.'

'Please hang it for me,' Kitty said when they were back in the house. 'I would like it in the drawing-room, on the wall by the mantlepiece. That way I shall be able to look up from my chair and see it, and it will remind me of you.'

She fetched him the tools and he hung it there and then. They both stepped back to look at it.

'It's perfect!' Kitty cried. 'It's quite perfect!'

'Not bad,' Albert conceded. 'Not at all bad. Not as good as the real thing, but quite nice. Anyway, I'm glad you like it, love. I promise you I shall come to see it every time I'm in London!'

'I shall hold you to that,' Kitty said.

In the early evening, before they went out to dinner, they made love again; unhurried and perfect. In the restaurant, between courses, they held hands under cover of the tablecloth.

'Like two young kids!' Albert said.

After dinner he saw her back to the house but she refused to ask him in.

' . . . and now you must go,' she said, kissing him tenderly. 'But I shall see you again tomorrow, however briefly.'

He planned to call on her immediately after breakfast, before he went for his train.

'In the meantime I shall look at my painting and think about you,' she said.

Dusk was falling, the long June day was almost over, when Kitty closed the door on Albert and he began to walk down the street, looking for a cab to take him back to the hotel.

He had gone less than a dozen yards when he heard the noise behind him: the sharp clatter of horse's hooves, the iron-rimmed wheels on the cobbles, the screams of terror. What he did then, he did without thought. There was nothing more in his mind than that somehow he must grab the reins of the runaway horse before the carriage it was pulling, and the people in the carriage, were overturned.

He turned swiftly and saw the horse bearing down on him at full gallop, dragging the swaying, tilting carriage behind it. He was dimly aware that the driver had lost the reins and that there were two women, both of them screaming, hanging on to the carriage for dear life.

All this he saw and heard in the split second before he leapt for the harness, grabbing it where he could, trying with all his strength to slow the animal down.

The horse was fresh and strong. It was also frightened. For several yards it dragged Albert along the street, bumping and banging him against the cobbles, until the harness slipped from his hands and he fell in front of the animal, stopping it in its tracks, but not before the full weight of its hoof had descended on his head. A second later the carriage banged into the back of the horse, and came to a stop, Albert's inert body lay in the road.

Kitty, hearing the screams in the street, ran out of the house.

'What is it? What's happened?'

'An accident, ma'am,' someone said.

In the confusion, it was the two women who had been in the carriage whom Kitty saw first. Onlookers had lifted them down to the pavement, seated them there, leaning against a house wall. A small crowd clustered around them. To all appearances they seemed unhurt, but the elder of the two was crying hysterically.

'He saved our lives! He saved our lives!'

'There now!' a man said. 'Don't you fret, lady. A gentleman has gone to fetch the ambulance.'

'Is he dead? Oh please say he's not dead?'

It was perhaps the thought of Albert Parkinson still fresh in Kitty's mind that accounted for the wave of sickness which suddenly engulfed her. In a flash, she left the women and ran to where the injured man lay, pushing her way through the crowd which had gathered.

'Let me through! Let me through!'

He was unconscious, and bleeding profusely. She knelt beside him on the ground and cradled his head in her lap, his blood staining her gown. With the hem of her petticoat she tried in vain to staunch the blood. It was an eternity before the sound of more horses heralded the arrival of the ambulance. When it came they lifted him in gently and, without asking anyone's leave, Kitty climbed in beside him.

'Poor lady, she must be his wife!' someone said.

In the ambulance she knelt by his side, anxiously watching the face so close to her own, stroking his matted hair. Then, at a moment when she feared he was entirely lost to her, he opened his eyes, and knew her.

He knew at once that there was very little time. Painfully, he moved his lips and she bent over to catch the words, so faintly spoken.

'I love you, Kitty!'

'I love you, Albert. Always!'

Her words were the last sound he heard. The ambulance had not quite reached the hospital before she knew he was gone from her. Her tears fell on his dead face and his life's blood soaked her skirt.

'Are you his wife?' they asked her in the hospital.

'No.'

It occurred to her, hazily, that someone would have to inform his wife, bring her from Helsdon. That being so, there was only one thing she could now do for Albert.

'No. I don't know him.' The denial pierced her to the heart. 'I just heard the noise and ran out into the street!'

'Oh forgive me, my darling Albert!' But the cry was inside her. It could not be allowed to reach her lips.

'It was good of you to come with him in the ambulance,' the nurse said. 'We'll find someone to take you home.'

When she reached her home a bloodstain on the cobbles was the only sign that anything untoward had happened. Everything else was back to normal. The two women, she thought, would perhaps never know who it was had saved their lives.

Albert Parkinson's identity was quickly established from a card in his pocket, which also bore the name of the hotel where he was staying. Thus, by the next day Mrs Parkinson had received a telegram in Helsdon, and from

251

there Drake was sent to fetch Sophia and David from their honeymoon in the Lake District.

'I shall most definitely accompany you to London,' David Chester said to his mother-in-law, 'though it would be better for Sophia not to do so. There will be the question of . . .' He stopped himself.

'Of identification, you mean? I am prepared for that,' Mrs Parkinson said quietly.

'And I would not for one moment allow you to endure it,' David said. 'That is one thing at least that I can spare you. But Sophia should stay at home with my mother and Roger.'

He dreaded the ordeal before him. He knew he wasn't a brave man. But duty was duty, and that he hoped he had never shirked. Besides, he was doing it also for his lovely Sophia, who, unlike her mother, had completely gone to pieces and had taken to her bed. But if such a terrible thing had to happen, he thought – and the thought consoled him a little – it was as well it had happened in the school holidays. He had not had to ask the Headmaster for leave, which would have been unwillingly granted. And poor young Roger was already at home.

'I could go, Mama,' Roger said uncertainly. 'I suppose I'm the man of the family now.' But at fifteen he didn't feel much like a man. In the last few hours he had felt suddenly a child.

'No need, Roger,' David said. 'I shall be the one. After all, I've been to London before. I know my way around.'

It was even worse than he had expected. He emerged from the ordeal of identifying his poor uncle's body white and shaken, trying hard not to be sick.

'Was he . . . was he badly mutilated?' Mrs Parkinson asked stonily. She must keep a tight hold on herself. Emotion, of which she had plenty dammed up inside her, would have to wait.

'No, Aunt,' he lied. 'He was not. Remarkably not.'

'I was told while I was waiting for you that a lady came

252

with Albert in the ambulance. I think I would like to see her,' Mrs Parkinson said. 'Shall we enquire if I might?'

'A lady?' He frowned.

'Oh, a stranger I believe. But it was a kind act and I should like to thank her. It appears the hospital has her name and address because a member of the staff took her home. She lives in Richmond.'

'Well, if you think it wise, Aunt,' David said. 'If you think we have the time.'

'I would like to see her,' Mrs Parkinson said. 'But there is no need for you to accompany me, David. I know you have other formalities to attend to.' Like sending my poor Albert's body back to Helsdon, she thought.

Standing on the doorstep, waiting for Mrs Shane to answer the bell, Mrs Parkinson wondered, not for the first time, what could have brought her husband to Richmond. It was a long way from the City. When Kitty Shane opened the door and saw the woman standing there she knew at once who it was. Though Albert had never described his wife, she had no doubt at all. I must be careful, she thought. For his sake *and* his wife's I must be careful.

'I'm sorry to trouble you,' Mrs Parkinson began. 'You won't know me. I am Mrs Albert Parkinson. You were . . . you were kind to my husband, I believe.'

Kitty Shane looked at the short, plump little woman, provincially dressed, standing on her doorstep. What did she know? What did those words mean?

'Please come in, Mrs Parkinson,' she said.

She led the way through the hall and into the drawing-room.

'Can I get you some tea?' she offered. 'It won't take a minute.'

'Nothing, thank you,' Mrs Parkinson said. 'I just wanted to see you, to thank you for being so kind to my husband, going with him to the hospital.'

Kitty's relief at the words was not only for herself, but for this plain, sad little woman who sat opposite her; relief that she wouldn't have to be hurt more.

253

'It was nothing,' she said. 'It was the least I could do. Oh, I am so sorry, Mrs Parkinson!'

'You were with my husband when . . . when he died?'

'Yes I was.'

'Did he . . .? Was he . . .?'

'I'm sure he suffered no pain in dying,' Kitty said gently. 'He was unconscious – and slipped away.'

'That at least is a comfort,' Mrs Parkinson said. 'I have been wondering why he was in Richmond. I don't think he knew anyone here. He only ever came to London for the wool sales. Wool was his life, Mrs Shane. Is there, perhaps, a woollen mill in Richmond?'

'I don't think so. But lots of visitors come here. It's a pretty place. Perhaps someone recommended it to him.'

Mrs Parkinson nodded. 'I suppose that was it.'

'Please change your mind and have some tea,' Kitty said. She had warmed to this woman. There was a dignity about her which quite outdid her ordinary appearance.

'Thank you kindly, but I won't. I have to get back to my son-in-law. There's a lot to be done.'

'Very well, then. I won't keep you.' Kitty rose to her feet.

'I've noticed your painting,' Mrs Parkinson said. 'It's very beautiful – and so like the moors at home. Albert loved the moors. You wouldn't consider selling it to me, I suppose?'

Somehow, she thought, it would be a bit of her husband from these almost foreign parts, where she had never set foot before and Albert had.

Kitty shook her head.

'I'm very sorry Mrs Parkinson, but I couldn't. It's one of my dearest possessions. It has very special associations for me.'

On the day of Albert Parkinson's funeral the sun shone from an early hour and the sky was an unbroken blue. The burial was fixed for dinner-time and the mill would be closed for an extra half-hour on to the dinner break, so that those of his employees who wished to do so could attend.

'There'll be some who'll take the extra half-hour and not go,' Mrs Barnet said. 'But I daresay most in the weaving will attend.'

'I want to,' Madeleine said.

She walked with Mrs Barnet and Sally, with most of the other girls also there, all of them keeping a respectful distance behind the family and other mourners more important than themselves.

'He were a good employer,' Mrs Barnet said. 'Not stand-offish like some. And very well respected, as you can see by the turnout.'

There were mill-owners and worthies, not only from Helsdon, but from all over the West Riding.

'He was good to me,' Madeleine said. 'How many men would have given me a job in the mill when I'd said I'd no longer work in the house?'

She genuinely grieved for him. She would never forget him. In some ways he had been almost like a father to her, but a very different father from her own. He had had understanding.

'Did you know he took me to Paris?' she asked Sally. And in Paris he had treated her almost as if she were his daughter.

'I must say, Mrs Parkinson is bearing up very well,' Mrs Barnet said. 'A bit different from Miss Sophia. She looks in a terrible state!'

Sophia certainly did look awful. Her face was chalk-white. She leaned heavily on her husband's arm and dabbed continuously at her eyes with a handkerchief heavily bordered in black. Mrs Parkinson, on the other hand, was impassive – until you noticed that her black-gloved hands were tightly clenched by her side and her chin was held unnaturally high.

'Miss Sophia would do better to offer her mother a bit of comfort,' Madeleine said sharply.

'Well, grief takes people different ways,' Mrs Barnet observed.

Madeleine glanced along the line of relatives – Roger

looking so young in spite of his height – and came to rest on Léon Bonneau, who was standing with the family, probably because he was still living in the house.

She wondered, not for the first time, why he and Miss Sophia hadn't made a go of it, and why the latter had married her cousin so suddenly. It had been a strange day, that Saturday of the birthday party. Even Emerald, who was close to Miss Sophia – or Mrs Chester as they'd now have to call her – didn't know the ins and outs of it.

'Do you reckon Monsieur Bonneau will go back to France, now?' Sally asked.

'I've no idea,' Madeleine said.

'We none of us know what will happen in t'mill wi' t'Master gone,' Mrs Barnet said soberly. 'It's more than a bit worrying!'

Then they kept silence while the earth was thrown on the coffin. Sophia cried out, and turned to bury herself in her husband's arms. Mrs Parkinson swayed slightly towards the open grave, then steadied herself, drawing her small figure as upright as a soldier.

'Monsieur Bonneau cut a very handsome figure,' Mrs Barnet said as they walked back to the mill when it was all over. 'I hope he *won't* be going back to France. I'm really enjoying working on his designs. I wouldn't take kindly to going back to run-of-the-mill stuff.'

'Me neither,' Madeleine agreed.

At Mount Royd sherry, tea, and lavish refreshments – stand pies, ham, ox tongue, jellies, fruitcake – were provided for those who went back there after the funeral, which a great many did, for once the ceremony was over spirits rose miraculously and the gathering became a social occasion. It was an opportunity for those who had known Albert Parkinson over the years to look back over their friendships, and for those who had not managed to set foot in Mount Royd to judge whether it was as fine as people said. It was also an occasion for almost everyone to speculate how much of a fortune the deceased might have left.

'I dare say his family'll come into a tidy sum,' one woolman said to another, looking appreciatively around the room they were standing in. 'There's no sign of shortage here, I must say!'

Léon Bonneau moved around, speaking to a few people he had met during his time in Helsdon, one of them a millowner from Shipley.

'I reckon Albert might cut up for a fair bit,' the man said.

'Cut up? Excuse me if I do not understand. What is cut up?'

'Aye, well, you being a Frenchie, how can you expect to understand the Queen's English?' the man said. '"How much will he cut up for?" means how much will he leave? In his will. Money!'

'I see!'

They were quite extraordinary, these Northerners. Kindhearted and hospitable, hardworking and honest, but blunt in the extreme; almost mannerless to Léon's way of thinking. He liked money as much as the next man – he had no intention of going through life without it – but they had no subtlety, no diplomacy.

He made his excuses and moved away.

Sophia, he noticed, seemed to have overcome completely the anguish she had shown at the graveside. She was circulating amongst the company, smiling and chatting in the most composed manner. Any minute now, of course, she would come into her inheritance. I wouldn't have had long to wait, he thought ruefully. All the same, he had no regrets. He couldn't have married her; he was more sure than ever now.

He moved over to where Mrs Parkinson was sitting. She was the one he felt sorry for. He doubted if she had shed a tear since the news first came. It was all bottled up inside her.

'Perhaps I should now move into an hotel, Mrs Parkinson,' he suggested. 'It was kind of you to insist on me staying at Mount Royd until after the funeral, but perhaps

I should now leave. As soon as things are sorted out at the mill, of course, I will return to France.'

'It's good of you to stay for a while,' Mrs Parkinson said. 'I doubt if anyone knows what should be done in the mill better than you do. Albert liked to run everything himself. He wasn't one for delegating or confiding.'

'Naturally I am at your disposal,' Léon said.

'Thank you. And there's no question of you moving into an hotel. You are always welcome at Mount Royd. Sophia and David will be returning to Thirsk tomorrow. Anyway, there isn't a decent hotel in Helsdon.'

She sounded so calm, so composed. These women are strong, Léon thought. It was how his mother had reacted when his father died. She and Mrs Parkinson were of the same breed – though his mother would not have countenanced that. She would consider herself way above this little Englishwoman whose only asset would seem to be her husband's wealth.

The feasting over, the company began to thin out until only the family, the lawyer, and Léon himself were left.

'I think we should foregather,' the solicitor said to Mrs Parkinson.

'Very well, Mr Ormeroyd,' she replied. 'In the dining-room, I think. Léon, you must come with us. There will be no secrets in my husband's will, and he thought very highly of you. He wouldn't have minded you being present and I shall be glad of your support.' She turned to the solicitor. 'Shall I send for the housekeeper? Mrs Thomas is sure to be a beneficiary.'

'Leave it for the time being,' Mr Ormeroyd said.

There were no surprises in the will, read in a grave tone by Mr Ormeroyd: a substantial sum to Sophia, in trust until she married; a similar sum held in trust for Roger; legacies to Mrs Thomas and to Drake; the rest, including all Albert's business interests, in trust to his wife and eventually to his children. Léon observed the smile of satisfaction on Sophia's face.

'When . . .?' she began.

The solicitor held up his hand.

'Bear with me a little longer, ladies and gentlemen. I have something further to say.'

The solicitor's manner was vaguely disturbing to Léon, but his disquiet was evidently not shared by the others. Now that they had heard the important provisions of the will, they sat around the large table with no more than mild curiosity on their faces.

'I hardly know where to begin,' Mr Ormeroyd said. 'You must all of you prepare yourselves for a shock.'

At that, they sat up suddenly, and gave him their full attention. Mrs Parkinson seemed the least concerned. No shock could compare to that she had received when the telegram came.

'The will,' Mr Ormeroyd began, 'which was made by the deceased some years ago, is valid. The truth of the matter is, there is no estate to leave! I have to tell you, with the greatest possible regret, that at the time of his death Mr Parkinson was penniless!'

The silence seemed to go on for ever, like the dropping of a stone into a bottomless well. It was broken by Sophia, who jumped to her feet, screaming.

'It's not true! It can't be true! You're cheating us! Mama! David! This man is cheating us!'

'Please sit down, Mrs Chester,' Ormeroyd said sternly. He had known Sophia Parkinson since she was a little girl. He would take no nonsense from her, sorry though he was for her predicament – which he knew to be worse, even, than she imagined.

'I have never cheated anyone in my life!' he said. 'And I am not about to begin. If you will now keep calm I will go into the situation in more detail.'

'Keep calm? How can I keep calm?' Sophia cried. 'You say I'm to inherit nothing, that I'm to be penniless, and you tell me to keep calm!'

'Sophia, behave yourself!' Mrs Parkinson said sharply. 'Let us hear what Mr Ormeroyd has to say.' She was riddled now with fear and anxiety. She could hardly believe what was happening. There must be some huge mistake.

'It's all very well for you, Mama!' Sophia shouted. 'You're old! You don't need money like I do. How can I be expected to live on a schoolmaster's miserable pittance?' She broke into hysterical sobs.

Léon saw David Chester wince at his wife's words. Poor devil, he thought. She'll make him pay for this. None of it is his fault, but she'll make him pay.

'For shame, Sophia!' Mrs Chester cried angrily. 'You have the best husband in the world in my son!'

'And I am not old,' Mrs Parkinson said coldly. 'I am not quite fifty, and I have to eat and to clothe myself without, henceforth, any support from a husband. So keep quiet. We will get nowhere, behaving in this fashion.'

She turned to the solicitor.

'All the same, Mr Ormeroyd, I don't quite understand. You say there's nothing, no money – but what about the mill? What about this house?'

'The mill is heavily in debt to the bank and there are sums owed to a moneylender,' Mr Ormeroyd said quietly. 'The house is not mortgaged, but I have no doubt that it will have to be sold to raise some cash. In any case, Mrs Parkinson, I'm afraid you couldn't afford to run it.'

'I see.' She didn't, in fact. It was all a terrible puzzle, a nightmare.

'The bank will not wait for its money,' the solicitor continued. 'They will undoubtedly foreclose. As for the moneylender – well, he might have to lose out. It remains to be seen. But I shall spare no compassion for him.'

He felt desperately sorry for this woman who had taken her husband's untimely death with more courage than he would ever have expected from her. And now this. It was cruel.

'He cheated us!' Sophia sobbed. 'My father knew what he was doing. He cheated us!'

Mrs Parkinson sprang to her feet, moved swiftly towards Sophia, and slapped her hard on the face. The mark of her fingers showed scarlet on her daughter's white skin.

'How dare you! How dare you talk like that about your father! He was the best father in the world to you. And if he'd not been killed saving someone else's life, it would have been all right in the end. I know it would. I have the utmost faith in my husband!'

Shocked by her mother's action, Sophia was sobbing quietly now, but when David put his arm around her to give her comfort, she pushed him away.

Mrs Parkinson went back to her chair, and now, for the first time since her husband's death, Léon watched her crumple. Her whole body went slack. Tears gathered in her eyes.

'Why didn't he tell me?' she murmured. 'Why did he let us go on acting as if we were rich? If he'd told me, I could have helped. I would have economized.' Suddenly she gave a loud cry, a terrible wail of anguish.

'Why didn't you tell me, Albert?'

And then the tears came. Great, gulping sobs convulsed her.

But she is not crying for the money, Léon thought. She is crying for her lost husband.

Her sister came and put her arms around her.

'I will look after you, my dear,' she said. 'You will always have a home with me – you and Roger, both. We shall manage, you'll see!'

Mrs Parkinson raised a ravaged face.

'But why didn't he tell me, Fanny? Why didn't he trust me enough to tell me?'

'He wanted you to be happy, that's why,' her sister said. 'He always wanted you to be happy.'

The solicitor gathered his papers together.

'I will talk with the bank so that I can put the situation more clearly in a day or two, dear lady. In the meantime I will leave it to you to break the news to Mrs Thomas and to Drake when you feel able to do so.'

'If there is any money at all,' Mrs Parkinson said, 'I

should like Mrs Thomas and Drake to have their legacies.'

'And now you and Roger must come and stay with me for a few days,' her sister said.

No one quite knew how the news got around. Perhaps through a clerk in Ormeroyd, Ormeroyd and Foster's? Perhaps Drake, down at the 'Black Swan' with too much ale inside him. But no matter how it got out, by breakfast-time next day everyone in Parkinson's mill knew about it, and long before the day was out, everyone in Helsdon and beyond.

'It's shocking! Shocking!' Mrs Barnet said, white-faced, echoing what everyone else was saying.

She turned to Joseph Bates.

'What ever shall we do if the mill closes? How shall we live?'

'We must trust in the Lord!' he replied.

And for his part he was going to begin at once to look for a job, before the rush started.

FOURTEEN

'What are we going to do?' Martha Bates said. 'What *are* we going to do?'

It was a question she had been asking herself all day. The news that Parkinson's would likely have to close had reached Priestley Street well before dinner-time. The women had gathered in little knots along the street, discussing it, and Martha Bates, who was known never to join what she called 'gossip groups', had been so far perturbed as to do so. Now, Joseph and Madeleine were home from the mill and she asked the question of them.

'What are we going to do? What's going to happen?'

'Nobody seems to know what's going to happen,' Joseph Bates said. 'I dare say the workers will be the last to be told,' he added bitterly.

'Perhaps they don't know themselves,' Madeleine suggested. 'The family, I mean. Perhaps the rumours aren't true!'

Her father shook his head.

'I reckon they are. Who would start such tales if there wasn't truth in them?'

'Plenty would!' his wife assured him. 'Some folk thrive on rumours! But why is it all so sudden? Surely someone must have had an inkling before this?'

'Not necessarily,' Joseph said. 'The Master kept his cards close to his chest, never confided much. He was a one-man band, the Master was. He ran everything himself. And I suppose the worse it got, the more he kept it to himself, waiting for things to come right again.'

'Which they might have, if he hadn't died so sudden,' Martha said. 'Anyway, sit you down and get your tea, the pair of you.'

How long would there be food to put on the table? she wondered. Today she had managed to buy threepennyworth of pie bits – scraps of meat, fat, gristle the butcher had left over which, with a few vegetables, had made the tasty stew she now served. Most of the mill families in Helsdon couldn't afford even threepennyworth of meat in the middle of the week. They were paid on a Friday, and by Saturday there wasn't a penny in the purse until the next wage day. So what will we all do when there's no work, no payday? she asked herself yet again.

'Well, I've made my decision,' Joseph Bates said, answering his wife's unspoken question. 'I'm going to seek work elsewhere. Tomorrow, before everyone else starts doing the same thing.'

'But you have to go to the mill,' Martha Bates said.

'Well I shan't go, shall I?'

It would be the first day off he had ever taken in his working life, except on the rare occasions when he'd been ill. But there was no other way, he could only call on other mills in working hours.

'It'll seem terrible to work somewhere other than Parkinson's,' his wife said.

'Do you think I don't know that?' he said roughly. 'Every day of my working life has been spent in Parkinson's. The Master was only a young man himself when he set me on as a lad. Do you think I don't feel it, woman?' He put down his spoon and pushed his plate away from him.

'Nay, I'm sorry!' Martha Bates said. 'I wasn't meaning to criticize. I know as well as you do that you've got to look for work. And you'll be lucky if you find it in Helsdon, at that!'

264

'I know it. I've no doubt I'll have to go further afield. But I shall go everywhere until I find something. You can depend on that. And if it's not in Helsdon, then we must all be prepared to leave Priestley Street, go wherever the work is.'

Madeleine looked up.

'Leave Helsdon?' It was a new thought.

'I don't want to leave Helsdon,' Penelope said. 'Not ever, as long as I live. All my friends live here.'

'We might have to, if the work is elsewhere,' her mother said quietly. 'And Madeleine, have you thought what you're going to do if you lose your job with Parkinson's?'

'I've been thinking about it all day,' Madeleine admitted. 'They've talked about nothing else in the weaving.'

She didn't in the least want to leave Parkinson's. In the eight months since that first day in the mill, when she'd known nothing more than the warp from the weft, when everything and everybody had seemed strange to her, she'd acquired both friends, and an unusual degree of skill in weaving. She and Mrs Barnet were working all the time on Léon Bonneau's designs now, and some lovely stuff they were turning out, cloth which was beginning to sell. She would hate to leave it. And who would give her another job with much more experienced weavers out of work?

'What have you decided?' Mrs Bates asked.

'I haven't, Ma. I want to wait and see what happens. Perhaps it won't be as bad as we think.'

'Of course it will,' her father said testily. 'You're living in a fool's paradise!'

'I think perhaps your father's right,' Mrs Bates said.

'Of course I'm right. And she should never have left Mount Royd in the first place. At least she'd have been sure of a job.'

Madeleine contradicted him.

'I might not have been. Who knows what's going to happen to them at Mount Royd? There's rumours around

265

about that, as well. Oh, I know Emerald's all right, since she's gone to Thirsk with Miss Sophia. Frankly, I'd rather starve than do that!'

'Don't let me hear you speak so glibly about starving, miss!' her mother said sharply. 'It might be all too true for some people!' It might be true for us, she thought – but that thought she'd keep to herself. The least she could do was show an optimistic front.

'I'm sorry, Ma!'

'I should just think so, too!'

'But I'm not going back into service,' Madeleine persisted.

'In the end you'll have to do what puts food in your belly,' Mrs Bates said shortly. 'You might not be able to pick and choose!' Right now she could well do without Madeleine being awkward.

I'll not do it, Madeleine thought. She would tramp all the streets in all the towns in the West Riding, take any kind of job, before she'd be a servant again.

Mrs Bates turned to her husband. 'Eat up your food, Joseph. If you're going to be traipsing around tomorrow you'll need all your strength. Where had you thought of going?'

'If there's nothing in Helsdon,' Joseph said, 'I thought I might try Salt's, at Saltaire. In fact I might go there first. It's the biggest mill there is, there's bound to be more chance of a vacancy. And Titus Salt is building houses for his workers, a whole model village, they say. I might get a job and somewhere to live at the same time.'

Pigs might fly, Martha Bates reckoned, but not for the world would she have said so. She was by no means sure that she had any vestige of love left for Joseph Bates – not the love of a woman for her man. There'd been times when she'd hated him, when he'd been on the point of turning Madeleine out, for instance; but because in the end he hadn't done so, she felt she owed him some loyalty. Also, since Irvine's leave had finished after Christmas she'd been allowed to receive his rare letters –

he was stationed a world away, in Brighton – and to sit at the table and reply to them openly, without causing trouble. She would have done it of course, trouble or no, for she was no longer afraid of Joseph – but because he left her in peace she felt she owed him something.

'So I'll be off in good time in the morning,' he said. 'We know the railway runs to Saltaire, but I shall try to walk it. We must save every penny we can from now on, just in case. And above all, we must remain strong and steadfast in faith, and assiduous in prayer. The Lord will provide!'

And I wish I could believe *that*, Martha Bates thought. Over the years she had seen too many cases in Helsdon where neither the Lord nor the devil had provided.

'And what about you, Madeleine?' she asked. 'What will you do?'

'I shall go to work as usual,' Madeleine replied. 'See what happens. Anyway, I'm halfway through a piece. I'm sure I'll not be expected to abandon it.' Such was her nature that she couldn't help but believe that somehow, something would turn up.

'What I'll also do, after work,' she added, 'is walk up to Mount Royd to see Mrs Thomas. I'd like to be sure she's going to be all right.'

Though they had put a brave face on the situation, neither Joseph nor Martha Bates slept much that night. Joseph, who usually went out like a light and slept almost without moving, tossed and turned the night long. Martha would have liked to have touched him, to have given him some comfort, but she couldn't bring herself to do so. In any case, like as not she'd have been rebuffed. She'd had plenty of rebuffs.

While the Bateses lay awake in Priestley Street so, unusually, did Léon Bonneau at Mount Royd. It was not in his nature to let troubles keep him awake, still less when they were not really his own. So far in his life he had not been one for shouldering other people's burdens. He had been profoundly saddened by Albert Parkinson's death, but since that occurrence it had been his intention

267

simply to go back to France as soon as he decently could. He had had no other idea in mind – until now, that was; until this hot night when he lay tossing and turning under the single linen sheet.

What was even stranger was that the thought of all those millhands who would certainly lose their jobs, disturbed him. He had glimpsed the poverty in Helsdon and knew that the closure of Parkinson's would be a tremendous blow. Also, he now knew some of the millhands; they were not just faceless creatures. How would Mrs Barnet who, he knew, worked to keep a crippled husband, fare? And the Bates family, if both Madeleine and her father lost their jobs? He liked Madeleine. Also, she was so talented at her job. It would be a shame to have that skill wasted.

'Though it is nothing to do with me!' he admonished himself. 'It is not for me to cure the ills of the world!'

But all his tossing and turning, all this thinking, was not without self-interest. Turning aside from his compassion for the millhands, he began to wonder if this was not, after all, a situation which might benefit himself. He had come to Helsdon to marry money, and that had not worked out: might there not now be a chance for him to make something from the present state of affairs? And if in making something for Léon Bonneau he was able to help some of the mill workers, so much the better!

From then, until the light of the new day crept into his bedroom, his mind whirled with plans: far-fetched, possible, impossible; practicable, useless – and all of them fraught with difficulty. He was glad when the day proper came, when, after breakfast, he could seek out Mrs Parkinson at her sister's house and put his ideas to her.

He was shocked by her appearance. Her face was grey, her eyes dull; she looked ten years older. Worst of all, she seemed to be in another world, not grasping what he said.

'I don't see how it will all work,' she said listlessly. 'I really don't feel competent to discuss anything, Monsieur Bonneau. Perhaps you should speak to Mr Ormeroyd. He will be here to see me any minute now.'

'Very well,' he said. 'I must say, you don't look well, Mrs Parkinson. I trust you have seen your doctor?' Clearly she had now begun to suffer from the shock of her husband's death.

'He has given me a sleeping draught,' she said. 'It makes my head ache.'

But she would take it. If her sister had not doled it out in the correct doses she thought she might have taken the lot. She would like to sleep and sleep; preferably not to waken. I was very good after Albert died, she thought. Now I'm too tired. Someone else must take over.

'Then if you permit it, I will wait and speak with Mr Ormeroyd,' Léon said.

At Mrs Parkinson's own request he stayed while the solicitor told her the result of his visit to the bank.

'I'm afraid I have little good news for you, dear lady,' Mr Ormeroyd said. 'The bank will foreclose, which means that the mill will have to be sold to pay your husband's debts. If we are able to make a sale – I say *if* – then possibly there will be enough left over for you and your son to live very modestly, though not at Mount Royd where the upkeep is high. I am sorry to be the bearer of such news, and to have to put it to you so bluntly.'

She took the news calmly. The fact was, she couldn't face it at all, so it was best to take no notice of what he was saying.

'There is one small piece of good news, though it will not affect you materially,' the solicitor went on. 'The bank is mindful of the catastrophe of all Parkinson's hands being thrown out of work immediately. They have therefore agreed to advance enough money to pay wages for three more weeks, thus giving the workers a chance to look for other jobs.' Though where they will find them, he thought to himself, God alone knows!

'I'm glad about that,' Mrs Parkinson said vaguely. 'Albert thought a lot of his workers.'

'The problem is that there is no one really to run the mill, even for three weeks,' Mr Ormeroyd said. 'As we've all agreed before, the late Mr Parkinson never delegated anything. And the bank naturally insists that someone must be in charge.'

He turned to Léon Bonneau.

'And here I have to beg your pardon, Monsieur Bonneau! Desperate for an answer, I told the bank that I would ask you if you would step into that position for the next three weeks. I know that in France you have experience of running a mill . . .'

'My brothers largely run our mill,' Léon interrupted.

'But you are not without experience. At least you understand the processes, you are able to advise. Monsieur Bonneau, I beg you to think of the difference it will make to the millhands if you agree to stay on and do this!'

'There is no need to beg me, Mr Ormeroyd,' Léon said. 'Of course I will do it. I could do no less. Which brings me to the proposal I have to put to you. Mrs Parkinson has agreed that I should discuss it with you since she feels unable to be involved, though naturally it could be to her advantage in the end.'

'If you don't mind I'll leave you to it,' Mrs Parkinson said. 'My headache is really quite tiresome.'

'Well,' Léon said when Mrs Parkinson had left, 'I will try to put my ideas as clearly as possible, though it would be easier in my native tongue.'

'I would welcome anything which will help in this sorry situation,' Ormeroyd said.

'First of all,' Léon said, 'I must tell you that, if it were possible, I would like to take over Parkinson's and run it for myself, with an interest for Mrs Parkinson, *naturellement*.'

He held up his hand at Mr Ormeroyd's gasp of disbelief.

'Yes, I know it seems impossible. But I start from the position I would like best. I would like to be able to keep on all the hands, and I am sure, given a little time, I could make a profit. But it is not possible that I can find enough money to pay the bank and to leave me with working capital. I wonder, therefore, if the bank might prolong the period of the loan until I am – how do you say it? – on my feet?'

'I think not,' Mr Ormeroyd said. 'The sum is too large. I am sure of that.'

'That is what I feared. Therefore I reduced my ideas. It seems certain that the business will have to be sold, and it is a large, perhaps awkward concern to sell as a whole, at this time. I therefore ask myself, if it is found better to sell it piecemeal, though there might be difficulties when it came to the actual building, whether I, Léon Bonneau, might raise enough money to buy the weaving and the finishing and run that as my own?'

Mr Ormeroyd was gaping at him, open-mouthed.

'Buy the weaving and the finishing?'

'Yes. It is the weaving which interests me most, especially the new designs I was working on with Mr Parkinson. I believe – he also believed – that they have a great future. Nothing quite like them is being done in the West Riding. It is a technique and designs that I have brought from France.'

'And what are the other mills going to think about that?' Mr Ormeroyd interrupted.

'I would not be in competition with your West Riding Mills,' Léon assured him. 'It is a different market. And it is a market which, given only a few months longer, I am sure will be most profitable. We already have several orders in our book.'

'Well I don't know, I'm sure,' the solicitor said.

'If Parkinson's sells as a whole, then I know there is no room for my proposition,' Léon said. 'In that case I will leave well alone. But if it does not, then what I propose to you will at least save something.'

'You've got a point there,' Mr Ormeroyd admitted. 'So what can I do to help?'

'Go to the bank with me,' Léon said. 'I will explain my idea to them, but your presence will be a strong support

271

when I ask them to let me buy the weaving, and also try to persuade them to lend me the money.'

'I don't think they'll do that, monsieur. You see, you're a foreigner.'

'Well we can try! Perhaps they will help a little. If not, or if I need more than they're prepared to lend, then I will go home to Roubaix and try to persuade my family to put some money into this concern.'

He was not optimistic about help from his family, but that he'd keep to himself. He would also keep to himself the idea which was deep inside him; that one day he would have the whole of Parkinson's. Whatever was sold, he would try to buy back. And if he could not buy back, he would build anew. There was nothing these Yorkshiremen could do of which he also was not capable. One day he would be as great a woolman as Titus Salt himself. But now was not the time to say so.

'Very well,' Mr Ormeroyd said. 'I'll make an appointment with the bank.'

'Today if possible. The time is short,' Léon urged.

'And someone must tell the hands that you are to take over for the next three weeks. Also that they will be given time off to look for other jobs. I suppose you will agree to that?'

'Of course!'

'Then we owe it to them to do it quickly,' Mr Ormeroyd said.

'*Certainement*! Will you accompany me to the mill at once? I will get the overlookers together first, and after that we will speak to all the hands.'

The first place Léon went into in the mill was the weaving shed. The first thing he noticed was that some of the looms were standing idle. The second was that Joseph Bates was missing. He walked over to Madeleine.

'Where is your father, Madeleine? I want him rather urgently.'

'He's not here, sir!'

272

'I can see he's not here, Madeleine. That's why I'm asking you where he is!'

'He's not come in today, sir!' He had no call to speak so sharply, even though she had said a foolish thing.

'Not come in? Is he ill?'

'No, sir.'

'Then why is he not here?'

He sounded so impatient, she thought, not a bit like his usual self. He was probably worried – but then weren't they all? He had a lot less to be worried about than most of them. He could pack up and go back to France, shake the dust of Helsdon off his feet and never give it another thought.

'He's gone to look for another job,' she said reluctantly.

'Look for another job? Already?'

'He's not the only one!' Madeleine said defensively. 'There's quite a few people missing this morning.' She didn't agree with her father's action, when did she ever? But there was no call for Monsieur Bonneau to sound so haughty about it.

'Ah! So that's why some of the looms are idle!' Léon said.

'It's not only the weaving,' Madeleine said. 'There's people missing in most of the sheds. They reckon it'll be first come, first served for any jobs that's going.'

'I see. So when are you going to look for another job, Madeleine?' Léon asked.

She didn't like the coldness of his tone. He didn't know what it was like to be out of work in Helsdon, did he? Nevertheless, she couldn't help but be on his side.

'I'm not going to look for another job,' she said. 'Not until I'm told to. I want to go on working here, monsieur.'

He smiled for the first time.

'I'm glad of that. I only hope you'll be able to.'

'There's another thing, sir.' She would tell him what she had decided when she'd lain awake during the night.

'Yes?'

'If I have to, if it's necessary, I'll work for lower wages.'

273

'You'd do *that*?' He sounded as astonished as he felt. Heaven knew the hands were paid little enough as it was. 'That is most good and loyal of you, Madeleine!'

She flushed at the warmth of his voice.

'Not at all!' she said levelly. 'Half a loaf is better than no bread.' It might well be literally true in the coming months!

'I hope you will have a whole loaf,' Léon said. 'We must wait and see what happens. In the meantime I am calling a meeting of all the overlookers.' He turned to Mrs Barnet.

'Would you come into the office, as Mr Bates isn't here?'

'I can't go to an overlookers' meeting,' Mrs Barnet said when Léon Bonneau had gone. 'I don't understand such things. I'd be all of a flummox!'

'Nonsense!' Madeleine reassured her. 'All you have to do is listen, then come back and tell us what was said. Somebody has to go. We're all anxious to know.'

'Then why don't you go?' Mrs Barnet said. 'You can explain things better than I ever could.'

'I can't go!' Madeleine protested. 'There are people who've been in the weaving ten times longer than I have.'

'Your father's the overlooker,' someone said. 'And you're the one knows Monsieur Bonneau best!'

'We'll put it to the vote!' Mrs Barnet offered. 'All those who'd like Madeleine to go in my place, put up your hand!'

Not everyone did so, but enough to make it a good majority.

'Very well, then,' Madeleine said. 'What shall I say to Monsieur Bonneau?'

'Tell him I'm suddenly not well. Tell him I asked you to take my place.'

As it happened, Léon Bonneau didn't ask. He raised his eyebrows when he saw her standing there among the overlookers, all men, but there was no time for asking questions. In any case it didn't matter, just as long as the

274

weavers were represented. He would talk to them himself, later.

'I suggest you take Mr Parkinson's chair,' Mr Ormeroyd said. 'And I will sit beside you and open the meeting.'

There was no need to call the men to order. They waited silently, not one amongst them whose face wasn't lined with anxiety.

'This is the situation, then . . .,' the solicitor began.

When he had explained the situation, as briefly and plainly as possible, confirming the worst fears of all of them, he called on Léon Bonneau to speak.

'I will do everything I can in the next three weeks,' Léon said. 'Anyone who wishes to take time off to look for another job may do so, including you overlookers.'

'What's going to happen at the end of the three weeks, sir? That's what we want to know.'

'I wish I knew myself,' Léon said. 'I have a scheme to put to the bank later today, but I cannot tell you about it, yet.' And if I could, he thought, it would be no comfort to most of you.

'I will also, as quickly as ever I can, contact other mill-owners in the West Riding and ask them to take on as many workers as possible. Some of you might have to leave Helsdon, but I dare say you will prefer that to having no job. Tomorrow I will meet with everyone in the mill and tell you how I have progressed. I wish you all the very best of luck, and I hope you wish me the same in my negotiations. In the meantime I suggest we carry on with the work in hand. We have several orders on the books, and every order filled brings in money.'

'Aye, but money for who?' one overlooker said to another as they filed out. 'Am I going to be working my guts out to keep them up at the big house?'

'They say they'll all have to leave,' the other man replied. 'They can't afford to live there.'

When Madeleine entered the weaving shed every pair of eyes looked towards her.

275

'You can stop your looms for a minute,' Mrs Barnet said, 'while Madeleine gives us the news.'

Though what she told them simply confirmed their fears, to have it said out loud was terrible. There were gasps of horror as Madeleine spoke.

'What are we going to do?' they asked each other. 'How will we manage?'

'Well I'm going off tomorrow, to look for another job!' one said – and then another and another.

'What are you going to do, Madeleine?' Sally Pitts asked. 'I'll do whatever you do!'

'I'm going to risk waiting a bit longer,' Madeleine replied. 'But you must do what ever's best for you, Sally.' Was she herself doing the right thing? No matter; she'd do it! 'I shall have to think about it,' Mrs Barnet said. 'There's my husband to consider, you see!' She was worried sick, but she tried not to show it. That sort of feeling could spread like wildfire.

After work Madeleine went to Mount Royd. When she walked into the kitchen Mrs Thomas was sitting at the table doing nothing whatsoever.

'Good heavens! This isn't like you!' Madeleine cried. 'Here I am, come to give you a hand if you want one, and there you are sitting twiddling your thumbs!'

'There's nothing to do, lass,' Mrs Thomas said. 'It's awful! And I cannot abide having nothing to do. There's only me and Monsieur Bonneau in this great big place, and he's out most of the time. Mrs Chester came in earlier to see if I was all right. By which I mean Mrs Fanny Chester o'course – not Miss Sophia. You'd not catch her bothering, even if she wasn't away to Thirsk, and not even her mother heard a word from her.'

'What's going to happen?' Madeleine asked. In all her life she had never heard that question asked so often.

'I don't rightly know. But Mrs Chester warned me I might have to go. They might not be able to live here – can you imagine that? When I think of the lovely times we've had here . . .!'

276

Speak for yourself, Madeleine thought.

'What will you do?' she asked.

'Oh I'll be all right, love. Don't you worry about me. I shall go to live with my niece in Morecambe. She keeps a boarding house and she's asked me often enough to join her. I shan't stick fast.'

'If you go to Morecambe I'll come and see you,' Madeleine promised. 'I'll come on the train. I've never been to Morecambe.'

'*You've* been to Paris!' Mrs Thomas reminded her. 'I'd have thought that was enough for anybody!'

'It *was* good,' Madeleine admitted. Nowadays when she thought of Paris she remembered only the good bits, never how horrid Miss Sophia had been to her.

'All the same, I shall miss Mount Royd,' Mrs Thomas said more quietly. 'I've been here since the Master and the Mistress was first married.'

She looked for a moment as though she might burst into tears. And she had been crying, you could see that from her red-rimmed eyes.

'Shall I make us both a cup of tea?' Madeleine suggested. 'And you wouldn't have a bit of your curd tart going spare, would you?'

'As it happens,' Mrs Thomas admitted, 'I have!'

She got up and went to the pantry to fetch it.

'You're looking better than you were, lass,' she said, cutting a generous piece of the tart. 'I thought you looked quite poorly a few months back. Round about the turn of the year. I said as much to your Emerald.'

'I wasn't too good,' Madeleine said. 'I'd had a . . . bad experience.' She shuddered, and felt herself go cold at the remembrance of it, then pulled herself together again. For a moment she wondered if she could tell Mrs Thomas. Sometimes she wanted desperately to tell someone; someone who would understand, and would reassure her. But Mrs Thomas, in spite of her title, had never been married. It would be a difficult subject, perhaps not a fair one, to broach with her.

'But I'm much better,' she said. She was too. There were days now when she forgot to feel dirty, defiled. As long as no man ever came near her she could manage.

'I've missed you,' Mrs Thomas confided. 'Your Emerald is a nice little lass, but she's not like you. We don't have the laughs that you and me used to have. Remember?'

When Madeleine arrived back at Priestley Street her father was already home, sitting at the table, eating his tea. He neither looked up nor spoke when she came in. But that didn't signify whether he'd had a good day or a bad, Madeleine thought. He was always the same with her.

Her mother, on the other hand, smiled a welcome.

'Your Dad's got a job!'

'Already? Why, that's wonderful! Where?'

At that her mother's face clouded.

'Salt's. In the weaving. Not as an overlooker, not yet. And there isn't a house in the village at the moment, though they're building all the time, nice houses. Some of them have a front garden, your Dad says – though they're mostly for the overlookers. We shall have to look for something in Shipley at first, so as to be in walking distance. It's too far and too expensive to go by train from here every day.'

'You mean . . . leave Helsdon?'

'Well we have to go where the work is, don't we?' Mrs Bates said. 'Stands to reason. Your Dad's very lucky to have got a job so quickly.'

'And if you've any sense you'll be off there tomorrow and see if you can't get one yourself,' Joseph Bates said.

'I can't do that,' Madeleine said quickly.

'What do you mean, "can't"?' her father asked.

'I've given Monsieur Bonneau my promise that I'll stay until something's worked out about Parkinson's. There was a meeting today with the overlookers. I took your place . . .'

278

'You took my place? How could *you* take *my* place?'

'Well I did!' Madeleine said flatly. 'The others voted for me to do so. Monsieur Bonneau is going to the bank to see what can be done. We're guaranteed wages for three weeks.'

'And after that, what?' Jospeh Bates demanded. 'There'll be a mad rush for jobs. No, my girl, you owe no loyalty to Monsieur Bonneau. You'd best tell him tomorrow that you're leaving with your family. I dare say sooner or later you'll get a job at Salt's.'

'I don't want to leave,' Madeleine said. 'I don't want to leave Parkinson's.' She was surprised to hear herself saying the words. She'd been at the mill less than a year, but she had not known it meant so much to her, not until now when she was threatened with leaving.

'Nor do I,' her father said. 'It's a question of needs must.'

'Your Dad says Saltaire is a lovely place,' Mrs Bates said. 'There's the river, and the canal, right by the mill – and you only have to walk up through Shipley Glen and you're on the moor. It sounds wonderful.'

'I dare say. I don't want to leave Helsdon!'

'But how can you stay in Helsdon without us?' her mother pleaded.

'If I have a job I dare say I'll find someone only too willing to rent me a room. Perhaps one of the women in the weaving. Don't worry, Ma, I'll manage.'

'And if you don't have a job?'

'Well, if there's nothing for me in Helsdon, then I'll have to think about Saltaire, won't I?'

'You'll be too late,' her father warned. 'All the jobs will be gone.'

'I'll just have to take my chance, that's all.' Her tone of voice dismissed the subject. 'What will you do about chapel, Dad?'

'The Lord is in every place!' Joseph Bates said. 'Though as yet there's no chapel in Saltaire, there'll be one in Shipley or Bingley where they will open their arms

279

to receive us all. Mr Salt is a devout man. I'm sure he will wish each and every one of his workers to attend a place of worship.'

When Léon Bonneau, accompanied by Mr Ormeroyd, went to the bank it was made plain to him at once that there was no way they would finance him, even in the short term, to run the whole of Parkinson's.

'Too much money is at stake, Monsieur Bonneau,' the bank manager said. 'Nor can we overlook the debt which Parkinson's mill owes to the bank. We have our shareholders to think of. No, we shall be obliged to put the mill on the market at once.'

'I see!'

Though it was exactly as Mr Ormeroyd had said earlier, Léon was strangely disappointed. Strangely, because up to the moment of Albert Parkinson's funeral it would never have occurred to him to stay in Helsdon. Now, in what was after all no more than a matter of hours, it was suddenly important to him that he should. He had seen a great chance within his grasp, and now, due to this hard-faced man sitting opposite to him, it was slipping through his fingers.

'And if the mill doesn't sell quickly?' Léon asked.

The bank manager shrugged his shoulders.

'Then we must persevere until it does sell. I repeat, Monsieur Bonneau, there is no way the bank can advance more money.'

'Is it possible that you might have to split the mill into lots to sell it – sell the machinery, for instance, or the yarn and cloth already there?'

'Alas, that is quite on the cards,' the bank manager said.

'Then I have a proposition to make,' Léon said. 'If it comes to selling it in lots, will the bank sell me the weaving and the finishing?'

'Excuse me for asking, but do you have the money, monsieur?'

'I would have to raise the money,' Léon admitted,

'which means I would have to go home to France for a week or so.' He was far from sure that he would be able to raise money from the Bonneau mill, but he would try to persuade his brothers that it was a good proposition. Also, he intended to go to other millowners in the West Riding and ask them for help, but he saw no need to tell that to the bank manager at the moment. 'The bank has guaranteed the wages for three weeks,' Léon continued. 'If the mill has not sold, will you give me an extra week's wages for the weavers, to cover the time I must spend in France?'

'Well, now, that I would have to think about . . .,' the bank manager said.

'I don't have much time,' Léon urged him. 'I have to know what to say to the workers tomorrow. I already know I must tell most of them they have to go, but I want to know what hope I can give my weavers.'

The bank manager lowered his chin on his clasped hands, as if praying. I am the one who should be praying, Léon thought. He turned to Mr Ormeroyd, sitting beside him and raised his eyebrows in query. Mr Ormeroyd slowly shook his head. At the same moment the bank manager looked up.

'Very well, monsieur. If the mill has not sold at the end of three weeks, then the bank will consider an offer from you for the weaving and finishing, and allow one further week's wages for the weavers. That is the utmost I can offer.'

'I appreciate that. Thank you, sir. I shall begin at once to put everything in hand.'

He would have to see yarn-spinners and dyers to discuss his requirements, and try for credit. There would be no processes before the weaving available to him in Parkinson's. As well as asking around the West Riding for money, he would have to go home to Roubaix. There was so much to be done in such a short time. But first of all, and most important, he must go at once to the mill and tell the workers what was to happen.

FIFTEEN

'Monsieur Bonneau wants everyone in the mill to assemble in the mill yard at the start of the dinner break,' Joseph Bates said to Mrs Barnet. 'Spread the word around the weaving. I suppose you'd better go, hear what he has to say.'

'We'll be glad to,' Mrs Barnet said. 'There's a good many very anxious folks in Parkinson's right now. Let's hope he has something good to tell us.'

'I wouldn't bank on it,' Joseph Bates said.

He was certain it couldn't be good news. How was that possible? But he himself would be well out of it by the weekend, ready to start at Saltaire on the Monday morning.

On the very first blast of the dinner-time hooter the workers streamed out of every department in the mill and stood in the yard. When Léon Bonneau came out of the office and mounted the platform, which had been hastily constructed from wooden boxes, he had no need to call for attention. The chattering ceased instantly. In total silence he faced a sea of upturned faces: grave, pale, worried faces. His heart sank at the thought of what he had to say to them. In that moment he wished he had done what he'd had every right to do – gone back to Roubaix the minute the funeral was over, not had this crazy idea with which his head was now filled. For once he wondered if his command of English would fail him. Would he be able to find the right words? And would the effort make him sound stiff and distant?

'I regret that I do not bring you good news,' he began. 'As your overlookers have already told you, Parkinson's is to be put up for sale – and that must happen immediately. I have failed to persuade the bank to lend me enough money to buy it as a going concern. It is now up to someone else to do so.'

He paused. If only one of them would say something, ask a question, even; but they stood in the cobbled yard, mute, rooted to the spot, their eyes fixed on him as if pleading with him to work a miracle.

'You will be paid wages in full for the next three weeks, starting from Monday, and as you already know, you may take what time you need, without loss of pay, to look for other jobs.'

'Does tha mean tha dooant expect onnybody to buy t'mill?' a man called out. 'Is that what tha means?'

Thank heaven someone had broken the awful silence, even though the questioner was belligerent and the answer was one Léon didn't want to give.

'Aye, tell us the truth!' someone else spoke up. 'Let's have it straight from the shoulder!'

'Mr Ormeroyd, here, who can answer some of your questions better than I can, since he knows the West Riding and the state of trade, thinks it unlikely that it will find a buyer as a going concern. The bank seemed to take the same view. I cannot tell you how sorry I am!'

'Being sorry won't put bread i' our childers' mouths,' the first man shouted angrily. 'Why wasn't we told anything afore?'

'Let me answer that!' Mr Ormeroyd interrupted. 'You weren't told earlier because Monsieur Bonneau, and I for that matter, didn't know anything. It's as simple as that. Monsieur Bonneau is doing us all a service in trying to make something of this sorry state of affairs. He has other

283

things to say to you and I would be grateful if you would give him a chance to say them!'

'Aye, give him a chance!' someone shouted.

'He's a foreigner! What the hell does he know about owt?'

The speaker this time was a man standing next to Madeleine.

'And you're an ignorant pig!' she said angrily. 'What do you know about anything?'

'Don't you talk that way to me,' he retorted, 'or I'll clout you one!'

'You dare lay a finger on me and I'll clout you back!' Madeleine flared.

By this time there were several small groups in uproar. Léon stood on the platform waiting for them to quieten down. He didn't mind the outburst. It unnerved him far less than the previous silence had done. When he wanted silence again he knew he was capable of getting it, so let them go on for a while, relieve their feelings. They had every right to be angry.

Madeleine was not so patient. When the noise had gone on for a minute or two she cupped her hands around her mouth, drew a deep breath, and yelled at the crowd.

'BE QUIET! Give the man a chance!'

The next second, as every eye turned on her, including Léon Bonneau's, she wished the ground would open and swallow her up. She buried her flaming face in her hands and tried to hide behind Mrs Barnet's ample frame. Nevertheless, her words told. There was a sudden hush.

'Thank you,' Léon Bonneau said to the crowd. 'I have two more things to say to you.' He was amused, and a little touched, by Madeleine, though he wished she had left him to deal with the matter himself.

'The first is that during the next two days I will go to other mill-owners in the West Riding and I shall beg of them to take on as many of you as they possibly can. I will post notices in each shed of any vacancies I can find for you. But do not, of course, let this prevent you looking for jobs yourselves.

'Secondly, but this will only affect some of you, I intend to try to buy the weaving and possibly the finishing, and to run these myself, though with fewer hands. I do not know, yet, whether this will be possible, and it will perhaps be another week or two before I can be certain. I will come to the weaving shed after dinner and speak further about this. For the rest of you, I wish you good luck, and I promise you that if I can do anything for you in the future, then I shall do it.'

There was no way he could tell them of his ultimate ambition. It was not the time to raise false hopes.

'I suggest that over the next three weeks we do everything we can to get out the orders on our books,' he concluded. 'That can only be to the good.'

For a few seconds the mill-hands stood there, willing the Frenchman to say something, anything, which would give them comfort; but when he stepped down from the platform and walked away, the crowd broke up. They moved silently back towards their places in the mill. The spirit had gone out of them. Even those who minutes before had had plenty to say, were dumb. The fears which had been in their hearts since the day of the funeral were now confirmed; the future was dark and threatening. Only the weavers had some vestige of hope, but sympathy for the rest of the hands kept them quiet until they were back in their own shed.

'Do you reckon we'll be all right?' Sally Pitts asked Mrs Barnet. 'Do you think we'll keep our jobs?' She dreaded to think what it would be like at home if she didn't bring in her wage packet.

'I don't know, do I, lass,' Mrs Barnet replied. 'We'll have to see what Monsieur Bonneau says. Nowt seems certain.'

'What will we do about an overlooker when Mr Bates goes?' someone else asked.

'There'll be no difficulty there,' Mrs Barnet said. 'There's plenty as'll want that job. I can think of someone meself.'

'It's a pity they don't have women overlookers,' Sally said. 'You could do it, Mrs Barnet!'

Mrs Barnet, who had hardly raised a smile all the last week, laughed out loud at that.

'That'll be the day, when they have a woman overlooker! I'll not live to see *that*! Why, it's against nature!'

The moment the hooter which signalled the end of the dinner-break had died away, Léon came into the shed.

'Please do not start your looms!' he called out. 'I wish to talk with you.'

They left their looms and came and stood around him. Joseph Bates stood aside, taking no part.

'I must tell you that if I am able to buy the weaving, I shall . . .,' – he searched for the word – 'concentrate . . . on doing the new designs which some of you are already working on. I see no future in doing the ordinary patterns here. Other mills are doing those, and on our small scale it would not be economic.'

No one spoke, but in the shifting of bodies, the shuffling of feet, he detected a feeling of apprehension, especially amongst those, and they were the majority, who had not worked on the new designs.

'You need not fear that you will not be able to learn the new patterns,' he assured them. 'The problem is, that in the beginning I think I would not be able to employ more than twenty weavers. Later, I hope it would be more, but not yet. Therefore I would like, when you have thought about it, to have the names of those of you who would like to work for me, if indeed there are any jobs to be had.'

'How soon would we know?' someone asked.

'Alas, it could be at least three weeks. I have to bargain with top-makers, dyers, yarn-spinners. All these processes will have to be carried out elsewhere.'

Even if he raised the money to buy the machinery and the present stock, and either to rent or buy the building, he would still have the uphill task of persuading the other processors to allow him credit until he was on his feet. And since they didn't know him, why should they? But that wasn't something he would say to these worried women standing in front of him.

'Are we to get our wages for three weeks, same as the rest?' Mrs Barnet asked.

'I have negotiated an extra week for the weavers,' Léon said. 'You have four weeks. But nothing certain beyond that.'

'We might miss other jobs in the meantime, sir!' another person pointed out.

'I know,' Léon replied. 'That is the snag – that, and the fact that I cannot employ all of you. So think carefully, and since Mr Bates is to leave us, let Mrs Barnet know and she will tell me. That is all, unless you have anything more to ask me.'

When he had left the weaving shed they all began to talk at once. Joseph Bates moved across to them.

'Get back to work!' he commanded. 'Get the looms going!'

'Nay, Mr Bates!' Mrs Barnet protested. 'Surely we can have ten minutes to talk among werselves? It's important!'

'So is the weaving,' he said. 'You can talk your heads off after work!'

'I'm sure Monsieur Bonneau would allow us ten minutes,' Mrs Barnet said bravely. She would not have dared to talk to him like this had he not been on the point of leaving Parkinson's.

'Well in this weaving shed, and for the moment, I'm in charge,' he said sourly. 'And I say, you set those looms on and get back to work, at once!'

Reluctantly, grumbling, they started up their looms.

'Awkward bugger!'

Madeleine looked up in astonishment. She had never heard Mrs Barnet swear before.

'I'm sorry!' Mrs Barnet said. 'I know he's your dad.'

'Don't be sorry, Mrs Barnet! I agree with you. He's exactly what you said!'

Madeleine was furious and ashamed. She was also determined that wherever she worked in the future, it would never be under her father.

'Not that he'll stop the lasses talking,' Mrs Barnet said. 'Not unless he gags us all!'

It was true. There was hardly a girl who wasn't talking to her neighbour or calling out across the shed. The words were drowned in the noise of the looms, but they were all able to read them, and the anxiety they felt swept through the weaving shed until it was almost tangible.

'What are you going to do, Madeleine?' Sally Pitts called across.

Possibly Madeleine was the only person in the shed who knew what she would do. She didn't have the slightest doubt. She had faith in Monsieur Bonneau – though what that faith was based on she couldn't have explained. It was just in her, strong as a rock.

'I'm telling Monsieur Bonneau I'd like to stay,' she said. 'I'm quite certain.'

'If you do, then I will,' Sally Pitts said. 'Though God knows what'll happen if I don't get a job in the end!'

'I've made up my mind,' Mrs Barnet said suddenly. 'Though it hasn't been easy. I'm going to take a chance on Monsieur Bonneau!'

'I think that's wonderful of you, Mrs Barnet,' Madeleine said. 'You're the one who could most easily get another job elsewhere, because you're far and away the best weaver!'

'Happen so,' Mrs Barnet agreed. 'But I like what we're weaving and I like Monsieur Bonneau. I reckon he's a genuine sort in spite of being a Frenchie. And another funny thing is, I feel a loyalty to Mr Parkinson, even though he's no longer with us, God rest his soul!'

'So do I!' Madeleine agreed.

'But if your folks are going to Saltaire, where will you live?' the older woman asked.

Madeleine frowned. It was the thought which troubled her most.

'I don't know. I shall have to get a room in Helsdon – but I can't afford to pay much.'

'Well don't worry about that,' Mrs Barnet said. 'You can have a room with me and my husband for the time being. You can pay for your food, and a bit extra when you can afford it for rent. It's nobbut a little room, but it's clean, and it's shelter 'til you can find summat better.'

Risking the consequences, Madeleine left her loom running while she flung her arms around Mrs Barnet.

'Oh, Mrs Barnet you are a love! You've saved my life! Do you really mean it?'

''Course I mean it, else why would I say it? And you'd better keep your eyes on your work, my girl! If you get a broken warp thread your dad'll have summat to say!'

Undemonstrative herself, she was nevertheless pleased by Madeleine's response, and the set of her mouth showed it. She liked the lass. She was a good little worker, always willing to learn more, and she didn't answer back.

In the end, ten weavers put their names down to back Monsieur Bonneau, some decided to start looking for new work the next day, and the rest voted to see what luck Monsieur Bonneau had with finding jobs for them in other mills before making any move.

Just before finishing time Joseph Bates walked over to Mrs Barnet.

'There's a message from Monsieur Bonneau,' he said truculently. 'He wants you to go and see him in his office. And Madeleine. I suppose you'd best stop your looms and go.'

'Whatever can he want wi' us?' Mrs Barnet wondered out loud.

'I don't know. But don't look so nervous, Mrs Barnet. He can't eat us!'

When they stood in front of Léon Bonneau's desk, Mrs Barnet was still apprehensive. In all her years as a weaver she had never before been summoned to the office.

'Please sit down,' Léon said.

'I'll stand, thank you kindly, sir!'

There was no way Mrs Barnet could bring herself to sit in his presence. He treated her as if she was a lady, but she knew she was no such creature, and mustn't presume.

Since her workmate remained on her feet, Madeleine did likewise; not that she didn't respect Monsieur Bonneau, but he had the knack of making you feel equal, and she would willingly have taken a chair. She was never in awe of him. Never since the moment outside Notre Dame cathedral when they had spoken together. And he was so handsome! So attractive.

Then her thoughts changed, darkened. He was a man, wasn't he? For all his handsome looks, his good manners and silver tongue, his sex was the same as that of the monster who had defiled her. Even now, as he was looking at her, she sensed in him the same passions, the same lust, that was in all men, hide it though they might.

She shivered at the memory. For months now she had kept it at bay, until she'd begun to think she was cured. But would she ever be cured? Would she feel like this every time a man looked at her?

Then just as swiftly her mood changed again. How ridiculous she was being! How conceited to think that Monsieur Bonneau would ever see her as anything other than an employee, and a humble one at that.

'I will not keep you long,' he was saying. 'What I want to say is that I would be very grateful if the two of you might find it possible to take a chance on me. I know it's asking much – it means you might miss other jobs – but you are the two weavers who know most about the new patterns. If I can find the backing, you are the two who could help me most to make this venture a success.'

Before he finished speaking they were both smiling.

How beautiful Madeleine Bates was when she smiled. It lit up her face, sparkled in her eyes. He felt in himself the first, faint stirring of desire; yet not the first, he remembered. That had been outside Notre Dame. It was a ridiculous notion and he put it from him at once.

'Nay, sir!' Mrs Barnet said. 'We've already made up our minds!'

'You have? Then please tell me what you have decided.'

'That we'll wait to see if there's a job with you, and if there is, we'll take it!'

He glanced at Madeleine.

'Me too,' she said. But he knew she would. Hadn't she told him this earlier?

'I am grateful to you both,' he said.

'Sir . . .' Madeleine began.

'Yes?'

'If you do start up, would you please take on Sally Pitts? She needs a job more than most. And she's already decided she'd like to stay with you.'

He looked at Mrs Barnet.

'Is Sally Pitts a good weaver?'

'One of the best,' Mrs Barnet affirmed. 'You wouldn't be sorry.'

'Very well, then.'

'There's another thing, sir . . .,' Mrs Barnet said. 'If you're going to be looking for an overlooker I've got a nephew who might be just what you're wanting. He's not as experienced as Mr Bates, of course – but he's young, and keen.'

'Then if I do start up you can tell him to come and see me,' Léon said.

Madeleine was already in the house when Joseph Bates arrived home.

'So what did he want – the Frenchman?' he demanded.

She hated his harsh tone; she hated his right to question her. For two pins she would tell him nothing. But he was her father, she lived in his house, she was not yet of age; she would have to tell him.

'Monsieur Bonneau' – she pronounced his name with deliberate clarity – 'asked me and Mrs Barnet to agree to stay on, hoping he'd be able to set up.'

He had gone through the cellar-head to wash his hands and face. Now he came back to the table to sit for his tea.

'And you refused, of course!'

'No, I didn't. I told him I'd be pleased to stay on, that I'd not look for another job in the next four weeks, give him a chance.'

Joseph Bates brought his clenched fist down on the table, the force of it setting the pots jangling.

'Then you're a fool! He'll never get the backing to buy the weaving. Who would entertain him for a minute? So you can walk right into his office tomorrow morning and tell him you'll be leaving with me; you'll be going to Saltaire in search of a job.'

'I'll do no such thing!' Madeleine contradicted. She tried to keep calm, to keep her voice level, though she was shaking inside. 'I've given Monsieur Bonneau my word and I'll not go back on it! And I'm not the only one who's done so.'

'Then you're all fools,' Joseph Bates said. 'Dazzled by a smooth-talking foreigner. Can't you see he has nothing to offer you?'

'And who is to say he won't have?' Madeleine demanded. 'Some of us have faith in him.'

'I place my trust in God, Who alone worketh miracles!'

'Then perhaps he'll work a miracle for Monsieur Bonneau!' Madeleine said hotly. It was no use, she couldn't keep her temper! 'I suppose He's his God as well as yours? I mean He does look after a few other people besides the members of your chapel?'

'Madeleine!' Mrs Bates cried out. Her daughter went too far. She had a genius for making things worse.

'Go and wash your mouth out, miss!' Joseph Bates thundered. 'Thou shalt not take the name of the Lord thy God in vain!'

'I'm not doing so,' Madeleine argued. 'I'm just claiming

a bit of His love and protection for a few other people besides your little clique!'

'Madeleine, please calm down!' her mother begged. 'Ask yourself are you wise, throwing in your lot with Monsieur Bonneau like this? Your father's right when he says it could come to nothing – and where will you be then? Wouldn't it be better to come to Saltaire with us?'

'I'm sorry, Mother, there's no way I'm going to Saltaire!' Madeleine said firmly. They'd have to drag her by the hair of her head, kicking and screaming every foot of the way, before she'd do that. 'I'll take my chance here in Helsdon.'

'But where will you live?' Mrs Bates felt eaten up with anxiety. She knew only too well why Madeleine wouldn't come to Saltaire – and how could she blame her? She hadn't had a civil word from her father in all the months she'd been living at home. If I could leave you, Joseph Bates, I would, she thought fiercely.

'Mrs Barnet's offered me a room. She'll just take for my food to begin with. I shall be all right.'

She would be if she got the job. Heaven knew what would happen if she didn't, but she'd face that when it came. Anyway it *would* be all right. She felt it in her bones.

'I've told you, you'll go to Saltaire, and no more nonsense!' her father said. 'That's my last word on the subject.'

Madeleine felt herself turn physically sick with apprehension. Was there something he could do to force her to go? But she'd fight him to the end.

'I'm sorry, Father,' she said. '*My* last word is that I won't go! I will *not* go!'

With that she pushed her plate away, leaving her tea untouched, and ran out of the house. She ran and ran, until eventually she found herself on the top of Helsdon moor. There she flung herself face down on the heather. It was in bud, waiting only for next month to burst into massed purple blooms. By the time the heather was out she would know the best or the worst. What would it be?

She stayed there on the moor until the July sun began to dip, then she got to her feet and made her reluctant way back to Priestley Street.

Immediately after breakfast next morning Léon Bonneau left Mount Royd.

'I'm not sure when I shall be back,' he told Mrs Thomas. 'I have a number of matters to attend to. Don't bother to prepare a meal for me.'

'It'll be no trouble, sir,' she assured him. 'In fact, it'll give me something to do. Time passes slow with nobody in the house.'

'When are you off to your niece in Morecambe?' he asked.

'At the end of the month, sir. As things are, I shan't be sorry to go. To think it should come to this!'

'I, too, shall have to look for lodgings in Helsdon,' Léon said. 'I can't stay here much longer.'

He had had no time to give a thought to where he might live. There were so many more important matters to take care of. Last night he had written to Roubaix to tell his family they might expect to see him within the week, but before he could attend further to his own affairs he must go in search of employment for the hands. That was his job for today, to visit the mills.

He had very little luck in Helsdon itself. The mill owners were sympathetic – as well as inquisitive as to what was to happen – but they had few vacancies.

'Who would have thought it of Albert Parkinson?' one said. Léon remembered him. He was the man who'd asked how much Albert would cut up for. Well now he knew, they all knew. Léon felt deeply sorry for his dead friend, for his humiliation.

'You've hit a bad time for jobs,' the man said. 'I could maybe take on a couple of wool-combers. I've had two wool-combers emigrate to America. But that's all for the time being.'

'Well that makes two men who will be grateful to you,' Léon said. 'All our wool-combers will be out of work, so you'll have plenty of choice.'

In another mill he found vacancies for two spinners and one weaver, and that was the lot for Helsdon.

After Helsdon he went to Bradford, to Bingley and Shipley. Once you left Bradford behind it was a pleasant place, this valley of the Aire; the river and the canal running through lush green fields, dotted with sheep and cattle; hill slopes on every side, sometimes steep and bare, sometimes gentler and tree-covered. And to the north, always there on the horizon, the high purple moors.

His last call was to Salt's of Saltaire. He stood in Victoria Road, gazing at the Italianate splendour of the mill. Everyone in Europe had heard of it, marvelled at the size of it, gasped in amazement at the reports of the party of three thousand guests which had marked its opening three years earlier. Well, he thought, as he was shown into the great man's presence, here's hoping Mr Salt will be as generous today as he was then, but this time in jobs, not food and drink.

'This is a sad business!' Titus Salt said, shaking hands. 'We feel the shock right through the trade when something like this happens. And I liked and respected Albert Parkinson.'

'Thank you,' Léon said. 'Mrs Parkinson will be pleased to hear that when I next see her.'

'As for jobs,' Titus Salt said, 'we must find a few for you. In fact I've been told that we've already set on one or two men from Parkinson's in the last day or two.'

'Certainly you've given our weaving-overlooker a job, though not as an overlooker, of course. You'll find him very skilled with the looms.'

'Good! Are you looking for jobs in every part of the mill?'

'Indeed, yes!'

295

'Then I will take on four spinners, and two hands in each of the other departments,' Mr Salt promised. 'I wish I could do more. As it is . . .'

'You've been very generous,' Léon said. 'I thank you.'

They talked amicably for a little while until Mr Salt stood to see Léon out.

'I was in your country for the Exhibition,' he said. 'I was very impressed.'

'And I was impressed by the exhibits from England,' Léon said. 'Your own among them. In fact, I was at the Exhibition with Albert Parkinson, which is why I am now in Helsdon.'

'And you are going back to France, of course?' Mr Salt asked.

'I am not sure, sir. Perhaps you might permit me to come and talk to you about that.'

Mr Salt looked puzzled. What was there to talk about?

'Certainly,' he said. 'By all means!'

By the end of the day Léon had promises of thirty-two jobs spread over several places. It was a pitifully small proportion of those who would be out of work. He could only hope that the promises he had been made, that Parkinson's workers would be remembered when further vacancies arose, would be kept. He had not yet been to Halifax, Wakefield, Dewsbury or the Huddersfield area, since he had visited only the mills where worsted cloth was made, as at Parkinson's. Perhaps he should take another day and go further afield?

He arrived back at Mount Royd tired and dispirited. As soon as he entered he heard voices, and as he stood in the hall Sophia came down the stairs followed by her husband, her mother and her aunt. Bereavement, he thought, had taken none of the bloom from Sophia. She was as pretty as ever, though a little thinner and more peevish in the face.

'Léon!' she said coldly. 'Might one ask what you are doing here?'

'Good evening!' he said. 'I'm not sure what you mean,

296

Sophia. For the moment, I am staying here. Didn't you know?'

'I most certainly didn't. May I ask by what right?'

Mrs Parkinson replied before Léon had time to speak.

'He is staying here because I invited him to. Good evening, Léon! How is everything?'

'When you can spare me a few minutes I will put you in the picture,' Léon said.

Sophia turned to her mother.

'Are you being wise, Mama? I mean, to have someone staying here when the family is not at home?'

'My dear!' David said.

'Are you mad, Sophia?' Mrs Parkinson said. It was strange how she had lost all fear of her daughter and her daughter's tantrums in the short time since her husband's death. 'What do you think Léon will do? Are you suggesting he'll steal the silver?'

'Well, he won't have the chance now, will he?' Mrs Chester said, then clapped a hand to her mouth. She was always saying the wrong things!

'What my sister means,' Mrs Parkinson said to Léon, 'is that we have come to Mount Royd to collect a few personal possessions. Since I shall have very little need of fine silver, Sophia is to take it to Thirsk.'

You could have sold it, Léon thought, if your greedy little daughter hadn't got her hands on it.

'In fact we have put together several bits and pieces in the drawing-room, a few of which are to come to my sister's home and the rest to go to Thirsk. I have told Mrs Thomas and I shall arrange for them to be collected. I hope you won't be inconvenienced by the lack of a drawing-room?'

'Not in the slightest,' Léon said. 'I seldom go in there. In fact, I shall be moving out of Mount Royd as soon as I have found lodgings in Helsdon.'

'Lodgings in Helsdon?' Sophia sounded horrified. 'Who could possibly live in lodgings in Helsdon?'

'Quite a number of people do, I believe,' he said smoothly.

'Well Léon, you are welcome to stay at Mount Royd as long as you like,' Mrs Parkinson said. 'Until it is sold over your head, that is! But I would have thought you'd be going back to France the moment all this business is over?' She turned to Sophia. 'You do realize, my dear, what a lot Léon is doing for us? How would we manage without him?'

'If I understood the business I would, of course, do my part,' David said eagerly. 'But I know nothing of wool! I have not been brought up to it.'

How do you live in Helsdon and escape wool? Léon asked himself.

'Well, Léon, if you would like to come into the study we can talk,' Mrs Parkinson said. 'After that I must see Mrs Thomas.'

Léon followed Mrs Parkinson into the study while Sophia continued her tour of the house, checking on what she could salvage.

'You must take no notice of my daughter,' Mrs Parkinson said when she and Léon were alone. 'I have come to the conclusion that we failed miserably in her upbringing, or why would she be so obnoxious?'

'Perhaps —'

She held up a hand to silence him.

'No, Léon, I have decided I do not like my daughter. As for you, you can be thankful you didn't marry her! Oh I know it was on the cards. I wasn't fooled! Just be thankful, that's all. Now tell me what's happening?'

He told her everything he had done and planned so far.

'Albert would have been very grateful for what you're trying to do for the hands,' she said. 'He thought more about the mill than about anything else. I believe that's why he lavished so much on us, to make up for the love he gave the mill.'

'I hope from somewhere there might be enough for a pension for you,' he said.

'That is Mr Ormeroyd's hope. And I should be grateful for it. My sister is kindness itself, but she is far from rich and I should dearly like to make my contribution. Anyway, Léon, I wish you every success in your own plans. I don't know where you'll get the money, but I hope you do. And now I must go and see Mrs Thomas.'

She is a changed woman, Léon thought as he watched her go. She is suddenly stronger; stronger by far than she was when her husband was alive.

Mrs Parkinson seated herself at the kitchen table, something Mrs Thomas had never seen her do before.

'Well, Mrs Thomas,' she said. 'We've come to the parting of the way. It's a sad day, after so long.'

'It is indeed, ma'am. You and me came to Mount Royd at the same time, if you remember?'

'I do indeed. I was a bride,' Mrs Parkinson said. 'And Briggs came not long afterwards. I'm glad he's found another job so quickly.' She sighed. 'Well there it is! I hope all goes well with you in Morecambe – and if ever I venture so far you can be sure I shall call to see you.'

They talked for a little while, until there was nothing left for them to say to each other, then Mrs Parkinson shook her housekeeper by the hand, and departed.

When her mistress had left the kitchen, Mrs Thomas put her head down on the kitchen table and wept. It wasn't a bit like her. Apart from when the Master had died, she didn't know when she'd cried last. Not since she was a little girl. But she'd be all right with her niece, she told herself. She was a kind girl.

The next day Léon went to the other side of the West Riding, Huddersfield way, where the county bordered on Lancashire. All in all he found seventeen jobs, though some of them were different from those in the worsted trade and who ever took them would have to adapt. They would also have to find somewhere to live. Still, it was the best he could do. When he got back to the mill he made out the lists and posted them in the appropriate parts of the mill. He wished they were three times as long.

*   *   *

There was a great deal to do in the next two days, before he sailed for France. His first call was on Mr Ormeroyd.

'Is there any sign of a sale?' he asked.

Mr Ormeroyd shook his head.

'Nothing. Which is as I feared. A few enquiries for job lots – machinery and so forth. Nothing whatever for Mount Royd, which might have provided some money for Mrs Parkinson. You see it's really a house for who ever owns the mill.'

'I'm sorry about that,' Léon said, 'but do you think I could now go ahead and try to raise the money to buy the weaving? I must move quickly if I am to do it at all.'

'I should think so. I wish you luck, I must say. It won't be easy.'

'I know that,' Léon said. 'My hopes are on the fact that I am going to do something different, not enter into competition. And I shall offer a reasonable interest, especially where the period of the loan is not too short. But first I must see the manfuacturers, check that I can get the yarn I want and get it in the colours I must have.'

'How will you do that?' the solicitor asked.

Léon shook his head.

'It will not be easy. It does not only depend on credit, it depends on co-operation. I want the tops, then I must have them dyed to my own colours. We have been doing that at Parkinson's, so if the dyer will give me credit, there will be no difficulty. Then, I have to find the spinner who will take those tops and spin them ready for my weavers. I shall want a say in how they are spun. I wish for the right mixture of colours in the yarn. We have also been doing this for the last few months in Parkinson's.'

If only, he thought – if only I could have bought the whole mill, a going concern, it would have been so much simpler, and given time it would have been *une mine d'or* – a gold mine.

'Well, we're not unused to complicated jobs in these parts,' Mr Ormeroyd said. 'There's plenty of skill in the

300

West Riding. Your main problem is getting the credit. Have you decided where you're going?'

'Yes.'

Léon felt in his pocket and brought out a list of names, which he handed to Mr Ormeroyd. The solicitor studied them, nodding approval at some, pursing his lips over others.

'I should take that last one off the list if I were you. He'll send you away with a flea in your ear!'

Léon took the pencil and scored the name from the list.

'And I'll add one name to it,' Ormeroyd said. He pencilled in a name and handed the list back.

'But you have put your own name,' Léon said.

'That's right. I'm willing to back you for a fair amount. I have a lot of faith in you, Monsieur Bonneau.'

'But . . . but that's wonderful!' Léon cried. 'I can not thank you enough!'

'You can tell the others I'm backing you,' Ormeroyd said. 'It might help a bit. Everybody knows lawyers don't run too many risks with their own money!'

Arranging with the top-maker, the dyehouse, the yarn-spinner was easier than Léon had expected, though it took him two days instead of the one he had set aside for it. It was quite clear that one reason for the co-operation he received was the liking these men had had for Albert Parkinson.

'If you get the money for running the business,' was the sum total of their offers, 'then we'll give you credit on the supplies.'

The third day, the day when he had to ask for money, was not so easy. He hated doing it, it went against his nature to go cap in hand to any man. But by the end of the day – and, he was quite sure, helped by the example of Mr Ormeroyd's contribution – he had raised a loan close to the amount he would need to go into business. It was near, but it was not enough. He would now be dependent on getting money from his own family in

Roubaix. Would they or wouldn't they part with it? Indeed, could they?

These were questions he continued to ask himself all the following day as he travelled south from Yorkshire, and finally took the cross-channel boat from Dover.

SIXTEEN

It was late afternoon the following day when Léon arrived at his home in Roubaix. His mother and his sister, Marie, were there to greet him. His sister, at eighteen the youngest of the family, fussed over him, but his mother was more contained. She kissed him on both cheeks, smiled a greeting, but otherwise her demeanour was as if she had seen him only yesterday. It didn't mean that he wasn't welcome. His mother was not a demonstrative woman, she found it hard to show her feelings; but they were there all right, hidden beneath her cool exterior. He knew that.

'Marcel and Pierre will be here to dinner,' Madame Bonneau said. 'Are you tired after your journey? Do you want to rest until then?'

'Not tired. But I will wash, and change my clothes.'

It would have been an insult to ask if his room was ready. He was sure it always was.

'I will make some fresh coffee. Or a *tisane* if you would prefer it,' Marie said. 'Shall I bring it up to you? Oh Léon, it's so good to have you back!'

'I'll come down for it quite soon,' he said.

His room was on the second floor of the tall house, at the back. He looked out of the window on to the pleasant courtyard, and beyond that to the vegetable patch and a small orchard with apple and pear trees. It was surprising

303

how many pockets of productive land were hidden away behind these houses which, unlike most of the houses in Helsdon, where the appearance of the front was what mattered, turned blind eyes and dour facades on to the streets, reserving their welcome for those who penetrated further. He liked that. He liked the feeling that family life was lived in private.

He turned away from the window, washed, chose a clean shirt from the chest of drawers and a suit from the massive wardrobe, just as though he still inhabited the room, had never been away. He liked his room. The small, personal possessions, the souvenirs scattered around, were the story of his life. None of them had been disturbed. He was fond of this house in which he had grown up. It had none of the richness of Mount Royd, but it suited him. How would he take to lodgings in Helsdon, which he must find as soon as he returned? He brushed his hair, gave a swift glance in the mirror, then went downstairs to join his mother and sister. How good it was to speak his own language again!

'Will Simone and Charlotte also be here for dinner?' he asked.

He looked forward to meeting his brothers but, since he wanted to talk business, he would as soon not have had their wives present. In his opinion Marcel and Pierre were both under the influence of their womenfolk, and those women would not be eager to part with money which they could spend on their own backs, even though he had a right to his share.

'I expect so,' his mother said.

She wondered what Léon's visit was about. He had given no indication in his letter. Had he grown tired of England and was ready to come home again? Or – and she hated the thought – was it possible that he had fallen for some Englishwoman and was here to prepare the way for bringing her to France? Well, they would know presently. The time for discussion would be after they had had their meal.

Marie broke in. There was so much she wanted to know.

'Léon, please tell me, what are the fashions like in England? How wide are the skirts and what are the fashionable colours? Have you seen the Queen? Or any of the royal children – is it eight or nine now?'

He laughed, and held up his hands in protest.

'Where shall I begin, *ma petite*? Well in the first place I have not seen the Queen, or any member of her family – which seems to increase all the time and I've lost count of them. The Queen wouldn't dream of coming to Helsdon.'

'Then what about the fashions?' Marie persisted. 'Tell me about the fashions.'

'My dear little sister, that's something else I don't see much of in Helsdon, the latest fashions!'

When Sophia had been at Mount Royd she had been fashionable enough, in her provincial way: now the women he saw were mostly mill-girls, in dark skirts and aprons, with shawls around their heads when they came to and from the mill. Into his mind came a picture of Madeleine Bates. Even in her mill clothes she managed to look different from the rest. She stood out from them, so alive, her face shining with intelligence. And in Paris, dressed for the theatre in Sophia's fine clothes, she had looked every inch the lady. Any man would have been proud to have been seen with her.

'But the women are pretty,' he added. 'Some of them are beautiful!'

'And have you fallen for any of them?' Marie teased.

Who could he fall for in Helsdon? *L'affaire* Sophia had come to nothing – and she had never surrounded herself with pretty friends in whom he might have interested himself. Apart from that, there were only the mill-girls. However attractive they were, that was not an idea to be taken seriously.

'Of course not!' he assured her.

His mother, keeping her head bent over her sewing,

noted the hesitation before he replied. He believes what he is saying, she thought, but I am not so sure. Her youngest son was closest to her heart, and sometimes she knew him better than he knew himself. Even so, she hoped she was wrong. She put her sewing away and rose to her feet.

'I must go and see what Brigitte is up to in the kitchen,' she said. 'We are making a *coq-au-vin*.'

'My favourite!' Léon exclaimed.

'Do you think I don't know that?' she asked dryly. 'And a *tarte-aux-pommes* for dessert.'

'In the meantime I will walk with Marie in the garden,' Léon said. 'She can tell me all about the young men I'm sure are queueing up for her, and who her favourite is!'

Léon's two brothers and their wives arrived together. Charlotte, Pierre's wife, was pregnant. Simone had not long since had her third baby. It was a race between them as to who should have the largest family.

'Dinner is almost ready,' Madame Bonneau said. 'Please be seated. I do not like to keep good food waiting.'

The people must wait for the food, never the food for the people. How often had Léon heard his mother say that?

The meal was a small miracle, and eaten in an atmosphere convivial and civilized. No talk of business was allowed to infiltrate the partaking of food, the drinking of wine.

'This is the best meal I've eaten in months,' Léon said. 'Since I left France, in fact.'

The *coq-au-vin* was something his stomach had craved. As for the *tarte*, with its lacing of apple brandy and exactly the right amount of cinnamon, it was perfection!

'A simple meal,' Madame Bonneau said, 'such as you would find in any home in France!'

She didn't add, 'but not in England,' though they all knew what she meant. Everyone knew that when it came to food the English were heathens.

'Shall we go into the *salon*?' she suggested when the meal was over. She was quite sure by now that there was a reason behind Léon's visit and the sooner it came out the better. She moved into the next room and everyone else followed.

They sat around, sipping their calvados, talking of this and that. They expressed regrets at the death of Albert Parkinson, about which Léon had informed them by letter. Madame Bonneau commiserated over his widow. 'I know what it is like,' she said. When Jean Bonneau died she lost her husband, her lover, her friend – and she had never ceased to miss him.

Darkness fell, the lamps were lit, and still Léon had not mentioned his reason for coming home.

'It's getting late,' Simone said. 'We must go soon. The baby will waken and I must feed him.'

Madame Bonneau looked at Léon.

'Before Marcel goes, is there something you want to tell us?'

'Thank you, *Maman*,' Léon said. 'You are quite right, there is. I should have mentioned it sooner.' He was relieved that she had broken the ground for him.

He told them, as succinctly as possible, wasting no words but leaving nothing out, what he had in mind – and while he told them he watched the expressions on their faces; incredulity, disbelief, apprehension, annoyance approaching anger on the part of Marcel and his wife. Only his mother's face remained expressionless. Marcel's anger burst out before Léon had finished speaking.

'Are you mad? Have you taken leave of your senses?'

'I think not,' Léon said. 'I have gone into it carefully. It is all feasible once you let me have my share of the money.'

'How can we give you that?' Pierre demanded. 'Our money is in the business. You know that.'

'Indeed I do know,' Léon countered. 'My inheritance was fed into the business while I was still too young to have any say in the matter. It might have seemed right at the time, but now there must be a way to give me back my money. I'm sure you can find a way.'

'It is taking bread from the mouths of our children!' Simone cried. 'We have three children to feed and clothe and educate! How shall we manage if you take your money out?'

You could start by having less finery on your back, Madame Bonneau thought. Her eldest son's wife was too extravagant, always buying new gowns, new hats. It was quite unnecessary. But she kept quiet. She would have her say when the right moment came.

'I wish to invest for *my* future,' Léon protested. 'One day perhaps *I* shall want to support a family. I see a good future for myself in what I propose. I shall make money in time; lots of money!' He had known there would be opposition and he was prepared to fight.

'So that is it,' Charlotte said. 'That is what is behind this mad idea! You wish to marry and you have not found the rich wife you sought?'

'At the moment I do not wish to marry. One day I shall, but for now, as I'm sure I've already made quite plain, I wish to set up in business. . .'

'At our expense!' Marcel interrupted. 'It can't be done, and there's an end of it!' He jumped up from his chair. 'Simone, get your cloak. We must go.'

'Then, before you go, I must remind you that this is money I have a right to!' Léon said firmly. 'I am speaking of the money left to me in the wills of my father and my grandfather. That money is mine!'

'But it is all tied up in the business,' Pierre persisted.

'And I now wish to take it out and invest it in a business of my own!' Léon said stubbornly. He had come back to Roubaix half believing that he wouldn't be able to get the money, but their attitude put iron into him. Nothing would stop him now. He would fight until he won!

Marcel turned to his mother.

'*Maman*, you have not spoken. You know the situation. Please tell Léon that what he asks is impossible!'

Madame Bonneau looked from one to another of her sons. Each one was out for himself, each one had inherited the ambition which had been in their father. There wasn't a pin to choose between them, but it was right that her youngest son should have his chance. It appalled her that he would leave France, live in that cold country across the channel. And when he married, her grandchildren would be English, and she would never know them. It was a terrible idea. Nevertheless . . .

'Yes, *Maman*, what do you say?' Pierre asked. 'You are always sensible!'

Every eye was on her; in every face, except little Marie's, she saw greed. In her daughter's was sadness, concern that her favourite brother might leave France and she would lose him.

'I am glad you think I am sensible,' Madame Bonneau said. 'I do not care for Léon's proposal one jot. . . .'

Now she watched the relief sweep over every face except Léon's. He looked even more determined, thrusting out his chin, clenching his hands until the knuckles whitened. He would fight me as well as the others to get what he wanted, she thought. Well, he wouldn't need to.

'Though I do not care for Léon's proposal, indeed I dislike it, I say that he has a right to his portion of the money. It was left to him and it is his. Bear in mind, also, that we have had the use of it these past years. Now a way must be found to raise it, even if it means selling something. Any other decision would be dishonourable. And it had better be done quickly. It is clear your brother is in a hurry. So get on with it!'

'Thank you, *Maman*,' Léon said quietly. He felt as if a heavy weight had rolled off his body. His mother's word was law. The family would not go against her, how ever much they grumbled.

'Well I don't know how we shall do it!' Marcel grumbled. 'The market is not right!'

'The market is never right,' his mother said. 'But I'm sure you're clever enough to find a way, Marcel.'

Simone gave her mother-in-law a baleful look. Why were the menfolk such putty in her hands?

'And remember that Léon needs the money quickly,' Madame Bonneau added. 'So waste no time!'

'*Maman*, I can't thank you enough,' Léon said when his brothers had left.

'You may not thank me in a year from now, if your business fails. You may wish I had decided otherwise!'

'No I shan't. Nor shall I fail. I have no doubt at all that I shall succeed.'

His mother sighed.

'I hope for your sake that you do. But whether you do or not, remember that your home is here, in France.'

Three days later, with black looks and tight lips, his brothers handed Léon the money. His sisters-in-law cursed him, but since that was behind his back it didn't worry him. The following day he packed, and left Roubaix.

Marie wept that the money had been found to allow him to live in England.

'I don't begrudge you the money. I want you to be happy,' she said. 'But why can't you be happy in France?'

'Don't cry, little one!' Léon said. 'As soon as I'm settled you shall visit me in England.'

'You promise?' she asked tearfully.

'I promise!'

It was harder parting from his mother. She, he knew, would never set foot in England.

'I shall visit you as often as I can,' he told her. 'See, I have left clothes in the wardrobe and in the drawers, so that you know I shall come back from time to time!'

'Your room will always be waiting,' she said quietly.

She would not break down in front of him. Her body was heavy with tears which asked to be shed; but not yet, not yet.

*　　*　　*

England was covered in a thick mist. What other country would have fog in the summer? Léon asked himself. As the train crawled slowly northward he peered out of the carriage window, willing the fog to part so that he could view the wide green landscape which he knew was there. He looked in vain. All he could see, from time to time, was the blurred shape of a few trees or the line of a nearby hedgerow. The rest was shrouded and silent. He leaned back in his seat and closed his eyes.

Was he quite mad? Returning to this place with its terrible weather, its lack of culture; where he had few friends and none at all of the opposite sex? How would he live without feminine company? But no, he was not mad. Work was the thing; to be successful, to make money. The rest – women, friends, leisure pursuits – could come later.

He was filled to the brim with optimism about his new venture. Everything good lay before him. The thickest fog would not be allowed to dampen his spirits now – and there was no fog in his future. It was clear and bright. Against the rhythm of the train he began to plan, to sort out the order in all that lay before him.

At Leeds he changed on to the branch-line for Helsdon. Albert Parkinson had always been met at Leeds by Briggs, but no such luxuries were available to Léon. Not yet, he thought; not yet. In Helsdon it was too late for a cab, and he was obliged to walk to Mount Royd, but the mist had cleared, revealing a fine, starlit night. When he reached the house Mrs Thomas was up, and waiting for him.

'Dear Mrs Thomas!' he said. 'I hadn't expected to see you. In fact I thought you might already have gone to Morecambe.'

'I go on Saturday,' she said. 'Now, monsieur, you must be hungry. I've kept a nice hot-pot in the oven for you.'

'I'm starving,' he agreed. 'I haven't eaten for hours. I wonder if the day will come when they serve food on trains?'

'Never, sir! That's for sure!' Mrs Thomas was adamant. 'It's an impossibility!' She was to make her first train journey on Saturday and she was not looking forward to it. Trains were unnatural; horses were the natural thing, else why had God created them?

The hot-pot, though he denied that it could come up to his mother's *coq-au-vin*, was delicious and filling. He ate the lot. When Mrs Thomas came to clear away he said, 'Please don't wait up any longer. It's time you were in bed!'

Me too, he thought, climbing the stairs to his room. He must be up early in the morning. First he would visit Mr Ormeroyd, find out how the land lay. With that thought came his only niggling anxiety, which he had pushed away from him until now. Supposing, just supposing, that it all fell through? Supposing someone had come along during his absence in France and bought the whole mill, lock, stock and barrel? He couldn't allow himself to hope that this had not happened; with so many people now out of work it would be a wicked wish; but if he didn't get the weaving now he would be bitterly disappointed.

In spite of his physical fatigue, he lay a long time awake, tossing and turning. In the morning he was up before daybreak and on Mr Ormeroyd's doorstep the minute the lawyer's office opened.

'There have been no offers for the whole,' Mr Ormeroyd reported. 'A few more for items of machinery. Also some more job vacancies have been sent to me in your absence, notably from Mr Titus Salt.'

'Then I can formally make my offer for the weaving,' Léon said. He felt almost giddy with excitement as he named the sum he would pay for the machinery and the stock. 'As for the building, I will offer a fair rent for that.'

'Very well,' Mr Ormeroyd said. 'Then the two of us will see Mrs Parkinson. I will send a messenger to ascertain if she will see us at once. If she agrees to the terms, we will put everything in writing. . . .'

' . . . And the weaving will be mine!' Léon said.

Mr Ormeroyd smiled at the young man's enthusiasm. 'I wish you well,' he said. 'And I'm sure you *will* do well. Our money – I speak for myself and the others – will be in safe hands.'

Mrs Parkinson agreed to everything without demur. What else can I do? she asked herself.

'If the sale of the other machinery goes through,' she said, 'and with your rent from the weaving shed, Mr Ormeroyd thinks there should be just enough money for me to keep Roger at his school, and for me to pay my way with my sister. Those are the two things I want most.'

With some difficulty Léon controlled his enthusiasm over his own affairs in the face of the widow. It was bound to be a sad day for her; the start of his hopes and almost the end of hers.

'Léon,' she said, when everything was signed and they were about to leave, 'don't hesitate to show your pleasure about this deal in front of me. I can imagine how you are feeling and I'm sure you're trying to hide it. But I congratulate you and wish you well. I am also very grateful for all you have done for me.'

'And now for the mill,' he said to Mr Ormeroyd as they left Mrs Chester's house.

'Do you need me there?' Mr Ormeroyd asked.

'I don't think so,' Léon replied. 'But I'm more than grateful to you for seeing to things in my absence.'

'You have a good work force there,' the solicitor said. 'It's a pity you can't use more of them.'

'It is my greatest regret,' Léon admitted.

In the mill he went into every shed and spoke to the overlookers and to several of the men. This would be their last week of work for Parkinson's. He gave out details of the new vacancies which had come in and a few men asked for permission to go after the jobs immediately.

'By all means,' Léon said. 'And I wish you luck!'

He left the weaving-shed to the last. When he went in, every woman and girl in the place looked up from her loom, trying to tell from the look on his face whether the news was good or bad, though it could be good only for the twenty chosen ones, that was for sure.

Léon walked across and spoke to Mrs Barnet.

'It is almost dinner-time. I will come into the shed then, when the looms are off. I want to talk to people.'

'Yes, sir. Is it . . . is the news . . .?' She felt the anxiety of all of them as if it were wound into one big ball inside her.

'Let us say, I am going to need a weaving-overlooker,' Léon replied, smiling. 'Can you get a message to your nephew as soon as possible? Ask him to come and see me?'

'Oh, sir! I will that! Happen I could send one of the lasses? If she went right away he'd be able to come in the dinner-time.'

'Do that,' Léon said. 'Now tell me, is everything going well?'

'Very well, sir. We've been working real hard while you was away. Madeleine here has finished a beautiful piece. Flawless, it was. A bit o'reight!'

He turned and smiled at Madeleine, working at the next loom.

'A bit o'reight, eh?'

Madeleine laughed outright, she couldn't help it, at the Yorkshire phrase on his French tongue. Then she blushed at her own temerity. It was nice to see him back, though. She would like to say that to his face, but she daren't.

'Well I will come and look at things later,' he said. 'At the moment I have several things to attend to.'

Back in the mill office he sat at the desk which had once been Albert Parkinson's. He had more than once felt the previous owner's presence when he sat at his desk, but it was a benign presence; he didn't mind it in the least. Now, as he sat there, a blank sheet of paper in front of him, a pen in his hand, he paused for a moment to think about the man who had brought him here in the first place. What a troubled soul he must have been in those last months of his life, knowing that one day everything must come crashing down. Or had he always remained optimistic, sure that it would all work out for the best? He sincerely hoped that this was the case.

He must never get himself into such a position. Keen as he was to expand, to build up the business, he must be watchful. He must obtain the orders, see them carried out promptly and get the money in. He must give very short credit, and as quickly as possible discharge the debts he was now incurring. Only then could he think about expansion. But expand he would, he was certain of it.

He started to write, making a list of the things he must do. As soon as possible he should visit the suppliers and set his orders in hand. He could send letters, of course – the penny post was reliable enough – but he had already learnt that in the West Riding it was better to establish good relationships face-to-face. Also, his written English wasn't good. That was another thing he must improve, his command of English.

When the dinner-time hooter went he put down his pen and left the office. Crossing the yard, he came face to face with Mrs Barnet, accompanied by a fair-haired young man in his early twenties.

'Monsieur Bonneau, this is my nephew, John Hartley,' Mrs Barnet said. 'He's come about the overlooker's job.'

'Well perhaps he and I should go back to the office for a few minutes,' Léon said. 'I will be down in the weaving shortly.'

'Now let us discuss a few particulars,' Léon Bonneau said when they were seated on either side of the desk. 'I suppose you live in Helsdon?'

'All my life, sir!' John Hartley said.

'You have not been an overlooker before?'

'No, sir. But I've worked under one. I know how to tune the looms. I can give you good references.'

'And could you manage twenty weavers? Perhaps more in time. All women, mostly young.'

He was too good-looking; he would set hearts a-flutter, they wouldn't be able to concentrate on their work with this young man bending over the loom!

'I think so,' the young man said. 'I've got four sisters. I can deal with them.'

Léon smiled.

'Knowing my own sister, that is quite a recommendation! I suppose Mrs Barnet will have told you that we are weaving designs and patterns different from those you must be used to?'

'She did that, sir. I'm very keen to try! You'll not find me wanting!'

In the end Léon said, 'Well, the fairest thing I can do is give you a month's trial. You can start next Monday. And now you might as well come down to the weaving shed with me and hear what I have to say. Let them have a look at you, too!'

On his handsome appearance and pleasant manner alone, John Hartley was immediately acceptable to most of the weavers.

'An improvement on old Bates!' one of them said.

'Handsome is as handsome does,' her neighbour replied. 'We shall have to see how he makes out as an overlooker shan't we? And don't go making remarks like that in front of Madeleine Bates.'

'Of course I won't, stupid! But I expect she feels the same way.'

She did. Madeleine was as pleased as punch when Léon Bonneau brought John Hartley into the weaving shed and announced that he had engaged him. She had already met John at Mrs Barnet's house. The Hartleys lived two streets away and, in the way of the West Riding, the two sisters and their families seldom passed each other's doors without popping in to pass the time of day.

While Léon Bonneau was visiting his family in France,

316

the Bateses had moved away from Helsdon, to a small, terraced house in Shipley.

'As soon as Mr Salt has built more, we're promised a house in Saltaire village,' Mrs Bates said. 'In the meantime, Shipley isn't too far away, only a shortish walk along the canal bank for your dad.'

But too far away from my lovely Madeleine, Martha Bates thought. She would miss her daughter so much.

'Promise you'll come and see us!' she begged.

'Of course I will, Ma! I'll come next Sunday afternoon,' Madeleine promised.

The day her family left Helsdon Madeleine took over the Barnet's back bedroom. It was small, and stuffy in this hot weather, but it was her own and that she liked. She liked Mr Barnet too. Though he was an invalid, and often in pain, he was such a cheerful man; always pleased to see her, always ready with a smile and a quip.

Apart from the setting-on of John Hartley, the rest of Léon Bonneau's news was received in the shed with mixed feelings. The weavers who now knew they would keep their jobs were deeply relieved; the rest had their worst fears confirmed.

'I am more sorry than I can say that at present I cannot employ all of you,' Léon said. 'But who knows, in time I might! I suggest that you all leave your names and addresses in my office and I promise you that if I have even one job free in the future I will engage someone from that list.'

'How much longer have we here, then?' someone asked.

'A week. The new weaving will start on Monday the first of September.'

'I wonder what it'll be called, then?' Sally Pitts asked Madeleine when Léon Bonneau had left the shed. 'They can't go on calling it Parkinson's, can they?'

'Bonneau's, I expect. Though it's a funny name for a Yorkshire mill,' Madeleine said.

'He can name it what he likes,' Mrs Barnet chipped

317

in. 'But folks round here will go on calling it Parkinson's till kingdom come! They don't like changes, especially foreign ones.'

Back in his office, Léon remembered that he needed to see Mr Ormeroyd again, on the subject of suitable lodgings in Helsdon. He couldn't continue to stay at Mount Royd after Mrs Thomas had left.

Sighing, he picked up his hat and left. What a nuisance all this to-ing and fro-ing was! When would someone invent a machine which would allow him to talk to Mr Ormeroyd instead of having to visit him? The telegraph was already in use; messages could be sent even from other countries as they had been in the recent war – but to communicate with someone no more than a mile away one had either to wait on the post or make the trip to see him face to face.

It was a hot August day. By the time Léon had reached Mr Ormeroyd's office in the centre of Helsdon he felt his clothes sticking to him, and said as much to the solicitor.

'It's a day for getting out on to the moors,' Mr Ormeroyd said. 'There's always a breeze up there, no matter how still it is down here in the valley. Now that you're going to be one of us you should explore the moors and the Yorkshire dales. There's plenty to see and enjoy hereabouts.'

'I'm sure of it,' Léon said politely. 'I shall do so as soon as I have the time.'

'Well, allow yourelf a little leisure,' Mr Ormeroyd advised. 'It is not good to work every hour God sends, especially when you have no family to go home to.'

'That is why I came to see you,' Léon said. 'I must leave Mount Royd very soon now. I presume it will have to be closed up as soon as Mrs Thomas goes. I shall need lodgings.'

'I thought about that when you were in France,' Mr Ormeroyd said. 'In fact I took the liberty of making enquiries, and I think I may have the answer – without in any way committing you, of course.'

'So?'

'There is a Mrs Lenham, a widow with a young daughter. You will have passed her house on the way down from the mill. If you are interested she would be able to offer you a bedroom and a small sitting-room. You would arrange with her whether you wanted to take your meals alone, or with the family. I've left all that to you.'

'I'm very interested and most grateful,' Léon said. 'When could I call on her?'

'I will give you a note of introduction and perhaps you might like to call on your way back to the mill. The house is called "Ashgrove". It stands a little back from the road.'

'I think I know it. I'll call at once,' Léon said. 'It will be good to have the matter settled.'

At the house he was shown in by a young servant. When he sent in his card Mrs Lenham, an attractive woman, perhaps in her thirties, came into the hall and greeted him with a welcoming smile.

'Monsieur Bonneau! I hoped you might come,' she said. 'Mr Ormeroyd told me about you. He is an old friend of my family. Would you like to see the rooms?'

'If you please!'

He felt sure he would like them. He liked the atmosphere of the house at once; he liked this pleasant-looking woman whom he now followed up the stairs to the first floor.

'They are adjoining rooms,' Mrs Lenham said. 'I think you would find them comfortable – and you would be quite private. I keep a cook and a maid – and then there is my daughter and myself. You would be well looked after.'

'Is your daughter at school?' Léon enquired.

Mrs Lenham laughed out loud at this.

'You flatter me, sir! My daughter is twenty!'

'I find that impossible to believe, madame!' Léon said politely. 'You are surely much too young?'

'Impossible or not, it is true,' Mrs Lenham said. 'My

daughter is not in the house at the moment or I would have introduced you.'

'Then I look forward to meeting her later,' Léon said. 'I'm sure if you will have me I shall be very happy here. Would it be possible for me to take over the rooms on Saturday?'

'Whenever you like, monsieur. As you see, they are quite ready.'

On Saturday afternoon Léon Bonneau moved his few possessions from Mount Royd to Ashgrove. Before leaving Mount Royd he took a last look around to see that everything was in order. He had not known the house long, but he was deeply saddened by the circumstances of his leaving. How must it have felt for Mrs Parkinson when she left, with no hope of ever returning? And for Mrs Thomas, who had left only half an hour ago?

Madeleine had undertaken to collect Mrs Thomas and to take her to the station and see her on to the train. They stood on the platform now, waiting for it to arrive.

'Is it safe, Madeleine? The train I mean?'

'Absolutely safe, Mrs Thomas,' Madeleine assured her. 'Why, I went most of the way to Paris and back on the train! And your niece will be on the platform to meet you at the other end. You've absolutely nothing to worry about!'

Except a new life, with different people, Madeleine thought. Mrs Thomas had been so long at Mount Royd, it would be difficult for her to change. She wished the train would come quickly. Words were so difficult to find.

It was Mrs Thomas who first saw the smoke from the engine in the distance, and then they both heard the sound. As it drew near Mrs Thomas clutched at Madeleine's hand.

'You will come to see me, won't you, love?'

'The minute I can save the train fare,' Madeleine promised. 'Now that I've got a sure job, that won't be too long.'

320

She found a compartment, a lady already in it, and helped Mrs Thomas in. Then she stood on the platform as the train left, watching and waving until it was out of sight.

Only a few months, she thought, walking back to Mrs Barnet's and everyone is somewhere different. Her parents and sisters, Irvine, Miss Sophia, Mrs Thomas, Mrs Parkinson, herself and Monsieur Bonneau. And Mr Parkinson. She would never forget him. It seemed as if the whole circle which had been her life had broken. How, if ever, would it come together again?

SEVENTEEN

'Give me your bonnet!' Mrs Bates said. 'Take off your cloak. Oh, this is going to be a lovely Christmas!'

Madeleine hung her cloak on the peg by the door.

'It's starting to snow,' she said. 'Am I the last to arrive?'

'You are, love. And no less welcome. Are you hungry?'

'Starving!' Madeleine admitted.

'Well I won't be a minute with your tea. We've had ours.'

'So when did you get here, Irvine?' Madeleine asked her brother. He was standing with his back to the fire; so tall and handsome in his uniform!

'Yesterday afternoon. My Queen and country decided they don't need me until after Christmas.'

'Then you've had plenty of time to warm up,' Madeleine said crisply. 'Move over and give me a chance!' She gave him a friendly shove, and when he moved away she held out her hands to the blaze, trying to get the life back into them. It was the sure way to get chilblains, of course, but never mind that now.

Emerald came down the stairs, which led straight into the small living-room, followed by Penelope. In a blue dress which her mistress must have handed down to her, her hair brushed and coiled, colour in her cheeks, Emerald looked quite the little lady. But what struck Madeleine most of all about her sister was her confident, almost pert, air. Every time she saw her, Emerald had more airs and graces; so different from the shy, weakly child who had gone to Mount Royd to help out while she herself was in Paris. It was amazing that anyone could thrive on working for Sophia Parkinson, but Emerald certainly did. Moreover, she seemed to be totally modelling herself on her mistress.

'How long have you been here, Our Emerald?' Madeleine enquired.

'I arrived from Thirsk this afternoon. Mr and Mrs David Chester have gone to spend Christmas with Mrs Chester senior and with Mrs Parkinson,' Emerald announced solemnly. 'My services are not required.'

'And I've been here all the time if you want to know,' Penelope said. 'I'm always here. What's more I hate it. I haven't a single friend in Shipley!'

'Cheer up, chicken! You soon will have,' Madeleine said.

'I don't like the place as well as Helsdon,' Mrs Bates admitted. 'But for the moment . . .'

She looked around her at her four children, pleasure and pride glowing in her face, showing in the brightness of her eyes and in the upward curve of her lips.

' . . . at this moment,' she finished, 'I dare say I'm the happiest woman in the West Riding!'

'You're like a mother hen with chickens,' Madeleine teased. 'All you want is your family under your wings!'

'I admit it. It's what most mothers want – and for a few hours I'm lucky.'

There was a radiance in her mother, Madeleine thought, that just now was not matched by any of her children, pleased though they all were to be together. And for the time being they were all the more at ease because Joseph Bates was not present.

'Where is Father?' Madeleine asked.

At her daughter's question Mrs Bates face clouded. As if a light had been dimmed inside her, Madeleine thought.

'Out. Something to do with chapel.'

It had taken her husband no time at all to be immersed in the life of the local chapel. Already it was as demanding of his time as ever it had been in Helsdon. And of his money. She didn't begrudge the time, she was happier in his absence, but the money was a different matter. As an ordinary weaver on piece work – though he minded two looms and could turn out good work quicker than most – his money was less than it had been at Parkinson's and their rent was higher than in Priestley Street. But come what may, the chapel must have its whack. It didn't matter to her husband that they could only afford meat once a week – and then only the scrag end of mutton, or a piece of fat belly pork – or that Penelope's boots were letting in the wet. Still, she thought, picking up the poker and giving the fire a good, purposeful jab, never mind all that now. Just please God everything would go smoothly over Christmas, that Joseph wouldn't spoil it for them.

'Madeleine . . .,' she began anxiously.

'Yes, Ma?'

'Madeleine, before your Dad comes in, will you promise me you'll go to chapel tomorrow, with the rest of us? To please me? To keep the peace.'

Madeleine put an arm around her mother's shoulders.

'Of course I will, Ma!' Eyebrows raised, she turned to her brother. 'Does that mean you're going, Irvine?'

'It does. It's peace on earth isn't it – so I'm doing my bit for peace at twenty-one Coomber Terrace. Won't hurt any of us.'

'Well I appreciate it,' Mrs Bates said. 'Not for the sake of chapel, but . . .'

She didn't need to finish. They all knew that the action would lighten the atmosphere a little, or at least remove another cause for dissension.

'But don't think I'm going to kowtow to him all along the line, Ma!' Irvine said. 'He hasn't spoken a civil word to me since I set foot here. I'll stand so much and no more, not even for you!'

324

Mrs Bates sighed. 'Well, do your best, all of you. Now Madeleine, you must come and eat.'

Madeleine sat at the table, bit into the flatcake, still warm and crisp from the oven, cut a piece of cheese, sipped the hot, strong tea. It was good to be home, even though she hadn't the slightest hope that her father would be cordial to her. He would never forgive her for defying him by staying in Helsdon, which was one of the reasons why she had wanted to spend Christmas with the Barnets.

'You haven't heard *my* bit of news,' Emerald said. 'Guess what, Madeleine?'

'I can't,' Madeleine said through a mouthful.

'Oh go on, guess!' Emerald urged.

'You're going to marry the Prince of Wales!'

Emerald pouted. Why did no one take her seriously? 'If you're going to be silly, I shan't tell you. I've told the others, but I shan't tell you. Anyway, the Prince of Wales has only just gone sixteen.'

'Ah! Then you'll have to wait until he grows up a bit. Come on love, tell me the news. I promise not to tease.'

'Mrs David Chester is expecting a baby! There now, what do you think about that!'

Not much, Madeleine wanted to say. It was an event which usually followed marriage, and sooner rather than later. Also, heaven help the child with Miss Sophia for its mother. But she wouldn't disappoint Emerald.

'Well I never! And when will the happy event take place?'

'April! And the Master says I must take extra special care of the Mistress from now on. Which I shall do, of course!'

How in the world could anyone as selfish as Miss Sophia inspire such loyalty in her servant? Madeleine wondered. Out loud she said, 'Well, mind you take care of yourself, Emerald. The winter's on us; mind you don't catch cold again!'

'I shall be glad when *I* can go into service,' Penelope said suddenly. She lived, now, for the moment when she could go out into the world. Would her mother possibly let her go next year, when she'd be twelve? Some girls did.

When Madeleine had finished her tea and cleared it away, they drew seats closer to the hearth, making a tight circle around it.

'Build up a good fire, Irvine,' Mrs Bates said. 'I bought a bag of coal this morning, so there's no need to stint over Christmas.'

Coal was only one of the things she had been saving for all the year, copper by copper, sometimes no more than a ha'penny or even a farthing at a time. She had kept the money in an ornament on the mantlepiece, an ornament Joseph had given her in happier times, just before they were married. A week ago, when she was alone in the house, she had taken down the ornament, rejoicing in its extra weight, and in one beautiful moment had tipped its contents on to the table.

Running her hands through the coins, picking them up and listening to the sweet sound as they dropped on to the table, she had at last disciplined herself into totting them up, dividing them into little piles. As well as the extra coal, there had been enough for oranges and nuts for the Christmas stockings, extra fruit for the mincemeat and the pudding and, the biggest treat of all – she had felt blissfully extravagant when she'd asked for it at the grocer's – a bottle of ginger wine! What with all that, and on the stone slab in the cellar a rabbit all cut up and prepared for the Christmas dinner, they would have a fine time.

For now, they chatted, hearing each other's news, telling their own.

'Brighton's a fine town!' Irvine said. 'And as barracks go, the barracks aren't bad.'

'It's a long way away,' his mother protested.

'Well one of these days,' he promised her, 'you might visit me there. See if you don't!'

'Get away with you!' Mrs Bates said. 'Pigs might fly!'

There were not enough seats in the house for all. Irvine

occupied his father's armchair and Penelope sat on the floor at his feet while Madeleine and Emerald sat on stools. It was thus, clustered together in comfortable companionship, talking and laughing so that at first they didn't hear him enter, that Joseph Bates found them. In the very first second he observed the tight semi-circle which contained no space for him, saw that his own chair, which no one else ever occupied, had been taken over by his son almost as if he had a right to it. Anger sparked in him, and might have exploded had not his wife, in the next second, and the rest of them by following her apprehensive gaze, seen him standing there.

'It's still snowing then?' Martha cried. 'You're covered!' She got up at once and went to help him off with his coat, giving Irvine a warning nudge which meant 'get out of your father's chair' as she passed him. Irvine made no move, and when Penelope started to jump to her feet he pressed his hand on her shoulder and kept her down. Martha hoped and prayed her son wasn't going to be awkward. All her own efforts would be useless if the others didn't try, though she had to admit it, Irvine had been on his best behaviour so far, in spite of the way his father had treated him.

While Martha Bates was seeing to her husband, Madeleine leaned forward and spoke sharply and quietly to Irvine.

'Move yourself! You know you can't sit there. And don't start anything, for heaven's sake!'

He grinned at her, but presently, and without the least haste, he rose to his feet, pulling Penelope up after him.

'Keep your hair on!' he whispered. 'I was only larking!'

'Well don't!' she warned him. Then she turned to her father.

'Good evening, Father. Merry Christmas! I hope you're well?'

His only acknowledgement was a brief nod in her direction. No reciprocal good wishes, no enquiry as to how she did. How in heaven's name would she manage to be civil to him right through Christmas Day?

'Sit you down,' Martha Bates said to her husband. 'I'll make you a cup of cocoa.'

'I'll give you a hand,' Madeleine said quickly. 'I'll make some for all of us.' Anything rather than sitting opposite to her father, enduring his cold silence. It was a silence which now filled the room. There was a chill over everything. Even the fire had turned sulky. Desultory remarks from her mother, whispered words between Emerald and Penelope, fell like stones in a pond, and then ceased altogether.

'You girls come to the table to drink your cocoa,' Mrs Bates said. 'If you're hungry you can have a piece of bread – and then it's bed.'

'I'll take myself off at the same time,' Madeleine said. There was no way she was going to stay up in this atmosphere – and it had been so pleasant until a few minutes ago.

'You'll have to get in with Emerald and Penelope,' Mrs Bates said. 'It'll be a bit of a squash . . .'

'We'll manage very well. Don't worry, Ma. Will Irvine sleep downstairs?'

'Yes. I'll make him up a bed on the floor,' Mrs Bates said.

Irvine stood by the table. His face was set. His hand, in his pocket, jingled some coins. His mother knew what was in his mind and prayed he wouldn't do it. She looked at him with entreaty in her face, but he turned away, refusing to catch her eye. He couldn't stand it. He couldn't stand this atmosphere. He wished he hadn't come home for Christmas, wished he'd never let on that he could get leave. He doubted if he'd ever come again. And in the meantime, no matter what, he was going down to the 'Black Horse' . . . The temptation to seek laughter, and goodwill, and a drink or two to liven things up, was too strong. And it was his sanctimonious sod of a father who'd caused the temptation. They'd been happy, as right as rain until he came in.

'I'm off out!' Irvine said, taking his greatcoat down from the hook.

'Irvine, *please*!'

Don't go, his mother wanted to say. And if you must go, please don't get drunk! She couldn't say it, of course.

Joseph Bates looked up and spoke for the first time.

'I lock the door at eleven o'clock!'

'You'll be back long before then, won't you Irvine?' his mother pleaded. He didn't answer. He looked at Madeleine, who gave him a barely perceptible nod of the head, which he knew meant she would come down and unlock the door. Thank God there was no way his father would wait up for any of his children. He didn't care enough for that; all he wanted was to rule them. Well he won't rule me, Irvine thought. Not ever again.

Mrs Bates saw the look which passed from Madeleine to Irvine and was partly relieved. She would have come down herself to let him in, even if Joseph had been awake and had forbidden her to do so. She would simply have defied him. But it was better if Madeleine did it. It might keep this so-fragile peace a little longer. She just hoped Irvine wouldn't return shouting and singing.

'I'm off to bed, then. Good night, Ma!' Madeleine said when Irvine had left.

They didn't kiss, it was not their habit, but there was a warmth and understanding in the looks they exchanged – and on Madeleine's part, pity for her mother, who could never escape.

'Good night, Father,' she said politely.

He grunted.

Madeleine lay awake long after her sisters had talked themselves to sleep. Three people in the too-narrow bed was uncomfortable at best, but in sleep Penelope and Emerald flung their limbs about with abandon, taking more than their fair share of room while Madeleine clung to the edge. She wanted to stay awake, to be able to creep downstairs at the first sound of Irvine returning. She had heard her father turn the key in the door before climbing the stairs, and now the rhythmic snores coming from the next room told her that he was asleep. There was no sound from her mother. Without a doubt, Madeleine thought, she would be wide awake, staring into the darkness, waiting for her son to come home.

In spite of herself, Madeleine must have fallen into a doze, because the sound of men singing hit her with the suddenness of lightning. They were outside the house, splitting the stillness of the night, rendering 'Christians Awake' at a volume which must have aroused the whole of Coomber Terrace.

Thank heaven there were several of them! The thought came to Madeleine at once, in the seconds it took her to get out of bed and creep down the stairs. If Irvine was amongst them – and she was sure he would be – then his voice wasn't distinguishable above the rest. All she had to do was open the door and get him inside while the others were still at it.

She was in the act of turning the key, which was large and stiff, when she realized that the reassuring sound of snoring from her parent's bedroom had ceased. She was uncannily aware of that small cessation of sound in spite of the cacophony outside.

Carefully, she opened the door, cursing it as it creaked on its hinges. She saw Irvine at once, a happy grin on his face as he stood with the others by the door, all of them singing at the tops of their voices. They had run out of words for 'Christians Awake' and had started on 'While Shepherds Watched'. Madeleine grabbed hold of Irvine, stretching up to cover his mouth with her hand.

'Shut up and come in!' she hissed.

He wasn't so drunk that he couldn't obey her. She led him into the house and closed the door, leaving the rest of the men still raucously singing. Let them! It suited her purpose. There was no snoring now from overhead, but the bed creaked. Her father was surely getting up. She took Irvine's cap and hung it on the peg – thank heaven it had stopped snowing – then pushed him over to the settee.

'Get under the blanket,' she ordered. 'Quickly!'

Amiably, he obeyed. She took a cushion and placed it under his head, then pulled the blanket high to his chin, covering his uniform.

'Don't dare say a single word!' she commanded. 'Go to sleep!'

She went back to the door, opened it, called out in a purposely loud voice.

'Merry Christmas lads, but please go away now. You're disturbing everyone!'

While she spoke she heard her father coming down the stairs. She held the door open until she knew he was in the room, then she closed it and turned around to face him.

'I'm sorry you were disturbed, Father. High spirits. I've sent them off. They'll be no more trouble! Goodness knows how Irvine slept through it!'

Joseph Bates glanced suspiciously at his son, lying under the blankets. As if on cue, Irvine began to snore. Was it real or was it feigned, Madeleine wondered? One thing was certain, it was as well her father had almost no sense of smell, for the little room reeked of liquor! There would be trouble in the morning, nevertheless. Her father knew very well he'd locked the door at eleven o'clock.

To Madeleine's surprise, her father left her and went back upstairs. She heard the bed creak again as he climbed in. Thank heaven that in the light from the dying fire, the only light in the room, he hadn't seen her brother's wet footprints across the floor. And now for Irvine! If he was awake, and it could be done quietly, she must get him out of his uniform.

She lifted the blanket and looked at him. He had stopped snoring, but there was no doubt he was deeply asleep. He looked so young in sleep, so untouched. The horrors he had gone through in the war had left no outward sign on him. But he *was* different. He was a man, with a man's experience and a man's independence. What a fool their father was to think he could treat his son like a child! Or treat me so, she thought. We're grown up, we're no longer tied to him.

She drew the blanket up again, around Irvine's neck. It would be cruel to disturb him now. She would will herself

331

to waken early in the morning so that she could come down and help him out of his uniform. She touched his cheek lightly with her finger. Never in her life had she kissed her brother, but there was love in her touch.

In bed she lay awake a little while. I am no longer tied to my father, she thought. He's forfeited that. But I'm not free. I'm tied to my mother by the bond of love – and even more tightly by her need of me. And it was her father who had created that need.

She wakened at six next morning, and crept quietly downstairs. It was perishing cold in the living-room. Moving as quietly as possible, she rekindled the fire and put the kettle on to boil before she turned her attention to her brother.

'Wake up, Irvine!' she whispered.

He stirred, grunted, but when he would have settled back to sleep again she shook him by the shoulder.

'You've got to waken! You must get out of your uniform!'

He sat up. Quickly, she started to unfasten the buttons of his tunic.

'Come on!' she urged. 'I can't do it all for you!'

'What's the matter?' he said thickly. 'What happened?'

'What happened is that you came in the worse for wear at heaven knows what time. I managed to get you in the house and under the blanket no more than a minute before father came down. You obliged by falling asleep at once. You'll still have to explain how you got into the house after he'd locked the door, but I'll think of something.'

'Oh Lord! Was I very drunk?' Irvine asked.

'Not very. But you and your friends between you could have wakened the whole of Shipley. I laid the blame on them!'

He grinned. 'I remember now! We decided we'd go carol singing!'

'Keep your voice down! I'm going to make a cup of strong tea, and when you've had that, and got undressed, you can go back to sleep again if you want to. By the way, Merry Christmas!' She had almost forgotten that it was Christmas Day.

It was not until they had all breakfasted, and were ready to set off for chapel that Joseph Bates asked the question Madeleine had been dreading. She had arranged with Irvine what should be said, but he was in an obstinate mood, more inclined to tell the truth and shame the devil than smooth things over.

'Please don't start another row,' Madeleine begged him. 'For Ma's sake!'

It was strange that her father hadn't mentioned the affair the moment he'd come down to breakfast and seen Irvine sitting at the table. Is he by some miracle going to overlook it? Madeleine wondered as the time went by and nothing was said. It was too much to hope for, of course. The long and the short of it was, he enjoyed keeping them on tenterhooks.

'Before we go to the Lord's house,' Joseph Bates said to Irvine at last, 'I would like an explanation of your behaviour last night.'

'My behaviour?' Irvine's tone was reasonable, innocent even, but Madeleine could see a muscle twitching in his cheek and knew he was holding his anger in check.

'You had not seen fit to return home at the time I ordered. But not only *your* behaviour, I think. Since you entered the house after I had locked up, you clearly had an accomplice!'

'I let him in!' Madeleine said quickly. 'You'd not long been in bed, Father. Not more than ten minutes or so – but I think you must have been tired, and gone to sleep quickly. I didn't want to disturb you.' She hated herself for her hypocrisy. She hated herself almost as much as she hated him.

Joseph Bates gave her a cold look.

'I might have known!' He turned to Irvine. 'You know my rule. No one comes or goes after eleven o'clock at night. Even that is far too late for decent people to be abroad. All who live in my house must live by my rule.'

Madeleine saw Irvine open his mouth, raise his hand. She tugged hard at his sleeve to restrain him, and he subsided.

'We must set off. We shall be late for chapel,' Mrs Bates said nervously.

'I suggest that in the Lord's house you throw yourself on His mercy and ask humbly for His divine forgiveness for your behaviour,' Joseph Bates said to his son. 'And you too,' he added, turning to Madeleine.

I won't go, I will not go, Irvine told himself angrily – but Madeleine, reading his thoughts, put her arm through his and dragged him along with her, walking behind their parents and the two younger girls.

Sitting in the chapel, which was if anything plainer and more sombre than the one in Helsdon, Madeleine thought: if I had stayed in Helsdon for Christmas I would have gone to Mrs Barnet's church, to the Catholic church of Saint-Mary-the-Virgin. She had not known when she'd first gone to lodge with the Barnets that they were Catholics. Religion had never been discussed in the weaving shed. When Mrs Barnet had seen Madeleine looking with surprise at the holy pictures in the living-room, the crucifix on the bedroom wall, she'd said, 'I didn't think to mention it. Perhaps I should have? Your dad being strong chapel.'

'It doesn't matter,' Madeleine told her.

The following week she said, 'Could I go to church with you, Mrs Barnet?'

Mrs Barnet seemed reluctant.

'I'm not sure as you should, love.'

'I'd like to,' Madeleine persisted.

'Well all right then! But don't blame me if your Dad finds out!'

'He won't,' Madeleine assured her. He was the last person in the world she'd tell.

334

Since that first occasion she had been several times to Saint Mary's and now, sitting in the chapel, she wished she could instead be in that small, equally poor, but very different place of worship in Helsdon.

Don't be stupid, she admonished herself. The Christmas story is just the same here as it is there. Nothing is different except the trimmings. But if there was no difference, why didn't everyone go to the same kind of church? Only half-listening to the long sermon, her thoughts chased each other far and wide, and came to rest on that morning in Notre Dame. From there it was a short step to the thought of Monsieur Bonneau. What was he doing this Christmas morning? Madeleine wondered. Did he feel lonely, homesick? So far from his own kith and kin, not even in his own country.

Léon Bonneau, though he would have quite liked to see his family at this festive time of the year, especially his mother and sister, had no reason to feel lonely. He was being exceptionally well looked-after. In his landlady's tastefully furnished drawing-room – though it was difficult to think of Mrs Lenham as a landlady, she was just not the type – he had been given the most comfortable armchair, next to the glowing fire, and Miss Florence Lenham had served him with a glass of very pleasant sherry wine.

'I do hope that both you ladies intend to take a glass with me,' he said. 'I would not wish to drink alone.'

'This being a special occasion, we will,' Mrs Lenham assured him. She handed a glass to her daughter, then poured one for herself. 'And you must propose the toast, Monsieur Bonneau. It somehow seems more fitting for a man to do that.'

'It will be my pleasure,' Léon said. 'Let us drink to a merry Christmas and a happy New Year, and the health and happiness of you ladies!'

'And of you, Monsieur Bonneau!' Mrs Lenham said quickly. 'You must be included!'

They raised their glasses and sipped the wine, then

Léon held his glass aloft, appreciating the quality of the engraving, the way the finely cut facets twinkled and sparkled like diamonds in the light from the window and reflected the orange and red of the firelight.

'This is beautiful glass,' he said.

'I'm glad you like it,' Mrs Lenham replied. 'English cut crystal is the finest in the world – or so my late husband always told me. These were a wedding present.'

'I dare say he was right,' Léon conceded.

'I must say, I do like beautiful things around me,' she went on, 'insofar as I can now afford them. And I have brought up Florence on the same lines, though perhaps that is not very sensible in view of our circumstances. One must cut one's coat according to one's cloth. But never mind that now! Drink up and have another glass, monsieur.'

'Only if you will, Mrs Lenham.'

'Very well!' She was not at all reluctant. 'Perhaps you will pour it, monsieur. And Florence may have another small one, though we mustn't sit down to Christmas dinner already tipsy!'

She gurgled with laughter. She had the most delicious laugh, Léon thought, and it was never far away. What an attractive woman she was! So warm and friendly, and with an appearance not far short of beautiful. Florence was also agreeable, though shyer than her mother, less vibrant. Her fair hair was a shade paler, her eyes not so deep a blue, her figure less sensuous. All in all, it had been a lucky day for him three months ago when he had knocked on the door of 'Ashgrove'.

'It's most kind of you to invite me to share your Christmas dinner,' he said.

Usually, he took his meals in his room, only going into the Lenhams' part of the house when he was invited, though that had happened more often recently. There had been cups of tea, glasses of wine, his opinion sought on this and that – and in return he had dealt with those few small things which needed a man's strength and

336

courage; a recalcitrant window which refused to close, a quite horrible spider on the wall.

'The pleasure is mine,' Beatrice Lenham said. 'Mine and Florence's.'

He was devastatingly attractive. She wished he was not so young – all of fifteen years her junior, she reckoned, though inside herself she felt not a day older than he. At thirty-eight her desires were still strong, as they had always been. In her marriage it was she who had been the passionate one, craving her husband on every possible occasion. It was amazing that she had conceived only the one child. And now she missed the marriage-bed so much that sometimes her body ached with desire. A man such as Léon Bonneau could assuage that need. She had no doubt of it. And she would make it good for him. Her age would count for nothing against her passion and experience.

She felt the longing rise in her, felt her breasts tingle with it – then she drew in a sharp breath and pulled herself together. She must be mad. It was an impossible idea. Léon Bonneau was for her daughter. She had made up her mind to that the moment he had walked into the house.

'If you will excuse me,' she said, 'I must go into the kitchen, see what Cook is up to.' She turned to her daughter. 'Florence, look after Monsieur Bonneau!'

'Of course, Mama!' Florence said.

She would be glad to have him to herself for a minute. It was the same with any young men who came into her life; her mother was always there, brighter, prettier and wittier. They started by calling on her, but in the end it was her mother they fell for. Perhaps, just perhaps, Monsieur Bonneau would be different?

She is very pretty, he thought; even-tempered, docile, obedient; all assets in a wife. But as yet he was not contemplating matrimony. He had neither the time nor the means. And to tell the truth, obedience and docility were not qualities he would look for when that time came. He preferred her mother's more provocative nature, though had he been looking for a wife she would have been too old. As a mistress, it was possible, but not as a wife.

There were times when he wanted a woman. No doubt in Helsdon, as in any other town, in any country, there were women to be had for payment, but he was fastidious. The thought of dirt and disease repelled him. As she smiled at him, he eyed, with appreciation, the fresh, wholesome prettiness of Florence Lenham.

'Please be seated, Monsieur Bonneau,' she said. 'Tell me what it is like to spend Christmas in France.'

At about the time Léon Bonneau, Mrs Lenham and Florence were sipping the glass of rich, ruby port which Mrs Lenham insisted they should take after the Christmas lunch, Madeleine and Irvine were striding over the moors beyond Baildon. Where the village gave way to the moors the children were sledging, and beyond that, as far as the distant horizon, the hills and valleys were white-covered. Nowhere, for it hadn't drifted, was the snow more than two or three inches deep, but it had frozen over so that on its surface a million crystals of ice sparkled like diamonds in the winter sun.

'I think if we turn left here,' Irvine said, 'and then left again in a little while, we can go down through Shipley Glen to Saltaire.'

'How do you know that?' Madeleine asked.

'When you've been in the army, you get a feel for these things,' he said. 'No! Actually, a fellow in the "Black Horse" told me last night!'

They walked for a while in silence, the snow crunching under their boots. Then Irvine said:

'So how many young men have you got in Helsdon? A dozen on a string?'

'None at all. I'm not interested in young men.'

He gave her a hard look. She strode forward, her face set, not even glancing at him.

'Why not? I can't believe they don't come after you.'

'You know why not,' she said tersely. 'You know what happened.'

'You mean George Carter?'

'Of course I do. Surely you can understand that?'

'To an extent,' Irvine said. 'Not entirely.'

'Surely you can understand that it's spoilt me for all men – and all men for me,' Madeleine said sharply. She didn't want to talk about it, but he wouldn't let it be.

'You're wrong, Maddy! You're quite wrong, that's one thing I *am* sure of.'

'There's really nothing more to be said about it, Irvine. Can we change the subject?'

'No we can't – because there is! You know that it was me beat up George Carter? You know it was me sent him packing?'

'I guessed. And I'm grateful, but it doesn't change anything.'

'Yes it does,' he persisted. 'If it didn't, I'd have been wasting my time, done it for nothing. You have to realize, Maddy, that most men aren't like George Carter. Not one in a hundred is, not one in a thousand! Most men are normal decent blokes. You're condemning them all because of him. Do you reckon that's fair? Do you?' She didn't answer. They came to the fork in the road, and turned left towards Shipley Glen.

'Well?' Irvine asked. 'Is it fair?'

'Perhaps not,' Madeleine agreed. 'It's the way I feel, but perhaps it's not fair. But what about the fact that I'm spoilt for them? You can't deny that!'

'I do deny it,' Irvine said. 'Men are loving, forgiving creatures, just as women are. What man worthy of the name would hold something like that against you? Even if he knew about it.'

'He would have to know,' Madeleine broke in. 'I'd have to be honest!'

'I suppose you would, being you. And I suppose you're right. But do you think there's no understanding? Think of the men you know. Not father – he's one on his own – but think of the other men you know . . .'

She didn't know many men. There was John Hartley, of whom she saw quite a lot because he frequently popped in to see his Aunt Harriet. There was Monsieur Bonneau. He was above her station, but that was no reason not to think of him.

'Well? Are they monsters, these men, who ever they are?'

'I don't know, do I?' Madeleine said. 'But I suppose it would be unfair to think that.'

'And do you think they're uncharitable, unforgiving, don't understand?'

She paused, considering his question.

'I don't know, do I?' she said in the end. 'But I think it goes deeper than that.' The fact was, she knew next to nothing about them – about how they thought, felt, saw the world.

It was almost dark by the time the two of them reached the bottom of the glen. Ahead of them the huge bulk of Salt's mill stood out, silhouetted against a slate-coloured sky.

'I reckon we can take the canal towpath to Shipley,' Madeleine said. 'That's the way Father walks to work.'

As they neared Shipley, Irvine spoke.

'Think about what I've said, Maddy. Promise you will.'

'I promise,' she said.

EIGHTEEN

It was Mr Ormeroyd who, on a day early in April when Léon Bonneau came to see him on a small matter of business, gave him the news about Sophia Chester.

'She has had a son. Eight pounds at birth, my wife tells me – which it seems is a substantial weight. I never understand why women are so interested in the weight of a new baby!'

'And the mother and child are well?' Léon enquired.

'So I am told. Sophia came to Helsdon to have the child, so with her mother and mother-in-law running around after her I'm sure she's well looked-after.'

'Then I must call,' Léon said. 'In any case it's time I went to see Mrs Parkinson again. Business has made me neglectful of her.'

Mr Ormeroyd emerged from behind his desk, went over to a cupboard and brought out a bottle of Madeira wine and two glasses.

'You will join me? I meant to speak to you about that – no, not about your neglect, if any, of Mrs Parkinson, but about the fact that in my opinion you are working far too hard. My wife complains that we never see you, you are always too busy to accept her invitations. We both feel that you are not meeting people, not giving yourself time to make friends.'

What his wife had really said was that it was high time

Monsieur Bonneau found himself a wife and settled down. She liked to see all her friends and acquaintances paired off, and Monsieur Bonneau would be a good catch for any young lady, even though he was a Frenchman. Also, she herself knew several young ladies who were looking for husbands. Mr Ormeroyd, from long practice, translated this into more tactful terms.

'Please don't take what I say amiss, Léon,' he continued. 'We have your interests at heart.'

'I know, and I thank you,' Léon said. 'And I suppose you are right. But over the last few months there has been so much to do, so many things to see to.'

'I understand,' Mr Ormeroyd said. 'And you are working miracles in building up your business. But allow yourself a little free time. I dare say you don't want to be bothered with all these little parties the women give . . . and thank heaven my wife can't hear me say that . . . but give yourself a day off now and then. Take a train to Skipton and walk in the Yorkshire Dales, for instance.'

'I assure you, I do appreciate your concern,' Léon said. 'And I'll follow your advice as soon as I can.'

'Good! Now tell me how you're getting on at 'Ashgrove'? Are you comfortable? Is Mrs Lenham looking after you adequately?'

'More than adequately,' Léon said. 'I couldn't be better catered for.'

Also, he thought, when it came to Beatrice Lenham there was more on offer than he had yet accepted. Nothing had been said – she was too sophisticated, too tactful for that – but he knew. He could read the message in her eyes, interpret the movements of her tantalizing body. At first, though she was incapable of suppressing her vibrant femininity, he thought she had tried to subdue it so as to give her daughter the limelight; but that was increasingly not so.

Did Beatrice Lenham know how provocative she was? Sometimes, when his whole body was responding to her attraction, when his desire was at its height, it was almost unbearable not to accept her unspoken offer. The fact of her age no longer mattered.

'Mrs Lenham is a splendid, brave little woman,' Mr Ormeroyd said, his voice warm with approval.

'Indeed!' Léon said. 'And now I must take my leave. I think perhaps I shall call on Mrs Parkinson and Sophia right away.'

An hour later a smiling Mrs Parkinson held out her hand to Léon as he was shown into her sister's drawing-room.

'How nice to see you, Léon! My sister is out. She will be sorry to have missed you.'

'Congratulations on being a grandmother!' Léon said. 'Is it a splendid feeling?'

'Indeed it is! The only thing is . . .' The smile left her face.

'I understand,' Léon put in. 'You are thinking of your husband.'

'Yes. Albert would so have loved having a grandson. Also, though my sister is the kindest person in the world, I would dearly like the child to have been born at Mount Royd. It would have been more fitting.'

Sometimes, without telling anyone, she went for a walk which took her past Mount Royd. She would stand outside the big iron gates, peering through at the house, now shuttered and desolate. The grass on the wide lawns, unattended, had grown a foot high. Albert had been so proud of those lawns.

If only someone, anyone, would buy the house, live in it, bring it back to life!

She took a deep breath and smiled again at Léon.

'But I mustn't allow myself gloomy thoughts,' she said. 'And particularly I mustn't let Sophia see them. She is nursing the child, you see, and so she must think only pleasant things. Would you like to see them both? The monthly nurse is a dragon, but I think she might let you in for a minute or two!'

In her mother-in-law's best bedroom, Sophia looked resplendent. She was propped up against snowy-white

343

pillows, her shoulders covered by a lace-trimmed bed-cape, her red hair falling in curls against her shoulders. When Léon came into the room she held out her hand and Léon bent to kiss her fingers.

He was as damnably attractive as ever, but she hated him. Though possibly no one other than her mother suspected it, he had humiliated her deeply, and she would never forgive him.

'I'm pleased to see you looking so well,' he said.

'Ah, if only you knew!' she said languidly. 'If only men experienced what women go through! I tell you. If men had to suffer so, there would be no children after the first!' In fact, though she would never admit it, the birth had been surprisingly easy.

'I have heard that said,' Léon replied. 'Yet it seems as though many women find the reward worth going through the experience several times.'

'They have no choice,' Sophia said tartly. As always, she thought, men had the upper hand.

'And how is your husband?' Léon asked.

'Like a dog with two tails! But then he didn't have to go through it, did he?'

That was a matter of opinion, Léon thought. He reckoned David Chester might have suffered as much as his wife over the last few months.

'And Thirsk? Do you like living in Thirsk?'

'Thirsk is a one-eyed place,' Sophia said. 'Every bit as bad as Helsdon! And speaking of places, I had expected you to be back in France by now, married to your betrothed.'

He looked her straight in the eye.

'Alas, she has married another! She could not sustain my long absence – but how can I blame her?'

I don't believe you, Sophia thought. It was impossible to say so, but she didn't believe there'd ever been another woman.

'May I take a peep at your son?' Léon asked.

'If you wish.' She waved an arm in the direction of the

344

white-draped crib at the side of the bed. Léon bent over the crib, observed the downy, dark hair, the puckered face. He put his finger into the baby's tiny hand, felt its fingers curl around his own in a surprisingly strong grip.

'Why, he's beautiful,' he said.

'Do you think so?' Her voice was cool. 'I think he looks like a little pink monkey.'

The nurse came in and began to straighten the bed-covers.

'Now that's not the way to talk, Mrs Chester! The gentleman is quite right, he's a beautiful baby!' She turned to Léon. 'I must ask you to leave now, sir. We mustn't tire the new mother!'

Downstairs again, Léon said to Mrs Parkinson, 'He's a fine boy. What are you going to name him?'

'Albert. Though Sophia will shorten it to "Bertie" I don't doubt.'

'He's a lucky child to have you for a grandparent,' Léon said. And with Sophia for a mother, he thought, the child would need some luck.

He hurried back to the mill. It was a beautiful day; a blue sky, with scurrying white clouds, for there was a fresh breeze; the grass as green as emeralds, the buds swelling on the horse-chestnuts. Ormeroyd was right, he should get out more. One day before too long, it would have to be a Sunday, he would definitely make for the country, spend the day there.

At the mill he stopped briefly in his office and then made for the weaving shed, looking for John Hartley. He was pleased with the new young overlooker. He wasn't nearly as experienced as Joseph Bates had been, not always able to find the root of a problem, but he was competent for his age, ready to learn, and would improve. In particular, he seemed well able to keep a shed full of women hard at work; happily at work, without the fear which had been apparent under Bates's regime.

When he entered the shed, John Hartley was standing

by Madeleine's loom, the two of them bending over, heads together, seemingly examining the cloth.

'Anything wrong?' Léon asked.

'The "pick" keeps breaking,' Madeleine said. 'It always seems to be the brown thread. I can't think why.'

'I've made an adjustment,' John said. 'I think it'll be all right, now.'

'Will there be a lot to mend?' Léon asked.

'I don't think so,' Madeleine said. 'I think I've noticed it every time, so it's been dealt with.'

'Good! How is it going apart from that?'

'All right, Monsieur Bonneau. I'm halfway through this piece and I've got two more to do to finish the order.'

'And do you like this new design?' Léon enquired.

'Yes, sir,' she said, ' . . . except . . .' She hesitated.

'Except what? Is there something you don't like about it?'

'Well, it's not for me to say . . .'

'Yes it is. I asked you.'

'It's the colours, sir. They don't seem quite right to me. I think it needs either a sharper green in the weft, or more of the one you've got. The colour needs lifting.'

She couldn't have explained how she knew this. It was instinctive. When she looked at a colour, she knew what had gone into it to make that particular shade. When she looked at a pattern – at a check, a fancy weave or a herringbone – she saw not only the whole effect, but how each shade contributed to the whole. And in this case where it fell short.

Léon screwed up his eyes, stared intently at the cloth on the loom; looked at Madeleine, and then back at the cloth.

'How do you know it's a better green it needs?' he asked her.

'I can see it in my mind, sir. I can see what it would look like.'

He looked at her again, intently.

'Can you? My word!'

346

She wasn't sure whether he was being sarcastic, but she would stick to her guns.

'Yes sir, I can!'

'Well, carry on with what you're doing,' Léon said. 'John, come with me. I want to take a look at some of the other pieces.'

When the two men had gone, an awestruck Sally Pitts, who had observed the episode, called out to Madeleine.

'Ooh Madeleine! I don't know how you dared! How could you say them things to Monsieur Bonneau?'

'Don't be silly,' Madeleine replied. 'I answered his questions and I told the truth. What's wrong with that?'

Nothing, Sally thought with admiration, except that she herself would have been struck dumb.

Madeleine was back at her loom, which seemed to be running better since John Hartley had made the adjustment, when the message came that Monsieur Bonneau wished to see her in his office.

'Whatever can it be for?' Sally Pitts wondered fearfully. 'Do you really think you said too much, Madeleine?'

'Of course not!' Madeleine replied. All the same, walking across the yard in the direction of the office, she was apprehensive. What could a summons to the office mean other than trouble?

'Come in!' Léon Bonneau called, answering her knock. 'Please sit down, Madeleine. I won't keep you a minute.' He was adding up a column of figures, frowning as he did so. When he had finished he laid down his pen then sat back in his chair and looked at her. She grew embarrassed under his gaze. What could it be?

'You sent for me, sir!' She couldn't help sounding defensive.

'Yes.'

'Is there something wrong, sir?'

'What? Oh no, of course not. Why should there be?'

'Then . . .'

'I was interested in what you were saying about the

347

designs you are weaving. I thought I would like to hear more, find out if you have any other ideas.'

'Do you mean about that design, or any of the others?' Madeleine asked cautiously.

'Any. I had not realized you knew about colours. You were quite right about that design. I saw it myself when I looked closer.'

'But I don't know about colours, Monsieur Bonneau. Not actually *know*. It's just that when I look at something . . . well, if it's to do with colour, especially weaving the colours into the cloth, then somehow . . . well I can *see* something. I can't explain it properly.'

As she spoke, struggling to find the right words, he heard the enthusiasm in her voice, watched her face light up with interest. Why had he not known this before? He had recognized she was a good weaver, one of the best for her short experience, but he had seen nothing beyond that, not until her quiet insistence about the pattern as they had looked at it an hour ago on the loom.

'What you mean is, you have an instinct?'

'I suppose that's it, sir. Is that all right?'

He smiled broadly.

'Of course it is! Do not sound so worried. I'm a great believer in instinct. So often it is another name for a gift. It may be that you have a gift for colour and design. Are you interested in such things?'

'Oh yes, Monsieur Bonneau! More than I am in the actual weaving, though I enjoy that too, especially working on the different designs and patterns.'

She was smiling now, clearly feeling secure again. She had changed, matured, since those days when she'd been a hardworked little servant in the Parkinson household. Paris had been the beginning of it, but leaving Mount Royd and also, he thought, getting away from her father, had helped her to change. He saw her now as a woman who would always seize the opportunity, always grow into her surroundings, and then outgrow them when the time

348

came. How different from Sophia Parkinson, who would never change.

'Then, do you have any further ideas about the designs?' he asked.

'Well, sir . . .'

'Please do not be afraid to say. I want to know or I wouldn't ask.'

'Well,' Madeleine said. 'It sometimes seems to me . . . I have thought . . .'

'Yes? Go on.'

'I've thought that if we did a smaller quantity of one design, say only a few pieces, then changed it – not changed it entirely, but made a variation on the basic design – then, we'd have a much bigger pattern book to show to the buyers. Also, in the end, the customer, the one who was buying the cloth for her dress, might feel she was getting something a bit more exclusive. She might pay more for it – though I don't really know about that side of things.'

'What about the extra setting up on the looms?' Léon asked.

'It wouldn't need much. Not if it was just a variation, not a whole new design, and almost always a variation in the weft. I reckon John could do it quite easily.'

'John?'

'Mr Hartley, sir.'

'Well, perhaps we should ask him. You get on well with John Hartley, do you?'

'Oh yes, sir,' Madeleine said. 'We all do!'

And he supposed she saw him outside the mill, since she lodged with John Hartley's aunt, Léon thought. He wondered how she was getting along there. He'd seen her in church once or twice with Mrs Barnet, and had been surprised.

'There's one other thing,' Madeleine said. She wondered at herself; how could she be so bold? But in for a penny, in for a pound!

'Yes?'

349

'I wish there were better colours, in the dyes, I mean. Most of them have been around for ever, and some of them are so crude, especially the purples and the reds.' In her mind's eye, and indeed in nature – in the mauve and purple of the heather for instance – she saw shades of softness, yet intensity, which never seemed to be reproduced in cloth.

'Oh, I agree with you!' Léon said. 'It is what I think every time I visit the dyehouse. But better things might well be on the way.'

'What do you mean, sir?'

'I read about a young man, name of Perkins, who has discovered how to make a dye from coal tar.'

'Coal tar?' She hardly knew what that was.

'Indeed! Though he was not thinking of dyes when he made his experiments. It seems he was looking for a way to make quinine, artificially – and instead he came up with a beautiful purple dye! He has called it "mauveine". So who knows what he will do next, once he has found the way?'

'Well, who would have thought it?' Madeleine said. 'A beautiful purple! I'd like to see that.'

'Tell me, do you like the cloth we make?' Léon enquired. It wasn't a question he should be asking her. The type of cloth a millowner chose to make had nothing to do with the hands – except that they made it, he reminded himself.

'Yes, sir, though it's a bit stiff. But I realize it's got to be boardy and quite strong to stretch over the crinoline frames. Is that why we use a cotton warp?'

'Partly,' he said. 'Not entirely. We should hope and pray that the crinoline never goes out of fashion. It will be a bad day for the West Riding if ever it does. Think of the amount of material it uses!'

'I know,' Madeleine said. 'But apart from that, I think it's a stupid, inconvenient fashion. And it hides a woman's shape.'

The moment the words were out of her mouth she felt

herself blushing. How could she mention a woman's shape in front of a man, and a Frenchman at that?

Léon Bonneau hid his amusement at her discomforture.

'Well, I will think about what you said, Madeleine – about the designs,' he promised her. 'You might have something there.'

'I hope I haven't spoken out of turn, Monsieur Bonneau?'

'Not at all. But now you had better get back to work.'

'Yes, sir! This won't buy the baby a new dress, will it?'

He looked at her open-mouthed.

'What did you say?'

'I'm sorry, Monsieur Bonneau. It's just something we say when we catch ourselves wasting time!'

As she went back into the weaving shed several heads lifted to look at her, several pairs of eyes held the question which Sally Pitts asked out loud.

'Is everything all right, Madeleine?' Sally could always think of a dozen things to worry about. 'Did you get into trouble?'

'Of course not!' Madeleine reassured her.

'Then what . . .?'

Madeleine hesitated. 'He . . . he just wanted to discuss the weaving of a design, that's all. Just a few questions because I'd spoken up about the colour.'

It was true, but it wasn't the whole truth. For some reason which she couldn't define, she didn't want to report all Monsieur Bonneau had said – not that any of it was private, couldn't have been said before the whole weaving shed, but because the short conversation had seemed somehow intimate, almost as if – though it was only to do with work – it was something just between the two of them. She knew she was being silly, it was nothing of the kind, but that was the way she felt.

'Is that all?' Sally persisted.

'Absolutely all. And I must get on with this piece, Sally.'

She turned to Mrs Barnet. 'Thank you for minding my loom! Has it been all right?'

'Perfect, love!'

She was one on her own, Madeleine Bates was, Mrs Barnet thought. Not that she didn't think the world of her, almost as much as if she'd been a daughter, but there ws no denying she'd been cast in a different mould from the other girls. Though she was open and friendly, didn't give herself airs and graces, there was always that bit of herself she kept back, a bit of her which stayed apart from the rest. 'Princess' was Mr Barnet's nickname for her. It suited. John Hartley came over to Madeleine's loom.

'Everything all right, then?'

'Yes, thank you. It's running fine!' It wasn't what he meant, and she knew it.

'Everything all right with the boss?'

'Absolutely,' she said. 'Why shouldn't it be? It was just about a design.'

'I see.'

He didn't, actually, but it was all he was going to get out of her for now. Perhaps when they were walking home he'd do better – for since he passed their house on his own way home, he walked with Madeleine and his aunt every evening. It wasn't just curiosity which made him want to know why Madeleine had been sent for to the office; he wanted to be sure that nothing was wrong, nothing had been said to upset her – though he had to admit, she didn't look the least bit upset.

'Don't wait for me, John, when t'mill looses,' Mrs Barnet called out. 'I've got to go straight to t'doctors for your uncle's medicine!'

So for once he would have Madeleine to himself! His spirits soared at the thought. He'd taken to her from the first day he'd set eyes on her in his Aunt Harriet's house, and each day he grew fonder, though somehow he never managed to see her alone. This would be his opportunity. He'd make the most of it.

'Right, see you later then, Madeleine!' He walked away with a new spring in his step.

Sally Pitts was green with envy.

'Ooh Madeleine, you are lucky! I'd give me back teeth to walk home with John Hartley, just once!' In fact, she reckoned, half the girls in the shed were sweet on him, but he only had eyes for Madeleine. As for Madeleine, she didn't seem a bit bothered.

'Well you can walk with us part of the way,' Madeleine said, 'until you have to turn off at Mossman Street.'

'I'm not playing gooseberry,' Sally said. 'He wouldn't thank me for it.'

Thus it was that Léon Bonneau, happening to look out of his office window as the weavers left for home, saw Madeleine and his overlooker walking side by side towards the gates. He could not have put a name to the feeling which suddenly came to him, nor did he try. John Hartley was a good fellow, he told himself, but he hoped that Madeleine wouldn't take him too seriously. Madeleine Bates was different. He felt in his bones that she was a young woman destined for better things. It had come to him strongly as he'd talked to her this afternoon. But, what things he didn't know, didn't even ask himself.

He turned away from the window and went back to his desk. There were still a few jobs to be done before he could leave. Usually he was happy to work on, sometimes long after everyone else had gone home, but this evening he was restless, and he recognized part of his restlessness as a desire for feminine company. It was a desire which came to him more often of late, and perhaps to get his head down and work was the best way to cure it. The only way, as far as he could see.

Into his mind came the thought of Beatrice Lenham. He tried to push the thought away, to concentrate on his work, but images, almost tangible, of her face and form superimposed themselves on the columns of figures he was staring at. He snapped the ledger shut, took up his hat and cane, and walked out of the office.

'Don't walk so fast, Madeleine!' John Hartley said.

'Don't tell me you can't keep up with me!' Madeleine

353

chivvied him, good-humouredly. 'You're inches taller than I am.' He was all of six feet tall, unusual in that part of the world; as strong as an ox yet as thin as a rail. If he was lagging behind it was deliberate.

'Of course I can,' he agreed. 'But what's the hurry? It's a beautiful evening and we've been cooped up all day. Why rush to get indoors?'

'Because I want my tea, that's why! Mr Barnet will have the kettle on, and if I make a start on the rest we can eat as soon as your auntie comes in.'

'Blow that for a tale! I want to talk to you, Madeleine!' He grabbed her by the elbow to slow her down – and was surprised by the vehemence with which she pulled away from his touch.

'Sorry!' he said. 'But please, Madeleine, I do want to talk.'

There was a serious note in his voice she didn't care for. She hoped he wasn't going to say anything silly.

'Well I'm here, aren't I? You can walk and talk at the same time.' Apprehension, though she told herself there was no need for it, made her voice sharp. Also, she was ashamed that she'd jerked away from him so roughly when all he'd done was touch her elbow.

'Well, since you're in such a rush,' John said, 'I'll come to the point – which is – will you come for a walk with me on Sunday afternoon?'

'Oh! Well . . . well I might be going home, to Shipley, on Sunday,' she said quickly.

'No you won't, Madeleine!' He wasn't letting her get away with *that*. 'You went last Sunday. You never go home two weeks in succession. I know that.'

'That's not to say I never will.'

'Please, Madeleine!' John pleaded. 'If there's some reason why you don't like me, then please tell me what it is. Otherwise, why not say "yes". All I'm asking is that you come for a walk with me.'

How stupid I am, she thought! Why should I be the least bit afraid of John Hartley? Into her mind came the memory of the conversation she'd had with Irvine on Christmas Day. 'Most men are not like George Carter,' he'd said. 'Most men are normal, decent blokes. You're condemning them all because of him.' He was quite right, and she *was* being unfair.

'Of course I like you, John,' she said. 'I'll be happy to go for a walk with you on Sunday.'

'Oh Madeleine, if only . . .'

She didn't want him to say any more. She'd stick to her decision, but between now and then she didn't want to think about it.

'In the meantime I do want to hurry home. I'm starving, even if you're not!'

Léon Bonneau let himself into the house and walked through the hall, passing the open door to the drawing-room on the way to his own quarters which were on the first floor. He'd just reached the stairs when Beatrice Lenham called out to him.

'Monsieur Bonneau!'

'Good evening, Mrs Lenham!'

He paused. Recognizing his state of mind, should he turn back, or should he continue up to his room? The short pause made the decision for him. Beatrice Lenham was now framed in the doorway of the drawing-room, smiling up at him. How attractive she was!

'Do come and take a glass of sherry wine with me, Monsieur Bonneau. Florence is out, visiting a friend. I should be so glad of your company!'

I had better not, he told himself; but ignoring his own advice he turned around and went towards her. He would take one glass of wine only, indulge in a little polite conversation, for no more than fifteen minutes, and that would be the end of it. Where was the harm in that? Surely he had earned a little relaxation, he thought, following her into the drawing-room.

'Please pour yourself some wine,' Mrs Lenham invited. 'And you can add a little to mine.'

The glass on the small table at the side of her chair was half-empty, and by the look of his landlady, by the pretty flush on her cheeks and the becoming sparkle in her eyes, Léon thought it might well not be her first glass of the evening. He picked up the decanter and helped himself.

'Do sit on the sofa,' she said. 'It is so much more comfortable than these silly chairs. And I do think you are looking a little tired. Or maybe not tired but, shall we say *distrait*? You have perhaps had a difficult day?' She had a low-pitched, quiet voice, with a slight huskiness which gave it added appeal.

'Most days seem to be busy, though that pleases me,' Léon replied. 'Do you speak French, then?'

'Alas, no more than the merest smattering! Would that I did, for it is a beautiful language! Perhaps you should give me lessons?'

'Perhaps I should,' he agreed. It was a prospect not without attraction.

'In which case I would need to repay you by giving *you* lessons in something or other! But what can an English-woman teach a Frenchman, I wonder?'

I could possibly teach you a great deal, she thought. I could give you pleasure. It was a fallacy that the English were cold, and didn't have the art of love. Not for the first time, she seethed inwardly that this attractive man – this passionate man, for she was sure he was – must be captured and kept for her daughter. Florence is not yet awakened, she thought. She had none of the needs which burned in her own body – and never more fiercely than at this moment.

'I am sure there is much you can teach me,' Léon said. He read the invitation in her eyes. He knew exactly what she meant. It was time he finished his wine and left. He picked up his glass and emptied it.

Beatrice Lenham rose quickly to her feet.

'Let me give you a little more sherry wine.'

He should have refused, but he didn't. When she had re-filled his glass she brought it over to the sofa, then sat down beside him. Her scent – some sweet-smelling perfume she had applied, plus the even headier aroma of her own aroused body – filled his nostrils. He drank deeply of his wine, then put the glass down on the sofa table.

'Why, monsieur, you have a thread of wool on your trouser leg!' she cried. 'Please let me remove it. It is lucky, you know. The one who removes the thread will have a letter in the post!'

As she leaned over to pick the thread he felt the soft fullness of her breasts against him. When she had picked off the thread her hand rested for the briefest of moments on his thigh. It was enough. Desire leapt in him, a desire he could no longer resist. In the next instant he had taken her in his arms, but it was she who, falling back on the sofa, pulled him down greedily on top of her. Oh God, how she wanted him! While his kisses forced her mouth open and his hands expertly explored her body, she writhed and moaned under him.

'Florence?' he said. 'What about Florence?'

'She will be hours!' Beatrice murmured. 'Oh Léon, don't stop! Please don't stop!'

'I don't want to. I don't ever want to stop. But we must go up to your room. We cannot stay here. Now, at once, Beatrice!'

She was out of the room and running up the stairs. He must give her a minute, his head told him. There were servants in the house. He must not follow too swiftly after her. But, oh God, he couldn't wait long!

When he went into her room she was lying on her back, naked on the bed, her crinoline and its frame in a heap on the floor. For a moment he stood there, staring at the incredible beauty of her body.

She held out her arms to him.

'Quickly, my darling! Quickly!'

She started to tear his clothes off until there was nothing between the two of them; they were body to body, and then fused into one person.

357

Afterwards, when he had left her, she buried her head in the pillow, tears running down her cheeks.

'Oh Florence, what have I done to you?' she cried. 'Florence, forgive me!'

But it would happen again. Of that she had no doubt. Already she was counting the hours.

NINETEEN

The minute the Sunday dinner was over and before anyone had had time to tackle the dirty pots, John Hartley walked into his aunt's house.

'Well then, Madeleine, are you ready?' he asked. He was raring to go.

'Give me a chance!' Madeleine protested. 'I'm still full of your auntie's delicious Yorkshire pudding. Sit down a minute while I help to wash up.'

'No need, love!' Mrs Barnet said. 'I'll see to that. You get out and make the most of the day.'

'Well, if you're sure . . .?'

'Course I am!'

From behind the lace curtains Harriet Barnet watched with approval as Madeleine and John set off.

'They make a lovely pair!' she said to her husband. Yet there was something in her, or rather, she detected something in Madeleine, which told her it wouldn't work out, much as she'd like it to.

I'm not sure that I want to go, Madeleine thought as they walked through the steets of Helsdon to join the track which climbed up to the moor. The real truth was, she was by no means sure that she wanted to be with John Hartley. She'd agreed to his request too quickly. To have been climbing up to the moor on her own would have been fine, for it was a glorious day, the sun shining, the sky high, the fresh, green bracken shoots curling at the sides of the track. But not with John Hartley.

Oh, don't be stupid, she chided herself. He was a nice young man, whom she liked, and she was simply going for a walk with him on a fine Sunday afternoon. There was nothing more to it.

But that wasn't quite true, was it? She knew very well, and everybody in Helsdon knew, that if you went for a walk with a fellow on a Sunday afternoon, just the two of you, it couldn't be counted as casual. Anyone who wasn't sleeping it off after their Sunday dinner, who'd seen them walking through the streets, would already be putting two and two together and making five! What an idiot she'd been not to insist on a foursome! She could have asked Sally Pitts and one of her brothers. Sally would have been in her seventh heaven.

'Isn't this grand?' John demanded. 'Just look at that view! You can see for miles.'

'It's beautiful,' Madeleine agreed.

The stony track had petered out now and they were in the middle of the wide moor. Up here in the winter, when snow blotted out every landmark, or at any time of the year when the mist came down and you couldn't see your hand before your face, and even the birds were silent, you could be totally lost up here. At such times the moor was hostile – but not today.

'We should have brought Sally and Tim Pitts,' she said.

'Why? Why should we do that?'

She didn't answer. He knew perfectly well why. He knew Helsdon as well as she did, and the way tongues wagged.

They walked to the crest of the moor. Here the downward slope started, suddenly and steeply, with imposing outcrops of dark rocks of millstone grit, and underfoot treacherously loose scree. John took Madeleine's arm to help her – and at once, at the very first touch, she pulled away from him, stepped sideways, putting a physical distance between them.

John stared at her in amazement.

'Why did you do that, Madeleine? I was simply trying to help you down the slope.'

'I'm sorry!'

'But why, Madeleine?' he persisted. 'It isn't the first time you've pulled away from me. What have I done?'

'Nothing, John! Nothing.' Leave me alone, she wanted to shout. Go away!

'Then why? Do you dislike me so much that I mustn't take your arm?'

'Of course not. Don't be silly, John!'

'Well that's what it looked like!' He was truly puzzled. Her movement had been so violent, so sudden.

'It's almost as though you're afraid of me,' he persisted. 'But that can't be true, can it? You know I wouldn't harm a hair of your head.'

How was she to tell him that it wasn't he she was afraid of, but all men? Yet somehow she must. It was unfair and cruel to let him believe that her aversion was to him. With a tremendous effort of will, fighting her reluctance as if it were a living enemy, she spoke.

'I'm sorry, John. It's not *you*. I'm just . . . afraid . . .'

'Of everyone?' He sounded incredulous. 'You, afraid?'

'Not of everyone.' She wished he would stop questioning her. She had apologized, so why couldn't he leave her alone?

'Are you telling me you're afraid of all men?'

She didn't answer. But she had no need to, it was there in her face, the horror in her eyes.

'Something happened, Madeleine?'

'Please don't ask me about it, John.' She had gone cold. She felt as though the sharp moorland air had taken the breath from her body.

He took hold of her by both arms, and when she tried to break away he held her in a firm grip and turned her to face him.

'Tell me who it was?' he demanded. 'I'll give him the hiding of his life!'

'He's been dealt with. He's left the district. Please John, don't ask me any more!'

'I'll not ask you about it now,' he said gently. 'But whenever you want to tell me, I'll listen. But I'll not ask. In the meantime, Madeleine, say to yourself that I'm not all men, I'm me, John Hartley. Tell yourself what you know is true, that I wouldn't harm a hair on your head. No, Madeleine, don't try to break away. Tell yourself, while I hold on to you, that you're safe with me. Quite safe. Tell yourself that, and believe it, and then I'll let you go.'

She stood there while he held her. He felt a shiver run through her. Madeleine felt the cold sweat break out on her, run down her neck on to her collar. Listening to his words, hearing his soothing tone, she tried to control her breathing, to calm herself.

'Do you believe it, Madeleine?'

It seemed a year and a day before she found her voice.

'Yes. Yes, I believe it of you.'

The instant the words were out of her mouth a tremendous feeling of relief swept over her. She realized that what she had just said was true, and with the realization came a tremendous rush of gratitude.

'You really believe it?'

'Yes.'

'Then I'll let you go.'

He loosened his grip. She rubbed her arms where he had held her so tightly.

'I'm sorry if I hurt you,' John said.

'It doesn't matter.'

She felt as if she had been in prison, and had come out again into the world – though whether he had freed her only in regard to himself she didn't yet know, couldn't tell. But with John she knew. How could she ever have been afraid of him?

'I brought you up here to ask you something,' John said. 'I'm not sure now whether I should – for your sake, I mean.'

'Please do so if you wish.' She didn't want to hear anything more but to let him have his say was the least she owed him.

'I've wanted to say it for a long time,' he confessed. 'What I want to say is, can we walk out together?'

She supposed, deep down, she had known he would say this. But to walk out was the preliminary, however long-drawn-out, to eventual marriage, and that she couldn't contemplate. The paradox was that though she no longer felt afraid of marriage with John Hartley, it was because he *was* John Hartley, and therefore not the man for her, that she didn't want it. It hurt her to refuse him, but she must.

'I'm sorry, John! I like and respect you, perhaps more than any man I know. And in the last few minutes you've put me in your debt. But I don't want to walk out with anyone. I'm not ready. Not yet.'

'You're twenty, Madeleine. I think you are ready, if you'll let yourself be.'

'No John,' she said firmly. 'I'm sorry. But please believe that it's not something against you. It's partly that I don't yet know what I want to do with my life.'

She had the feeling – how could she explain it to him? – that around some corner, which at any moment she might turn, something new awaited her. How could she explain it to anyone? She scarcely understood it herself.

'Perhaps we should turn back now,' she suggested. 'Make for home.'

'I won't come in,' John said when they reached the door of his aunt's house. 'Tell Uncle Charlie I'll pop in and see him tomorrow evening.'

Harriet Barnet looked up in surprise from the shirt she was mending when Madeleine walked into the house on her own.

'I've got the tea all ready,' she said when Madeleine delivered John Hartley's message. 'I thought he'd be stopping.'

There were questions in her face which Madeleine hoped she wouldn't ask. Had Mrs Barnet known what was in John's mind or was she just guessing?

'Well sit to and we'll have our tea, anyway,' Mrs Barnet said.

Normally Madeleine would have found no difficulty at all in eating the high tea, with meat and pickles and current teacakes and parkins, even after the substantial Sunday dinner they'd all demolished only a few hours ago. Everyone, given half a chance, ate like this, and her appetite was as healthy as the next person's, but for once she wasn't hungry.

'I'll just have a cup of tea and perhaps a square of parkin,' she said. 'I thought I'd go to church.'

'Chapel?' Mrs Barnet said.

'No. Saint Mary's.'

'I see.'

But Mrs Barnet didn't quite see. Though her religion meant a great deal to her – she was not a born Catholic but had gone over before marrying Charlie, promising they would bring up their children in the true faith, and then never having any – she was uneasy at Madeleine's increasingly frequent visits to Saint Mary's. It was no good doing the right thing for the wrong reason and it was her belief that Madeleine's interest was largely made up of defiance of her father. Not that anyone could be blamed for defying that pig of a man – but it was a wrong reason. So far she had hesitated to say much to Madeleine, but before long, she thought, she must.

'Are you going, Mrs Barnet?'

'Not this evening, love.'

I need to go, Madeleine told herself. The events of the afternoon had disturbed her and now she craved the balm and peace which she knew the church would bring her. She knew the peace would come, yet following it would come a dozen more questions which cried out for answers, questions which came so often now. They were not questions to do with John Hartley, or with anyone else; they were questions about herself, about what was happening to her, about what she must do.

Soon, now, she must talk to someone who would help her find the answers. Would Mrs Barnet do so? She was the only Catholic Madeleine knew to talk to. There was Monsieur Bonneau, of course; sometimes she saw him in church; but she couldn't possibly talk to him. In her heart she knew she must talk to the priest, but that she shied away from. It seemed an irrevocable step, one she was not yet ready for.

St Mary's was a poor church, poorer even than the chapel her family had attended in Helsdon. It had been built largely on the sacrificial gifts of the Irish population of Helsdon who had come over starving and penniless after the potatoes had failed in their own country. It was a miracle that it had been built at all, but it was a congregation not afraid of miracles, optimistic enough to expect them. And there was in it a richness of feeling and atmosphere, compounded of Madeleine knew not what, except that it had nothing to do with money. Now, Benediction over, she continued to kneel after everyone else had left, until she heard Father O'Malley's footsteps approaching.

She rose to her feet at once.

'Is there something I could be doing for you?' he asked in his soft voice. He had noticed this girl for several weeks now, sometimes with Mrs Barnet, often alone. She wasn't one of his flock.

'No. No thank you, Father,' Madeleine said quickly. 'Are you waiting to lock up? I was just going.'

'There's no hurry at all, now,' he said. 'Take your time.'

She heard the words, and felt another meaning behind them. There *was* no hurry. She would take her time and it would sort itself out in the end. When she looked into the priest's quietly smiling face, she just knew it would.

'Shall I pray for you?' he said.

'Please do.'

How often had her father said those words, yet in his case always as a threat, always giving her the feeling that whatever she'd done it was past redemption . . . . Well, in her father's eyes, what she was doing now was certainly unforgivable.

Léon walked back from the mill in the almost certain knowledge that Beatrice would be waiting for him the moment he set foot in the house. It had been so since that first afternoon, several weeks ago now, though how she managed to get Florence out of the house so often he couldn't imagine, and hadn't asked. There was also something about his relationship with Florence – if relationship was the right word for something so nebulous -- which was not as it had been. She was as polite as ever, but distant, avoiding him when she could. He was sure he didn't imagine. He wondered how much she suspected, or perhaps even knew. Did she voluntarily absent herself so often in the late afternoon and early evening.

When he walked in at the front door Beatrice rushed to meet him, taking his hands in hers.

'You're late, dearest! I thought you were never coming!'

As politely as he could, he disengaged himself. He wished she wouldn't greet him like this. There were two servants in the house, either of whom might see or hear. When he'd first known Beatrice Lenham here he'd taken her for a woman of the greatest discretion, but now she was clearly not so.

'We are very busy in the mill,' he said. 'All the time trying to get out our new patterns.'

'"All work and no play . . .,"' she quoted. 'Now come and have your glass of sherry wine.'

He had quickly discovered that she had almost no interest in his work. He would have liked, sometimes, to have talked to her about how things were going, especially as they were going so well. It would have been pleasant to relate some of his triumphs, to have received her congratulations. He was ambitious, and the more he succeeded, the more he felt the lack of someone with whom to share his success. But Beatrice was certainly not the one.

'Here you are then!'

She handed him his glass of sherry wine, poured one for herself, and sat close beside him on the sofa. With her free hand she began to stroke his thigh, rhythmically, ever more insistently. In spite of himself, in spite of the fact that in his heart he didn't want to make love to her, and on the way home he had made up his mind not to do so, he felt the passion rise in him. Before he had finished his wine she took the glass from him and put it on the table; then she took his hand and laid it on her breast, pulled her low-cut dress still further down so that he could fondle her.

'Not here, Beatrice,' he murmured. 'Not here! It is not . . .'

'You're right, dearest!' She jumped to her feet. 'Follow me upstairs in five minutes. No longer! You know I can't wait.'

Nor, by this time, could he. Within five minutes he was in her bed – or rather on her bed, for she refused, as always, to make love under the bedcovers.

'I want to see you!' she said. 'I want to see us both! If I could watch us in a roomful of mirrors I'd be delighted.'

'You are quite shameless!' he told her.

'I know! But don't tell me you don't like it because I wouldn't believe you!'

At first, because she was impatient, they climaxed quickly, she with a great shout of triumph as she came. After that they began again, she knowing every art of how to enslave and conquer him, so that in the end he was avid for her.

When it was over she said, 'Oh Léon, it was wonderful – as always. You are the best lover in the world. What would I do without you?'

There was no fear in her voice as she uttered the words, but in her heart she was beginning to feel fear. She wasn't stupid. She was clear-headed enough to know that what was between the two of them was purely physical. Outside of that they were very different people. And whereas at first he had been as eager as she to make love whenever she could create the opportunity – which she did frequently and without shame – of late she had sensed a reluctance in him. It was a reluctance to start, shown in a late arrival home from the mill, for instance, so that there was no time for lovemaking. But once the start was made, once she had touched him and he her, his eagerness was equal to hers. She dreaded the day, and knew it might come, when it would no longer be so.

'Did I please you?' she said. 'I did please you, didn't I? But you must go now. Florence will be home soon.'

When he had dressed and gone to his own room she looked at herself long and hard in the mirror. She was flushed from their lovemaking, her eyes still shining, her lips full and red. But was she – she hardly dared ask herself the question – was she *coarsened*? There were no new lines on her face, thank heaven – but her jawline was not as firm as it had been at twenty. She turned away from the mirror, cursing the fate which made women less attractive as they grew older and did nothing of the kind to men.

Every day, sometimes two or three times a day, Léon Bonneau went into the weaving-shed, walked around – sometimes with John Hartley, often on his own – examining things, asking questions, checking how the work was going.

'But he doesn't make you feel he's spying on you,' Sally Pitts said to Madeleine. 'Trying to catch you out. I used to be as nervous as a cat when he first did it. I was sure he was looking for something I'd done wrong.'

It was the dinner break. Those few weavers who didn't get home for dinner had brought their food outside and were sitting on a low wall, enjoying the summer's day. Mrs Barnet always scurried home – she had Charlie's dinner to attend to – but Madeleine stayed. Because of the distance, she had had to do so when they'd lived in Priestley Street, and she had grown to appreciate the precious oasis of free time in the middle of the working day.

'He'd soon see if you had done something wrong,' Madeleine replied. 'What's more, he wouldn't hesitate to tell you.'

That wasn't quite true, she thought on reflection. With Sally, because she was so nervous of the whole world, he'd probably get John Hartley to break it to her gently. But with me he'd come straight out with it! To be fair, he'd also come straight out with it if she'd done something he liked. Ever since the day when he'd had her in his office and talked to her about the designs she'd had a very direct and open relationship with him. He'd never sent for her to the office again, but when he came around the weaving-shed he'd stand by her loom and talk to her about the work; ask her opinions, which she was never afraid to give.

'He comes around a lot more than Mr Parkinson ever did,' Sally said. 'We used to see Mr Parkinson, of course, but he didn't stop and have a word – well not with the likes of me.'

'Mr Parkinson had the whole mill to attend to. Monsieur Bonneau only has the weaving,' Madeleine pointed out.

'I was a bit frightened of Mr Parkinson,' Sally confessed.

'Well you'd no need. He was a lovely man.' It was a year now since he had been killed. So much had happened in that year, but she didn't forget him.

'I don't feel as frightened of Monsieur Bonneau,' Sally said. 'I'm in awe of him, of course, because he's the boss. And he's so tall and handsome, and sounds so French and looks so rich! Do you think he is rich, Madeleine?'

'Well, getting richer all the time,' Madeleine conceded. 'But I doubt it's all cut and dried yet. I dare say he has a way to go, but the thing is, he's on the way – which is more than can be said for you and me!'

'What do you mean?'

'Well, however hard we work at the job, where will we be in five years' time? Exactly where we are now! We'll be doing the same job, for the same money, day after day from now until then.'

'We might be married and have children,' Sally said hopefully.

'*You* might. I doubt I shall.'

Since Irvine had talked to her last Christmas, and since she'd been for the walk with John Hartley – something not so far repeated, though he was always asking her – Madeleine had done a lot of thinking about marriage. She thought now that in the right circumstances, whatever those were, it was just possible she might not be afraid. She didn't know, and there was no way of proving it, but it was possible. If she could cure herself of that fear, then she determined to do so. But she would never marry, as so many did, to be rid of the drudgery of working in the mill.

'You don't seem a bit in awe of Monsieur Bonneau, the way you talk to him,' Sally said enviously.

'I'm not,' Madeleine agreed. 'I respect him because he's good at what he does, but I'm not in awe of him. He's only a man, like the rest of men.'

And that was another thing which wasn't quite true. He wasn't like all other men. He was different from anyone else she'd ever met. She'd known that, at the back of her mind, ever since Paris. Oh, she wasn't soppy about him, not like poor little Sally with John Hartley, who went tongue-tied and almost swooned whenever the overlooker came near her. There was nothing like that. Nevertheless, Monsieur Bonneau *was* different.

'We've ten minutes before the hooter goes,' she said to Sally. 'Shall we walk up the road, stretch our legs?'

When they were back at work after dinner and Monsieur

370

Bonneau came into the weaving-shed, he mentioned a new order he hoped to get. It wasn't unusual for him to do this. As far as he could, without going into too much detail or breaking confidences, he believed in keeping his workers in the picture. As Mrs Barnet sometimes said, it made them feel part of things.

'This could be a most important order,' Léon said. 'Garston's of Leeds is one of the biggest wholesale clothing manufacturers in the country – though I dare say most of you know that even better than I do.'

'That's right,' Mrs Barnet said. 'They allus have been, that I remember.'

'Yes. Well I have an appointment with Mr Henry Garston on Friday of next week. If he likes our cloth I suppose he could buy miles of it!'

Henry Garston had the reputation of being a tough man, not easy to please, but a man with great power. And our designs can't fail to please him, Leon thought. I'm confident of that. All he needed was the chance to show them to this man – and that, with incredible luck, he'd been given. Everything now depended on the meeting.

On the following Tuesday evening Léon Bonneau arrived home from the mill with a splitting headache and a general feeling of wretchedness. He was shivery, and felt as though his legs didn't belong to him. As usual, Beatrice Lenham came into the hall to meet him.

'I feel unwell,' he said at once. 'I think I must go to bed.'

She gave him a wide smile.

'To go to bed will do you all the good in the world!' she said. 'And I will provide an almost instant cure!'

'No Beatrice,' he said wearily. 'Not that. I tell you I feel ill.'

She looked at him narrowly. Was it an excuse? But when she noted his flushed face, his over-bright eyes, she realized he was speaking the truth – in which case it was quite the best thing for him to go to his bed before she herself caught whatever it was ailed him.

'I'll grant you don't look well,' she conceded. 'I shall send Jane up with a hot toddy and I'm sure you'll feel better in the morning.'

'I'm sure I shall,' Léon said.

Though the rest of him felt cold, his head was as hot as fire, and there was a tightness in his chest which sent a pain through him with every breath. He undressed, and crawled thankfully into bed, but then a fresh bout of shivering came, so violent that it shook the bed. When the maid brought his hot toddy she was alarmed by his appearance.

'I think you should have the doctor, sir!' she said – and hurried downstairs to tell her mistress.

'Do you really think so?' Mrs Lenham asked. 'I dare say it is just a chill and will be much better by morning. I don't think Monsieur Bonneau would thank me for making a fuss.'

'She's as hard as nails, that one,' Jane, back in the kitchen, said to Cook.

'Not only that,' Cook said. 'She's just got no experience of sickness. The late Mr Lenham died sudden, on a trip abroad. Her being in this country, she never even had the trouble of burying him!'

'Well I'm worried about Monsieur Bonneau, and that's a fact,' Jane said.

'Not our place for the likes of us to worry about our betters,' Cook said comfortably. 'But you can take him a cup of cocoa later, when I make ours.'

In the night, when Léon slept fitfully in between bouts of burning and shivering, his dreams were of a giant man with a purple face and flame-coloured hair, who stood brandishing an order book, which he himself could never reach because he was so small that he came no higher than the man's knee. The man was very angry, and Léon wakened from each dream in a state of terror.

When morning came he tried to get up. He *must* get to the mill. But as he stood by the bed the room whirled round, blackness swept over him, and he dropped to the floor. He was aware, dimly, of people running, and of a voice saying, 'You'll have to send for the doctor, now, ma'am!'

Later, standing by Léon's bed, the doctor said, 'I'm afraid you have a nasty chest infection, Monsieur Bonneau!'

'It cannot be!' Léon protested weakly. 'I must not be ill. I have a most important appointment in Leeds in two days' time which I can not possibly miss!'

'And you can't possibly keep,' the doctor said firmly.

'I must!' Léon urged. 'You must get me better!'

'I am Helsdon's best physician,' the doctor said dryly, 'but even I cannot work such a miracle. Though you needn't take my word for it – you will find yourself quite unable to go. But if you were so foolish as to make an attempt, you could find yourself with pneumonia. I need hardly tell you how long that would take you away from the work you are worrying about.'

When the doctor had left, except that Jane came and remade his tumbled bed and brought him a drink of hot lemonade, he was left very much alone. At one point Beatrice put her head around the bedroom door and spoke to him from afar.

'I'm sure you'll soon feel better,' she said. In the meantime she had totally forbidden Florence to go near the sick-room. One mustn't take foolish risks. And if he was no better tomorrow then a professional nurse must be called in. She couldn't be expected to nurse him.

From the moment of the doctor's visit Léon was racked with worry about the appointment. The anxiety loomed larger than his burning head, the shivering and the pain in his chest all put together, and it never left him. What should he do? If he couldn't go, then he must let Henry Garston know. But if he didn't go, then there might never be such another chance. Someone else might beat him to the post.

Could he send someone in his place? But who? His was so much a one-man business. He worked – he now thought perhaps foolishly – without a deputy. There was no one. John Hartley wouldn't do. He was good at the looms and good with the weavers, but he was not the kind of man who could go in and sell an idea. Nor did he really understand too much about design.

It was mid-afternoon when the thought of Madeleine came to Léon, and at first he dismissed it as a feverish fantasy. She was twenty years old, she had no experience whatever of selling. Worst of all, she was a woman. It was inconceivable that a woman could do such a thing. He put the idea from him, but it returned again and again. Don't be stupid, he told himself. You must be delirious!

But she knows the work, he reasoned with himself. She understands the designs and the patterns; she can talk about them. I was impressed when she talked to me. But would Henry Garston be impressed, or would he be insulted that I'd sent a woman? What shall I do? What shall I do? Léon asked himself.

'I am desperate!' he cried out loud.

But desperate diseases must have desperate remedies, he reminded himself. And what more desperate a remedy than sending a young, untried woman to do his work for him? But he would do it! He would definitely do it! What alternative had he? What had he to lose?

He rang his bell, and when Jane promptly appeared he said, 'Will you tell your mistress that I would like to see her. As soon as possible, please.'

Beatrice Lenham stood by the bedroom door while he spoke to her.

'I want to send Jane down to the mill at once and ask Miss Madeleine Bates to come here to see me. She is to bring the batches of all the new designs with her.'

'But surely you're not well enough to think of work?' Mrs Lenham protested. 'I have already sent a message to tell them that you won't be at the mill for several days.' And who was Miss Madeleine Bates, she wondered, that he should send for her from his sick-bed?

'Please do as I ask,' he said. 'And quickly.'

When, an hour later, Beatrice Lenham showed Madeleine into Léon Bonneau's bedroom he said, 'Will you please remain, Mrs Lenham, while I talk to Miss Bates?'

'Well . . .,' Mrs Lenham began. She didn't want to stay in the sick-room, on the other hand she was curious about Miss Bates, who was not at all what she had expected. Exactly what that was, she wasn't sure, but certainly not this tall girl with the beautiful face and dark hair who carried herself as if she was the equal of anybody. Nor, at first glance, was she dressed like a weaver. She had taken off her apron; her dark dress was neat, and fitted her well, showing off the curves of her figure. And unlike all the mill-girls Mrs Lenham had seen in Helsdon, she didn't wear a shawl over her head. She was not to know that Madeleine had rebelled against the shawl after her first few weeks in the mill, and now, in spite of the comment it caused, wore a bonnet to work. She could have been any class of person, Mrs Lenham thought. It was quite confusing.

Léon Bonneau's thoughts were similar to his landlady's. Really, Madeleine looked quite presentable. If she were to wear her best dress, whatever it was, and perhaps some gloves to hide her hands – and of course dress her hair differently, for in the mill she must always wear her hair well tied back under a kerchief – yes, she would do nicely! In appearance she would certainly not disgrace Bonneau's.

'I'm sorry to see you so poorly, Monsieur Bonneau,' Madeleine said. He looked awful! Face flushed, hair all over the place, his eyes bright with fever.

'It is the biggest nuisance in the world!' he said. 'I have never been ill in my life, and I cannot afford to be now.'

'Unfortunately, Nature doesn't take much notice of what we want or when we want it,' Madeleine said. 'Anyway, I brought the patterns, as requested. But do you really think you ought to be working, sir?'

'I have said exactly the same thing to him,' Beatrice Lenham interrupted. 'I think it most unwise. And now if

375

you don't mind, Monsieur Bonneau, I must leave you to it. I have things to attend to, downstairs.'

She simply wasn't going to stay in this germ-laden atmosphere just to observe the proprieties for a mill-girl.

'If Miss Bates doesn't mind,' Léon said. Beatrice Lenham was co-operative when it suited her, and not otherwise.

'Not in the least,' Madeleine said cheerfully. 'In any case, here are the samples. If you'll just check that they're what you want I can be off and leave you in peace. I hope you'll soon feel better.'

'No, you must not go,' Léon said as Mrs Lenham left the room. 'I have to talk to you. There is something I want you to do for me, Madeleine.'

'*Me* – do something for you?' she asked. 'Oh, you mean like shake up your pillows, or pour you a cold drink? Well of course I will!' She moved over to the small table and began to pour a glass of water.

'No, I do not wish you to attend to my pillows! Or to give me a drink. Please sit down and listen to me.' He wished she would do as she was told. It really was an effort to talk. And was he doing the right thing after all?

'Very well, sir.' He sounded quite cranky, not a bit like himself. 'What is it, sir?'

'I cannot keep my appointment with Mr Garston on Friday. I want you to go in my place.'

Her jaw dropped. She stared at him open-mouthed. His illness had affected his brain! 'I can't possibly do that, Monsieur Bonneau!'

'Yes you can, Madeleine. Do not interrupt. Next to myself you know more about the designs and the patterns, *and* what's involved in the weaving, than anyone else. I will write a letter for you to take to Mr Garston, explaining the circumstances. It might be enough to just deliver the letter and the samples. Perhaps he won't wish to see you – but if he does, then I am quite sure you can answer any questions he may have.'

'But . . . but I'm a woman, sir!'

'Of course you are! Do you mean that makes you incompetent?'

She flushed with anger.

'I do not, sir! Only that a man will assume I'm not competent! It's the way of the world. He'll not listen to me.' But Monsieur Bonneau was right in what he'd said. After him, she *did* know more about the subject than anyone else in the weaving shed.

'Then we will show Mr Garston that it is not the only way of the world. I shall not, in my letter, apologize for the fact that I am sending a woman in my place – and for your part you will not behave like one!'

A wide grin split her face.

'Do you mean I'm to act like a man, monsieur?'

'No I do not!' She couldn't if she tried. She was the most feminine of creatures, for all her competence. 'Now come along, Madeleine. Please don't argue with me. Your job is to get Mr Garston to listen to you, so just let me inform you about what you have to say.'

'I might not remember it,' she said, a mite frostily. 'Will it not do if I say what comes naturally to me?'

'Of course it will – so long as you keep to the subject. And I shall give you money for your fares – you must not hestitate to take a cab from the station, and enough to buy yourself a meal in Leeds.'

'Am I to take it that you're ordering me to do this?' Madeleine asked.

'If that makes it easier for you to carry it out, then yes. You know how important it is to Bonneau's mill – which means, to you and me, Madeleine; and the rest of us.'

The silence which followed his words seemed so long that he thought she was going to refuse. He couldn't make her do it, other than by threatening her with dismissal – and that he wouldn't stoop to.

'Very well, sir,' she said at last. 'Since you trust me to do it, I will, to the very best of my ability. And now if you'll permit me I really must shake up your pillows for you. You look dreadfully uncomfortable.'

As she leaned across him, arranging the pillows, straightening the counterpane, he felt the first minutes of ease he had known in the last twenty-four awful hours.

TWENTY

On Friday morning, with the precious samples and the letter to Mr Garston in a drawstring bag hung over her wrist, Madeleine stood on the platform in Helsdon station waiting for the train. She was far too early, of course – but better that than being late. Several times during the night she'd wakened, worrying that she'd oversleep, miss the train, something terrible like that.

'How could you possibly?' Mrs Barnet said at breakfast. 'Seeing as how I have to be up far earlier than you to get to the mill, did you think I'd be daft enough to leave the house with you still in bed? And don't think you're going out without a bite inside you, because you're not!'

'I couldn't possibly eat any breakfast,' Madeleine protested. 'It would choke me!'

'You can and you will! Nobody gives of their best on an empty stomach, so get it down you!'

Madeleine gagged on the bread and lard, but an unusually fierce Mrs Barnet watched until she had eaten the last crumb.

'That's better!' she said. 'And I must say, you look very nice. You'll be a credit to Bonneau's.'

'Oh I do hope so, Mrs Barnet!'

'And I'll put up a little prayer for you.'

Perhaps I don't look too bad, Madeleine thought, viewing herself in sections in the small square of mirror in the bedroom after Mrs Barnet had left. She had sponged and pressed the green dress she had worn in Paris and it looked reasonable. Mrs Barnet had rooted around in her sewing chest and found a piece of good-as-new ribbon with which she'd trimmed Madeleine's bonnet. John Hartley, to Madeleine's surprise, had presented her yesterday with a brand new, white linen handkerchief, edged with lace. She had had very few new handkerchiefs in her life and certainly never one as fine as this.

'I'll keep it for show,' she told him. 'I couldn't possibly blow my nose on it!'

And now here she was on the platform, and just when she'd decided the train wasn't ever coming, it steamed into the station. Moving quickly, she found a seat, back to the engine, so that the smuts wouldn't blow in and land on her clothes or, worse still, in her eyes. Sitting upright so as not to disarrange the becoming bunch of ringlets at the back of her head, she dwelt for a time on the awful prospect of arriving for the appointment with a lump of soot in her eye. Next she considered whether the draught she was sitting in might cause her to lose her voice, and after that whether the train might collide with another, or might run out of steam, so that she would be hours late. She was agreeably surprised when it drew into Leeds station exactly on time and she was none the worse for the ten-mile journey.

As firmly instructed by Léon, she took a cab outside the station, eyeing the horse with suspicion, wondering if it might be frisky, and run away with them.

'Garston's Clothiers, if you please!'

It was the first time in her life she had ever given an instruction to a cabbie! She rather liked the feeling. But when the cab drew up at the entrance to a tall building less than ten minutes drive from the station, her first thought was that she could have walked, and saved the money. Still, she reckoned, counting out the coppers to pay the driver, put it down to experience! Experience gave you confidence which now, faced with this imposing entrance, she could certainly do with.

Just inside the entrance there was a glass cage, with a man sitting inside.

'I have an appointment with Mr Henry Garston,' she told him. 'That is . . .,' she corrected herself, 'I have come on behalf of Monsieur Léon Bonneau, who has the appointment, but is ill.'

'So you don't have an appointment?' the man said disagreeably.

'No, but . . . well, perhaps you had better take this letter.' She fished it out of her bag and handed it over reluctantly. She didn't trust him an inch. 'It's very important,' she emphasized. 'I feel sure when Mr Garston reads it he will want to see me.'

She didn't feel in the least sure, but she wasn't going to be put off by this dour man. Also, she would hang on to the samples. That might give her a better chance of getting into Mr Garston's presence.

The doorman took the letter.

'Wait here,' he said.

He handed the letter to a clerk, who disappeared with it. Madeleine hated to see it go. She hadn't the least faith in it reaching its rightful recipient.

In his office Henry Garston read the letter quickly, then looked up and spoke to the clerk.

'There should be samples with this. Where are they?'

'I wasn't given any, sir,' the clerk said.

'Then go and get them.'

Then, as the clerk was leaving, Henry Garston said, 'Wait a minute! It says here a woman brought the letter. Did you see her?'

'I caught a glimpse, sir.'

'Was she young? Was she pretty?'

'A very pretty young lady, sir.'

Henry Garston smiled.

'Then on second thoughts she can bring in the samples herself!'

It was nonsense sending a woman on such an errand – but there was no accounting for what the French would do, and he'd enjoy looking at her. Miss Madeleine Bates, eh? Perhaps she had a bit of French 'Ooh la la' in her. At any rate she'd make a pleasant change from all these dull clerks he was surrounded by.

When Madeleine was shown into Henry Garston's office – a much bigger room than Monsieur Bonneau's at the mill, she thought, with a carpet on the floor and two or three comfortable chairs – she saw a broad-shouldered man with dark hair flecked with grey, and a handsome face set in a stern expression. She stood just inside the doorway, not liking to advance, conscious that he was studying her from top to toe. Well, rich and powerful he might be, she decided, but he was also rude!

'Well, don't just stand there,' he said when he'd looked his fill. 'Come over here and sit down. I won't eat you!'

He was less frightening when he spoke. He had an honest, plain Yorkshire voice, with a hint of humour in it.

'Thank you, sir.'

He indicated a chair and she perched on the edge of it.

'So you are . . .' he referred to the letter, ' . . . you are Miss Madeleine Bates? And you've come on behalf of Monsieur Léon Bonneau?'

'If you please, sir?'

'Well I'm not sure whether I'm pleased or not, Miss Bates. I don't do business with women . . .'

There was no answer to that. She kept quiet.

' . . . as a rule,' he amended. 'Tell me, young lady, why did Monsieur Bonneau not send a man?'

She was suddenly furious at the purring condescension in his tone. She wanted to get up and walk out, slamming the door behind her. She was halfway to her feet when she came back to her senses.

'Monsieur Bonneau sent me because he thought that in his own unavoidable absence I would be of the most help to you. I know about the designs and patterns, I understand the weaving – actually more than any man

Monsieur Bonneau could have called upon.' She spoke as calmly as she could, though inside she was shaking, not now with fear, but with rage.

'Well, well!' Henry Garston said. She was a spirited filly, this one! He liked a bit of spirit whether in horses or women. Let's see if she's as knowledgeable as she makes out.

'And are the samples you've brought in that bag you're clutching? If so, let's have a look at them.'

She spread the samples on the desk, then watched his face while he examined them, picked them up, felt them between thumb and finger, squeezed them in his large hands. She hadn't the slightest qualms about this bit of the affair. The quality was one hundred per cent. She was proud of the samples; proud of them as a product of Bonneau's mill, proud of the part she had played in producing them, in the weaving and even in the design, for Monsieur Bonneau had taken notice of her ideas on colour.

Henry Garston's face gave nothing away. He studied the samples for a long time without speaking, then referred to the price list Léon Bonneau had enclosed with the letter. At long last he raised his head.

'I agreed to see Monsieur Bonneau because I'd heard he was doing something new, something a bit special —'

'So he is,' Madeleine interrupted. 'It's the French influence, you see. I don't think there's anything quite like them in this country.'

'I know that, young lady,' he said dryly. 'I dare say I know every design and pattern that's done in the West Riding, and a lot more from outside as well.'

'I'm sorry, sir!'

'You needn't be. I'll agree they're a bit special. I'm interested in the colours. They're good colours. I quite like this one which has a slight colour variation in every design. Do you know anything about that one, then?'

Madeleine felt herself grow pink with pleasure.

'Yes, sir, I do indeed! In fact . . . in fact I had

383

something to do with that design myself.' She was sure Monsieur Bonneau wouldn't mind her saying that. It was true, and from the look on his face Mr Garston seemed interested.

'Did you indeed?'

'Yes, sir. The idea is that we won't produce many of each variation, so that the cloth's a bit more exclusive. It doesn't entail a lot of extra work on the loom.'

'I see,' Henry Garston said quickly. 'So if there's not a lot of extra setting up involved you wouldn't expect to charge me more?'

'That's up to Monsieur Bonneau. I don't have anything to do with the costing,' Madeleine said. 'But he's an honest man. He'd give you a fair price.'

For the first time, he gave her a broad smile.

'And he has a very good ambassador in you, Miss Bates. Tell me, what's your position with Monsieur Bonneau?'

'I'm a weaver, sir.'

'A weaver?' She'd seemed a cut above that.

What in the world was the man thinking of, sending a weaver, a millhand, to do his business for him? On the other hand she could certainly speak up for herself. She was a novelty, it made a change – rather like these samples which he was also quite taken with. Well, he'd have a bit of fun, see what she was made of!

He started to fire questions at her, about production, design, processes. To his amused surprise, and to Madeleine's delight, she answered most of them without hesitation. And in answering his questions she lost her fear of him, and was able to look him straight in the face.

'So you'd be able to do some exclusives for Garston's?' he said in the end. 'Special patterns that no one else would be offered?'

'I'm sure of it, sir – if your order was big enough.'

'And the price was right!'

He smiled again, and stood up, holding out his hand to Madeleine.

'Well, I'm not going to give you an order to take back

with you, much as I dare say you'd like that. Tell your Monsieur Bonneau that I'll be in touch in about a week.'

Madeleine gave him her hand, which he crushed in his strong grip.

'Good day, sir. Thank you for seeing me.'

When she was at the door he called out to her.

'If ever you find yourself looking for a job, Miss Bates, come and see me!'

Leaving Mr Henry Garston's office, walking down the stairs and past the morose-looking man in the entrance, Madeleine felt as light as a piece of thistledown floating through the air. It wasn't until she was out in the busy street, fighting her way along the thronged pavement, that she was suddenly brought down to earth by a gnawing hunger. She had never been so hungry in her life! While she searched for an eating-house into which a woman might go, visions of food came to her like a mirage: pies, steaks, chops, puddings. She was almost back at the station before she found what looked a suitable place, a small café with steps ascending from the basement.

'Get yourself a good meal,' Monsieur Bonneau had said when he'd handed her the money. Now, studying the bill of fare chalked on the board, she needed no persuading. It was simply a matter of choosing between steak-and-kidney pudding, roast beef and Yorkshire, or meat-and-potato pie. She could hardly choose all three, more was the pity.

She went down the stairs and took a seat at a long table with several other people.

'I'll have the pie,' she said to the waiter. She had seen it sitting on the range, crisp and golden, with a spiral of fragrant steam issuing from the hole in the top.

She followed the pie with a generous helping of jam roll and a cup of strong sweet tea. Never had food tasted so delicious, and never did she feel she had earned it more! How much easier it was to stand at her loom and weave, do what she'd been taught to do, know the boundaries.

But less exciting, oh, infinitely less exciting! She could hardly wait to get back to tell Monsieur Bonneau what had happened.

He was still in bed when she arrived. His head ached less and the shivering bouts had almost ceased, but the tightness in his chest was still there and when, earlier, he'd tried to get out of bed he'd been amazed by his weakness. Now, when Madeleine was shown in by Mrs Lenham, it felt as though the sun had entered the room. He had spent the whole of the day wondering how Madeleine was faring, whether he'd been right to send her.

'Madeleine! How good to see you! Please sit down and tell me all about it!' He turned to his landlady. 'Mrs Lenham, do you think Miss Bates might be brought a cup of tea? I'm sure she's had a most tiring day!'

Beatrice Lenham raised her eyebrows. Tea for one of his mill-girls?

'I'll see if Jane has time,' she said frostily.

'Please do,' Léon ordered.

'Well?' he said to Madeleine. 'How did it go? Tell me everything. Did Mr Garston like the samples? Did he give you an order?'

'He didn't give me an order,' Madeleine said. 'But he did like the samples. He was very interested and asked me a lot of questions . . . .'

'And were you able to answer them?'

'I was. Most of them, anyway. I couldn't talk to him about prices, but he asked me about the weaving and the designs and so on. In fact once he'd got over the shock of me being a woman, it all seemed to go well.'

'He liked you, then?' Léon asked.

How could Henry Garston, or any other man, not have done so, he thought, looking at her sitting there, her lovely face flushed and alight with eagerness, her dark hair curling from under her bonnet in an unruly but infinitely becoming manner, her voice lilting with enthusiasm? Impulsively, he stretched out his hand and took hold of hers.

'How could he fail to like you?' he said.

For a second, just for a second, she wanted to snatch her hand away, to hide it behind her back where he couldn't reach. The breath almost left her body with the strength of the feeling. She clenched her teeth and willed herself not to move – and then, as quickly as it had come, the panic was over. She experienced a tremendous sensation of relief, of reprieve. It swept over her and through her. She wanted, almost, to cry.

Her hand was still in his. She let it lie there for no more than a second, then withdrew it gently. On his part it had been an impulsive, friendly gesture, no more. Nothing for her to worry about and all over quickly. By now he probably didn't know he had done it. But it would not be seemly, and it would be embarrassing to both of them if she were to leave her hand in his.

'Thank you, monsieur,' she said. 'I think perhaps he did like me. At any rate, his last words were to offer me a job, if ever I wanted one.'

Léon Bonneau was amazed at the agitation which Madeleine's words, so lightly spoken, aroused in him. She couldn't leave him? He wouldn't hear of it. She was his best operative; better now than Mrs Barnet, for her talents were wider. She had imagination, and almost a painter's talent for colour. Bonneau's mill needed her, and if he had thought Henry Garston was going to steal her away he would never have let her go to Leeds.

'And what did you say to that?' he asked carefully.

'Oh, I didn't answer. I was half out of the door.'

For a moment he was relieved, but at the back of his mind there was to remain, long after Madeleine had left, a nagging anxiety.

'Anyway,' Madeleine continued, 'he'll be in touch with you. In about a week, he said. I feel sure it will be good news, Monsieur Bonneau.'

'Well, I cannot tell you how grateful I am,' Léon said. 'You have done so well. I shall try to find some way to repay you.'

'There's no need,' Madeleine assured him. 'After the

387

first few minutes I quite enjoyed myself, it was interesting. I'd do it again any time I was asked.'

'I shall bear it in mind,' he said. Perhaps it would be a way to keep her? But really her job was in the mill. He needed her there.

When Madeleine had left, Mrs Lenham came in to see him. Now that his fever was over she had given up the idea of getting in a professional nurse. It would only cause a lot of extra work and fuss, and Jane could cope quite well with his needs. He wasn't a demanding patient.

'How are you feeling?' she asked politely.

'Much better. I'm over the worst.'

'Then we'll soon be back to normal, Léon.' She sat on the edge of the bed and took his hand in hers. Immediately, though he didn't withdraw his hand, she felt him shrink away from her. So what she had feared had come to pass!

'Dear Léon, you'll feel quite differently when you're well again,' she cajoled him.

He knew what was in her mind; she wasn't difficult to read since she was the most unsubtle of women. But it was no use. Lying there over the last few days he had decided that the affair between them must end. He didn't really even like her, and he doubted if she liked him. Apart from their lovemaking she seemed more and more indifferent to him. All they had were bodies which cried out for each other, bodies which met in perfect unison. Beyond that, there was nothing.

Physical gratification – though from Beatrice Lenham it was available to him whenever he desired it – was not enough, he had discovered. It was nothing to do with the difference in their ages, indeed he was thankful for that now, since otherwise he might have been inveigled into promising her marriage. The truth was, she bored him. Even Sophia Chester, whom he disliked, was less boring than Beatrice Lenham.

'I have been thinking', he said, 'that when I am well again I must move on from here.'

'Move on? Leave Helsdon?' Now she *was* startled.

'No, not leave Helsdon. But leave "Ashgrove". It is time I set up my own establishment.'

He wasn't, he couldn't, it was *impossible* that he should marry that Miss Bates he'd been so inordinately pleased to see. Whatever else, he was a gentleman. Surely he couldn't contemplate marrying a weaver? But who else was there? She was sure there were no other women in his life.

'I had no idea you planned to marry!' she said.

'Marry? Of course I haven't. Perhaps I used the wrong phrase. I simply mean that I think now of having an establishment of my own. I shall have a housekeeper.' He already had an idea in his mind of what he would do. As soon as he could see his friend Mr Ormeroyd he would put it to him.

'Oh really? Whatever you think, of course.' Her voice was cold. 'I must say, this is a surprise!'

It wasn't, actually. She had seen it coming. And if he had gone off her there was no point in him staying. To her lasting and bitter regret she had spoiled him for Florence and she would continue to feel guilty about that. But for herself someone else would turn up, of that she had no doubt. He wasn't the only pebble on the beach. And if ever I can pay you out for this, Monsieur Léon Bonneau, she said to herself, you can be certain I'll do so!

'I shall not forget you, Beatrice,' he said more gently. 'We have been good friends.'

It wasn't true. They had never even approached friendship – but he didn't want to hurt her.

'Of course!' she said, her insincerity matching his. 'And we shall continue so.'

The next day Mr Ormeroyd came to the house.

'I hope you are feeling better, Léon?'

'Every day. I should be back in the mill by this time next week. And I am glad you came. I was about to ask Mrs Lenham if she would send for you.'

Mr Ormeroyd raised his eyebrows.

389

'Nothing wrong, I hope?' A lawyer was a bit like a doctor. People only wanted to see him when they had problems.

'Nothing wrong,' Léon assured him. 'Just an idea I wanted to discuss with you. But first let me tell you about Henry Garston's. You know I sent Madeleine Bates to keep my appointment?'

'Madeleine Bates?' Could he be hearing aright? Mr Ormeroyd still thought of Madeleine as he had known her longest, as a servant at Mount Royd.

'Yes. Let me tell you about it!'

When Léon finished speaking Mr Ormeroyd said:

'Well, I must say, you do surprise me! I look forward to hearing that you've got an order.' Privately, he doubted that it would hapen. Henry Garston was known throughout the West Riding as a tough nut to crack. 'Was that why you wanted to see me?' he asked.

'No. Something quite different. I've decided I want to leave "Ashgrove". I want to set up on my own.'

'On your own? Léon, you are full of surprises today! Are you not comfortable here?'

'I am very comfortable, but I have a desire to be . . . shall we say, more independent. I would need a housekeeper, of course.'

'Well, you sound as though you've made up your mind, thought it all out. I can't at the moment think of any property which would be suitable. You wouldn't want anything large, would you?'

Léon chuckled.

'What you're trying to tell me, my friend, is that I cannot afford anything large. Well, for the moment that is true, though Bonneau's is becoming more and more successful, and if we get a good connection with Garston's, who knows what might happen! But I understand you – and I already have an idea about where I might go.'

'You do?'

'Yes. What do you say to the suggestion that I might take over two or three rooms in Mount Royd? A small number of rooms, plus the kitchen for a housekeeper, would make a more than adequate apartment; easy to run. It could easily be closed off from the rest of the house. It would be handy for the mill – and also it would give Mrs Parkinson a little more income by way of rent. So what do you think? It is feasible, is it not?'

'It's feasible if Mrs Parkinson will agree,' Mr Ormeroyd admitted. 'And indeed, why shouldn't she? We are no nearer to getting either a buyer or a tenant for the whole house. As it stands now, it's a white elephant.'

'And will fall into disrepair,' Léon pointed out.

Mr Ormeroyd eyed Léon carefully.

'Tell me,' he said slowly, 'do you have it in the back of your mind, eventually, to take over the whole of Mount Royd?'

'That is what I would like to do,' Léon confessed. 'Though the time isn't ripe yet. Everything for the moment must go into the business. If all goes well, before too long, I also want to open up the spinning again – not on a large scale at first, but with enough frames to supply my weaving. But one day, believe me, I shall have enough to take on Mount Royd. Is there anything against that?'

'I do believe you,' Mr Ormeroyd said. 'You are a very determined young man. And no, I see nothing against it. In my opinion Mrs Parkinson would delight in seeing the house occupied by who ever was running the mill.'

Those were exactly Mrs Parkinson's sentiments when a week later, as soon as he was fit to visit her, Léon put forward the idea of an apartment for himself in Mount Royd. He made no mention of eventually wanting the whole house. That was too far off.

'I would welcome it,' she said. 'And by no means only for the rent. I can't tell you how it saddens me when I walk past the house and see it deserted. We will come to an amicable arrangement about which rooms you will use, and what furniture you would like to have. After that, the sooner you move in, the better.'

391

'It should not take long,' Léon said. 'And I am truly grateful. I will take great care of everything, you can trust me for that.'

'I know I can,' she said.

'Tell me, where do you think I should start looking for a housekeeper?' Léon asked.

'I have an idea,' Mrs Parkinson said. 'It came to me the moment you explained your requirements. Why not see if Mrs Thomas would come back? She loves Mount Royd and was sad to leave. I dare say Madeleine Bates is in touch with her and will have a notion as to whether she might be willing.'

'Why, that is wonderful!' Léon exclaimed. 'I shall look into it. And now tell me how Sophia is faring. And the baby?'

Mrs Parkinson was suddenly transformed. The sadness which in this last year seemed to have settled on her permanently, vanished as a radiant smile lit her face, and at the same time every inch of her plump little body seemed to perk up, come alive.

'Why, she's splendid! They're both splendid! I was able to go to Thirsk last week to spend a few days and I think I have never seen Sophia so happy!'

'I am glad to hear it,' Léon said. What in the world could have brought it about?

'I would never have thought it, I would never have believed you if you'd told me it would happen – but once Sophia was in her own home, why, she took to motherhood like a duck to water! She is in her element with the child.'

It was incredible, Léon thought.

'And David? Is he happy?'

'David is happy when Sophia is happy. It's as simple as that.'

'I must say, your news about Sophia surprises me,' Léon said candidly. The last time he had seen Sophia, when the baby was a few days old, she had been very offhand about the poor little thing.

392

'Oh, it surprised me, Léon. I have never thought of my daughter as the maternal type.' In fact she had never thought of Sophia as loving anyone except Sophia. 'Of course,' Mrs Parkinson continued, 'there's good reason for it. My grandson is quite the most beautiful baby I have ever seen in my life. And so good! So even-tempered!'

'A paragon!' Léon said.

'Indeed, yes,' Mrs Parkinson said seriously. 'A little paragon!' And now, she thought, with a little rent coming in from Mount Royd I shall be able to spoil my grandson.

'What splendid news,' Léon said. 'And now I must go. Thank you for agreeing about Mount Royd. I will speak to Madeleine about Mrs Thomas when I see her on Monday.'

In fact, he saw Madeleine in church on Sunday morning, but the moment the Mass was over she scurried away, not waiting to speak to anyone; almost as if she didn't want to be seen. Mrs Barnet was in no such rush, and as they emerged into the sunshine he passed the time of day with her.

'I'm glad to see you looking better, sir,' she said.

'I look forward to being back in the mill tomorrow,' he informed her.

And by tomorrow there might be a letter from Henry Garston. It was just over a week since Madeleine had been to Leeds. Was it wrong, he thought, that in the Mass he had prayed for the letter to come?

Halfway through the morning the letter was delivered. Léon opened it with trembling hands. The yea or nay of it could make all the difference in the world to Bonneau's.

'Dear Monsieur Bonneau . . .,' he began to read.

Halfway down the page he stopped reading and raised his hands in a shout of triumph. Then, waving the letter aloft, he rushed from his office and into the mill.

'Stop the looms,' he ordered John Hartley.

When the weaving-shed was so quiet that you could have heard a length of yarn fall to the floor, he held up the letter.

'I received this only a few minutes ago,' he said. 'I want you all to hear the good news. Garston's of Leeds have just given us the largest order we have ever had and, if we deliver on time and the goods are satisfactory, there will be more to come. Mr Henry Garston is coming himself to inspect us and to discuss our long-term prospects. I want to thank every one of you for the good work you've done, and will be doing in the future. If all goes well there will be a bonus for each of you at the end of the year.'

He waited until the cheers had subsided, and then said, 'But now back to work! As I have learned to say, "This won't buy the baby a new dress!"'

With the laughter still in his ears, he left the shed, on the way out saying to John Hartley, 'Please ask Madeleine Bates to come to my office.'

While he waited for her, he read the letter again. He wanted to thank her especially, but already he had decided he would not, could not tell her of the last sentence in the letter.

'If ever this young lady wants a job, send her to me,' Henry Garston had written.

He couldn't tell her. It was unfair of him, but he mustn't lose her now. And when she walked into his office, her face shining with joy, he knew for the first time that it was not only because she was a good weaver that he couldn't let her go.

He stood up to meet her.

'Madeleine, I don't know how to thank you. Perhaps my English is not good enough. You clearly did a splendid job in Leeds. Mr Garston is full of compliments. . . .' He paused, willing himself to do what was right, to show her that last sentence – and couldn't.

'I'm glad it came off, Monsieur Bonneau,' Madeleine said. 'But it was the samples that did it. Mr Garston knows a good thing when he sees it.'

'So it seems,' Léon said. 'So it seems!' It was nearer the truth than she knew.

'Well, I'd best get back to work,' Madeleine said. 'There'll be a lot to do from now on.'

'Indeed yes! But before you go there is one other thing.'

He told her, then, about his plans for moving into Mount Royd, and of Mrs Parkinson's suggestion that Mrs Thomas might be persuaded to keep house for him.

'It will be nice to think of you living in Mount Royd,' Madeleine said. 'More fitting.'

Also, he'd be better out of the clutches of Mrs Lenham. She hadn't liked Mrs Lenham. There was something about her which rankled. And it wasn't just that she treated me like dirt, Madeleine thought.

'Shall I give you Mrs Thomas's address, so that you can write to her?' she asked. 'Her niece will have to reply. Mrs Thomas can't write.'

'No,' Léon said. 'I have a better idea. I'm very grateful to you for what you did in Leeds, and you're clearly such a good ambassador, that I thought it would be good if you were to go to Morecambe next Saturday – you shall have the day off – and see Mrs Thomas for yourself. Bring back her answer.'

'Me, go to Morecambe?' She could hardly believe it.

'Why not? It's not all that far. And by now you're a much-travelled young lady. You could stay overnight – I'm sure Mrs Thomas or her niece would find somewhere – and come back on the Sunday. Naturally I would pay your expenses.'

'It's very good of you . . .,' Madeleine began.

'Nonsense! Apart from the fact that you will be doing me a service, I shall be pleased if you find it a little treat. You deserve one.'

'Well I would quite like to see Mrs Thomas,' Madeleine admitted.

'Good! And if anyone can persuade her to come back to Helsdon, you can. So it's settled!'

From his office window he watched Madeleine as she walked across the mill-yard, back to the weaving-shed.

Had he cheated her? What was a trip to Morecambe, and the rise in her wages which he intended she should have, compared to what Henry Garston might do for her? When she was out of sight he turned back to his desk. His thoughts about Madeleine were confused. Somewhere in him was a hint of the desire he had felt for Beatrice Lenham, yet not the same, for Madeleine was a totally different creature. She is also a mill-girl, he told himself. One of your workers. But one thought stood out clearly above the rest. He didn't want her to leave Helsdon. He didn't ever want her to leave.

TWENTY-ONE

Ten days after Léon had replied to Henry Garston's letter, and without so much as a word of warning as to the day, let alone the hour, when they might expect him, the great man's carriage, drawn by a pair of perfectly matched black horses, rattled over the cobbles of Bonneau's mill-yard and came to a halt outside Léon's office window.

Léon jumped to his feet, gave a swift glance out of the window, and ran to the door. Henry Garston had already stepped down from his carriage and now advanced with outstretched hand towards Léon.

'You must be Monsieur Bonneau!' he said. 'Henry Garston. Will someone show my man where he can attend to the horses?'

'I am delighted to meet you,' Léon said. 'This is indeed an honour! Please be seated. If I had known when you might be coming — '

'You'd have had everything spick and span,' Garston interrupted. 'Everyone on their best behaviour! Well that's not my way. I like to see things as they are, form my own judgements.'

'Of course you are welcome at any time, without any prior warning,' Léon said. 'What I meant was that I would have had some refreshment waiting for you. But it can soon be arranged.'

'Don't bother, monsieur,' Henry Garston said. 'I've had a hearty breakfast and I need nowt else until dinner. There's too much time spent eating and drinking when folks could be working. So you were pleased with my letter, eh?'

'Delighted, sir! And truly grateful for the honour of serving you!'

What fancy talk these Frenchmen had, Henry Garston thought. Well, fine words buttered no parsnips with him. He was a plain man, and proud of it.

'I'm a plain man,' he said. 'I say what I think, call a spade a spade. I liked what I saw of your cloths. We can argue about prices – for I warn you I'm not one to pay through the nose. . . .'

'And I am not a profiteer,' Léon said quickly. 'I set what is the right price for best quality goods.'

'Aye, well, we'll discuss that,' Henry Garston said. 'Now there's one or two matters I need to sort out.'

'Certainly! Such as?'

'In the first place, if I continue to place orders with you, can you supply me? Can you supply me on time? For I don't like being kept waiting. Can you fulfill your commitments?'

'I assure you that I shall not take on any commitments I cannot fulfil,' Léon said.

'As long as that's understood. And now I'd like to take a look around. I don't know your set-up, though I must say I've heard your name mentioned once or twice in the trade recently.'

'Favourably, I hope?'

'I suppose you could say that. We don't go in for much flannel in Yorkshire.'

'Flannel?'

'Flattery!' Pity the man didn't understand real English. 'But I've heard nowt against you.'

'Then permit me to show you my mill,' Léon said. 'Though as you know, at present I have only the weaving and the finishing. As soon as I can I hope to start up the spinning, but it will not be just yet.'

'So what do you do for yarn, now?' Henry Garston asked. 'Albert Parkinson did some good spinning.'

'I know. And one day I will. At present I buy the tops and choose the colours I will have them dyed. That is very important to me and I have a good relationship with Robert's Dyeworks. They take a lot of trouble to get the colours I want.'

'Well there's no better dyeworks than Robert's,' Henry Garston conceded.

'And after that, Brogden's spin the yarn for me. They do very well – you have seen the results – but if I had my own spinners I would be able to make more experiments, produce even more designs. The other problem, of course, is that sometimes Brogden's have to keep us waiting. They have other customers.'

'And your weavers get pent for yarn,' Henry Garston said. 'Aye, I can see the problem. Well lead the way, then, and let's see what you've got.'

They crossed the yard and walked into the cacophony of the weaving-shed, every loom working at top speed.

'Shall I stop the looms?' Léon shouted.

'Certainly not! Never stop production! And you needn't shout. I dare say I've spent more hours in weaving-sheds than you have. I can hear perfectly well.'

He walked around, looking keenly at the cloth on the looms, watching the operatives. As he stood close to Sally Pitts she shook with nerves and prayed that she wouldn't do something stupid.

'What's this on the looms, now?' he asked Léon.

'An order we are just finishing. When this is done we shall be free to start on yours.'

'How about putting this aside and starting my stuff sooner?'

'I'm sorry,' Léon said firmly. 'That I cannot do, Mr Garston. This order has been promised for a certain date and I intend to deliver it on time.'

If the man thought he was going to bully him into neglecting his other customers, into always putting Garston's first, then he was wrong. Even at the risk of losing a valuable order, the most valuable he'd ever had, he wouldn't do it. Bonneau's was his; he would run it as he thought fit, and that included loyalty to all his customers, not just to his biggest.

'Good!' Henry Garston said emphatically. 'That means you'll never put my work aside to fit in somebody else who might be nagging at you. Though you'd be a fool if you did, of course, considering the size of order I can give you.'

'I wouldn't do it to you or to anyone. When I have given my word I keep it.' Léon spoke coldly, annoyed that Garston had tried to catch him out.

'Quite right, lad!' Henry Garston said mildly.

He was approaching Madeleine's loom now, but at first he didn't recognize her. She was wearing her mill-skirt and apron, with her hair totally hidden beneath a kerchief. She kept her head down, her eyes on her work, watching the shuttle as it flew from side to side. She knew he was there, but it would be wrong to push herself forward.

'Madeleine!' Léon Bonneau said.

When she looked up Henry Garston saw the same beautiful face, the same dark eyes shining with intelligence, which had so impressed him in his office in Leeds. She was wasted here.

'Good morning, Miss Bates!' he said.

'Good morning, sir!'

'When are you coming to Leeds again?'

'I have no plans,' she said, blushing. 'I'm busy enough here.'

He watched her for a minute, then said,

'Well I'd best let you get on with it.' He moved off after Léon Bonneau who seemed impatient to be away.

Back in the office Garston said:

'I'm quite impressed by your little set-up, Monsieur

400

Bonneau. It seems all right to me. And I've made a decision I dare say you'll like. You'll discover I'm a man of quick decisions, good or bad – and mostly good! I don't believe in wasting time.'

'Nor I,' Léon said. 'What is this decision, Mr Garston?'

'I'm going to help you set up the spinning, young man! I reckon it'd be to my advantage as well as yours, because the first stipulation I'd make is that I have first refusal of your new designs. I won't be greedy, I won't take everything. I expect I won't like everything. But first refusal, eh? So what do you say?'

Léon stared at him, shook his head.

'I don't know what to say! I can't believe it, Mr Garston! You really mean you're going to help me set up the spinning? Is it true?'

'I've said so, haven't I? Are you telling me you doubt my word?'

'Of course not. It's just . . .'

'And do you want this or don't you?'

'But of course I do, Mr Garston!'

'Then let's get down to business. Money and dates,' Henry Garston said. 'I haven't much time. I want to be back in Leeds by dinner-time.'

In less than half an hour, in which the preliminaries were completed, Léon saw Henry Garston to his carriage.

'I can never thank you enough,' Léon said.

'Oh yes you can, lad! I mean to see you do! You're going to make money for me the same as I am for you! I'm not in business for toffee apples!'

'Toffee apples?'

'Just a saying, lad! Just a saying.'

The driver flicked the whip and the horses walked forward. While they were still in the mill-yard Henry Garston turned and called out to Léon.

'That Miss Bates is wasted where she is! You should do something about her! If you can't, I will!'

On Saturday Madeleine went down to the station and took the train for Morecambe. It would be the longest journey she had ever undertaken on her own – nearly sixty miles so they said – but she was much less nervous than when she'd made the short journey to Leeds. Well, she'd nothing to worry about at the end of it! All she need do was sit in the train and look out of the window at the scenery for as long as it took to get there, and eat the sandwiches which Mrs Barnet, before leaving for the mill, had packed for her. She wasn't sure of the way from Morecambe station to where Mrs Thomas lived – the instructions Mrs Thomas's niece had sent were vague – but she had a tongue in her head, hadn't she?

In fact, when she left the train at Morecambe, there was Mrs Thomas, with a young woman beside her, standing on the platform. Madeleine rushed forward to meet her.

'Oh Mrs Thomas! Oh, it's grand to see you! You don't look a bit different – well that's not quite true, you look *better!*' She had colour in her skin now, Madeleine noted, as if she'd spent time in the fresh air and sunshine, instead of being cooped up in a kitchen every hour God sent.

Mrs Thomas looked Madeleine over.

'Well, you've lost weight, you're too thin, my girl!' Mrs Thomas criticized. 'Are they working you too hard in the mill?'

'We're very busy,' Madeleine admitted. 'It's all go at the moment, with overtime as well. But I like it there.'

'Oh dear, where are my manners!' Mrs Thomas said suddenly. 'I haven't introduced you. This is my niece, Flora.'

Flora Herbert was a small, frail-looking creature with a welcoming smile.

'Pleased to meet you,' she said. 'We don't live more than a few minutes' walk away, just back from the sea – but I dare say you'd like to walk along the seafront.'

'Oh yes, please!'

She had seen the sea before, of course. Unlike most people she knew, she'd actually crossed it, but Morecambe Bay was quite different from the English channel at Newhaven. It was so wide, and at the moment so calm, with miles of golden sand, and in the distance the Lakeland hills, slate-coloured against the sky.

'You can walk all the way across the sands to Grange,' Flora said, 'if you start at low tide, that is.'

'But don't you ever try it, love,' Mrs Thomas advised Madeleine. 'It looks quiet enough now, but the tides can be very treacherous!'

'Well, I'm not likely to,' Madeleine assured her. 'Seeing as how I have to go back tomorrow! Were you able to find me lodgings for the night?'

'You're staying with us,' Flora said. 'There's a spare bed in Auntie's room.'

When they reached the house, a small terrace house in a narrow street, Flora said, 'I'll make a cup of tea and then I'll leave you to it. I want to go and see a neighbour who's poorly. But I expect you'll have a lot to talk about anyway.'

When her niece had left, Mrs Thomas sat back in her chair and gave Madeleine a satisfied smile.

'Well, this is a right treat, and no mistake! I'd never reckoned on you coming here to see me, Madeleine.'

'I couldn't have as yet, not if Monsieur Bonneau hadn't paid for me,' Madeleine admitted. 'So what do you think of his idea? How do you feel about coming back to keep house for him at Mount Royd?'

Mrs Thomas shook her head.

'I couldn't, love! I'm happy here – and I must say, Flora seems pleased to have me. She's kindness itself.'

'Oh, Mrs Thomas!' Madeleine had felt so certain that she would jump at the chance. She'd not even entertained the thought of her refusing. 'Oh, Monseiur Bonneau will be so disappointed!'

'I'm sorry, love. But it's been a while now, hasn't it? Things change. You get used to different ways. I'm practically my own boss here.'

'I'm sure you would be with Monsieur Bonneau,' Madeleine said. 'He'd leave everything to you.'

'No. I'm sorry,' Mrs Thomas repeated. 'But give Monsieur Bonneau my very best respects and thank him for the offer. I'm sure he'll find someone.'

'He'll be lucky to find someone as good as you,' Madeleine said.

'Well, there it is. Now tell me about everybody: your Ma, Emerald, Miss Sophia – who never writes to me, though Mrs Parkinson sent me a bit of the christening cake . . .'

Madeleine told her everything she could remember about everyone she had known in Helsdon, finishing up with an account of how well they were doing in the mill.

'I don't like to see any one in the Master's place,' Mrs Thomas said. 'But I allus thought Monsieur Bonneau would make a go of it.'

In the evening the three of them walked down to the sea to watch the sunset over the bay, the sea a shimmering pink and gold, the lakeland hills darkened now to black and purple.

'It's incredibly beautiful,' Madeleine said. 'I don't wonder you don't want to leave!'

'Auntie,' Flora said, 'why don't you go to Helsdon for a month or so, to settle Monsieur Bonneau in, then come back here before the winter starts?'

'Well I hadn't thought of that,' Mrs Thomas admitted. 'Happen he wouldn't want me just for a month?' She looked enquiringly at Madeleine.

'He'd rather have you for good,' Madeleine said. 'But half a loaf is better than no bread! You'd be able to put someone else in the way of things.'

'Well let me sleep on it,' Mrs Thomas said. 'I'll tell you tomorrow before you go back. What time do you go?'

'Straight after dinner.'

When Madeleine came down to breakfast next morning, Mrs Thomas had her answer ready.

'I'll do as Flora suggests. I'll come for a month or so.

Just until Monsieur Bonneau gets someone else to take it on.'

'Oh, Mrs Thomas, that's marvellous!' Madeleine cried. 'Monsieur Bonneau will be so pleased!'

'Then you're to write and let me know when he wants me to start. Flora has said she'll see me on to the train in Morecambe . . .'

'And I'll meet you in Helsdon,' Madeleine promised.

'But mind you come back here well before the cold weather sets in!' Flora said. 'I don't want you spending the winter in Helsdon.'

'Oh I'll be back all right,' Mrs Thomas promised. 'I'll be back in good time.'

Going home in the train, Madeleine's eyes were on the scenery. There was a late summer feel about the fields and the trees, a lushness, and a change of colour. The trees were heavy and dense with foliage, the leaves a darker green. In places, the fields showed a brownish tinge. Autumn would soon be here, for it came early in these parts. But though her eyes were on the scenery her mind was elsewhere, filled with thoughts she didn't want to face, which she tried to push away. Deliberately, she turned her mind to Mrs Thomas, Monsieur Bonneau, the mill, anything which might distract her.

Nothing could. She had known for some time that she must talk to Father O'Malley. She had tried to persuade Mrs Barnet to advise her, but Mrs Barnet had been evasive, refusing to be drawn. Madeleine recalled the conversation they'd had less than a week ago.

'I'm not the one to ask,' Mrs Barnet had said.

'But you must know what I'm feeling,' Madeleine protested. 'You weren't always a Catholic. At one stage you made the decision to be one.'

'That's as maybe. But I'm not clever enough to answer questions. All I'd like to say, lass, is don't do the right thing for the wrong reasons.'

'Is that what you did? Oh forgive me if I'm prying!'

405

'No, it's not. What I did was right for me, and I hope for the right reason. But I'm not so sure about you.'

'What do you mean?'

'Well if you must know, Madeleine, I'm not so sure that all this isn't something to do with your dad. I don't know whether it's that he's pushed you in the opposite direction, pushed you away from the chapel because you don't like what *he* does, or whether you're trying to pay him back, get your revenge. They're both bad reasons, love. You've got to bring more to the church than that.'

Is she right? Madeleine wondered, as the train ate up the miles between Morecambe and Helsdon. Is it to do with my father? Would I ever have felt like this if it hadn't been for him? But she felt inside her it wasn't revenge. It was longing.

By the time the train drew into Helsdon station she had made up her mind. She would go to see Father O'Malley, and she would do so now, straight away, before the ounce of courage she'd mustered had evaporated.

Knocking at the door of the presbytery, waiting for the housekeeper to answer, her heart thumped so loudly against her ribs that she thought it must be audible. And when her knock wasn't answered in the first few seconds she decided, with relief, not to wait. After all, any time would do. She had half-turned away when the door opened and the housekeeper was standing there.

'Well?' She was tall, thin, fierce-looking. Madeleine had seen her in church without knowing who she was.

'I wanted to see Father O'Malley,' Madeleine said. 'But if it's not convenient that's quite all right!'

'He's resting,' the housekeeper said, 'which is a sure sign that someone will come knocking on the door.'

'Then I'll come some other time,' Madeleine offered eagerly.

'Oh no, Miss!' the housekeeper said. 'If I didn't tell him you were here it'd be trouble for me and no mistake. You'd better step inside!'

Within five minutes Madeleine had been shown into Father O'Malley's study. He rose to greet her. In his shabby black suit he seemed smaller, less impressive than in church, wearing his vestments and celebrating the Mass. His voice, as he welcomed her, wasn't so powerful. It was quiet and gentle, more Irish than when he was preaching from the pulpit.

'What's your name, child?'

'Madeleine Bates, Father.'

She had never called a clergyman 'Father' before. It sounded strange on her tongue. She shuddered to think what her own father would say if he could hear her doing it.

'Madeleine. And what did you want to see me about?'

'It's difficult to explain,' she said. 'I don't know where to begin.'

It wasn't difficult for him to guess why she was here. He'd seen her often enough in church to expect this visit, sooner or later.

'The beginning's usually a good place to begin,' he said. 'I've seen you in Saint Mary's, isn't that right?'

'Yes that's right.'

'But you're not a Catholic? Am I right about that too?'

'Quite right.'

'And don't you lodge with Mrs Barnet?'

She was thawing a little, he thought. Looking less scared.

'Well if you don't want to tell me why you've come – and there's no rush, to be sure – why not tell me a bit about yourself, Madeleine. Have you been in a Catholic church before Saint Mary's?'

'I've been in Notre Dame cathedral, in Paris,' she replied.

Father O'Malley gave a long whistle.

'Have you now? Well that's more than I can say for myself! And what did you think of it?'

He had it all out of her. Hesitantly at first, but then with the words flowing, so that he hardly had need to ask her anything, she told him about the morning in Notre Dame, about her home, her father, the chapel, the mill. He saw quite quickly where the trouble lay, but now wasn't the time to discuss it.

'So you work for Monsieur Bonneau?' he said. 'I believe he is a good employer.'

'The best!' Madeleine said.

'I'm glad to hear it. My word, you must have found Notre Dame a very great contrast to Saint Mary's!'

She'd hardly thought of that. It was the contrast with the chapel in Helsdon which had struck her most.

'Mind you,' Father O'Malley went on, 'God isn't present any more effectively in such splendid surroundings, with all that music and spectacle, than He is in the plainest, humblest place. People find God in different ways. But I'm sure you've worked that out for yourself.' The gentleness of his voice took the edge off what might have been a rebuke.

'I didn't mean to criticize,' Madeleine said. 'It's more that I'm confused. I'm . . . searching.'

'Perhaps God is searching for *you*,' Father O'Malley said. 'Think about that, Madeleine.'

He rose from his chair.

'I have to go now. I have a visit to make. Will you promise to come and see me again? There is no hurry. God is very patient.'

'I will,' she said.

Walking back to Mrs Barnet's, Madeleine realized that she had asked Father O'Malley none of the questions which had been in her mind all these weeks and months, yet she felt as though some of them, a few of them, had been answered.

On Monday morning, in the breakfast-time break, she went to Monsieur Bonneau's office to tell him the outcome of her visit to Morecambe.

'I'm sorry that's the best I could do for you,' she said when she'd given him the details. 'Perhaps you'll be more persuasive when Mrs Thomas comes here. There's another thing, though. . . .'

'What's that?'

'If you leave it too late, I mean until the weather turns, she might not feel like coming.'

'I will not do that,' Léon said. 'There is no reason why I should not be in Mount Royd very soon.'

He would be pleased to leave 'Ashgrove' as quickly as possible. Relations between himself and Beatrice Lenham were strained and even Florence had turned cold towards him. He wondered what her mother had told her?

'Thank you, sir,' Madeleine said. 'I'll get back to work. Shall we be starting Garston's order this week?'

'Tomorrow, I hope.'

The mention of Garston's, the memory of Henry Garston's words as he'd been leaving, pricked Léon's conscience again, but he put the thought from him.

In the end it was Beatrice Lenham who hastened Léon's departure from 'Ashgrove', and on the very next day, waylaying him after breakfast as he was leaving for the mill – she no longer served his meals herself but left it entirely to Jane.

'I've been wondering, Monsieur Bonneau, when you might be thinking of leaving? The point is, I have another paying-guest very anxious indeed to move into your room as soon as you vacate it.'

'Then I shall leave quite soon,' Léon said readily. 'I will see Mrs Parkinson about Mount Royd today. I would certainly not wish you to miss the opportunity of another guest.'

'Oh, that is not the difficulty, monsieur,' Mrs Lenham said sweetly. 'I really do believe I could fill a small hotel with the people who wish to take up residence here! People, alas, I have to turn away! It's just that the gentleman concerned is rather pressing!'

In fact, she had every hope that the said gentleman might be the answer to her prayers. He was middle-aged, not really handsome, but rich and lonely; a man who would not have as high an opinion of himself as this Frenchman. But of course, she thought sadly, not nearly so exciting!

'Then I will give you a firm date this evening,' Léon promised.

It was all arranged quite quickly. Mrs Parkinson put at his disposal a sitting-room, bedroom, and the study which could be converted to a small dining-room, together with a bedroom and the kitchen for the house-keeper. With the exception of the basement kitchen, all the rooms were on the ground floor and made a cosy apartment.

'I thought you wouldn't want the big dining-room,' Mrs Parkinson said.

'You're quite right,' Léon agreed. 'I shan't be doing any entertaining. All this will suit me very well indeed.'

'I'm glad Mrs Thomas is going to see you in,' Mrs Parkinson said. 'Meanwhile I shall keep my eyes and ears open for a permanent housekeeper.'

Back at the mill, he spoke to Madeleine.

'I am writing to Mrs Thomas today and I hope she will agree to come on Saturday. Would it be possible for you to meet her at the station after work and bring her to Mount Royd? I shall be occupied, moving in.'

'Certainly,' Madeleine agreed. 'I'd be pleased to.'

The train arrived on time. Madeleine stepped forward to greet a pink-faced Mrs Thomas and took her bags.

'Monsieur Bonneau has hired a cab to take us to Mount Royd,' she said. 'It's waiting for us.'

When the cab drew up in front of Mount Royd Mrs Thomas stepped down and stood there for a minute, looking up at the house. All the windows except a few on the ground floor were shuttered, giving it a sad, blind look. Also, there was too much ivy climbing over the walls.

'Ivy doesn't do a house any good,' she said critically. 'If the Master had been alive he'd have had that seen to, sharp!'

But he wasn't, was he? And it was no use looking backwards, not more than you could help.

'Perhaps Monsieur Bonneau will see to it,' Madeleine suggested.

Léon had heard the cab, and came out to greet them.

'How pleased I am that you've come, Mrs Thomas!' he said, shaking her by the hand. 'Now the place will immediately seem more like home.'

'Thank you, sir!' She felt doubtful. Everything was bound to be different and she wondered if she had been wise to leave the comfortable niche she had made for herself in Morecambe.

'Would you like me to come in to give you a hand, Mrs Thomas?' Madeleine asked.

'I would that!' Mrs Thomas said eagerly.

When they were in the house Léon said:

'First of all, Mrs Thomas, you might like to make yourself a cup of tea. Mrs Parkinson has seen to buying in stores, and if there's anything else you need, please tell me. Then whenever you are ready I will show you my apartment and your own room.'

'It's funny, being back here,' Madeleine said minutes later, as the two of them sat at the kitchen table. 'I never thought to set foot in Mount Royd again.'

'Nor me,' Mrs Thomas confessed. 'And I'm not sure I should have. Any road, it's not for long. I expect Monsieur Bonneau will soon get suited.'

'I must say, I like this house,' Madeleine remarked. 'I wouldn't ever want to be back as a servant, but I do like the house.'

'Aye, it's a nice enough house,' Mrs Thomas agreed. 'But wasted on one man.'

When Monsieur Bonneau showed them around the apartment he had carved out for himself, the rooms furnished with choice pieces of furniture Mrs Parkinson had been only too happy for him to use, Madeleine and Mrs Thomas were full of approval.

'I wouldn't have believed it could feel so snug,' Mrs Thomas said.

'Now let me show you your room,' Léon said to the housekeeper. 'I hope you will think it an improvement on climbing up to the attic!'

A vivid memory of that tiny room in the roof, where she had been almost frozen to death in the winter and baked alive in the summer, came back to Madeleine. She remembered, too, the morning when she had walked into Monsieur Bonneau's room and found him stark naked. On the rare occasions when she'd previously recalled this incident it had been with amusement; but now the feeling was different. He'd been remote then, belonging to another world. Now that she knew him better, knew him as a man – though they still lived on different levels – such thoughts were disturbing.

'If you will excuse me, I must go,' she said. 'I promised to do some shopping for Mrs Barnet. Mr Barnet is not at all well.'

'You'll come and see me, love?' Mrs Thomas asked anxiously. She was used to company. She didn't relish being alone.

'Of course I will!' Madeleine promised.

Monday morning saw the start of work on Garston's order. Léon Bonneau was like a cat on hot bricks, in and out of the weaving-shed all day, asking questions, offering encouragement, checking on progress.

'Everything's going fine, sir!' John Hartley assured him.

'Good! It means a lot to all of us. But shall we finish in the time allowed?' It was his chief anxiety. They were on a tight schedule. It needed very little – a breakdown of one or two looms, a few weavers off sick – to result in the cloth not being ready.

'We've only just started,' the overlooker pointed out.

'We can never say for certain what might happen, but a few of us are prepared to put in all the overtime necessary to make sure it's done to schedule.'

'I think Monsieur Bonneau would feel better if he could stand at one of the looms and weave the cloth himself,' Madeleine said to Mrs Barnet. She hadn't meant him to hear, but he did.

'And do not think I couldn't!' he answered.

Each time he saw Madeleine he was pricked by the thought of what Henry Garston had said. Now, as he stood beside her loom, and watched as she worked with such skill, he determined he would say something, give her a chance to better herself. He would do it at the very first opportunity, which would not be just yet for they were all, Madeleine included, far too busy.

It was almost three weeks before the opportunity came. They were three weeks in which Léon settled in at Mount Royd, thankful to have Mrs Thomas to look after him when he came home from the mill; in which Beatrice Lenham and her new lodger found themselves totally compatible. They were weeks in which Madeleine, bone weary with the long hours they were now working, yet still with her mind on the church, went twice more to see Father O'Malley, and took another step or two along the way. They were also weeks towards the end of which Charlie Barnet's health deteriorated, and it was this last factor which gave Léon his chance to talk to Madeleine.

Garston's order was almost completed, great rolls of beautiful cloth ready for delivery to Leeds. On this last night only Mrs Barnet and Madeleine, with John Hartley to oversee, were required to work late – but Léon Bonneau did so, too. There was no way he would go home until it was completed. It was already dropping dark when a boy came to the mill gate and spoke to the night watchman.

'It's Mr Barnet! He's been taken real bad! Mrs Barnet has to come home at once. And Mr Hartley with her.'

When the watchman brought the message to Léon Bonneau he hurried to the weaving-shed.

'You must go at once, Mrs Barnet,' he ordered. 'And you too, John!'

'Then you'd better come, Madeleine,' John Hartley said.

Madeleine thought for a moment, then said:

'No. You'll be better without me. I'm not family and I'll be in the way. Besides, I'd like to finish this last piece.'

'I don't want you going home on your own, in the dark,' John Hartley persisted.

'Don't worry about that,' Léon broke in. 'I will see Madeleine home. Now please go, both of you.'

Madeleine put her arm around Mrs Barnet's shoulder.

'You know I would come if there was anything I could do.'

'I know. But you're best here,' Mrs Barnet agreed. 'Will you be able to see to my loom for me, love? And let Monsieur Bonneau bring you home. I'd feel easier if you did.'

'I'll do both those things,' Madeleine promised. Really, she didn't need anyone to see her home. Though it might be quite late when she finished, and it was a lonely way in the dark, she wasn't frightened.

It was almost eleven o'clock before she was through. Léon had been constantly in and out of the weaving-shed, keeping an eye on her, but now he was back in his office. She breathed a deep sigh of relief that she had come to the end – and thankfulness that everything had gone well – but oh, she was so very tired! She walked across to where the buffets stood against the wall, and sat down, hanging her head, letting her whole body go limp. She'd just give herself a minute to recover and then she'd go to the office, tell Monsieur Bonneau she was done.

It was thus, coming quietly into the shed a minute or two later, that Léon found her. She was so still that at first he thought she had fallen asleep where she sat. He stood motionless, looking at her. There was weariness in every line of her slender body, and as he watched her he was filled with remorse, and with a great tenderness towards her. They were feelings new to him. He cursed himself that he could work anyone into this state for his own ends; for his own ambition and profit.

He went quietly towards her, and when she heard the movement she lifted her head and looked at him. She looked at him as if she was seeing him for the first time, and feelings which she had not known were in her, not for him or for anyone, showed in her face, in her soft bright eyes, in the curve of her parted lips. Léon caught the look and knew that the shining light which seemed to be in her, illuminating every facet of her beauty, was for him. He knew also, for good and for all, that he could never let her go to Henry Garston; but neither could he deceive her about that any longer.

He stepped towards her and took her hands in his. It seemed entirely natural that he should do so and she made no protest.

'I should not have let you work so hard, Madeleine,' he said. 'Now I must take you home.'

'I don't mind,' she said. 'I wanted to finish. Do you want to look at it?'

'Not now,' he said. 'I'm more concerned about you. Madeleine, you shouldn't be doing this job. You can do so much more. I have been selfish to keep you in the mill. If you want to leave me and go to Henry Garston I shall have only myself to blame.' The words rushed out. There was so much more he wanted to say, and the look on her face both encouraged him and made him tongue-tied at one and the same time.

'I don't want to go to Garston's,' she said quietly. 'No matter what Mr Garston will do for me. I don't want to leave here – not unless you wish me to, that is.'

'Oh Madeleine!' he said. 'How could I ever wish that?

I never want you to go. I want you always in my life, for ever. Do you understand, my dear one?'

They stood looking at each other. It was a long time before she could speak, and when her voice came it was no more than a whisper.

'I understand. And I will never leave you!'

'Promise me!' he said urgently. 'Say "Léon, I will never leave you". Say the words!'

'Léon, I promise I will never leave you!'

It was the first time she had spoken his name. In her heart she had said it before, but it had never passed her lips – and now that she had spoken it she wanted to say it again and again.

'Léon, Léon, Léon!' she cried. 'I will never leave you!'

He took her in his arms and kissed her, at first gently, no more than brushing her lips with his, but then harder and fiercer until she knew he must bruise her, yet she welcomed it and it seemed the most natural thing in the world, the only thing in the world.

He let her go, ran his fingers over the lips he had just kissed, traced the contours of her mouth.

'Oh, my darling Madeleine!'

'Léon!'

His name was magic to her. She would never tire of saying it.

'Father O'Malley was right,' she said suddenly. 'The love which lies between a man and a woman is good, he said. Though it is only a reflection of God's love for us, it is still sublime. And true love casts out fear.'

'Father O'Malley said that to you?' Léon asked. Why should that be? he wondered idly.

'Yes. And now I know it's true.'

She realized she had not shuddered or pulled away at his touch. She had wanted him to go on touching her, holding her.

'Of course it is true,' Léon said. 'How could anyone think otherwise?'

416

It was not the time to explain. Sooner or later she must, but not now, not yet.

'I must go home,' she said. 'It's very late.'

Arm in arm they walked through the dark street towards Mrs Barnet's house. Madeleine felt gloriously alive, and safe, and contented – and as Léon kissed her good night she felt as though everything in the world was singing.

Later, lying in bed, when the thought came that the affair was unsuitable, that she was a mill-hand and he the mill-owner, and that there were other, deeper reasons for not becoming involved, she pushed them from her as if they had no importance.

'I'm in love!'

Lying in the dark she whispered the words out loud, while Charlie Barnet was fighting and winning the battle for his life in the room below.

'I'm in love, I'm in love, I'm in love!' she repeated.

TWENTY-TWO

'Madeleine, I do not understand!' Léon said. 'Why will you not marry me? I have told you I love you. I believe you love me, and you have not denied it. So why?'

He had asked her to come to his office, ostensibly to discuss some patterns, and though he must sometime soon discuss work with her, nothing counted beside the urgency of his love for her. It consumed him like a fire, the spark of which, he now recognized, had been kindled many months ago. Why had it taken him so long to know it?

After he had taken her home on the previous evening he had walked back to Mount Royd like a man in a dream. Not until the night was almost over had he gone to bed to snatch an hour or two of exhausted sleep. Most of the night he had paced the floor, wrestling with his feelings, fighting the emotions which threatened to lead him into a most unsuitable alliance. In the end he had lost the fight, and been thankful to do so.

This morning he had come to the mill determined to ask Madeleine Bates to marry him. Common sense warned him that such an action was ill-advised, rash, and to his family would be unthinkable. But no matter. He loved her so. The gap which yawned between them, with Madeleine a servant-turned-mill-girl on one side and himself a mill-owner and her employer on the other – to say nothing of their religious differences – would be bridged by their love. It would overcome all obstacles. And now she had refused him.

'But why?' he repeated. 'Why, Madeleine? I love you. Please do not deny that you love me!'

She stood in front of him, silent.

'Look me in the eye and tell me you do not love me!' he insisted. 'Tell me that what happened last night meant nothing to you!'

'I can't say that,' Madeleine answered. 'The fact remains that I can't marry you.'

He took both her hands in his, and love and desire shot through her at his touch.

'Madeleine, I know there are obstacles. Do not think I haven't faced them. But we will overcome them together. If you are thinking of the differences in our positions, it doesn't matter. When you are my wife nothing else will matter!'

Madeleine shook her head. Because she loved him, these differences were no obstacle to her. But it was impossible for her to accept him. She had known that as soon as she'd wakened this morning, as soon as she had opened her eyes to the cold light of day.

She was spoilt; she was defiled. What George Carter had done to her could not be ignored. She knew she was no longer afraid of physical love, indeed she welcomed it, longed for it, but to go into marriage with Léon without telling him the truth was, she now knew, out of the question. Yet to tell him was equally unthinkable. If she were to do so, not only would he no longer want to marry her, he would cease to love her. She couldn't bear that.

'I can't,' she persisted. 'Please don't ask me why.'

'Madeleine, I *have* to ask you why! You're not being fair to me. Is it because I am a Catholic?'

'Oh no!' she assured him. 'I want to tell you, I was going to do so presently, that I hope to be received into the Catholic church before long.'

'Well, I can't tell you how pleased I am about that –

though not as surprised as you might think. But since there's no barrier there, I'm more than ever puzzled! Surely you realized last night that I am in love with you, that I would want us to be married?'

She had realized it, but she'd pushed the knowledge away, wanting only to experience the fact of being in love, not looking to the future.

'Léon, please don't mention marriage to me,' she begged. 'Let things be as they were!'

'There's no way we can do that, and you know it, Madeleine. If I thought you did not love me I would never speak of it again. But I know you do.'

'Then give me time, Léon. Please give me time!'

'I do not understand,' he said slowly. 'Nevertheless I will do as you ask. But I will not wait long. For a few days I won't mention the subject, but after that I shall ask you again.'

It was no good, she thought. She couldn't stop him – and in her heart she didn't want to.

'May I go now?' she asked.

'No. I have to talk to you about work. I suppose I am allowed to do that?'

The sharpness of his voice stabbed her. I don't want to hurt you, my darling, she longed to say. I don't ever want to hurt you. Instead, in a controlled voice, she said:

'Of course!'

'Very well, then. You know, Madeleine, that Henry Garston said you could apply to him for a job when ever you wanted one? Well, he mentioned that offer in the strongest possible terms when he visited Bonneau's. I have told you I do not want you to go, but I am now telling you that I must not, and will not, hold you back. You are free; you are not a bondswoman.'

If she persisted in refusing to marry him, would it not be better if she went to Garston's? he asked himself. How could he bear to see her every day, yet keep his distance?

Madeleine looked at him in surprise.

'But, I told you I didn't want to go to Garston's. I said I wouldn't leave Bonneau's . . .'

'You said you would not leave *me*!' he interrupted.

'And I won't! Not unless you tell me I must.'

'That day will never come,' Léon said. 'But since it's what you want, let us continue to talk business. I have decided, if you wish it, that you should come out of the weaving and concentrate on design. The fact that we are very soon to have our own spinning means there will be more opportunities for design, and I truly believe you're the person to do it. You understand not only what looks good, what will be fashionable, but whether and how it will be possible to weave it.'

Madeleine's face, sad until this moment, was suddenly lit by a smile.

'Oh, Léon! Oh that's wonderful, it's truly wonderful! But who will do my work in the weaving?'

'That is the immediate problem,' Léon acknowledged. 'I can not take you out of the weaving until we have trained someone else, and I do not know who that someone else will be. You are the best weaver I've ever come across; it will be difficult to find anyone as good. But if we can find the right person, and if you and Mrs Barnet between you can train her, then we have to hope it will work out all right.'

'There's Sally Pitts,' Madeleine said quickly. 'She's a good little worker – quite talented in fact.'

'Sally Pitts? She's such a little mouse!'

'She's come on a lot in the last six months,' Madeleine said. Come to think of it, Sally had been coming out of her shell ever since John Hartley had set foot in Bonneau's as overlooker.

'Well I will consider her,' Léon said doubtfully. 'I will get Mrs Barnet's opinion, and also John Hartley's.'

'There's another thing . . .,' Madeleine began.

'Yes?'

'Since you've been kind enough to mention my work . . . I don't want to push – and I don't want to run

421

before I can walk – but if ever there was a chance of me going on the road, selling the cloth . . . well, I'd really like that! Not instead of designing, of course. I could do that also.'

He wasn't surprised at her request, but he was doubtful.

'I am not sure,' he said. 'It would be a novelty, a woman selling – but would it be acceptable? Oh, I know you did well with Garston's, but Henry Garston is a law unto himself! Other customers might not see it the same way.'

But unless he believed it might harm his business, he would hold her back from nothing she was capable of doing. He had made that promise to himself and he meant to keep it, though what he deeply desired was that she should marry him, build his home, bear his children. Oh, why must she refuse him?

'Where shall I do my designing?' Madeleine asked.

'I don't know. I must find you a corner somewhere.'

It couldn't be in his office, much as he would have liked to have had her always with him. But as well as such a move being unsuitable, he knew he couldn't bear the nearness of her, hour after hour, day after day.

'I'll think of something,' he promised.

Both Mrs Barnet and John Hartley gave good accounts of Sally Pitts, and so it was arranged that she should train to take Madeleine's place, alongside Mrs Barnet, on the most special designs.

'But I'm right sorry you're moving on, Madeleine,' Sally said. 'I've enjoyed working with you. We've been good friends.'

'We still shall be, silly,' Madeleine chided her. 'I'm not going to the moon. I'm still working for Bonneau's, same as you!'

'Not quite the same, love. But you always were clever and you deserve a leg up.'

That, it seemed, was the opinion of most of the weavers. There were very few who didn't wish Madeleine well when they heard the news. The one who liked it least was John Hartley.

'Well you've outgrown us, Madeleine,' he said. 'I suppose that's that between you and me!'

'You do talk rubbish,' Madeleine said. 'We're friends, aren't we? And we were never anything more. I was honest with you about that from the beginning.'

She owed John Hartley a debt for showing her that a man could be decent with a woman, a debt there was no way she could repay.

'You'll keep an eye on Sally, won't you?' she asked him. 'She needs encouragement. She doesn't always have a lot of confidence.'

'Oh, I'll look after Sally, don't you worry,' he said. 'She'll be all right. In fact she's a much better weaver than she thinks she is.'

If only he would turn his attention to Sally! Sally was dotty about him, and it seemed to Madeleine that they were made for each other, only John hadn't realized it.

She was saddest of all to part from Mrs Barnet.

'You've been a true friend to me. You've taught me everything I know about weaving,' she said to the older woman.

'Get away with you, soft!' Mrs Barnet said brusquely. 'I never knew anybody need less teaching. And I didn't give you your talent, you know. Talents are God-given. Anyway, I'm not getting shut of you altogether, am I? I take it you're not looking for fresh lodgings?'

'Of course not,' Madeline assured her. 'You know how I like being with you and Charlie. Isn't it grand that he's picking up?'

'Praise the Lord!' Mrs Barnet said. It had been touch and go on the night they'd fetched her from the mill.

A week later, Léon found a small room which had once been a storeroom and, with a drawing-board, a table, a chair and some shelves, fixed it up for Madeleine.

'It's wonderful!' she said. 'A room of my own to work in!' Oh, there'd be no end to the splendid designs she'd turn out here!

'Mr Garston was delighted with his cloth,' Léon said. 'I

heard from him today. He has put in another big order and he wants to see some fresh samples, so for the moment I am leaving you to start work on that. I need to concentrate on getting the spinning going.'

He was halfway out of her room, and then turned back again.

'Madeleine, I have to talk to you. We can't talk in the mill – it's too public. Will you go for a walk with me on Saturday afternoon?'

'I don't think . . .'

'Please Madeleine! It is important. I am not asking for the earth. Just for a proper chance to talk to you. If you don't want anyone to see us together, we can meet on the top of the moor, wherever you say.'

'Very well.' She owed it to him.

For the rest of that week, though by day she concentrated on her work, anxious to prove herself, in every minute of spare time she thought about what she must say to Léon. She knew the question he would ask her, but how could she answer? Night after night she lay awake, everything churning in her mind. In the end, when Friday night had given way to Saturday morning and she had not slept, she made up her mind. She would tell him the truth. She would tell him the real reason why she refused to marry him.

The decision brought her no peace. She pictured the look on his face when he heard the ugly truth. He would see her with new eyes; she would be as unclean to him as she was to herself. But that was something she must learn to bear. She had determined that, whatever the cost, she must be honest with him. She must let him know that the fault wasn't in him, but in her.

Saturday afternoon was drizzly, with a thin mist which grew thicker towards the top of the moor where they had arranged to meet. At least in weather like this the whole of Helsdon wouldn't be up there! Léon had arrived before her. When she reached the gate in the wall at the top of the first rise he was already waiting. He walked towards

424

her and took her hand, tucking it into the crook of his elbow.

'You're late,' he said. 'I worried in case you weren't coming.'

'Only five minutes. I said I'd come, didn't I?'

She wished he would let go of her hand. His touch took the strength away from her. How would she say what she had to say?

'Do you want to walk?' Léon asked.

'I'd rather not. Let's get it over, please.'

'You make it sound unpleasant. There's no reason why it should be, Madeleine.'

But there was. She knew that only too well. She took her hand from Léon's and stood at a short distance from him. While he continued to touch her she felt helpless.

'Madeleine . . .' he began.

'No, Léon! Let me speak!'

'Very well.'

She took a deep breath and forced the words out. In her own ears her voice sounded flat and cold, though it was not the way she felt. Inside she was crying, her heart was breaking.

'You do me a great honour in asking me to be your wife. No one has ever done me such an honour before. More than anything in the world I should like to accept. I beg you to believe that, even though I must say "no". I would rather not have to tell you the reason why, but I shall do so because it is only fair to you. You have a right to know.'

She stopped. She wasn't sure she could go on. Léon took a step towards her but she held up her hand and fended him off.

'No, don't touch me! Please let me finish.' Her voice was trembling. With the utmost difficulty she brought out the words which she knew would cut her off from him for ever.

'I cannot marry you because I am not . . .' she hesitated, searching for the words . . . 'I am not fit for your marriage bed. I am not a virgin.'

She had said it. She had uttered the words – and now she wished she could die. She had never been so unhappy in all her life. It was the end of her hopes. The tears streamed down her face now and she lowered her head, not daring to meet Léon's eyes.

'Madeleine! What do you mean?'

'Exactly what I said.'

'I don't understand you. I do not believe it! Are you telling me that you have already given yourself to another man?'

She heard the shock in his voice, and though she had expected it, it still angered her.

'No, I do not mean that! I do not mean that at all. I gave nothing. What I would have given willingly, and with love, to my husband in marriage was taken from me by force!'

'By force? You mean you were . . . raped?'

She nodded her head, no longer able to speak. Because she now buried her face in her hands, sobbing, she saw nothing of Léon's expression. All she knew was the shock in his voice. He will never touch me again, she thought – and who can blame him? Then she felt his hands grip her arms, his fingers digging into her so hard that, had she not been hurt beyond endurance already, she would have cried out with the pain.

'Madeleine! Madeleine, look at me!'

He spoke sharply, and when she refused to meet his look because she was afraid, he put his finger under her chin and raised her head so that she was forced to see him. He's angry with me, she thought. It was what she expected; but was it too much to hope that he might also have been kind?

'Madeleine! You must tell me all about this. When did it happen? Where? Was the brute caught and punished?'

'Oh yes,' she said dully. 'My brother saw to him all right!'

'I would have killed him with my bare hands,' Léon cried. 'I would have thought the world well rid of him.'

426

She had never seen him so angry, so hard. His voice shook with rage.

'My brother almost did,' she said. 'Though it was too late for me.'

'And is that why you will not marry me, Madeleine?'

'Yes.'

'Do you love me, Madeleine?' he asked in a quieter voice.

'With all my heart, Léon!'

'And if I had sinned – I am talking of sins of the flesh – if I had sinned with another woman, if I had taken another woman – though never against her will – would you still love me? Would you forgive me and want to marry me?'

'That's different,' Madeleine said. 'You're a man.'

'And do you think it should be different for a man?'

'I don't – but the world does.'

'But you would forgive me? You would still want to marry me?'

'Yes. I would forgive you because I love you.'

'And yet you cannot forgive yourself,' Léon said. 'Though you have not sinned at all, my dear. The sin has been against you. Did you think I would love you any less because someone has hurt you? Is that how you see my love – as less generous, as meaner than yours?'

He was looking at her now with hurt, angry eyes.

'I couldn't believe, *can't* believe, that you would want me,' she said.

'Then, my darling, you do not know the strength of my love. The only thing that has changed between us, if such a thing is possible, is that I love you more because of what you have suffered.'

How could she believe what she was hearing? How could it be true?

'It can't be true!' she whispered.

'It can be and it is!' Léon said. 'If there was anything to forgive I would forgive it, as you would for me. But there is nothing. And I am asking you again, will you marry me? Will you do me that honour, Madeleine?'

427

There was a moment in which she said nothing. All speech, all feeling, left her while the world stood still. Then with a joyful cry she found her voice.

'Oh I will!' she said. 'I will indeed!'

He took her in his arms and held her close. When he bent to kiss her she raised her lips to his with eagerness. She pressed her body against his, exulting in the hard masculinity of him. She had no idea how long she stood there in his embrace, only that eventually she realized her face and her hair were wet from the mist which was coming down thickly now.

'We must go,' Léon said. 'I cannot allow you to catch a chill. When can we be married, Madeleine? Soon, I hope.'

'I would like it to be soon,' she said. 'But not until I belong to your church.'

'Tell me something,' Léon said. 'When you mentioned Father O'Malley, when you told me what he had said to you about love between a man and a woman, had you been talking to him about us?'

'Oh no!' Madeleine was shocked. 'I wouldn't have done that. I told him . . .' She hesitated. 'I told him what had happened. I had to tell him. I thought it might be a bar to my acceptance. Afterwards I was glad I'd done so.'

'And you believe what Father O'Malley said? That perfect love casts out fear?'

'With all my heart. And I've proved it, and will continue to do so.'

'When did we really fall in love?' Léon mused. 'I want to remember every minute of the time we have spent together.'

'I know when it was,' Madeleine told him, 'though I didn't at the time. I fell in love with you on the morning we went to Notre Dame.'

'Yes, you are right!' Léon agreed. 'And when we go to France we will visit Notre Dame again. Where better to give our thanks?'

She felt a chill at the thought of visiting Léon's family in France. Whatever would they think of her? And she had also to face her own family, not only about Léon, but about what to them might be an even greater shock – her entry into the Catholic church. To break that news was the first hurdle, and must be cleared soon. She dreaded the moment. Even her mother would not approve of this step.

'I must visit my parents next weekend,' she said.

'Let me come with you,' Léon urged.

'No, my dear. I should like our engagement to be kept secret from them – and therefore from everyone else – until I've been received into your church. That will be a bitter enough blow for them to begin with. So will you be patient and allow me that?'

'If it is your wish, my love. For my part I would prefer to shout it from the housetops. But you will permit me to write and tell my own family?'

'They will object to me, I'm sure of it,' Madeleine said.

'Not when they have met you,' he assured her. 'I shall take you to Paris and then to Roubaix as soon as we are married.'

On an evening in the following week Madeleine came out of the church after a period of instruction with Father O'Malley. She was glad of the anonymity which the darkness gave her, for Helsdon was a small place and tongues wagged. It was a miracle that she had kept this particular secret so far. Other than Mrs Barnet and Charlie, she had so far chosen to tell no one, afraid that something might come between her and what was now her strong desire. She would be glad when she could proclaim her membership of the church to the whole world; and soon after that the other secret which she hugged to her breast, her engagement to Léon.

Descending the steps from Saint Mary's she heard footsteps, and saw a figure – a man – carrying a lantern. She was halfway down the steps when the man stopped in his tracks and lifted the lantern to see who was there. He had expected to see Father O'Malley, or the priest's housekeeper or some other devout member of his flock:

429

instead he saw Madeleine Bates, daughter of Joseph Bates.

He and Joseph Bates had been members together of Helsdon chapel for many years. He disliked Bates intensely, and the feeling was mutual. He disliked him because he was everlastingly superior, always a step ahead: more devout, stricter in his observances, always, seemingly, supported by his wife and family, while he, Walter Butler, lagged behind in every sphere. Even in the matter of employment Bates had been lucky, landing a job with Salt's when Parkinson's had closed. He himself was still out of work. And now, here was Joseph Bates's daughter leaving the Roman Catholic church! This was something *quite* different! Mind you, it was no more than you could expect if you let your daughter go gadding off to Paris. It was well known that foreigners were all papists.

'Why, if it isn't Madeleine Bates!' he exclaimed. 'I didn't expect to see you around here!' He gave a significant look in the direction of the church to make sure she got his point. The Bateses weren't going to get away with this one!

'Good evening, Mr Butler,' Madeleine said. 'Nor I you.'

'Well I live in the next street, love. I hear you're lodging with Harriet Barnet?'

'That's right.' She could perhaps make the excuse that she had been to the church on an errand for Mrs Barnet – but she wouldn't bother, she wouldn't stoop to it. She disliked Mr Butler.

'And how is your dad, then? How are things going for him?'

'Very well indeed. He likes working for Titus Salt, and I believe he's due to get one of the new houses in Saltaire village quite soon.'

She wasn't to know that she'd said quite the wrong thing. If she'd been able to say that things were going badly for her father, that might have satisfied Walter

430

Butler. As it was, she fanned the flame of Walter Butler's hatred of him.

'Well he seems to have landed on his feet, your dad!' But he could, if he chose, put him flat on his back.

'Good night then, Madeleine!' he said. 'I'm pleased to have met you.'

Yes, I'm sure you are, Madeleine thought, walking away. How long before he told half of Helsdon – and when he did it would spread through the chapel folk like a forest fire. It would catch up with her father in no time at all. Therefore she must go to Shipley after work on Saturday. It would be cruel to let the news reach her parents as a piece of gossip.

But Walter Butler decided, and it took him no more than a few minutes that same evening, not to rely in the first instance on gossip. That would come later. No, it was his immediate and solemn duty to inform Joseph Bates just what his daughter was up to. He cleared a space on the table and began to write:

'Dear Mr Bates,
    After much wrestling with my conscience I
am, with the greatest reluctance, writing to
inform you . . .'

By the time he had signed his name at the bottom he felt better, much better.

Taking the train to Shipley on Saturday afternoon, Madeleine felt sick with apprehension. She could remember nothing she had had to do in her whole life which had frightened her more. Since Tuesday evening when she had met with Mr Butler it had hardly been out of her mind. She had told Léon about it, but he viewed the matter much less seriously than he did.

'You are not committing a crime, dearest,' he pointed out.

'In my father's eyes,' Madeleine said, 'there can be few

431

more serious crimes. I do believe he'd rather see me dead at his feet!'

'But there is nothing he can do to you. You have made up your mind.'

'I know I have,' she agreed. 'And nothing will change it. I am quite resolved. I don't think I care what he does to me; it's what he will do to my mother which frightens me. He will take it out on her, and she has to live with him.'

'Please change your mind and allow me to come with you,' Léon begged. 'Let us tell them everything, and let me be in my rightful place, by your side. There is no need ever for you to stand alone again, my love!'

'Oh Léon, you can't know what that means to me! But this is something I must do on my own. I'm sure of that.'

'Then be equally sure that I shall be thinking of you,' he said.

Saturday's weather did nothing to help Madeleine's state of mind. It was foggy, getting thicker by the minute. There was no way she'd be able to get back to Helsdon tonight for she doubted if a train would run. Though it would mean yet another sleepless night, perhaps she should put off breaking the news until morning so that she could escape more quickly from her father's wrath?

When she walked into the house in Shipley it was already too late. She knew it at once. The frightened expression on her mother's face told her everything. She had hoped to find her mother alone, but it was not to be. Penelope sat at the table, pale and scared, her hands clenched. Her father, stiff as a ram-rod, stood with his back to the mantlepiece, his dark-skinned face almost black with fury. They must have been quarrelling until the minute before she entered, Madeleine thought. And there was no need to wonder what the quarrel had been about. The look of hatred on her father's face as soon as he caught sight of her, said it all.

For a moment no one spoke. The only sound, magnified a thousand times in the stillness, was the ticking of the clock Martha Bates had brought with her as a wedding present. It was Penelope who broke the silence. She got down from the table, rushed towards Madeleine who stood motionless in the doorway, and flung her arms around her.

'Oh Madeleine, I can't bear never to see you again, not ever see you as long as I live! Not even if you *have* been the most wicked person in the world!'

So that was the way it was? Madeleine bent down to her sister and took her in her arms.

'Now why should you say that, love? Of course I haven't been wicked. And of course you'll see me. We're sisters. We'll see each other as long as we live. Whatever anyone says.'

'Father says—'

'Be quiet! Leave the room at once!' Joseph Bates shouted.

'I don't want to leave the room!' Penelope whimpered. 'I want to stay with Madeleine!'

'Go upstairs and take your book, love,' Madeleine said. 'Just for a few minutes. I promise I'll still be here when you come down.'

When Penelope had reluctantly left the room, Madeleine looked directly at her father. She was trembling from head to foot with fear and anger, but not for a moment would she give him the satisfaction of knowing it.

'Well,' she said. 'What have you heard?'

He took Walter Butler's letter from the mantelpiece and flung it at Madeleine. It fluttered to the floor at her feet.

'Read this! Tell me not a word of it is true. Tell me you weren't seen coming out of a Roman Catholic church. Tell me Walter Butler is lying!'

She picked up the letter from the floor and sat at the table to read it, her legs suddenly too weak to support her. As she read, anger rushed into her, coursed through her body.

'The snake!' she cried. 'The snivelling, crawling snake! Oh, how he has enjoyed writing this!'

433

'Is it true?' her father demanded.

Her anger had achieved something; she was no longer afraid. It was rage which caused her body to tremble now. 'You've already decided that it's true! You've already decided to believe this . . . toad . . . without waiting for my explanation.'

'I don't need an explanation,' Joseph Bates said. 'I want to know only one thing, did Walter Butler see you coming out of that . . . place?'

'He did. The reason . . .'

'I want no reasons,' he shouted.

'Well you're going to get the reason!' Madeleine yelled. 'Whether you want it or not!'

'Madeleine, *please*, I beg you!' They were the first words her mother had uttered.

'No Ma, I'll have my say. I might have been in the Catholic church for a number of reasons. I might have been taking a message, or fetching the priest to a sick person – but my father can be guaranteed to think the worst of me! And in this case the worst – or rather, what he sees as the worst – is the truth. I had been to see the priest. Father O'Malley is giving me instruction and I am shortly to be received into the Catholic church!'

'Madeleine!' Martha Bates's horrified whisper dropped like a stone in the silence.

'I'm sorry, Ma. I didn't mean you to hear it like this. I came to tell you peaceably, to explain things.'

'I don't understand!' Mrs Bates said.

'I'd hoped you would understand when I'd explained. Of course I never hoped for a minute that my father would.'

With a stream of abuse, shouting words that Madeleine had never before heard on his lips, her father lunged at her. Though he had never in his life laid a finger on her, she was certain he was about to attack her and she ran to put the width of the table between them.

'You are not too big to be beaten!' he said savagely. 'I should have beaten the devil out of you when you were a child. I have sinned in not doing so. But it is not too late!'

434

'If you so much as touch me,' Madeleine said, 'I shall call the police! Nothing will stop me.'

She stood in front of him, ram-rod-straight and defiant. He backed away. She watched the effort he made to stop himself striking her. Then in a tightly controlled voice he spoke to his wife.

'Fetch Penelope down!'

'Why? I don't want her down.'

'Do as you're told!' he shouted.

What does he intend? Madeleine asked herself. He had some purpose, that was plain, but what? She watched as he went to the dresser and took out the family Bible. He placed it on the table and took pen and ink from the mantelpiece.

She knew now what was to happen. She knew, and he knew, that there was no action of his which could affect her more. He had chosen well. She had hurt him deeply and he had found the perfect punishment.

'Stand around the table!' he ordered when they were all there.

While they stood in silence, Martha Bates gripping the back of a chair to support her, he opened the Bible and read aloud through the list of names in the front. Every one of them was there, even Irvine's. He read out the dates of birth and the few but important anniversaries. He read slowly, with deliberation, as if he were in the chapel. Then he took the pen and in the stony silence of the little room he crossed through Madeleine's name.

At first he drew one line through it, but then, his blood mounting, suffusing his face, he drew another and another and another, until her name and every detail about her was totally obliterated.

'You are no longer my daughter,' he said. 'Your mother is not your mother; your sisters are not your sisters. As far as this family is concerned it is, from now, as if you have never been born, never lived.' He intoned the words as if he was reciting a curse.

It was as if a knife had been plunged into the depths of

Madeleine's being, as if by crossing out her name he had killed her, taken her life. She sank to the floor and lay there sobbing, and was still sobbing when he took his coat from the hook, and put it on.

'I am going out,' he said. 'I am going to the chapel. I shall no longer pray for you, you who were once my daughter, whose name I shall never speak again, because you are past praying for. You have surrendered to the devil. When I return I shall expect you to be gone. I shall never see you again, nor will your mother or your sisters.'

When he had left the house Mrs Bates helped Madeleine to her feet, took her in her arms.

'Oh Ma,' Madeleine sobbed, 'you won't cross me out of your heart, will you?'

'Of course I won't, love! Didn't I give you birth? Of course I won't. But oh, Madeleine, why did you have to do it? Can't you change your mind?'

'I did it because I had to, because it seemed right, the only right. I shall never change my mind, Ma!'

'I'll write your name in my Bible,' Penelope cried. 'I won't ever let father see it!' The tears were streaming down her face.

'Bless you!' Madeleine said. 'And don't fret, Penelope. I might not see you as often from now on, but I *will* see you. I promise you that and you must believe me.'

'You must be gone before your father gets back,' Mrs Bates said anxiously.

'I know,' Madeleine agreed. 'I won't make it worse for you. Shall you be all right, Ma? I mean afterwards?'

'I'll be all right.' She would manage. Somehow she would get through – because she had to, there was no choice. But she hated him all the time now. She hated him more than ever.

Madeleine went to the door and looked out into the street.

'The fog's thicker than ever, Ma! You can't see a hand in front of you. I'll never get a train back to Helsdon. What shall I do?'

Mrs Bates thought for a moment, then said:

'I'll go and ask Mrs Turner at number twenty-three if she can give you a bed for the night. She's a nice woman. She'll understand.'

She was back within a few minutes.

'It's all arranged. She'll give you breakfast before you go for your train in the morning. But stay here a bit longer. He'll not be back for an hour or so.'

As they sat, they tried to talk everyday things. The time was past for questions and answers. Madeleine longed to tell her mother about Léon, but it must wait.

After an hour or so Mrs Bates said:

'Time you were off, love. Give me a kiss before you go.'

They clung to each other as if they could never part, and then each to Penelope, and then all three of them together. With tears streaming down her face Madeleine put on her cloak and bonnet, took one last look around the room, and went out into the fog.

'You and I will go to bed, Penelope,' Mrs Bates said. She could not bear another moment of this worst day of her life.

She fell asleep more quickly than she could have hoped. It was the chimes of the clock from the living-room downstairs, striking midnight, which wakened her. Turning in the bed, she realized that Joseph was not with her. It was not like him to sit up late. She lit the candle and went downstairs. He was not there. He was nowhere in the house.

TWENTY-THREE

Martha Bates opened the house door and looked out into the street. The fog hung like a dark curtain, making it impossible to see a yard in any direction. She stood there in the doorway, in her nightshift, calling her husband's name.

'Joseph! Joseph!'

It was a ridiculous thing to do, she knew that. If he'd been within earshot, if he'd fallen and was hurt, he'd have made himself heard hours ago. Even so, she shouted his name again and again, each time the wall of fog absorbing the sound of her voice. It was useless. She went back into the house and closed the door. Stirring the dying embers of the fire into a blaze, putting more coal on until there was a pyramid through which the flames could take hold, she wondered what to do.

In all the years of their marriage, Joseph had never stayed out late. That much could be said for him. He always came straight home from chapel, and the chapel meeting would have finished more than three hours ago. At his usual pace the walk from Coomber Terrace, along a short stretch of the canal bank, over the bridge and up Buck's Lane, across the main road and then up a short hill to the chapel building, took no more than fifteen minutes. So where was he? What had happened to him? What could she do? He had not taken a lamp – he seldom did – but in any case it wouldn't have penetrated the fog.

It was now nearly one o'clock in the morning. To go out and look for him would mean leaving Penelope alone in the house, and Penelope frequently wakened, screaming, frightened out of her life by nightmares. She couldn't be left alone. Yet supposing Joseph was lying somewhere out there with a broken leg?

There was only one solution. Madeleine must be fetched from Mrs Turner's to stay with Penelope, then she herself would go in search of Joseph. She didn't like knocking up Mrs Turner at this time of night, but there was nothing else for it.

Madeleine heard the knock at once. So far she hadn't slept a wink, going over and over in her mind the terrible scene with her father. She heard Mrs Turner get out of bed, muttering, and go down the creaky stairs to answer the door. And when the door was opened and she recognized her mother's voice she jumped out of bed and ran downstairs herself.

'What's wrong? What's the matter? Is someone ill?'

'No. I don't know. Your father hasn't come home!'

'*Not come home*? Oh Ma! Whatever can have happened?'

'I must go and look for him,' Mrs Bates said. 'You'll have to come home, Madeleine. You'll have to stay with Penelope while I go out.'

'You're not going out on your own, Mrs Bates!' Mrs Turner declared. 'It's not fit! Apart from the fact that it's the middle of the night, the fog's as thick as my best blankets!'

'I *must* go,' Mrs Bates stressed. 'For all we know Joseph's lying there in Buck's Lane with a broken leg, or he's been knocked down by a cart on the road. I've got to find him.'

'Then Madeleine must go with you,' Mrs Turner pronounced. 'I'll come round to your house in case Penelope wakens.'

'I don't like to bother you,' Mrs Bates said hesitantly. 'It's bad enough to waken you up at this time of night, let alone drag you out.'

'Stuff and nonsense!' Mrs Turner's reply was brisk. 'Now give me a minute to get dressed and I'll be with you.'

'Well, if you're quite sure, I'll go back and get a few things together,' Mrs Bates said. Bandages, she thought; a bottle of water; a shawl. What else? Who knew what she would find?

'I'll be ready in two ticks, Ma!' Madeleine said.

Ten minutes later the two of them set off, arm in arm, Madeleine carrying a lamp, though it was of little use. The thick wall of fog seemed impenetrable.

'We'll make for the chapel,' Mrs Bates said. 'We're bound to find him between here and there.'

Because of the fog they could walk only slowly, but all the time they called his name.

'Joseph! Joseph, are you there?' Mrs Bates shouted.

'Father!' Madeleine cried – then remembered that only a few hours ago he had told her she was no longer his daughter. Well, he had disowned her but she would not disown him. She continued to call, and, for what it was worth, she shone the lamp into the corners, up against the wall which bordered the lane, and into the ditch at the other side – searching any and every place where he might be lying.

Much of the time they were not sure of their own whereabouts, so much had the fog disorientated them, but when Buck's Lane gave way to the main road they felt the different surface underfoot and knew it wasn't far now to the chapel. There was no traffic, everything was eerily silent. Nor, though they searched diligently along the road, did they find Joseph Bates there. Now there was only Chapel Hill to climb.

When, minutes later, the dark shape of the chapel loomed up suddenly out of the fog, they knew they had reached the end. There was no sign of Joseph Bates. They felt their way around the perimeter of the building, searching every inch. He was not there. Where else could they look?

'Perhaps he's inside the chapel,' Mrs Bates said, clutching at straws. 'Perhaps he stayed behind to do something, after everyone else had gone. Perhaps that's what he did – and was then taken ill?'

Madeleine went to the chapel door, tried it, shook it hard.

'No Ma,' she said gently. 'The chapel's locked!'

Martha Bates's eyes were wide with fright as she stared at her daughter.

'What shall we do?' she cried. She could hardly believe that they hadn't found him.

'We'd better go to the police station, Ma,' Madeleine said. 'They'll know if someone has met with an accident, been taken to hospital.'

'But in that case why wouldn't they have sent someone to Coomber Terrace to tell us?' Mrs Bates queried.

Madeleine shook her head. 'I don't know. Perhaps father had nothing on him to say who he was or where he lived. Perhaps we should have gone to the police station in the first place?'

But a startled policeman, confronted in the middle of the night by two women with damp hair falling from underneath their bonnets, faces black-streaked from the fog, deep anxiety in every line of them, could give them no news at all.

'We've had nothing in here,' he said. 'No reports of any accidents. I reckon nobody's ventured out in this fog, and I don't think you should have either!'

'But my husband didn't come home,' Mrs Bates said. 'Would you expect me to do nothing?'

'Husbands don't always come home when they're expected,' the policeman said. It was nothing new to have wives in here, seaching for errant husbands, though this didn't seem that sort of set-up. In spite of her bedraggled appearance, this woman didn't look that sort. 'But I dare say he's found a bed with friends, someone he went home from chapel with; on account of the weather,' he added.

441

'Not my husband,' Mrs Bates said firmly. 'My husband always comes home!'

'Well, I'm afraid there's not much else we can do until morning,' the policeman said. 'Happen the fog will have lifted a bit then. I suggest you two ladies return home. And mind you go carefully at that!'

'He's right, Ma!' Madeleine admitted. 'There's nothing else we can do.'

By the time they reached home, still searching, still calling out Joseph Bates's name all the way, it was almost three in the morning and the fog as thick and damp as ever.

'You look perished!' Mrs Turner said. 'I've got the kettle on. What you need is a good hot drink, and off with those wet clothes. And Penelope hasn't stirred, bless her. I went up and looked and she's lying there peaceful as can be!'

'I'm very grateful to you,' Martha Bates said. 'I don't know what we'd have done without you.'

She felt so weary now, so hopeless! Where could he be? Something terrible *must* have happened.

'If only the fog would lift!' she said.

'Happen it will when the daylight comes,' Mrs Turner said. 'In the meantime I reckon you two should get a bit of sleep, so I'll be off and let you get to bed.'

'I'll sleep with you, Ma,' Madeleine offered when Mrs Turner had left. 'We'll be company for each other.'

She busied herself making cocoa, and as they sat to drink it she looked around the room. She had not expected to see the inside of this house ever again. Still less would she have dreamt of the reason why she now sat here in the middle of the night.

'First thing in the morning,' she said, 'we'll go and see the Minister. He'll at least be able to tell us what time Father left the chapel.'

They slept only fitfully, much of the time each of them aware that the other was lying awake. Neither of them could summon the courage to put their deepest thoughts

442

into words, lest even the mention of them should have the power to make them come true.

They were up again before daylight. Madeleine looked out of the window.

'I do believe the fog's lifting! It's swirling about and there's a bit of a wind, which is a good sign,' she said. 'Yes, I can just about see across the street.'

'Then we must get to the Minister's house as quickly as possible,' her mother said. 'Can we ask Mrs Turner to come in again and look to Penelope?'

'I'm sure we can,' Madeleine said. 'I'll pop round and fetch her.'

When Mrs Turner came they were ready to leave. Why am I not taking the water-bottle, the shawl, the bandages? Martha Bates asked herself. Why am I assuming they'll no longer be needed?

The Minister was a long time in answering the door, and when he did so he was wearing a dressing-gown over his night-shift.

'We're sorry to be here so early,' Mrs Bates apologized. 'It's a matter of urgency.'

He sat them in his study and listened to what they had to say, then shook his head.

'I'm sorry to have to tell you, Mrs Bates, that your husband didn't attend the chapel meeting last evening. A number of members failed to arrive, presumably because of the inclement weather. I knew, of course, that no weather would have kept your husband from his duties, but I assumed that he was unwell, or that some urgent family matter had prevented him.'

'He left the house as usual,' Mrs Bates said dully.

Where could he be? He had now been missing twelve hours – on a fifteen-minute journey. She refused to entertain the thoughts which were now crowding her mind.

'We'd better go to the police station again,' Madeleine said. 'Come along, Ma!'

'Let me offer you some refreshment before you leave,' the Minister said. 'A cup of tea?'

443

'No thank you, sir,' Madeleine said. 'I think we must go.'

'Then I shall visit you after this morning's service,' he promised. 'And I hope you will have better news for me.'

There was no news at the police station.

'Nothing's been reported,' the policeman said. 'Since the fog's lifting, we've started a search. Perhaps something will come of that.'

He had very little hope. There wasn't all that much ground to cover.

'As it is,' he continued, 'I'm afraid there's a question which has got to be put. What I mean is . . .' He floundered, searching for the words to put to this poor woman. 'What I mean is, has your husband been depressed lately? Worried about something? Work perhaps – or upset about family matters?'

He noticed at once the deep flush which swept over the younger woman's face.

'If you're trying to say, would my husband be likely to take his own life, then the answer is very definitely no!' Mrs Bates's voice was strong and firm. 'That's the last thing my husband would ever do. Nothing upset him to that extent. He wasn't that kind of man.'

Despair, remorse, she thought, were not in Joseph's character. He was always conscious of being in the right, never troubled by doubt, as lesser mortals were.

'No,' she said emphatically. 'He'd never do that!'

'I see. Well as soon we have any news, we'll let you know at once,' the policeman said.

When the two women had left he turned to his colleague.

'There *was* an upset! Did you see the girl's face? But if what the wife says is true, then all I can think is that he walked into the canal in the fog. What other explanation is there, I ask you?'

The other man nodded.

'I reckon you're right. In which case we'd better start searching the canal before the fog comes down again.'

Within minutes of Madeleine and her mother returning home – Mrs Turner had managed to spread the news along Coomber Terrace – neighbours organized themselves into small search parties and set off to explore every inch of the neighbourhood.

'But you and Madeleine should stay here with Penelope,' Mrs Turner advised. 'You'll want to be here when news comes.' It could only be bad news now, she thought.

It was while they sat, Penelope still sleeping in spite of all the disturbance, that Madeleine decided to tell her mother about Léon. It was a strange moment to choose, she knew that, but she felt a compulsion. And though it wasn't the reason, if she'd wanted to create a diversion, to break the heavy silence which lay between them, then she couldn't have done better.

'Oh, no Madeleine, I can't believe it!' Mrs Bates cried. 'I just can't believe it! First the Catholic church – and now this! What has come over you, Madeleine?'

'I thought you might have been pleased for me,' Madeleine said quietly. 'I've fallen in love. I never thought I would, but I have.'

It had not seemed possible, after George Carter, that she could ever love any man, still less that any man could love her as she knew Léon did. She had resigned herself to spending her life without a partner. Now all that was changed. The past was a lifetime away.

'Yes, I love Léon with all my heart,' she said. 'And I know he loves me!'

'Oh! It's easy enough to fall in love . . .' her mother began impatiently.

'For me it wasn't,' Madeleine interrupted. 'For me it was hard.'

'What matters is whether you're suited,' Mrs Bates said. 'Can't you see that?'

Love, she thought – how long does it last? Joseph Bates had been in love with her, more than she with him, but it hardly lasted beyond Madeleine's birth.

When she'd turned out to be not the kind of wife he wanted, love had soon flown. Duty remained, but duty was dry and cold.

'And how can you possibly be suited?' she asked her daughter. 'You come from two different worlds! Oh he's a nice enough young man – but how can you know you're suited?'

'I assure you we are,' Madeleine said gently. 'We love each other very much. And we plan to marry at Easter.'

'Easter! But Madeleine, that's only a few months away! You can't do that!'

'I'm sorry, Ma – but it's what we intend. Oh, I didn't mean to blurt it all out like this, especially not now, but nor did I think it would upset you.' She had taken for granted that her father would oppose it, but she hadn't expected it from her mother.

'Oh Ma!' she pleaded, 'I don't want to quarrel with you, that's the last thing I want! But I do mean to marry Léon at Easter. I'm twenty-one, now. Nothing can stop me!'

The moment the words were out of her mouth the terrible thought came, she was jerked back to the reality of the moment, the reason why they were sitting here waiting. In the last few minutes she had thought of no one but herself, herself and Léon. But supposing . . . just supposing. . . . And in that case, who else would support her mother except she?

'It would have killed your father!' Mrs Bates said desperately – and then gasped with horror at the form of words she had used. 'Would have killed him,' she thought. As though he was already dead. In her heart, though she couldn't bear to think of the why's and the wherefore's, or what would happen to her or how she would live, she thought he was.

It was at about the time that the congregation would have been leaving chapel after the morning service – the main topic of conversation on all lips being the disappearance of Joseph Bates – that a policeman presented himself at the door of twenty-one Coomber Terrace with the news that the body of a man, believed to be that of Joseph Bates, had been taken from the canal.

'Just by the bridge,' he said. 'Not more than five minutes' away from here. We can't be sure it's your husband, Mrs Bates. That's why we'll have to ask you to identify him – unless there's some male member of the family could do it for you.'

It can't be true, she thought. It can't be! Yet wasn't it what, in her heart, she'd expected?

'My son is away in the army,' she said stonily. 'I will come with you.'

'But not by yourself,' Madeleine said. 'We'll go together.'

'Nasty job for two decent women to have to do,' the policeman said to his colleague later, when the identification had been made. 'A good thing we found him afore he'd been in the water too long, else it'd have been nastier still!'

In fact, during the ordeal Martha Bates had kept remarkably calm. The identification had simply confirmed what she had feared since the early hours of the morning. She was calm also because she was numb, and mercifully numb because she couldn't bring herself to consider what would happen to her now. It was something she would have to face – but not yet. She didn't think even now, looking at his dead face, that she would mourn Joseph, but without him there would be the practicalities of staying alive, of putting food in their stomachs, keeping a roof over their heads. But not now. What she would like at this moment was to go to bed and to sleep and sleep.

With Madeleine it was different. The sight of her father lying dead in this terrible place – her father who had been so handsome, so powerful – was more than she could bear. With difficulty, she held her feelings in check until they had left the mortuary and then, walking side by side with her mother down the road, she burst into loud tears, caring nothing for the passers-by who stared at her.

'It's my fault!' she cried. 'It's my fault! If he hadn't

447

been angry with me he wouldn't have gone, he wouldn't have stormed out of the house. If he hadn't had me on his mind he wouldn't have lost his way and walked into the canal! It's my fault and I shall never forgive myself!'

Mrs Bates took her daughter firmly by the arm and held her close.

'It is nothing of the kind, Madeleine! Don't speak so foolishly! Whether you'd been there or not, and whatever the weather, your father would have gone out to chapel exactly when he did. You know that as well as I do. A more sensible man might have stayed at home in such weather, or at least have taken a lamp, but your father behaved as he always behaved. What happened to him had nothing to do with you. It was the fog which killed him.'

The words made sense, Madeleine knew that – so why could she not take comfort from them? Was the anguish she felt, for some other reason than her father's death? Was it her own situation which so appalled her? She faced the fact that now it would be up to her to support her mother, and Penelope also until she was old enough to get a job. It was quite unlikely that a suitable job could be found for her mother. Jobs were scarce and she had no experience of anything.

But if I must support my mother, how can I marry Léon? she asked herself. And if I can't marry Léon, how can I bear to live? Her father, she thought bitterly, not content with punishing her in life, would now do so from beyond the grave.

Penelope cried loudly on hearing the news, but she would, Madeleine knew, get over it more quickly than any of them. Penelope had disliked her father, had wanted nothing more fervently than to leave home and escape from him.

'You should go to bed for an hour or two, Ma,' Madeleine said. 'Get some sleep.'

'Not yet,' her mother said wearily. 'There are things to see to. The undertaker and so on. Thank God your father always paid into the burial club.'

'I think Irvine might be given compassionate leave,' Madeleine said. 'We could telegraph.'

At that, Mrs Bates felt the first small lightening of her spirits. If she could see Irvine she would feel so much better. Irvine would see to everything.

'And Ma . . .' Madeleine took a deep breath. It had to be said. 'Don't worry about anything – about what you'll do, I mean. I'll always look after you. You know that. My job's quite good now. I can find some rooms to rent in Helsdon and you can live with me. You'll be all right!'

It was the moment she should have put her arms around her mother, drawn her close for comfort. She knew that, but she couldn't do it. She crossed the room, turned her back on everything and looked out of the window, clenching and unclenching her hands which she kept in front of her so that her mother shouldn't see. The words she had just spoken sounded in her ears like a death sentence. With all her heart she longed for Léon, longed to be in the comfort of his arms, away from this situation which was more than she could bear.

Mrs Bates shook her head.

'I don't want to do that, Madeleine. I don't want to be beholden to you. You've got your own life to live.'

But between Madeleine and her mother unspoken thoughts hung in the air. And in those thoughts Helsdon Workhouse loomed large. There was no other place for anyone – man, woman or child – who couldn't support themselves. Not many people who went in through those doors came out again. It was a life sentence, though for all but the strongest, not a long life, since the work was hard driving graft, and the food not enough to keep a cat alive. No, Madeleine thought, I can't let that happen to my mother, no matter what.

'Don't worry about it, Ma,' she said reassuringly. 'We'll be all right. But for the moment I must get back to Helsdon, let them know at the mill. I'm sure I'll be allowed a couple of days off and I'll be back sometime tomorrow.'

'Bless you!' Mrs Bates said. 'I don't know what I'd do without you, love!'

They were not the words Madeleine wanted to hear.

She returned to Helsdon later that day and went at once to Mount Royd, ostensibly to see Mrs Thomas, but wanting so desperately to see Léon.

'Well I'm real sorry to hear about your dad,' Mrs Thomas said. 'What a shock to you all, especially to your poor ma! Here, sit down love and I'll get you a bite to eat while you tell me how it happened.'

'We don't rightly know,' Madeleine said. She didn't want to go over it all, she couldn't bear it, but Mrs Thomas would expect to be told. Nor, until she had done that, could she reasonably ask to see Léon. The thought that they were under the same roof, that he didn't know it, that she couldn't rush into him, was torture. But Mrs Thomas knew nothing of what was between them, though it had been agreed that, as his housekeeper, she must be amongst the first to be told. But what was there, now, to tell? Madeleine asked herself miserably. In the last twenty-four hours her whole future had changed. For herself and Léon there *was* no future.

'If Monsieur Bonneau is at home, perhaps I could have a word with him,' she said when she could wait no longer. 'If he wouldn't mind, then it would save me going into the mill to see him in the morning and I could be back in Shipley all the sooner.'

'Nay love, I'm sure he'd not mind. He's in his study. I'll just pop and ask him.'

Five minutes later Madeleine knocked on his study door and he called out to her to enter.

'Close the door,' he said.

He was halfway across the room to her already, and in the next instant she was in his arms.

'Oh Madeleine!' he said. 'My dearest little Madeleine, I am so sorry! Mrs Thomas has told me. Oh *ma pauvre petite!*'

Her head was on his shoulder. He was stroking her hair,

and then he put a finger under her chin, tilted her tear-stained face to his and kissed her gently on the lips. She returned his kiss, parting her lips to meet his, filled with longing for him, for his love, for the safety of his arms. She wanted to leave the rest of the world and be only here, with him, nothing and no one ever to come between them.

Eventually he loosed her, and led her by the hand to the sofa, where they sat side by side.

'Was it very bad, my darling?' he asked.

'Oh Léon, it was terrible! I had to . . . we had to . . .' The memory of how she had stood in the mortuary, looking down at her father, swept over her and she broke into fresh tears.

'I'm sure you were very brave,' Léon said. 'And now it will be good for you to cry.'

'I shall have to go back to Shipley until after the funeral,' she said presently, drying her tears. 'I shall have to be off work.'

'Of course you will,' Léon agreed. 'I don't want to intrude on your mother's grief, but I would like to take you back myself.'

'Oh no!' Madeleine said quickly. 'No, that wouldn't do at all!'

'Then, at least I shall come to your father's funeral – after all he did work for me – and afterwards bring you back to Helsdon.'

'No, you mustn't!' Madeleine protested. 'People would talk!'

'Does it matter?' he asked. 'Very soon now we will give them even more to talk about. It cannot be too soon for me, my dearest one!'

She drew away from him, freed herself from the circle of his arms.

'Léon,' she said, 'I can't marry you now. You must see that.'

'What are you talking about, my darling? What do you mean?' Then relief swept over his face. 'Oh I see! You

451

mean because you will be in mourning? Well, I shall not like waiting, but if we must, we must, though you must not expect me to be patient!'

'You don't understand, Léon,' Madeleine said. 'It has nothing to do with mourning – indeed I don't mourn my father, nor shall I ever, only the manner of his dying. And if I observe any outward mourning it will only be to please my mother.'

'Then why . . .? You are quite right when you say I don't understand, my love.'

'Surely you see that from now on I am responsible for my mother? And for Penelope. They have no one else. My brother is in the army, and who knows where that will take him? Emerald is in Thirsk, and earns far too little to help anyone else.'

Every word which rushed out of her stabbed her to the heart. She had never felt so unhappy in her life. Her eyes, looking into Léon's, were dark with despair. When he began to smile it hardly registered with her. She could think only of her own misery. Then he put his arms around her again, and when she tried to pull away, held her closer.

'What a little goose you are!' he said tenderly. 'There is no problem about your mother and Penelope. I will give them what ever support they need!'

'Oh but Léon, I couldn't let you!' she protested. 'It wouldn't be right. If we were already married it would be a different matter, but I can't come to marriage accompanied by two dependants. As it was, I was bringing nothing. I'm sure your family would expect your bride to bring a dowry, but I was bringing nothing. Do you think that hasn't been on my conscience?'

'You were bringing yourself,' he broke in. 'That is all I want.'

'And now you say I should bring my mother and sister! I couldn't do that. Even if I could, I know my mother wouldn't agree.'

'I think you are wrong,' Léon said. 'But you have had a shock, and you are not yourself, so I shall not continue to argue with you. There is nothing here which cannot be solved, but we will talk about it when you come back after the funeral.'

'It won't make any difference,' Madeleine said. Everything seemed dark; she could see no light ahead.

'I am grieved that you should consider giving me up with so little struggle,' Léon said quietly. 'I wouldn't give you up if the whole world stood against me!'

'Please, Léon, don't try to make me feel ashamed,' she begged. 'I can't bear any more.'

By mid-morning on Monday Madeleine was back at Coomber Terrace. When she went into the house a man she had not seen before was seated at the table, cap in hand, talking to her mother.

'This is Mr Gibson,' Martha Bates said. 'He's come from Salt's mill. One of the neighbours let them know about your father first thing this morning. Mr Gibson has been exceedingly kind.'

'You must thank Mr Titus Salt, not me,' Gibson said. 'I'm only his messenger. Yes, Mr Salt is the most considerate of men when anyone's in trouble.'

Mrs Bates pointed to a basket on the floor.

'He brought me these groceries,' she said. 'But what's more, Mr Salt has sent me five pounds!'

Her voice shook; she felt overwhelmed by gratitude. Never in her life before had her purse contained as much as five pounds.

'It'll tide you over for a bit,' Mr Gibson said. 'That was Mr Salt's idea.'

'It'll pay the rent and buy the food for six weeks, if I'm careful,' Mrs Bates said. 'I can't thank him enough, and please be sure to say so – though I'll write to him myself after the funeral.'

'I'll convey your thanks,' Mr Gibson promised. 'And that won't be all, mind you. They'll be making a bit of a collection in the weaving. It might not be much of course, but every little helps.'

'It does indeed,' Mrs Bates agreed. 'I'm more than grateful. And if any of Joseph's workmates have time to be at the funeral – it'll be at dinner-time on Wednesday – they'll be more than welcome.'

'How are you, Ma?' Madeleine asked when Mr Gibson had left.

'Not so bad, love. Everyone's been very kind – the neighbours, and people from the chapel. I shall get through, don't you fret!'

But for how long, Madeleine asked herself? Six weeks would come and go quickly – and what then? Perhaps after the funeral she would tell her mother what Léon had said. Now was not the time.

Later in the afternoon Irvine came. Watching mother and son embrace, Madeleine thought – though without rancour – he means ten times more to her than I do! If only he wasn't in the army, stationed so far away!

'They're bringing your father back later today,' Mrs Bates told Irvine. 'I was dreading that, but now that I've got all my family here, I dare say I can face things.'

'All except Emerald,' Penelope reminded her. 'She's not here.'

'I dare say she will be,' Mrs Bates said. 'I'm sure Mrs Chester will spare her to come home for her father's funeral.'

It was about the only thing she would come home for. These days Emerald was totally wrapped up in the Chester family, and blissfully happy to be so. She belongs to them far more than she ever belonged to me, Mrs Bates thought.

Long after her mother and sister had gone to bed that night, Madeleine sat in the living-room talking to Irvine. She was reluctant to go to bed. Her mother and Penelope were squeezed into the latter's bed, while Madeleine would have to sleep on the narrow strip of floor beside them. Her father lay in his coffin in the main bedroom,

454

where tomorrow a stream of chapel folks and neighbours would come to pay their last respects.

'There'll be some among them who've hardly known him,' Madeleine said to her brother. 'But they'll still come!'

'And not a few who disliked him heartily,' Irvine said. 'Hypocrites, I call 'em!'

'If that Walter Butler is amongst them I'll be fit to scratch his eyes out,' Madeleine snapped. 'And I reckon he'll come all right.' He would also spread the news about her – as much as he knew. Thank goodness she had persuaded Léon to stay away.

'I'll be glad to get back to Brighton,' Irvine confessed. 'Father was the one who drove me away in the first place. I'd never have left but for him. But now I don't like it up here any more. It's a different life in the south. And I've got a bit of news for you, our Madeleine – only I don't want to tell Ma just yet.'

'News? What news?'

'I'm getting married! A Brighton lass. We hope to get married quarters.'

Madeleine's spirits plummeted. So much for the faint hope, the dream she had had, that by some miracle Irvine might share the burden of caring for their mother. It had never been more than the faintest hope, but while she'd had it there had been something, however frail, to cling to. With her brother's words that hope died.

'I wish you every happiness,' she said. Her lips were almost too stiff to frame the words.

TWENTY-FOUR

In contrast to the night of his death, the weather on the day of Joseph Bates's funeral was clear and dry. It was cold, though, with a touch of frost. Madeleine, standing in the graveyard around the small hilltop chapel, shivered, and drew her cloak closer around her.

The funeral procession from the house to the chapel had been a small one – family and one or two neighbours only; Irvine supporting his mother and Madeleine walking behind with her sisters, every step of the way reminding her of the night she had searched this same route for her father.

A group of people had been waiting to greet the cortège at the chapel. Among them she at once saw Walter Butler.

'Do you see who I see?' she whispered to her mother. 'How can he have the effrontery?'

In Madeleine's mind, though she knew that the fog was the real culprit, it was Walter Butler's letter which had sparked off the sequence of events leading to her father's death. Certainly it had been the reason why her own last encounter with her father had been such a bitter one. And now, the burial being over, the cheap coffin consigned to the ground, the prayers ended, the revolting man was edging closer to herself and her mother, obviously intent on speaking to them.

'A sad day, Widow Bates,' he said unctuously, wringing

his black-gloved hands. 'Who would have thought of our dear Brother being taken so suddenly?'

'Who indeed?' Martha Bates murmured. She had no time for Walter Butler and his false sympathy. Everyone knew how much he had disliked Joseph, though presumably no one outside the family knew about the disgusting letter.

'Of course, he had a troubled mind,' Walter Butler continued. 'Who knows what a troubled mind can do to a man?'

'Yes indeed,' Martha Bates said smoothly. 'Conscience pricks us all at times, Mr Butler – those who have a conscience about their deeds, that is.'

'I don't quite understand, Widow Bates,' Walter Butler said.

'Don't you?' Martha said. 'Don't you really? But I'm sure it will comfort you to know that my husband was his usual self when he left the house that night.'

And only his family knew what his usual self was, she thought.

Walter Butler, not the least bit discomfited, turned his attention to Madeleine.

'Well,' he said confidentially, 'there are some things I suppose it's a mercy your poor father didn't live to see!'

'Ah, Mr Butler! You mean my conversion to the Catholic church?' The clearness of Madeleine's voice, as if she didn't care who heard her, took him by surprise. 'Don't feel obliged to whisper it! Anyone who means anything to me already knows, so you can feel quite at liberty to tell the rest!'

It was true. She had told Irvine and Emerald last night. Emerald had been totally disapproving. 'I don't know *what* Mrs Chester will think,' she'd said. Irvine had been indifferent.

'Well, it takes all sorts!' he said. 'But I'd have thought you'd have had enough of religion from Our Dad. I know I have!'

'Since you are so very interested,' Madeleine said now

457

to Walter Butler, 'I dare say I could give you an invitation to the service, when it takes place. I *think* you'd be allowed in!'

She could have laughed out loud at the indignant expression on his face. She knew full well that he would rather die than enter Saint Mary's.

'Well, Mr Butler,' Martha Bates broke in. 'I'll bid you farewell. I won't ask you to come back to the house because I'm sure you'll want to get back to Helsdon.'

It was the ultimate insult, and she knew it, to bar him from the house after the funeral. Deliberately adding to it, when he held out his hand she ignored it and turned away.

The little house had been packed to the door, her own family relegated to sitting on the stairs, for the funeral tea which custom had obliged her to provide. It had used up entirely what was left of the burial-club money after the undertaker had been paid, and had eaten a little into Mr Salt's donation. But what else could she do? Not to have provided a decent funeral tea would have been a disgrace.

When it was over, when everyone had eaten their fill, praised the standard, and taken themselves off home, it was almost time for Irvine to catch his train. But first he had something to say to his mother.

'I've got a bit of news for you, Ma!'

'News? What news? Is it good?'

Oh, if only he was about to tell her that he was coming back to the West Riding! What joy that would be! Nothing could delight her more.

'*I* think it is, Ma. I hope you will. I've met the girl I'm going to marry!'

Martha Bates drew a sharp breath. For a moment she couldn't answer. She was confused about what she felt. Dismay, yes – and at the same time, pleasure. She wanted her son to marry, of course she did. She wanted grandchildren, whom she could love and spoil. But not yet. And not to hear of it today, of all days. He shouldn't have told her today.

'You'll like her,' Irvine said. 'Her name's Bessie!'

'I see. It's . . . it's a nice name!'

And will Bessie like me, she wondered? Or will she part me from my son? But that was a stupid thought; she mustn't condemn the girl before she'd even set eyes on her.

'So when shall I meet her?' she asked.

'When you come to the wedding, Ma. In the early summer, we reckon. We'll get married in Brighton, of course, and I dare say Bessie's family will be only too pleased to put you up.'

'I see. So you'll live in Brighton?' No one knew the effort it took to keep her voice level.

'That's right. As long as I'm stationed there. You will come to the wedding, Ma?'

'I'll have to see, won't I?'

Brighton felt a thousand miles away. She had never been out of the West Riding; since she'd married had never even left Helsdon except when circumstances moved them to Shipley, and that still felt a foreign country to her. Why couldn't he have chosen a Yorkshire girl?

'Of course you'll go, Ma!' Madeleine said. 'If Irvine can find somewhere for us to stay, and we can save for the fare, I dare say we'll all go!'

Madeleine watched the conflicting emotions in her mother's face. What an idiot Irvine was to blurt it out like this, and today of all days! Then she saw her mother square her shoulders and lift her head in the proud gesture which was so characteristic of her.

'You're right!' Martha Bates said firmly. 'I wouldn't miss my son's wedding, would I?' And she would love her daughter-in-law, she decided. They'd get on well, why not? And perhaps one day, if God was good, Irvine's regiment would be moved to Yorkshire and she would see her grandchildren grow up.

Madeleine turned to her brother.

'Well if you're ready, I'll walk with you to the station.'

'I'll come too,' Mrs Bates said. She had not intended to

459

do so, it seemed right to stay indoors for the rest of this day of the funeral, but now she wanted to see Irvine on to his train.

'No need to trouble, Ma,' Irvine said.

He would far rather she didn't come. She seemed to have taken the news about Bessie all right, but she wasn't *quite* herself.

'It's no trouble,' his mother said. 'I'd like to come.'

But when the moment came to say 'goodbye' – she knew better than to hug him in full view of everyone and contented herself with a cool kiss on his cheek – and when the train drew out of the station and they waved until he was out of sight, she wished she had, after all, remained at home.

'I must return in an hour or two,' Madeleine said as the two of them walked back to Coomber Terrace. 'And before I go I have something to put to you.'

She had decided, after thinking about it most of the time since he had made it on Sunday, to tell her mother of Léon's offer of support. She doubted that it would be acceptable, and it was not ideal, but it now seemed to her that it was the only chance she had of making a life with Léon.

'What ever is it?' Mrs Bates asked anxiously. She had caught the nervousness in her daughter's tone. I have reached the end of what I can bear in one day, she thought.

'It's about Léon,' Madeleine said. 'He has offered to look after you – and Penelope – as long as you need; to support you financially and in every way.'

They had been walking arm in arm. Now Mrs Bates pulled away from Madeleine and stood stock still in the middle of the pavement.

'Madeleine! I couldn't! I couldn't possibly! Why, Monsieur Bonneau is a stranger to me! I couldn't be beholden. I hope you told him so at once!'

'Léon is the man I love,' Madeleine said quietly. 'We want to be married – but how can you expect me to marry unless I know you are provided for?'

460

Mrs Bates flushed to the roots of her hair. Why must everything come down on her at once? As if the funeral itself wasn't bad enough; first Irvine and now Madeleine. And Walter Butler called her 'Widow Bates', she thought inconsequentially. Why was everyone reminding her so cruelly of her position?

'I shall not stop you marrying,' she said hotly. 'Go ahead and do it! Don't think twice about me; I shall be all right!'

'Oh Ma, please don't be so angry!' Madeleine begged. 'You know how much I care about you. You know I wouldn't leave you unprovided for. But I dare say, like Irvine, I've spoken at the wrong time.'

'You have indeed,' Mrs Bates said. 'It could have waited.'

'But these things have to be said, Ma. We have to plan. If you won't accept Léon's offer – and believe me, I do understand, though it was made with the best of intentions on his part – then I must start looking for somewhere for you and me and Penelope to live in Helsdon. There's no time to waste. You do see that, surely? Please don't be unfriendly, Ma. I didn't mean to hurt you!'

She put out a hand and touched her mother's arm.

'I'm sorry,' Mrs Bates was contrite. 'I shouldn't have flown off the handle. You're a good daughter to me, the best a mother could have. And I don't want to stop your marriage to Monsieur Bonneau if you're sure it's what you really want. . . .'

'Oh it is, Ma! It is!'

'But I don't see how I can accept his offer. It wouldn't be right. What would people say?'

Madeleine shook her head. It was turning out exactly as she had feared. 'Does it matter what people say?' she asked sadly.

She put her arm through her mother's and they began to walk again, at first in silence, each deep inside her own unhappy thoughts. Mrs Bates was the first to speak.

'With the money Mr Salt gave me, and the collection

from the weavers, I've enough to last a few weeks. So during that time, you need do nothing, love. What *I'll* do is look for a job – any sort of job as long as it brings in the money. There must be something, somewhere, I can do!'

'But supposing . . .' Madeleine began.

'Listen, Madeleine,' her mother said. 'Try to understand. For more than twenty years now I've been dependent on a man. Many's the time, and you know it, I'd have left your father, but I was imprisoned by my dependence. Where there's love, it's different; you don't talk of independence then. But in my case – well, speak no ill of the dead, I suppose. Only now, if I can, I want to stand on my own two feet: not yours, not Monsieur Bonneau's. Do you understand?'

'Yes I do.'

'Then let's not talk about it any more for the present,' Mrs Bates said. 'Let's see what happens.'

'If that's what you want,' Madeleine acquiesced. Talk, they might not, but would the subject ever be out of her mind or her mother's in the coming weeks?

'I have two favours to ask you,' Madeleine said to her mother when it was time for her to leave for Helsdon.

'And what might they be?' her mother asked apprehensively.

'In the first place, will you let me bring Léon to see you, Ma? He so much wants to, and I don't believe you can judge him until you know him. And whether I'm to marry him or not, I'd like you at least to meet him.'

Mrs Bates stayed silent for so long that Madeleine thought she was never going to utter again, but at last she spoke, though reluctantly:

'Very well. But leave it for a week or two, love. And what's the next favour?'

'When I'm received into the church – *if* I am, because there's no guarantee yet – will you be present? It would mean so much to me.'

'I shan't understand it,' Mrs Bates demurred. 'Even if

I approved – which I'm by no means sure that I do – I wouldn't understand anything.'

'There'll be very few people there. It would mean a lot to me to have you there,' Madeleine pleaded. 'Please, Ma!'

Impulsively, Martha Bates leaned forward and kissed her daughter.

'Of course I will, love!' Religion had brought enough trouble to this house. It wasn't going to bring any more, not if she could help it.

On the next morning, when Léon came into Madeleine's small workroom, ostensibly to discuss patterns, she told him what her mother had said.

'She's adamant that she won't take help from you – as I knew she would be. She's also determined on finding a job. I have very little hope that she'll manage that, but if she doesn't . . .'

She left the sentence unfinished. It was quite clear to Léon what she meant; that it was the end of their engagement.

'Well I refuse to look on the black side,' he said. 'At least she has agreed to let me visit. Perhaps when we get to know each other it will be different?'

'Perhaps,' Madeleine said – though she didn't believe it.

Yet who, faced with Léon – so strong, so handsome – so clever yet so kind – would not succeed in liking him? Only someone like her father could fail to do that. But it would need more than liking to change her mother's mind on the subject of Léon's support.

'I understand her feelings,' Léon said. 'They do her credit. But I will not let them keep you and me apart.'

'We shall have to wait and see, then,' Madeleine said.

When the money ran out, if there was no job in the offing, then her mother would have to make a choice. Surely her independence wouldn't allow her to opt for Helsdon Workhouse? That was unthinkable. Her mother in the Workhouse? I couldn't live with that, Madeleine thought.

'But for now I have to get on with my work,' she said to Léon. 'There's a lot to do.'

She must try her hardest to suppress the thoughts which had milled around in her mind over the last few days. She must concentrate on the new designs.

'How do you plan to approach it?' Léon asked. Like her, he was all business now, cool and impersonal.

'Well, in the first place,' Madeleine said, 'the designs have to be original, different. They have to make a quick appeal to the woman who's going to wear them. Also – and this is very important – they have to be as trouble-free as possible in the weaving. I can't put these qualities in any order; they're equally important.'

'The designs also have to appeal to Henry Garston,' Léon reminded her. 'He will be our first and biggest customer. It will be no good if *he* does not like them.'

'But some of that's in the selling,' Madeleine said swiftly. 'You might have to use a little persuasion to get him to like them.'

Léon pulled a face.

'I don't see Henry Garston being persuaded into anything he does not like.'

'Oh I don't agree,' Madeleine contradicted. 'Especially when you're confident that he'll like it in the end.'

She took samples of yarn from the shelves, choosing first the colours which seemed to have a natural affinity with each other, then adding a few which at first sight seemed to scream at the rest. She piled these on the table, arranging them in careless heaps, then rearranging; all the time scrutinizing them in the clear light from the north-facing window.

'I wish we could get better dyes,' she said. 'There are colours in my head, and colours in nature, which I've never seen in yarns. But at least it won't be long before we get Perkins's new "mauveine". I look forward to that. A good purple shade is what's needed with some of these other colours.'

'And it will also be better when we get our own spinning,' Léon said. 'We'll be able to make different mixes. Best of all, we'll be able to experiment more –

which isn't possible on someone else's frames and in their time.'

'How long do you think, now?' Madeleine asked.

'I don't know. I expect to hear from Mr Garston any day – but I dare say he's not a man you can hurry. He will choose his own time. Now, I will leave you to get on with your work. Remember, you have a free hand with this set of patterns. I shall not interfere and we shall see what you come up with. But if you do want any help, just ask.'

'Thank you, I will.'

She badly wanted to do it alone. It was her chance to prove herself and she relished it. But she must get it right. She must justify not only Léon's faith in her, but her own faith in her ability to do the job. A let-down was unthinkable.

When Léon left the room Madeleine began picking up the samples again, then dropping them haphazardly against each other. She surveyed them for a long time, sometimes changing their position, sometimes adding one, or taking one away. Then she began to arrange them more formally, first in swathes of colour and then narrowing the colours down into single strands of yarn. By the time she turned to her drawing-board all thoughts other than those of the job in hand had left her. Her mother, her father, even Léon, receded into the distance and she was left alone with her design.

It was the sound of a carriage being driven into the mill-yard which made her look up – and see Henry Garston arriving. Through the window she watched him jump down from the carriage, not waiting for his coach-man to assist him, and stride into the mill. The man had an air of urgency and excitement about him, as if there were things to be done and he wanted to get on with them. She hoped he had called to talk about the spinning.

'Well!' Henry Garston said, striding into Léon's office after no more than a peremptory tap on the door.

Léon jumped to his feet.

'Good morning, Mr Garston! This is indeed a pleasant surprise!'

'Ah! Thought I'd forgotten, did you? Not a bit of it! Not a bit of it!'

'Of course not, Mr Garston. In the meantime I have been making some enquiries – sources of supply and so on.'

'So have I, lad, only mine have been financial ones. You'll be pleased to hear I've had good reports so there's nothing to stop you going right ahead. As I see it you'll have to rent the space. . . .'

'No problem there,' Léon interrupted. 'Mrs Parkinson and the bank will be only too pleased.'

'And what about the machinery?'

'Some of the frames were sold, but not all. There'll be enough to make a start. I reckon we should use what there is, then when we get going see if we need anything different, and look around to see if there's anything new on the market.'

'Good thinking!' Henry Garston said approvingly. 'Exactly what I'd have suggested meself. And the operatives?'

'That is the easiest of all,' Léon said. 'There are spinners still out of work from being laid off when Parkinson's closed down. I shall be a very popular man in Helsdon when I can set some of them on again.'

'Right! Then let's get down to brass tacks!'

'Brass tacks?'

Henry Garston looked at Léon in disbelief.

'You don't know what brass tacks means? Nay, you'll have to learn the language if you want to get on here! It means . . .,' he hesitated. 'Well, it means . . . I suppose it means the important facts. Brass tacks!'

'I see!' Will I ever learn this strange language, Léon thought. 'Then let us do the brass tacks, Mr Garston.'

'Not *do* them, lad. Get down to 'em!'

He took a piece of paper from his pocket and pushed it across the desk to Léon.

'These are my terms, then. If you agree, and you'll be a

fool if you don't, it's up to you to get going. I'll see that the money goes into your bank tomorrow. You'll see I'm guaranteeing wages and the rent and anything else you need to start up. In moderation of course! Naturally I shall want the money back, and with interest, but I'm not in a tearing hurry. You can pay just the interest as long as it suits you. I shall also want a share in the mill profits as a whole, but since I believe you're going to be very profitable in the future, I'll settle for a modest percentage. I'm not a greedy man.'

'I do not know how to thank you!' Léon said.

'By getting on with it, young man! The sooner we make a start, the sooner you'll be into profit. There's no profit in idle space and idle machinery!'

'Oh I will, I will!' Léon promised. 'I shall make a start this very day.'

'Good! And now tell me how the new designs are coming on.'

'Very well, I think. Miss Bates is working on them,' Léon said.

'Miss Bates? So you've seen sense and given her a decent job? I'm glad to hear it. And think on you look after her or I'll likely take her away from you!'

Oh no you will not, Léon thought. You will never take her. Madeleine is one thing your money cannot buy!

'Well, perhaps we should go and see her, see the designs,' Henry Garston suggested.

'Certainly, sir!' Léon jumped to his feet.

When they entered Madeleine's workroom she was intent on her drawing-board. She raised her head, then at once made a move to stand up.

'No! Carry on,' Henry Garston said. 'I'm interested in what you've got there. It looks very different.'

'It is,' Madeleine said. 'I thought you might like something no one else had. But it's also going to be beautiful.' She was amazed at her own confidence when it came to the designing.

'And supposing I don't like the designs when you've

done them?' Garston asked, studying the drawings closely. 'What then? You must bear in mind I'm the customer.'

'Certainly,' Madeleine agreed. 'But if you didn't like them at first sight, first of all I'd explain why I chose them, why I think they work. Then I'd ask you not to make an instant decision but to keep them for a few days, see if you grow to like them.'

Henry Garston nodded appreciatively.

'Well said, Miss Bates! Well said! Any road, keep up the good work. And as I've just told Monsieur Bonneau, if he doesn't treat you right, if you're looking for another job, think on you come to me!'

'Thank you, sir. You're very kind,' Madeleine said.

I would never want to leave Bonneau's, she thought when the two men had left. Never. And yet . . . and yet. If her mother didn't get a job, if she refused Léon's offer of support, if I have to give up the idea of marriage – wouldn't it be best if I left Helsdon, she thought? How could I bear to see Léon every day, longing for him, yet apart from him.

Léon, having said farewell to Henry Garston, sat at his desk thinking the same melancholy thoughts. Perhaps it would be for the best if she went to Leeds. But no! He wouldn't have it. There must be a better solution, and he would find it!

The very next day after her husband's funeral, with Irvine returned to Brighton and with Madeleine back in Helsdon, Mrs Bates decided to look for a job. She had no idea how to set about it, where to go; she had never had to do such a thing in her life. She knew there was no point in applying to the mills because she had neither training nor experience, and even those who had were being laid off.

'I think I'll start with the Minister,' she said to Penelope. 'It seems to me the only thing I know how to do is housework. He just might know someone who wants a charwoman.'

'If only I was older,' Penelope said unhappily. 'If only I

468

could go out to work and earn enough money to keep us both!'

'I know you're willing, love,' her mother said. 'And I dare say next year you'll be able to get a position, but you'd be a while before you could earn enough to keep a home going.'

Her youngest daughter would get either a job in service, or the lowest-paid job in the mill, and in spite of the fact that Madeleine had taken to it like a duck to water, Penelope hated the thought of going into the mill, so service it would have to be.

Mrs Bates ironed her skirt, put on a clean blouse and brushed her cloak. She had worn black for years now, so that was all right. Anyway, there wouldn't have been enough money to buy new mourning.

'Do I look tidy?' she asked anxiously.

'You look very nice,' Penelope assured her. 'If I had a job going I'd give it to you!'

But according to the Minister, when Martha Bates had at last summoned the courage to ring his bell and he'd appeared on the doorstep and asked her in, there were few, if any, jobs to be had in the whole of Shipley.

'When people get a job these days they tend to stick to it,' he said. 'Times are hard, as I don't need to tell you, Mrs Bates. However, there is a lady, a Mrs Appleton, who might be wanting a charwoman. I'll give you her address and you can call on her.'

He was truly worried about Mrs Bates, as indeed he worried about any widow of a poor man. The future was black for her, and there was little he could do.

'Well, thank you. I'll try Mrs Appleton at once,' Mrs Bates said.

'One moment,' he said as she rose to go.

He opened the drawer of his desk, took out a tin box and unlocked it.

'I have a small fund here from which I might be able to give you a little help. I'm afraid it would not be more than five shillings, but perhaps that will buy some food.'

'Thank you very much, sir!' Mrs Bates said. 'It's kind of you.'

She hated taking charity – which was what it was – and then she remembered all the years in which she and her children had gone short because Joseph gave too much to the chapel. With that thought she minded less.

Mrs Appleton lived in the expensive part of Shipley, in a hilly, tree-lined road with big houses. Martha Bates was amazed that she should be a chapel-goer. From this kind of place she would have expected a Church of England member. However, church, chapel, or heathen Chinese, it made no difference because the job was already taken. She didn't even set eyes on Mrs Appleton. A servant answered the back door and gave her the news at once.

Over the next few days Martha Bates did a round of most of the shops in Shipley. She felt sure she could hold down a job as a shop assistant. She was reasonably spoken; she could add up and give change. But if there were any vacancies – and mostly there were not – it was clear that what the shopkeeper wanted was a young, bright, pretty assistant who would bring in the customers.

'So it will have to be housework,' she said to Penny. 'A pity. I'd quite worked myself up to serving in a shop. Still, never mind. Something will turn up!'

Because she didn't want to worry Penelope she deliberately sounded more hopeful than she felt. It was for that same reason that she didn't tell her daughter what she proposed to do the next day.

She set off immediately after breakfast.

'I've got one or two more addresses,' she lied. 'So don't worry if I'm not back for dinner. I probably won't be. But I'll be back before dark.'

'Can't I go with you?' Penelope begged.

'No, love. It wouldn't help my chances,' she said.

What she determined was to go to every house in the better areas of Shipley, ring the bell at every tradesman's entrance, and simply ask if they had a job for her. Any sort of job. Nor could she be fussy about whether it was a permanent job, one for a few weeks, or even one she could do just today. She *must* find something! She also knew that on a charwoman's wages she would have to work all day and every day to keep the two of them in the simplest fashion – but she didn't mind that. She was strong, and more than willing.

She found no work, except that towards the end of the morning a housekeeper said she could sweep and swill the yard, since the handyman who usually did it was ill.

'Make sure you do a good job!' she said. 'No scamping!'

Martha Bates cleaned the yard as though it was her life's work, working the brush into every corner, then swilling it with bucket after bucket of water drawn from the outside tap. Her hands were red and swollen from the cold and the water seeped through the soles of her boots. Nevertheless, she told herself, as she presented herself at the door for payment, it was a job! She'd get paid.

'Here you are then!' the housekeeper said.

She thrust twopence into Mrs Bates's outstretched hand, and then followed it with a packet of sandwiches.

'Twopence!' Mrs Bates was dismayed.

'That's right,' the woman said. 'You've got the sand-wiches extra. It's your lucky day.'

Martha Bates could hardly believe it. It had taken her an hour-and-a-half to do the yard. Her back ached and she had a raging thirst from the clouds of dust she'd swept up.

'Do you think I could have a drink of water?' she asked.

'Wait there!'

The woman returned a minute later with a pint mug filled to the brim with water, which Mrs Bates drank greedily before handing back the mug.

'I won't charge you for the water,' the woman said graciously.

Leaning against a field gate at the top of the hill where the road gave way to a farm track, Martha ate half the sandwiches, and wrapped up the rest to take home. She was tired and would have liked to have sat down, but the ground was soggy from the November rains. When she'd eaten she tidied herself up again as best she could and set off to call on more houses.

It was strange, she thought, how seldom the person who answered the door actually believed that she was looking for work. Mostly they thought she was begging. Might that be what I'll come to in the end, she wondered fearfully? If so, she wouldn't be very good at it, for all she was given in the whole of the afternoon was a penny piece at each of two houses, some cast-off baby clothes – though she declared she hadn't a baby – and a slice of bread and lard. She'd never really believed the tales that women borrowed babies to go round begging, but now she thought it was probably true! Anyway, there was no work.

It was while she was passing the 'Fox Inn' on her way home that she saw the notice in the window, 'Barmaid wanted'. Could I possibly? she asked herself. Not only had she never been in a public house, she was a lifelong teetotaller. Nevertheless, here was a genuine vacancy. She went around to the back door of the 'Fox' and rang the bell. If Joseph could see me now, she thought fearfully, he would rise from the grave and strike me down!

When she stated her business she was shown into a dingy little room behind the bar where the landlord sat. He was fat and jolly, and looked as though he'd enjoyed several pints of what he sold. He was quite polite, and invited her to sit down, but when she made her application he shook his head.

'It's not the job for you, love!' he said. 'You see, you wouldn't know one drink from another, nor the prices of anything, let alone how to pull a pint.'

'But I could learn!' Mrs Bates said eagerly. 'I'm quite a quick learner!'

'Well I'm sure you are, love,' he said kindly. 'But it's not the job for you. They're a rough lot, the customers here. You're . . . well, not to put too fine a point on it, love, you're too refined!'

What he wanted, what he'd get, was a young piece, tough; a wench who'd give as good as she got and wouldn't take offence at a bit of larking about. And a lass who would also encourage the customers to buy more drinks.

'I'm sorry, love,' he said.

'I understand,' she said. 'It's a funny world, though. All afternoon I've been taken for a beggar, now you tell me I'm too refined!'

When Saturday came, Madeleine journeyed over from Helsdon to see her mother. Mrs Bates had hoped to greet her daughter with news of a job, but there had been nothing, nothing at all. Madeleine walked into the house, put her arms around her mother's shoulder and kissed her on the cheek.

'How's it going, Ma?' she asked.

'Well I haven't found a job yet,' Mrs Bates replied. 'But it's early days. Something might turn up next week.'

For a moment, just for a moment, she wanted to give in. All she wanted was for someone to look after her, tell her everything was going to be all right. But she wouldn't give in, no indeed she wouldn't. Somehow or other she had to keep her independence.

'Let's not talk about it. We promised we wouldn't,' she reminded Madeleine.

'Very well,' Madeleine agreed. 'Then may I ask Léon to come to tea next Sunday?'

'Oh Madeleine!' Mrs Bates was completely flustered. 'Oh Madeleine, I can't! It's too soon!'

'No, it's not too soon,' Madeleine said firmly. 'In fact if it bothers you that much you'd be best getting it over with – for I'll not let you off this one, Ma. I fully intend that you shall meet him. It's only fair to me.'

Mrs Bates sighed – and relented. 'You're right, love. Very well then.'

'Don't worry about the food,' Madeleine said. 'I'll come down on the Saturday and bring something. Only . . . if

473

you could bake some of your currant teacakes . . . nobody makes better teacakes than you.'

'I'll bake teacakes,' Mrs Bates promised. If only everything was as easy as baking teacakes!

TWENTY-FIVE

On the following Saturday Madeleine arrived at Coomber Terrace bearing a basketful of groceries – tea, sugar, butter, currants.

'And there's a dish of home-made potted beef from Mrs Barnet *and* a jar of her own lemon curd. She makes delicious lemon curd.'

Mrs Bates took the basket from her daughter and eagerly began to unpack it.

'It's very kind of her. People *have* been kind – neighbours, I mean, and one or two from the chapel and the mill.' She was particularly glad of the potted beef. Mr Salt's diminishing money couldn't be spent on meat; they hadn't tasted it since the funeral.

'Ooh, doesn't it all look lovely?' Penelope's eyes sparkled at the sight of the food on the table. 'Shall we have our tea right away, then?'

Mrs Bates shook her head.

'I'm sorry, love, but we can't break into this lot! This is for tomorrow, when Monsieur Bonneau comes to tea.'

She felt terrible, seeing the disappointment on her youngest daughter's face. Penelope was growing fast, shooting up by inches; she needed good food and plenty of it.

'Well, go on, then,' she said, relenting. 'Cut yourself a slice of bread and you can spread some lemon curd on it;

only don't be greedy with it. I'd like some left for tomorrow!'

'I'm not greedy!' Penelope protested. 'I'm just hungry.'

'Léon won't mind if there's no lemon curd,' Madeleine said. 'He's not coming for the food, Ma.'

'Happen not. All the same . . .'

Mrs Bates was determined that Monsieur Bonneau should have as good a spread as she could possibly manage. It was a matter of pride, and she still had a bit of that left, though her total failure to find a job was fast denting it.

'As long as you've made the teacakes!' Madeleine teased. 'You have made the teacakes, Ma?'

'No.'

'Ma! But you promised!'

'I'm making them tomorrow,' Mrs Bates said.

Madeleine's eyes widened.

'Tomorrow? But tomorrow's Sunday! You don't mean you're going to *bake* on a Sunday!'

It was unheard of. Nobody, but nobody, baked on a Sunday. And in this particular strict, chapel-going house nobody did anything on a Sunday. It was forbidden to sew a button on, or to sing anything other than a hymn or sacred song. Madeleine had learned, from the first time as a little girl she had struggled to cast on the stitches, that to pick up her knitting on a Sunday was a quick and certain way to the devil. And here was her mother, calmly talking about baking!

'Well no need to look at me as if I'm about to be struck by lightning!' Mrs Bates said defensively. 'I want those teacakes fresh out of the oven, so I'm going to bake them tomorrow. What's more, while the oven's hot I shall also make potato scones!'

Madeleine threw back her head and laughed. It was a long time since she'd felt like laughing, and now that she'd started it was difficult to stop. She grabbed hold of her mother, who started to laugh with her – and then Penelope, until the three of them were rolling around the kitchen in paroxysms of healing laughter.

'Oh Ma!' Madeleine gasped. 'If you could have seen

your face! You looked so defiant! As if you were going into battle!'

'If Heaven's going to strike me down for teacakes,' her mother said, 'it might as well include potato scones! And while I'm about it, let me also tell you I shan't be going to chapel in the morning. I shall have far too much to do. Everything's got to be spick and span.'

'I'll help you,' Penelope offered quickly.

'Not by staying away from chapel, you won't!' her mother countered. 'You'll attend as usual; and if Monsieur Bonneau leaves in time, I shall go in the evening.'

'And make peace with God for having baked on a Sunday!' Madeleine chaffed. 'Ma, you're priceless!'

'Don't run away with the idea that I'm giving up chapel just because I'm missing one Sunday morning,' Mrs Bates said. 'Nothing's further from my thoughts.' In fact, it was her belief that the chapel might come to mean more to her now that she wouldn't be forced into going.

On Saturday evening, when they had cleared away the tea things, all three of them drew up their chairs as close as they could get to the warmth of the fire. The weather had turned cold and a sharp draught came straight under door into the little room.

'The fire's burning frosty,' Mrs Bates observed. 'If the weather turns bad, might Monsieur Bonneau not come?' She almost wished for it. She didn't look forward to tomorrow, though she was determined to see it through, to do her very best, for Madeleine's sake.

'Not a hope, Ma!' Madeleine said. 'He'll come whatever the weather. But I just wish you'd stop worrying.'

'I want him to come,' Penelope said. 'I've never met a rich man before. Will he arrive in his carriage and pair?'

'Certainly not!' Madeleine said. 'He'll come by train, like I did.' She had particularly asked Léon to do so. The less fuss, the better for her mother – and the less for the neighbours to see. A carriage in Coomber Terrace would be a talking point for days.

'And he's not rich,' she declared.

It was true, for now. But one day he would be, she was certain of that, and was not sure that she liked the idea. She'd not been one to indulge in the poor girl's dream of marrying a rich man and being transported into another world, nor had she ever thought to meet a man like Léon. And if in the end I can't have him, she asked herself, shall I wish we'd never met?

The answer to that was a swift and decisive 'No'. If it were all to end tomorrow, what she had so far with Léon was worth any unhappiness the future might hold. It was hers to remember for ever.

Mrs Bates suddenly put down her work – between them they were doing the week's mending – and reached up to the mantelpiece to take down the pen and ink.

'Who are you going to write to?' Madeleine asked.

'No one,' Mrs Bates said. 'Come to the table, both of you.'

Puzzled, they did as she ordered. There was something in her voice which demanded obedience.

She waited until they were seated, then went to the sideboard, opened the top drawer and brought out the family Bible. Then she sat herself at the table, between her daughters, and opened the book in front of her, opened it at the fly leaf, where the names were listed.

Madeleine looked down and saw the thick black lines which obliterated her name, and felt sick. All the horror of the scene which had preceded her father's departure from the house, the leaving which had led to his death, swept through her, turning her insides to water. She jumped to her feet and would have left the table, run out of the house, even; but her mother caught at her hand and drew her back.

'No Madeleine! Wait. Sit down again.'

'I can't, Ma! I can't!'

'Yes you can!'

Trembling, Madeleine did as she was told. She hardly recognized her mother in this commanding mood.

Mrs Bates dipped the pen in the ink and began to write.

First of all, beneath Joseph Bates's name, she wrote the date of his death.

'No Ma!' Madeleine protested. 'I don't want to watch this!'

'Wait!' her mother said. 'I haven't finished yet.'

Then on a new line, below the obliterations which her husband had made, she wrote in Madeleine's name afresh, adding the date of her birth.

'This is to show you, Madeleine, that whatever you do, whether I approve of it or not, you are my daughter and a much-loved member of this family. Nothing can change that and you must never forget it.'

'Oh Ma!'

She spoke with difficulty. She was near to weeping; and when she looked at her mother, and then her sister, she saw that their eyes were bright with tears also.

Mrs Bates took a deep breath and was the first to recover herself.

'I wonder how long before I write in the date of Irvine's marriage?' she said, more brightly than she felt.

And will you ever be able to enter the date of my marriage to Léon? Madeleine asked herself. But there was one event in her life which she now knew was to be certain.

'Ma,' she said hesitantly. 'When I'm received into the Catholic church, will you write that in the Bible also?'

'Of course I will,' her mother promised.

On Sunday morning Mrs Bates roused her daughters early.

'Come along!' she chivvied. 'There's plenty to do!'

'But Ma, Léon won't be here until three o'clock this afternoon!' Madeleine protested.

'Nevertheless, there's plenty to do,' Mrs Bates repeated. 'So rise and shine, the pair of you!'

She hurried them through breakfast, then set them to work, sweeping, dusting, polishing.

'I don't believe this place wasn't cleaned within an inch of its life only yesterday morning,' Madeleine grumbled.

'It certainly was,' Penelope affirmed.

479

'No reason why it shouldn't be done again today,' Mrs Bates said. 'You know how quickly things get dirty in Shipley, from the smoke. I wouldn't want Monsieur Bonneau to think your mother was a slut!'

Madeleine screamed with laughter.

'You! A slut? Oh Ma!'

'She took all the curtains down and washed them yesterday, before you came,' Penelope said. 'Do you suppose we'll have to do *that* again this morning?'

'Less of your cheek, young lady!' Mrs Bates said sharply. 'And when you've finished polishing the sideboard you can go and get ready for chapel.'

'Must I?' Penelope pleaded. 'I'd rather polish six sideboards than go to chapel.'

'Yes you must,' her mother said. 'And you can say a prayer for me while you're there.'

'Shall I explain to God that you can't come because you're busy baking teacakes?' Penelope said pertly.

'If you were a bit younger you'd get a smacked bottom for that!' Mrs Bates retorted. She was on edge. She just wished the whole day was over and done with.

Does the fact that my mother's going to all this trouble mean that she's actually going to welcome Léon? Madeleine wondered. But no, she was sure it didn't. It was simply her mother's way of keeping her anxiety in check. In a way, Madeleine too wished that the day was over – and wondered for the hundredth time what the outcome would be.

'Ma,' she said, when Penelope had at last gone off to chapel, 'Ma, you will try to like Léon, won't you? For my sake!'

'Good heavens child, what do you take me for? Of course I'll try to like him. According to you he's a paragon of all the virtues, so why shouldn't I?'

But what difference will it make whether I like him or not, Mrs Bates thought. I'm still not going to accept his patronage; I can't be expected to. If there was to be a solution to this dilemma which fate had thrown at her, it would have to be something other than that.

480

At five minutes past three in the afternoon there was a knock on the door. When Madeleine, her heart thumping in her chest, went to answer it, Léon stood there. She wanted to leap into his arms, be enfolded in his embrace, and she knew by the look in his eye that it was what he wanted too. Oh, if only everyone else would melt away and they might be alone! They were so seldom alone and it was what she yearned for. As it was, she held out her hand, and in the French manner which he had not outgrown, despite his time in Helsdon, he raised it to his lips.

'Please come in!' Madeleine said.

Mrs Bates stood, as if to attention, in the middle of the room.

'This is my mother,' Madeleine said. 'Mother, this is Monsieur Léon Bonneau.'

Mrs Bates held out her hand, but instead of taking it in a handclasp he bent low and brushed it with his lips.

'I am delighted to meet you!' he said.

She felt herself flush scarlet to the roots of her hair, and was glad that he turned away to be introduced to Penelope. When he kissed Penelope's hand, Penelope thought she would faint with pleasure! Nothing so romantic had ever happened to her in the whole of her life. Oh, lucky, lucky Madeleine!

'Why don't we sit down?' Madeleine said.

'I'll make the tea,' Mrs Bates flustered.

'No Ma, stay where you are. *I* will make the tea,' Madeleine insisted.

In fact, the kettle was singing on the hob, almost ready to boil. There was nothing to be done aside from pouring the water into the pot. The table had been laid for the last hour; first with the fine white cloth with the deep crocheted edge, a seldom-used wedding present from Martha's parents, and then, placed on it, food enough for a feast. There was fresh white bread, lemon curd, potted beef, plain and currant teacakes, and a madeira cake which Madeleine had brought. The only space left on the table was for the potato scones, at this moment keeping hot in the oven.

'There is a most delicious smell in the room!' Léon said.

'Mother's been baking,' Penelope said. 'Of course she doesn't usually bake on a Sunday but in this case . . .'

'Penelope!' Mrs Bates was mortified! It was one thing to make an effort for company; it was quite another to let them know you'd done so.

'Well I'm pleased she has,' Léon said amiably. 'And if everything tastes as delicious as it smells, then I'm afraid I shall eat far too much!'

It was a measure of Penelope's instant devotion that, hungry as she was, she would willingly have sacrificed everything on the table to him; and it was she who, when the meal began, pressed everything on him, handing him one tempting plate after another.

The fact that he ate heartily, praising the light-as-air teacakes, wolfing down the potato scones until the butter ran down his chin and drinking three cups of tea, put Mrs Bates at her ease more than any words could ever have done.

'That is the best tea I have ever had!' he said, sitting back in his chair. 'You must forgive me for eating so heartily, Mrs Bates.'

'I'm pleased you did,' she said. 'It's one of the nice things in life when someone enjoys a meal you've prepared.'

In all her married life Joseph had never praised a meal she'd cooked. 'We eat to live,' he'd reminded her. 'We do not live to eat!' If Monsieur Bonneau were there just to take tea with them, it would be a pleasant, carefree occasion: but there was more to it than that, and they all knew it.

'Penelope, since everyone has finished, you may clear the table,' Mrs Bates said in the end.

'And I'll help you to wash up,'. Madeleine offered. She was determined that her mother should spend a few minutes alone with Léon.

'There's no need,' Mrs Bates said quickly. 'I can help

Penelope – or indeed it can all be left until later. We mustn't neglect Monsieur Bonneau!'

'No, Mother,' Madeleine said firmly. 'Penelope and I will do the dishes. I'm sure you and Léon can entertain each other for a few minutes!'

'Of course we can, Madeleine!' Léon agreed.

Every time he spoke to her daughter, Martha Bates heard the love and the care in the tones of his voice: every time they looked at each other, as they did now, she saw the devotion and the longing in the eyes of both of them. Because of her own position, their love was the last thing she wanted to observe. But it was there, patent, undeniable; the air was full of it. And looking at Léon Bonneau as he sat opposite to her now, she could understand why Madeleine felt as she did. He was, she thought, the most attractive man – in looks, in manner, in disposition – she had ever met. How could she possibly, ever, part them? And yet how could she bring herself to take his support?

'Mrs Bates,' Léon said quietly, 'I know that you and I have a lot to talk about, but I also know that this is a bad time in your life. For that reason, if you wish, we won't speak much today, but wait for another time. But this much I must say. I want you to know, above everything else, that I love Madeleine deeply, with my whole heart. It would be my life's work to bring her happiness. And because I love Madeleine so much, it would be easy, and a privilege, for my care and protection – indeed affection – to embrace you and Penelope also. Will you please, when you think about me, remember this?'

'I will,' Mrs Bates promised. 'I can see that you love my daughter and I know how much she cares for you. Seeing you together is . . .' Words failed her. 'But things are by no means straightforward. If I can find employment, then the problem will be solved – but so far I've found nothing. I'm grateful, therefore, that you're giving me a little more time.'

Madeleine and Penelope had been washing the dishes in the sink at the cellar-head, a few feet only from the living-room, just out of earshot of the words being said. When Madeleine realized that the conversation between her mother and Léon had petered out, she came back to join them. Anxiously, she looked from one to the other, but could read nothing in their faces.

'I must go,' Léon said. 'Are you to accompany me back to Helsdon, Madeleine?'

'No,' she replied. 'I shall catch a later train.' She was not yet ready to be seen travelling with him, but when that moment came, if ever it did, she would be the proudest woman in the West Riding.

She saw him off at the door, longing to embrace him but forced to make do with no more than a touch of his hand, though even that made her tremble. When she had closed the door on him she stood by the window, watching until he was out of sight.

'Well,' she said, turning eagerly to her mother, 'did you like him? Oh, please say you liked him!'

'Of course I did,' her mother answered. 'He's a very nice gentleman.'

'And do you believe now that we're suited?'

Mrs Bates hesitated, then said:

'Yes, love. I don't have any doubts about that.' Who could have? Seeing them together.

'Then Ma, will you reconsider his offer? Will you let him look after you and Penelope once we're married? Please, Ma!'

'I don't know! I can't say!' Mrs Bates felt frightened, imprisoned. 'Do you realize what you're asking?'

'I do,' Madeleine said. 'Do *you* know what you're asking if I have to give him up?'

'I do. I don't want you to give him up. Why should I want to be the cause of your unhappiness?'

'But if you won't accept his help, what else can I do?' Madeleine demanded. 'You *know* I can't leave you destitute. You *know* that!'

Mrs Bates clasped and unclasped her hands in agitation, pulling at the brooch at her neck.

'You must give me a little more time,' she pleaded. 'Monsieur Bonneau has offered to do so. I believe you can do no less.'

'Very well,' Madeleine said reluctantly. 'But please, Ma, remember my feelings as well as yours.'

'I promise!'

It was a downhearted Madeleine who travelled back to Helsdon an hour later. She knew she ought to go straight home to Mrs Barnet, who would be expecting her, but with all her heart she longed to see Léon. How could she bear to wait until the mill started tomorrow morning?

I'll go to see Mrs Thomas, she thought. Once I'm there I'll think of some excuse to see Léon.

It was freezingly cold and as dark as pitch as she walked from Helsdon station to Mount Royd. She was glad to step into the brightness of the kitchen.

'My word, love, you look perished,' Mrs Thomas said. 'Take your cloak off and come to the fire. And then tell me what brings you here this evening. I didn't expect to see you.'

'I thought of it in the train, coming back from Shipley,' Madeleine said. 'I suddenly thought I must come and see how you were.'

She felt ashamed, deceiving Mrs Thomas so, and when the latter said, 'Well I must say, that's very kind and thoughtful of you,' she felt worse than ever. But she *had* to see Léon, she just *had* to see him.

'So how are you, Mrs Thomas?' she asked.

'Jogging along, love. Jogging along. I can't say more than that. And how's your Ma?'

'Desperately looking for a job,' Madeleine said. 'There don't seem to be any. Why do you say you're only jogging along? It's not like you to be down.'

'It's not, is it? But to tell you the truth, I'm finding it a bit lonely here, especially with the dark nights on us. The fact of the matter is, I want to go back to Morecambe. I've stayed much longer than I intended when I first came. If

485

you remember, it was to be only until Monsieur Bonneau had found someone else. But it's my opinion he's stopped looking.'

'He knows when he's on to a good thing,' Madeleine said.

'That's all very well – and he's a nice gentleman, I won't hear a word against him – but my home's in Morecambe now. I certainly don't want to be here when Christmas comes, so he'll have to find somebody sharp, choose how! There must be somebody.'

It was at that point that Madeleine and Mrs Thomas, both struck at the same moment by the same thought, stared at each other – then spoke simultaneously.

'Your Ma!'

'My mother!'

'Why didn't I think of it before?' Mrs Thomas said. 'Though of course I didn't know your Ma was looking for a job, did I?'

'And I'd overlooked that you were only here temporarily,' Madeleine said. 'You seemed so settled.'

The truth was that, immersed in her own affairs, she'd hardly spared a thought for Mrs Thomas, except as someone who was fortunate enough to live in the same house as Léon.

'So do you reckon your Ma would like to take it on?' Mrs Thomas asked.

'I don't know,' Madeleine confessed. There were complications Mrs Thomas wasn't aware of. 'Do you think she could do it?'

'Of course she could!' Mrs Thomas sounded astonished. 'She's run a home all these years, brought up a family. The meals here might be a bit more fancy, but she'd soon get into that. As for the housework, there's a daily help for that. There's only one gentleman to see to, after all – and Monsieur Bonneau isn't difficult.'

'Yes, you're right. I'm sure she could do it,' Madeleine agreed. The question was, would she? The other question was, would Léon agree?

Mrs Thomas answered the last, unspoken question.

'Should I go and have a word with Monsieur Bonneau, do you think? Strike while the iron's hot? I shall put it to him fair and square that he's got to find someone soon.'

'I think you should,' Madeleine agreed. 'The sooner the better!'

While Mrs Thomas went to speak to her employer, Madeleine paced nervously up and down in the kitchen. Would it work? Would Léon be agreeable to having his mother-in-law actually working for him? Might he want some other housekeeper? And if Léon agreed, would her mother? Oh, but she must! She was determined she would do her utmost to persuade her.

Mrs Thomas was back within ten minutes.

'What did he say?' Madeleine asked quickly.

'He said he was very sorry I wanted to go. He liked having me here and I'd been more than satisfactory. He said I'd made him very comfortable . . .'

'I'm sure you have,' Madeleine interrupted. 'What did he say about the idea of my mother taking the job?'

'He seemed to think it would be all right. He wants to see you, have a word with you about it.'

'I'll go to him at once!' Madeleine said.

As Madeleine swept like a whirlwind out of the kitchen, Mrs Thomas looked after her in some surprise. She was certainly very keen to get her mother a job of work!

Madeleine tapped on the door of Léon's room and walked in, closing the door behind her. He came towards her and she ran into his outstretched arms, lifting her face for his kiss. He rained kisses on her, on her lips, her cheeks, her closed eyes; gentle, tender kisses, which grew more passionate until his mouth was hard on her lips. He kissed her on her neck and down the length of her throat to where the hollow between her breasts was visible. There his kisses became gentle again as he sought to explore the softness of her breasts. As his hands moved over her, sensations she had never known before ran through Madeleine's whole being. She pressed herself against him, exulting in the hardness of his body against her own.

'Oh Madeleine!' he murmured. 'We must be married! I want you so! I cannot live without you – you must know that!'

'Nor I without you,' she said.

At last, reluctantly, for she wanted never to leave his arms, she pulled away from him, put a distance between them.

'I must go,' she said. 'Mrs Thomas will wonder what's happening.' In fact, she had no idea how long she had been there. All sense of time had left her.

'Very well, my darling,' he said. 'Though I long for the day when you do not have to leave me ever again.'

'Not one bit more than I do,' Madeleine assured him. 'But for now, what about my mother? Mrs Thomas says you are agreeable to having her here as housekeeper. Is that true? Would it work?'

'In the first place,' Léon said, 'I am more than agreeable, I am eager, for anything which brings our marriage closer. Apart from that, I am more than happy to have your mother – and Penelope – living here for their own sakes. I liked your mother. I believe, in spite of the fact that I pose a threat to her, that she liked me.'

'Oh, she did!' Madeleine assured him.

'There is plenty of room here,' Léon said. 'Your mother could live quite separately, and in comfort. I intend in any case to see Mrs Parkinson about taking more rooms when we marry.'

'*If* we marry!' Madeleine said.

'No, my love. *When* we marry! I refuse to let you go!'

'Then, may I write at once and tell my mother that there is a job for her here if she wishes to take it?'

'No!' Léon said forcefully. 'You may not write! I am too impatient to wait for the post. I want a quick answer. You must go and see her tomorrow. However busy you are, you must take time off work. And if you won't go, then I shall!'

'It would be better coming from me,' Madeleine said. 'I'll go to Shipley, tomorrow.'

When Madeleine arrived at Coomber Terrace Mrs Bates was dressed for going out. She was alarmed at the sight of Madeleine, in the middle of a Monday morning.

'What's wrong?' she asked. 'What's happened?'

'Nothing's wrong, nothing at all!' Madeleine assured her. 'Quite the contrary, in my opinion. But where were you off to, Ma?'

'I was going to look for work,' Mrs Bates said.

She had no plan. It was simply a case of knocking on more doors; of perhaps being offered some small, menial job for which she'd be paid a few coppers, or, worse still, of being taken for a beggar and, according to the whim of the householder, either being given a crust of bread, or being ordered to take herself off before the police were called. She was sick to the heart at the thought of it, but once again she must make the effort.

'Then sit down and listen to me!' Madeleine ordered.

What was it all about? Mrs Bates wondered. Her daughter sounded full of confidence this morning, so different from the mood in which she'd returned to Helsdon yesterday. She was not to know that inside Madeleine's breast her heartbeat quickened with fear and apprehension until she felt likely to choke.

'You're very bossy today!' Mrs Bates said.

'I'm sorry, Ma. I don't mean to be. But I want you to listen very seriously to what I have to say. It's important to both of us.'

Quickly, the words tumbling out, she told her mother of Léon's new and different offer.

'This is a businesslike affair,' she pointed out. 'You will do a job, perhaps sometimes it will be an exacting job, and you will be paid a wage for doing it. Mrs Thomas is leaving and Léon *needs* you. There is no question of charity.'

'And you? What will you do?'

'I shall continue to lodge with Mrs Barnet until Léon

489

and I can be married, which would be at Easter. Oh yes, I realize that technically I shall still be in mourning then, but I propose to ignore that, though of course we will be content to have a quiet wedding. Then I would live at Mount Royd.'

How strange it would be, she suddenly thought, to live as mistress in the house where she had for so long worked as a servant. Her mother was not the only one who would have to make adjustments.

'I can see that it would be all right until you were married,' Mrs Bates said thoughtfully. 'It would be, as you say, a business arrangement. In other circumstances it's a job I'd be ready to accept at once. But when you are married, how will Monsieur Bonneau feel about leaving his mother-in-law under his roof?'

'The idea is his,' Madeleine said. 'The invitation comes from him. It isn't, after all, a very unusual situation – or it wouldn't be if I'd already been married. Most widowed mothers move in with one or other of their children. And in your case you'd have much more independence than most. *You* would be earning your keep!'

Mrs Bates was silent for a long time. Madeleine watched her mother's face, but it gave nothing away.

'I, too, will have to make adjustments when I marry Léon,' Madeleine persisted – and noted also that she said 'when' and not 'if'. 'I will have to come to terms with living as mistress of Mount Royd. That won't always be easy and to have you there would often be a comfort to me. Please, Ma, tell me what you think! Give me an answer!'

'Very well,' Mrs Bates said. 'I had already decided, before you came, that you and Monsieur Bonneau must marry. I want you to believe that. I knew when I saw you together yesterday that it would be wicked if any action of mine were to part you. What I didn't know was how to work it out – and now you have shown me.'

'You mean . . .?'

'Yes, Madeleine! You may tell Monsieur Bonneau that I

accept his offer, and with gratitude. Also that I will do my best to be a good housekeeper!'

'Oh Ma!'

They were in each other's arms, tears running down their faces. Mrs Bates felt that the fog which had been on her soul and on her spirit since the night of her husband's death had lifted, cleared. Madeleine felt as if a window had been flung open on to a view of a world full of beauty and light and sunshine.

'Oh Ma, I know you'll be happy! I just know it! When will you come? Mrs Thomas is anxious to leave as soon as possible, and you'll want a day or two with her so she can show you the ropes.'

'I can come as soon as Monsieur Bonneau wants me,' Mrs Bates said. 'There is nothing to keep me here. I was never happy in Coomber Terrace and I shall be glad to leave!'

Within the week, Mrs Bates and Penelope were installed at Mount Royd, sharing the kitchen quarters and a large bedroom.

'When I have seen Mrs Parkinson about extra space, there will also be a small sitting-room for you,' Léon said. 'I really don't expect you to spend your life in the kitchen. And when Madeleine and I are married you will naturally have the freedom of the whole house, even though you have your own private part of it.'

He had also, from the very first day, said that when Penelope left school at Christmas she could be found a job with her mother and be paid a wage, unless and until she wished to go into service elsewhere.

'The next thing I must do, dearest, is to see Mrs Parkinson,' Léon said to Madeleine. 'I long to announce our engagement to the whole world, but as far as Mrs Parkinson is concerned, she must hear it first from me.'

'And I must tell Mrs Barnet,' Madeleine said. 'I've felt uncomfortable all these months, keeping it from her.'

They had let Mrs Thomas go back to Morecambe, still in ignorance.

'If she knew,' Madeleine pointed out, 'without meaning the slightest harm, she'd not be able to keep from telling the daily women, and then it would be all over Helsdon in no time. But I'll write to her the minute we announce it. Dear Mrs Thomas! What a lot I owe her, one way and another!'

Mrs Barnet showed less surprise than Madeleine expected.

'No, I didn't know it had gone so far,' she admitted. 'But I've seen the way he's looked at you. I've known for months that he was head over heels for you, but you never showed a thing.'

'I tried not to,' Madeleine said.

'And I had hoped that you and our John would have made a go of it,' Mrs Barnet went on. 'But then I saw it wasn't to be. You weren't really suited. And I dare say Sally Pitts will make him a good little wife.'

'Sally? Do you mean that John and Sally . . .?'

'You haven't been here at weekends for a bit, have you? So you wouldn't know he's been taking her for walks on a Sunday afternoon.'

'But that's wonderful!' Madeleine cried. 'It's absolutely wonderful!'

'Oh, it's far from settled,' Mrs Barnet said. 'But straws show which way the wind blows!'

A day or two later Léon went to see Mrs Parkinson. As far as he could tell, she was still happy with her sister.

'We get on well together,' Mrs Parkinson said. 'And have you heard that Roger is to be articled to Mr Ormeroyd? I think a solicitor's life will suit him.'

'I had heard,' Léon said. 'It should work out well.'

'And how is the mill going?' she asked.

'Splendidly, I must say. Any day now the spinning will be in production, and the weaving is going exceptionally well. Garston's of Leeds are giving us a lot of work, and we have more than a foot in the door of several other cloth merchants.'

'So you're well on the way to being a "warm" man?' Mrs Parkinson said.

'A warm man?' What had his temperature to do with anything?

Mrs Parkinson laughed at the puzzled expression on his face.

'It's another of our north-country phrases. A "warm" man means you're making money – perhaps not yet rich but on the way.'

'Ah! I should never have guessed it! But yes, I suppose that is true,' Léon said modestly. 'And now I have a piece of news for you, dear Mrs Parkinson. I wanted you to hear this first, before I tell the whole world.'

'Tell the world? My word, that sounds important!'

'It is the most important thing in my life,' Léon said.

'Then tell me at once!'

'I am to be married!'

Mrs Parkinson's mind at once ran over all the eligible spinsters in Helsdon, then, failing to find one to fit, started on the young widows. But there was no one. He must have looked further afield – perhaps even found a bride in France.

'Do I know the lucky lady?'

'You do indeed,' Léon said. 'I am to marry Madeleine Bates!'

'Madeleine Bates?' She tried hard to hide her astonishment. 'You mean Madeleine Bates who . . .'

'Who worked for you and now works for me. Yes indeed. But it is not she who is the lucky one, it is I who am the luckiest person in the world!'

Conflicting emotions whirled in Mrs Parkinson's head. It was not so much that he was marrying beneath him – it wasn't the first time in the West Riding that a mill-girl had married the Master, and it wouldn't be the last. She knew of cases herself, and very well some of them had worked out. No, it wasn't that, though it had taken her breath away; it was the fact that Madeleine Bates would be living at Mount Royd, or presumably so.

It should be Sophia I was hearing about, she thought. It is my daughter who should be marrying this man and living at Mount Royd.

'I hope you wish me well,' Léon said, breaking the silence.

'Oh, oh yes, well of course I do! I congratulate you. Madeleine Bates is a nice girl, and very competent.'

It took her all her time to force out the words, though they were essentially true, she thought. As for Sophia – well she had made her choice, and by some miracle, and contrary to all expectations, she seemed happy with her little son. She was certainly easier to deal with than she had been once. But how would she take this?

'I wanted you to know,' Léon continued. 'I also wanted to discuss with you about renting more of Mount Royd.'

'I see. Well I'm sure we can come to some agreement.'

And so they could, and it would bring her in yet a little more income which, added to what she would get from the spinning, would see her quite comfortable. All the same, she would never get used to Madeleine Bates being at Mount Royd. Shall I be expected to visit her, she wondered?

The announcement to the rest of the world – or to that bit of the West Riding which might be interested – of Madeleine's engagement to Léon caused a swift stir, a ripple of astonishment, which died down almost as quickly as it had risen. Amongst her colleagues in the mill it caused much less surprise than she had expected.

'I admit you didn't do so in the beginning,' Mrs Barnet said, 'but for the last week or two you've been wearing your heart on your sleeve, love! So it hasn't exactly come like a thunderclap. And I know for a fact, everyone wishes you well.'

That seemed to be true enough. She was showered with congratulations.

'Oh Madeleine, it's wonderful news!' Sally Pitts said.

'I hope one day it will happen to you,' Madeleine replied. 'I couldn't wish you anything better.'

Before Christmas, Madeleine was received into the Catholic church. Léon, her mother, Penelope and Mrs Barnet were present. Over many weeks and months Father O'Malley had patiently instructed her, had gone over not only the requirements of her new faith, but the very words which would be used. But when the solemn moments came it was not the details which mattered to her. What struck her most of all, what invaded her heart and mind and was to stay with her, was the overwhelming feeling that she had come home; that she had arrived at the place where, from the very beginning, she was meant to be.

'I didn't do this to be nearer to you,' she said to Léon later that same day. 'I did it because I knew I must. But it has brought me immeasurably nearer to you in a way I can't describe.'

'You don't need to describe it,' Léon answered. 'The same feeling is in my heart, also. It will help me to bear the next four months while we wait to be married.'

TWENTY-SIX

Mrs Parkinson had kept from Sophia the news of Léon's engagement to Madeleine Bates, and she had begged her sister to do the same.

'Please do not mention it when you write to David,' she said. 'It will upset Sophia mightily.'

'Well she's bound to find out, and sooner rather than later,' Mrs Chester pointed out. 'Someone will write with the news.'

'I don't think she corresponds with anyone in Helsdon,' Mrs Parkinson said hopefully.

'Anyway, why should she be upset?' Mrs Chester said defensively. 'She's married to David now – and a better husband never trod shoe leather!' Who did she think she was, the little madam?

'It isn't that, sister. It's the thought that they'll be living at Mount Royd. I feel it myself. Sophia will do so a hundred times more.'

'Well, I can promise I won't breathe a word,' Mrs Chester said. She would keep quiet for her son's sake, not for Sophia's.

And now, quite unexpectedly, Sophia had arrived, with little Bertie, for one of her rare visits, having taken advantage of the offer of a seat in a friend's carriage going to Helsdon and returning next day. For once, Mrs Parkinson thought, she is not welcome.

'So!' Sophia said, yawning. 'What's the news?'

She was sitting in an armchair, sipping tea, while her mother devoted herself to Bertie. There wouldn't be any news. Helsdon wasn't much better than Thirsk in that respect. Practically nothing happened.

Her mother and aunt looked at each other. Mrs Chester gave an almost imperceptible nod.

Yes, she will have to know, Mrs Parkinson thought. If I don't tell her now, the person she travels home with tomorrow will surely do so.

'As a matter of fact . . . ,' she hesitated, ' . . . there is some news.'

'Oh do tell me, Mama!'

Sophia could hardly disguise her lack of interest. No doubt two of her aunt's cronies had fallen out over which of them had been asked to sing at a musical soirée, or some such nonsense.

'Léon Bonneau is to be married!' I will feed her the news piecemeal, spread the shock, Mrs Parkinson thought.

'Léon, married!' Sophia squealed with surprise. 'Then he is going back to France?' There was no one in Helsdon he could possibly be marrying.

'No my dear, he is staying on here.'

'So he is bringing a wife from France? Well, it was always on the cards. But heaven help the poor woman, exchanging France for Helsdon!'

'He is not bringing a wife from France,' Mrs Parkinson said.

Oh, why don't you get on with it, dear Sister, Mrs Chester thought impatiently – and then decided that since her sister seemed incapable of speaking out, she would do it for her.

'He is marrying a Helsdon girl,' she informed her daughter-in-law.

Sophia stared in astonishment.

'Who could he possibly marry in Helsdon? There's just no one! Oh Ma, for goodness' sake, do tell!'

497

'He is to marry Madeleine Bates,' Mrs Parkinson said levelly.

A split second's silence hung in the air before Sophia found her voice.

'Madeleine Bates!' There was fury, agony, outrage in her cry. 'I don't believe it! He can't do that!'

He can't do that to me, she thought. It was unbelievable. The humiliation of it was unbearable!

'He can and he will,' her aunt said briskly. 'And he won't be the first mill-master to marry one of his weavers. Anyway, they say she's moved up from the weaving. Designing, if you please!'

Mrs Parkinson sat in silence. The worst had not yet been said. Sophia looked at her mother and saw her troubled eyes. There was more to it. *She* wouldn't be so deeply concerned at the prospect of Léon marrying the Bates's girl. So what was it?

'There's something else, isn't there Mother?' she said. 'What are you not telling me?'

And then, before her mother could say a word, it came to her, hit her like a blow between the eyes.

'Where are they to live?' she asked slowly.

Mrs Parkinson looked her daughter straight in the face.

'They will live at Mount Royd,' she whispered.

There! It was out, it was said. She picked up Bertie from the rug and held him close, as if he could protect her from the storm she knew must break.

It came at once. Sophia sprang to her feet. Her face was chalk-white – but inside her rage flamed and burned.

'It's not true! It can't be true! You can't have agreed to let them live there! You could have stopped it!'

'I *have* agreed,' Mrs Parkinson said quietly. 'There was no good reason that I could give for doing otherwise. Léon Bonneau has been good to me. How could I say, "You can't have the rooms because my daughter will be jealous"? Don't think I don't feel for you, because I do – but there was no other way. Besides, I need the money,' she added.

Sophia hardly listened. 'You've betrayed me!' she screamed. 'You've let Mount Royd go. The house where I was brought up, where my son should be brought up. You've let it go to a . . .' She searched for words and could find nothing bad enough.' . . . to a low-class, guttersnipe mill-girl!'

'There was no prospect of your son being brought up at Mount Royd,' Mrs Parkinson said. Now that it had come out into the open she felt better. 'You know that as well as I do. If you thought otherwise you're living in a fool's paradise. And though Madeleine Bates may be a mill-girl, she is *not* a guttersnipe. She shows better class than you are doing at this moment. Your father would have been ashamed of you!'

'My father? It's my father's fault! It's all his fault!' Sophia stormed. If he'd been more competent. . . 'What did he do with his money anyway?'

'He spent it on you!' her mother retorted. 'And don't let me ever hear you speak of your father like that again. He was the best of parents to you.'

But only according to his lights, she thought sadly. He had indulged and spoilt his daughter, and so had she. They must take some of the blame for Sophia. But she was sick of taking blame, of making excuses for her daughter, who was now ranting and raving, pacing up and down the room like a madman while her child screamed in fear, and with some of the temper he had inherited from his mother.

'She shan't have it! She shan't!' Sophia cried. 'I'll see to that!'

She ran to the door.

'Sophia, where are you going?' Mrs Parkinson cried. 'Sophia, come back!'

Sophia was already out of the house, running, running. Where else would she be going except to Mount Royd? She kept on running – Helsdon was all hills – but ever since Bertie's birth she'd carried too much weight and she was out of condition. Quite soon her breath gave out and

499

she was obliged to slow down. And this, though it did not cool her rage, gave her time to think. She had not thought at all before rushing out of the house.

How would she get in? Was Mrs Thomas still there – if so, she didn't want to see her. The little side door to the conservatory used to be always left unlocked. Would it still be so? If she could enter unheard and unseen, so much the better; but if not, then she was prepared to break a window, hammer down a door if necessary. She would get in all right. It was *her* house; hers, not that trollop's.

Luck was on her side. The conservatory door was unlocked. She entered quietly, and stood there, looking around.

The memory of her nineteenth birthday when, on this very spot, Léon Bonneau had so cruelly jilted her, was vivid in her mind. She would never forget it. There had been beautiful flowers in this place then, and on her bosom Léon's rose. Now the place was neglected; only ferns and other greenery struggled to exist.

What should she do now? How should she take the revenge which was burning inside her? She would like to set fire to the whole place, to burn it down so that if her son couldn't have it, no one else should. But to start a fire you needed matches, a taper. She should have thought more carefully before rushing out of her mother-in-law's house.

In a sudden flash of frustration and temper she turned and tore at the plants, stripped the leaves and threw them to the floor, pulled such plants as she could out of the soil and sent them flying. When she had wreaked what havoc she could in the conservatory, though she stopped short at smashing the windows, she moved quickly into the drawing-room. If she could not set the place on fire, then she would do all the damage she possibly could, and here, in this beautiful room, this place where she had once held sway, was where it mattered most. But she would have to move quietly. She had no idea whether there was anyone in the house. She might not be alone, might at any moment be discovered, though there were no sounds.

She tugged at the long brocade curtains, trying to tear them down, but in spite of the extra strength which her temper gave her, they were too much for her; they remained implacably in place. Frustrated, she turned to the mantelpiece and picked up a vase from the shelf. . . .

Madeleine had arranged to meet Léon at the house. They were to discuss new covers for the drawing-room.

'I would like something which is *ours*,' she'd said to him. It would make it easier to settle if the room was not exactly as she'd known it when she was a servant there. He had understood at once.

'You are quite right, *ma petite*,' he'd said. 'We will change whatever you wish!' She had spent time with her mother in the kitchen but she was still early. Léon would be a quarter of an hour yet. No matter, she would sit for a while in the drawing-room, and try to visualize what it might be like living there in a few months' time; try also to allay the apprehension which came over her every time she thought of living in this house.

When Madeleine opened the door and stepped into the drawing-room Sophia Parkinson was standing by the fireplace, a vase held high in her raised hand, her body tensed and taut, a frenzied look on her face. Madeleine gasped with fright. It was like seeing a ghost.

There was an infinitesimal pause in which the two women stared at each other, before Sophia let fly. The vase hurtled across the room and smashed into a hundred pieces at Madeleine's feet, a sliver of it cutting her hand on its way down. Without looking at it, for she was transfixed by the sight of Sophia, she felt the blood trickle down the back of her hand. Madeleine was the first to speak.

'What are you doing here? By what right . . .?'

'What are *you* doing here?' Sophia shouted. 'What right have you to be in this house? This is *my* house!'

'It is not your house,' Madeleine answered.

She tried to keep her voice from trembling. She must somehow keep calm. It was not the first time she had had to deal with Sophia Parkinson's temper, though she had never before seen her in a state like this. But to keep calm was the best way, if only she could do it.

'It is not your house, Mrs Chester,' she repeated. 'And I am not aware that you rang the doorbell, therefore I think you must have somehow broken in.'

'It will take more than the likes of you to keep me out,' Sophia said scornfully.

'I have more right here than you,' Madeleine said, 'for in three months' time I am to live here. However, it somehow seems to me that you already know that.'

'*You*, live here! *You*, a servant, a mill-girl, set yourself up as mistress of Mount Royd? You can never do that. Oh yes, you might try. I'm sure you will – you always were brazen enough for anything. But once a servant, always a servant!'

'Nevertheless, when I marry Léon I shall be mistress here,' Madeleine said. 'It is I—'

'*If* he marries you!' Sophia interrupted. 'I don't *really* think he will, though you've done your best to get him. Oh, don't think I didn't see what you were up to in Paris! I saw it all right!'

'I can quite see why you don't like the idea . . .,' Madeleine began.

'Like it? It's impossible! No one will visit you, you know. You'll be an outcast. Your own lot will hate you for getting above yourself, and your betters won't have anything to do with you.'

'I shall have my husband,' Madeleine said.

'I wouldn't place any faith in him. All he's doing now is taking revenge on me because I jilted him. That's what he's doing. You know he probably has a wife in France? I jilted him for that very reason.'

Oh Léon, please come, Madeleine prayed. Please come! She didn't know what to say next, what to do.

502

'But never mind *him*! I don't care a fig about him! It's that you are taking what belongs to my son! All this . . . everything here should belong to my son! My son is the most precious thing in the world to me, and you have stolen his inheritance! I hate you, Madeleine Bates!'

She was shrieking now. Why doesn't my mother hear, and come running from the kitchen? Madeleine cried inwardly.

'I think you should go,' she said as firmly as she could. 'You're beside yourself.'

She felt threatened, frightened, as if the waves of hate from Sophia were beating into her, doing her actual physical harm.

'You think you'll have it all for *your* son,' Sophia cried. 'That's what you think, isn't it? You've got it all planned. But you won't, you know. It won't work. I shall curse you, Madeleine Bates! I curse you so that you never have a son! Never, never, never!'

Madeleine felt suddenly sick, fearful for a dreadful moment that she would vomit on the carpet . . . How could anyone have such hate in them? And all of it directed at her. Oh, why didn't Léon come? But she mustn't give in, she mustn't let herself be so frightened by what was, after all, no more than Miss Sophia in one of her paddies. But it didn't feel like that. Though common sense told her it was nonsense, at this moment Sophia's curse felt real.

'I must insist that you leave, Mrs Chester,' she said again. In her own ears her voice sounded weak, and a long way off. She tried to strengthen it, to pull herself together. 'I regret that you have no right here. What's more, my fiancé' – she used the word with deliberate pride – 'is due any minute. I'm sure you wouldn't wish him to see you in such a state.'

Nor me, she thought. I must get rid of her even if I have to use force, and I must see to my hand. It was bleeding freely and the blood had stained her skirt. Though earlier she had wanted Léon to come, now she was glad he hadn't. She didn't want him to see her like this – nor would she ever tell him all that Sophia had said.

She was too late. As she finished speaking the door opened and Léon entered. He stood in the doorway staring at Sophia; then, from her to Madeleine, at the ghastly pallor of her face and at the broken vase scattered around the floor, blood on her hand.

'*Mon Dieu*! What the devil is happening?' He put his arm around Madeleine and gently took her hand. 'My love, are you hurt? Are you all right?'

'I'm quite all right, my dear. It's nothing. As you see we have a visitor. Mrs Chester is not well and she is just leaving. Perhaps you will show her out, Léon?'

'You will regret this,' Sophia said fiercely. 'You have taken my home; you have stolen it from my son. God will punish you, both of you!'

Swiftly, Léon crossed the room, took Sophia none too gently by the elbow and propelled her out of the room. The moment they had gone Madeleine collapsed on to the sofa, weeping, and was still weeping when Léon returned.

'Now, tell me all about it, my love,' he said gently.

'I can't,' Madeleine sobbed. 'I don't want to think about it. Oh Léon, she said such terrible things! I want to forget it!' But she felt sure in her heart that she never would.

In the three months which passed between the encounter with Sophia, and her own wedding, Madeleine, though she said as little as possible to Léon, thought long and often, and never without a shudder, about the affair. In the end, though inside her she was still a little afraid of the venom in Sophia's words, she came to think about it more rationally. After all, she reflected, I am marrying the man Sophia wanted. She remembered the day of the birthday party and was quite sure, though she would never ask him, that it was Léon who had done the jilting. I am to live in the home which Sophia thought would be hers, she reminded herself. I am happy. I love, and am loved. What more can I wish for?

Sophia, she reasoned, is not happy, except with her son, whom she will spoil as she's been spoilt. She will go back home, and if I know her aright, she will pretend that all is well, keep up appearances. But she doesn't have the gift of happiness. So though she still disliked Sophia, and though she always would, she could forgive her. And I *will* have sons, she told herself. Léon and I *will* have sons.

And now it was the eve of her own wedding.

Mrs Barnet lit the candle and passed the candlestick to Madeleine.

'Well, not long now, love. Get off to bed and get some sleep. You want to look your very best tomorrow.'

She reckoned, though, that Madeleine Bates would be one of the bonniest brides Helsdon had seen in a long time – and the bridegroom certainly the handsomest man. Oh, they'd make a lovely pair!

'I don't expect I'll sleep a wink,' Madeleine said. 'I'm far too excited, not to mention nervous!'

And if the truth be told, she was a little afraid, though that was nonsense! How could she be afraid when it was Léon she was to marry next day, Léon whom she loved so deeply and who adored her? She was not afraid of him. She was not even afraid of her wedding night and what it would bring; it was marriage itself which made her apprehensive.

'Shall we be happy, Mrs Barnet?' she asked anxiously. 'Do you think we'll be happy?'

'Good heavens! What a thing to say!' Mrs Barnet's voice was brisk, but when she glanced at Madeleine, saw her pale face, read the anxiety in her eyes, she changed her tone, spoke gently.

'Of course you'll be happy, love – why wouldn't you? And you'll make Monsieur Bonneau happy as well.'

'Not all marriages are happy,' Madeleine said. She thought of the long misery of her mother's marriage. Yet presumably her mother, on her wedding day, had expected happiness.

'But a lot are,' Mrs Barnet answered. 'Look at me and Charlie. We've never had what you'd call a smooth passage. We didn't have the children we'd looked forward to, and then there was Charlie's illness – but I've treasured every minute of being wed to Charlie.'

'And he to you, I'm sure,' Madeleine said. 'Yes, you're right; and as always, such a comfort. Oh, I don't know where I'd have been without you over the last year or two. I can never thank you enough.'

'Get away with you!' Mrs Barnet brushed the thanks aside. Both she and Charlie were going to miss Madeleine, more than she liked to think about. Madeleine had felt like the daughter they'd never had, a daughter any parents would have been proud of.

'Get off to bed!' she ordered.

'Very well!'

Climbing the stairs, candlestick in hand, Madeleine thought: before this hour tomorrow I shall be Mrs Bonneau! Or will I be *Madame* Bonneau, since everyone still called Léon 'Monsieur' in spite of the time he'd been in Helsdon? 'Madame Bonneau!' Going into the bedroom she said the name out loud – and then wondered fearfully if it was unlucky to do so before it actually happened. She hadn't realized until recently that weddings were hedged about by all kinds of things which were either lucky or, more usually, unlucky. Sally Pitts had urged her not to put the final stitches into the hem of her wedding dress until the day itself. Well, she hadn't. This was no time to take risks.

The dress – lilac moiré, because officially she was in mourning for her father – hung on the wall under one of Mrs Barnet's clean white sheets to protect it from the dirt, and now she went across and lifted the sheet to take another look. She had made it herself, with her mother's help, as she had also trimmed her new bonnet with lilac ribbon and small artificial violets, which matched the tiny bouquet of fresh violets she would carry.

She knelt to say her prayers, then got into bed. It was

the last time she would sleep alone, hopefully for the rest of her life. What would it be like, sharing a bed with a man? And was it right to have such thoughts not five minutes after she'd said her prayers? But of course it was, Father O'Malley had said that marriage, and all it entailed was a natural state and pleasing to God. So she would cease to worry, and go to sleep.

She slept soundly, could hardly believe the night had passed when she opened her eyes on the sight of Mrs Barnet coming into the bedroom, carrying a tray.

'Breakfast in bed on your wedding day!' Mrs Barnet said cheerfully.

'Oh I couldn't possibly eat!' Madeleine said. 'I'll drink a cup of tea, but I couldn't eat a thing!'

'You can and you will!' Mrs Barnet ordered. 'Even if I have to lock you in until you've done it! You'll need all the strength you can get, today.'

'Well I'll try,' Madeleine said reluctantly. 'What's the weather like?'

'A beautiful spring day! I've known some terrible Easter Mondays in my time – rain, hail, even snow – but this one is extra special. Now while you're eating your breakfast I'll bring some hot water, and then when you're washed, if you want me to help you with your dress you have only to shout.'

'Oh Mrs Barnet, you're spoiling me!'

'Well it's the last time I'll be able to do so,' Mrs Barnet said.

'Then stay and talk to me while I eat my breakfast.'

Struggling with the meal, Mrs Barnet watching every mouthful, Madeleine's fears began to return.

'Oh Mrs Barnet, will I ever get used to living in Mount Royd, where I was a servant?' she cried. 'Would it have been better to have lived somewhere else, made a fresh start?'

'Of course you'll get used to it, love! And in no time at all. Anyway, it's a bit late in the day to worry about that after all that's been done there.'

'I suppose you're right,' Madeleine said doubtfully. 'I dare say I'm being silly.'

The extra rooms had been agreed with Mrs Parkinson. There was a large bedroom, overlooking the garden, for herself and Léon, and they were also to have the drawing-room, the dining-room and the conservatory. A further room had also been prepared as a guest-room.

'Though who will come to stay I can't imagine,' Madeleine had said.

'Well, my love,' Léon pointed out. 'I do rather hope that from time to time members of my family might visit us!'

'Oh Léon, I'm sorry! Of course, I hope they will too! We shall welcome them.'

But would they ever come? Léon had written to tell them of his engagement, but if there had been a reply, then he hadn't informed her, from which she deduced that if it existed it was unfavourable. He had also sent invitations to the wedding, which had been politely refused on the excuse of the distance.

'Oh Mrs Barnet,' she asked now, 'do you think Léon's family will ever take to me?'

'They'll take to you when they see you. No fear about that,' Mrs Barnet assured her.

'That's what Léon says. All the same, I dread meeting them.'

Mercifully there was no immediate prospect of that. Léon had hoped that they might spend a short honeymoon in France, visiting his family, but they were now so busy in the mill that it was impossible to spend more than two nights away from Helsdon.

'I am disappointed,' Léon had confessed. 'I wanted so much to show you to my family. But perhaps at Helsdon Feast week, in August, when the mills close down . . .'

'Perhaps so,' Madeleine agreed. Anything, so long as it was far enough into the future!

'There!' she said, pushing the breakfast tray away. 'I can't eat another thing!'

'Well, I'll let you off the last bit,' Mrs Barnet conceded.

'I must hurry and get ready now,' Madeleine said. 'I don't want to be late.'

In the absence of a male member of Madeleine's own family, John Hartley was to give her away. Even if her father had been alive, he would have refused to enter Saint Mary's, or indeed take any part in the festivities. She knew that. He would have turned her wedding day into a day of mourning. It had seemed that Irvine might be able to do the honours, until at the last moment his leave had been cancelled. Léon had suggested that Mr Ormeroyd would be happy to oblige, but Madeleine had preferred John, whom she knew.

'The carriage will be here at half-past ten,' Mrs Barnet said. 'You've plenty time.'

It would be Léon's carriage, and it would first take him, and her own family, and then come to fetch her and John. Mrs Barnet had expressed a preference to walk to the church.

'It wouldn't be seemly for me to share the bridal carriage,' she pointed out.

A little later Madeleine stood in her wedding dress as Mrs Barnet knelt to put the final stitches into the hem. Then Mrs Barnet got to her feet and stepped back to take a look.

'There!' she said. 'You're as bonny a bride as I ever saw. I'm sorry that you couldn't be married from your Ma's house, but her loss is my gain!'

But when this radiant girl left her little house, it would be for the last time, Mrs Barnet thought.

'Remember I shall be back in the mill in a few days' time,' Madeleine said, seeing the shadow on her friend's face, understanding its cause. 'I shall see you quite often.'

It had been agreed between herself and Léon that until she conceived her first child, she would continue to work in the mill, at her designs.

'I love the work,' she'd said. 'Also, my mother is a competent housekeeper, so I won't be needed for that.

509

Anyway,' she teased him, 'what would you do in the mill without me?'

'You're quite right. I don't want to lose your talent,' Léon agreed, smiling. 'Though when we have children . . .'

'They will be my first consideration,' Madeleine assured him. 'But no! My second. You will always be first in my life.'

The guests filled no more than two pews at the front of the church. In addition to her mother, her sisters and Mrs Barnet, Sally was there, and Léon had invited Mr Ormeroyd. He had also invited Henry Garston, who had politely refused owing to a previous engagement, but had sent them a magnificent silver teapot as a wedding present. Mrs Parkinson had sent them a vase. How ironic, Madeleine thought, since it was almost a twin to the one Sophia had smashed to pieces, though Mrs Parkinson presumably knew nothing of that. Léon had invited her to the wedding, but she had tactfully refused on learning that the small reception afterwards was to be at Mount Royd.

When Léon, waiting at the front of the church, turned around to watch his bride walking down the aisle towards him, her face lit by an eager smile, he thought she had never looked so beautiful. If she was nervous, no trace of it showed now.

Léon's own nervousness had him trembling from head to foot, but when Madeleine drew level with him and briefly touched his hand, it was as if she passed on to him a share of her own serenity. From that moment, all agitation left him. The two of them made their responses, their promises to each other, in clear, steady voices. To Madeleine it felt as though her whole life had been leading towards this point.

Emerging into the spring sunshine after the ceremony she was thrilled and delighted to be met by a group of almost all the girls from the weaving. They were dressed now, not in their mill-skirts and shawls, but in their

510

Sunday best, so that to Léon, who knew them less well than did Madeleine, they were almost unrecognizable. They crowded forward, touching Madeleine, stroking the material of her beautiful dress, and the bolder ones among them daring to touch the bridegroom for luck.

'My word!' one of them called out, 'I don't half envy you tonight, Our Madeleine!'

At Mount Royd Mrs Bates had laid on a cold collation in the dining-room.

'It looks marvellous, Ma!' Madeleine said. 'Ma, I want to thank you – not just for the meal, but for everything. I'm a very happy woman!'

My daughter's earned her happiness, Mrs Bates thought, watching. She thanked God that in the end she had done nothing to come between Léon and Madeleine. Well, they'd be all right now. What mattered was that they were together. Together they could cope with anything. Nothing could go wrong.

THE END

The House of Bonneau, a sequel to *Madeleine*, is currently in preparation.